Books by James Broom Lynne

ROGUE DIAMOND   (1980)

JET RACE   (1978)

COLLISION!   (1973)

THE MARCHIONESS   (1968)

THE WEDNESDAY VISITORS   (1967)

As James Quartermain

ROCK OF DIAMOND   (1972)

THE MAN WHO WALKED ON DIAMONDS   (1971)

THE DIAMOND HOOK   (1970)

Rogue Diamond

ROGUE DIAMOND

James Broom Lynne

Atheneum   NEW YORK   1980

Library of Congress Cataloging in Publication Data

Lynne, James Broom.
   Rogue diamond.

   I. Title
PZ4.L9894Ro 1980 [PR6062.Y62] 823'.914 79–55621
ISBN 0–689–11048–0

Manufactured by American Book–Stratford Press, Saddle Brook, New Jersey
Designed by Harry Ford
First American Edition

For Michael Sissons

ACKNOWLEDGMENTS

My thanks to Richard Dickson and Robin Walker of the Diamond Corporation for their friendly and helpful cooperation; to Kenneth Harrington of Woodbridge, and to Eric Bruton, F.G.A., and S. Tolansky, F.R.S., whose works of reference were essential to the writing of this book. J B L

BOOK ONE

CHAPTER 1.

TEN degrees above the equator a man, apelike in his stance, stood on the banks of a wide river whose distant shore could not be seen. A few meters upshore the river had eroded a ridge of land into a series of terraces in one of which a cave had been scooped out. Inside the cave a woman slept with a child.

The man on the beach was rock still, his spear held in striking position as he waited for the monitor lizard now scrabbling up from the river edge unaware that the rock held the power to kill.

A few inches from the man's feet the lizard paused and raised its head, and the man struck downward, pinning the lizard to the muddy, pebbly riverbank. In its death throes, the lizard twisted and disturbed the alluvial deposits on the ground.

The man reached down to pick up his prey. As he did so the heel of his long-toed left foot scuffed back the mud and exposed a bright glasslike faceted stone. Clutching the dead lizard, the man straightened up, then loped back up the beach to his family sleeping in the cave.

It was one hour after dawn, two million years ago.

Dr. Arthur Appleby found his next foothold and lowered himself down the last three feet of the angled terraced cliff. Above the cliff and a hundred yards from the edge, he could hear sounds from the camp he had set up a little before nightfall after the hundred-mile trek from a site that had proved to be a whited sepulchre.

Fifty yards away from the terraced cliff he turned and looked back. Now he could see the contour of the low hill and the extent of its rise and fall. He panned his gaze along the cliff. To his left the terraces petered out a mile or so away as the higher ground swung out to project into the flatland. It was the same on Appleby's right, so that the terrain within his view resembled a bay. In his imagination he filled the flatland with river water and could see its flow carving out the baylike undulation in the course of the river.

It was geologically interesting—the low hill curved like a whale's back, the terraces with their steep fall, and the pocket formed by the twin projections of land. After breakfast he and Ernst Blohm, his fellow geologist, would use a theodolite to measure the precise height of the hill and then, with the aid of tyrannical Colonel Magasi and his security guards and field-workers, begin the long process of sampling the area —weeks of patient work all too often disappointing.

In his mind's eye Appleby envisaged the land as it must have been untold millions of years ago. A great river, six hundred yards wide, eating its way at the rising ground behind him, and yet it would have been a shallow river, twenty feet at its deepest to judge by the fall of land from where he stood, unless silt had been brought down from some distant point. And then some natural diversion of the water had, over the years, slowly decimated the river flow until it became what he now saw, a dried-up riverbed.

He turned away from the scrubby, thorn-bushed landscape and looked back at the terraces carved out of the cliff face, and wondered how many years it had taken that river to sculpt the cliff into its present form.

The cold of the night and early morning was rapidly dispersing under the rays of the sun, low on the horizon, and Appleby slowly walked away from the cliff, his eyes on the ground now, observing the sand and gravel at his feet. A hundred yards away from the cliff he turned and looked back again. Now he could see the low hill, some two thousand feet in diameter, rising up from the cliff. Again Appleby looked out across the expanse of the extinct river. This was the most inhospitable part of Angwana, he thought. No settlements of friendly or unfriendly tribes, just thousands of acres of desolate land littered with thorn and scrub and the debris from land upheavals a long way back in time. It was this debris that had led him here with Ernst Blohm.

A light breeze stirred the wings of white hair that surmounted Appleby's ears, and carried on the breeze was the sound of Magasi's whistle summoning his men to breakfast.

Appleby walked back to the terraced cliff. Thirty feet from the cliff he paused as a movement a few inches away from his right foot caught his eye. A small lizard—Appleby recognized it as a descendant of a much larger ancestor—was waddling toward him. Instinctively Appleby moved back, the heels of his field boots scuffing the pebbly ground. Startled, the lizard took evasive action and darted away. Appleby watched it disappear, then brought his gaze round to where his feet had scuffed the ground, raising a mound of gravel and sand. Then he frowned, bent down, and picked up the largest pebble. As he picked it up it ceased to be a pebble.

Roughly faceted in octahedral form, it glinted in the sun, sending out a bright spark of fire. He held it between thumb and forefinger, doubting his eyes, doubting the evidence of its structure, its transparency and color. He pushed back the excitement that was growing in him, an excitement that was physical, so that his breath quickened. Still holding the stone, he scoop-fingered his left hand through the mound and then extended his hands to search beyond the mound. Three orange-red granules and larger particles of blackish-brown stone appeared on the palm of his hand as the dross sieved through his fingers.

There was no doubt about the orange-red and blackish-brown stones—garnets and ilmenite. Appleby straightened up, a bubble of excitement centered between his chest and stomach. It was almost unbelievable; in his left hand he held the clue to what he had been seeking; in his right he held that to which the clues would have led him. How odd that the solution should have come before the puzzle.

He looked at the crystal again, turning it this way and that so that its sides caught the sun and flashed back pale prismatic colors. Suspicion dulled his excitement. Was it simply an alluvial find? Had the diamond—for that surely was what it was—had it been washed down the river from its source many miles away or was this the place, the terraced cliff and hill beyond? And the garnets and ilmenite, were those too brought down by the ancient river?

Controlling both suspicion and excitement, he walked to the foot of the cliff, and placing the diamond in his right tunic breast pocket and the garnets and ilmenites in his left, he bent down and gathered a handful of gravel. Nothing. Another handful sieved through slightly parted fingers revealed two more tiny garnets and ilmenite fragments. Five minutes later his left tunic pocket contained two dozen garnets and chips of ilmenite.

Unhurriedly Appleby began to climb the sloping face of the cliff. As he neared the top he became aware that Colonel Magasi was standing on the edge silently observing his progress.

CHAPTER 2.

"NEAR perfect," Ernst Blohm said, and took his eyes away from the Gemolite binocular microscope. "A commercial white, I would say—of good quality."

The diamond was held by a clip on the microscope's stage; over the stage and the diamond a color-grading lamp shone. Blohm had used the microscope's zoom lens and a proportional grading eyepiece; he had taken his time to reach a calm, considered opinion.

Blohm tweezered the diamond out from under the clip and placed it in Appleby's hand. "I would advise hiding it from Magasi," he said. "The less we tell him at this moment, the better."

"I'd no intention of telling him," Appleby said. He held the diamond up to the light. "If I were a betting man, I'd lay every penny I own on the chance that this is a perimeter find—that we've found a pipe and it's not far away."

Blohm glanced through the opened back of the prospecting truck. "Put the stone in your pocket, Arthur—Magasi comes."

Framed against the sun beating through the back of the truck, Magasi was a black silhouette. He ascended the steps and entered the truck.

"Well, Doctors?"

"Yes, Colonel?" Appleby slipped the hand holding the diamond into his trouser pocket.

"You found something, I think."

"Nothing of consequence. One or two clues, but hopeful."

"It must be reported to the president."

"In good time."

"It is now three months since you began this expedition."

"To the day, Colonel."

"You were given two months."

"By you," Blohm said. "Not by President Sotho."

6

Appleby smiled. "And Rome wasn't built in a day." He turned to Blohm. "How about diamonds, Ernst?"

"Two hundred million years—give or take a million years either way."

"You see, Colonel?" Appleby said. "What's three months compared with two hundred million years—give or take a million?"

"The president will not be pleased."

Blohm exploded. "You mean *you* are not pleased!"

Appleby laid a hand on Blohm's shoulder. "Come now, Ernst—we owe the colonel a great deal. In this wild country we need his protection. He's naturally anxious that we should succeed. I'm sure Colonel Magasi will forget what you've said."

"He must understand that diamonds do not grow on trees," Blohm said. "Very well, Colonel. I spoke in anger."

"I neither forgive nor forget," Magasi said. "I shall record your insult, Dr. Blohm—and use it if necessary."

"Understood." Blohm dipped his head in acknowledgment. "How well I understand."

And Blohm did understand. To be in Magasi's black book meant that the balance between the dispensable and the indispensable was hairline thin; that in Angwana and under Magasi's law skin color had no significance—white, brown, and black all came under Magasi's dictum that subservience only guaranteed a relatively painless existence.

Ernst Blohm was in his middle forties. His manner was as stolid as his appearance. Of middle height, he carried not an ounce of excess fat, yet was broad and thickset. What little hair he had fringed the base of his skull and formed unruly tufts about his ears. He was bilingual, and in both his native German and acquired English he was correct to the point of pedantry, avoiding colloquialisms and portmanteau words except when his native language demanded such usage. He seldom wasted words even when his temper rose—inevitable in a hot climate.

In part Arthur Appleby shared Blohm's precise speech form; this was apparent when definitions and words necessary to their profession were essential. When they were not, Appleby used a looser English.

In everything else, in their methodical, scientific approach to mineralogy, geology, and gemmology, they were one; a stone was simply a stone until its structure had been examined and tested until it could be formally identified as zircon or diamond, tourmaline or topaz.

Angwana's President Sotho had joked about their serious attention to detail. "If I asked you to identify chalk from cheese," he had said, "I would expect you to report the difference after many hours of microscopic study."

It was in the area of human behavior that the difference between the two men was marked. Where Appleby's attitude was to think well of any man until that man had proved unworthy, Blohm was suspicious of men's motives until he had depth-probed character and behavior. The difference between them resembled the contrast offered by British and French law; for the one, a man was innocent until proved guilty; for the other, a man was guilty until proved innocent.

Blohm had quickly made an exception in Appleby's case. When they had met and Appleby had asked him to partner him in Angwana, he had fought against an immediate liking for the tall, stringy man with the deep-set gray eyes, and failed in the fight. The years they had worked together had done nothing to alter Blohm's first impression.

There was a kind of innocence about Appleby; Blohm would have called it "missionary blindness." That innocence allowed Appleby, a man as English as any man could be, to take out Angwanan citizenship when the British pulled out and gave Angwana its independence. In a rare moment of humor Blohm had said, "Arthur, if you are so intent on becoming an Angwanan, why do you not stain your skin black?"

It was a good partnership, and now, as they faced Magasi, their solidarity in dislike of the man was apparent.

Magasi said, "Dr. Appleby, I saw you pick something up when you were below the cliff. You will show me what you found."

"Certainly." Appleby dug into his tunic pocket and withdrew the garnets and ilmenite. "Not much, I'm afraid."

"What are they?" Magasi took the stones and looked at them.

"Pyrope garnets and ilmenite. Of little value, but significant."

"In what way?"

"Simply that we may have stumbled on a good site. They're a diamond's bedfellows, Colonel. Finding them means that we will be here for some considerable time."

"How much time?"

Appleby hunched his shoulders. "Who can tell? Sampling will take weeks—months."

"There must be a time limit," Magasi said. "I cannot spend my time shuttling between here and the Kundi Mine where security is weak."

"Then leave us in peace," Blohm said quietly.

"There can be no time limit," Appleby said. "Tell the president that I am reasonably sure that we have found what we have been looking for. That the chances are good—very good."

Magasi fingered the garnets in his hand. "You will not be moving to yet another site?" he asked.

"No."

"These stones—you say they have no value?"

"Some value. They're very good garnets. The ilmenites you can throw away."

Magasi slipped the stones into his tunic pocket. "Then I will return to the palace and tell the president he can expect good results?"

"No," Blohm said. "Tell him that prospects suggest further investigation." Then, as Magasi turned to leave the truck, Blohm said, "Colonel, you still have the garnets."

Magasi turned and smiled, showing an expanse of white teeth in his dark face. "If they are of little value, why should you want them back?"

"Just for the records," Appleby said.

"In that case," said Magasi, "I will keep them—just for the records."

Watching Magasi walk away from the truck, Blohm said, "How much has he stolen from the Kundi Mine—just for the records?"

"Insufficient to harm Angwana's economic stability."

"Which is neither good nor stable," Blohm said.

Appleby went to the open end of the truck and looked out over the site. Many weeks of sampling lay ahead, and basic plant had to be brought up from the Kundi Mine; workers, too, would be needed.

"I shall see the president," said Appleby. "Once we can make a fair assessment and agree on full development, I'll ask Sotho for full backing. If I can show him evidence that this site is as rich as I think it is, perhaps he'll divert funds from his other projects." He turned and looked at Blohm. "You've never met Arnold Mackenzie, have you, Ernst?"

Blohm shook his head.

"One of the best mining engineers in Africa. He's an old and trusted friend. I'd give a lot to have him with us."

"So ask him to come."

"Soon. Mac's under contract to the government diamond mines in Sierra Leone. I'm seeing Sotho in a few days' time. I'll phone Mac from the palace and sound him out."

Blohm got to his feet. "Meanwhile an inspection of the area is in order—and a look at the terraces, I think. I would like to see where you found the diamond. Perhaps it is a perimeter find."

CHAPTER **3.**

A RELIC of the colonial days, Angwana's presidential palace was small but grand in manner, and now, after ten years of independence, it was showing signs of neglect. As Appleby mounted the steps leading to the entrance he compared the building's present state with his memory of it in the days when Angwana was a colony. Then, the lawns had been carefully tended and the palace kept spick-and-span, shining with authority and the constant attendance of an army of maintenance men. True, Sotho did his best to keep the fabric of the building in good shape, but the patches of replaced stucco standing out like sores suggested both laziness on the part of staff and lack of funds in Sotho's treasury.

The palace interior was little better. Desultory repainting showed up areas that had been without paint for the ten years of independence. The patterned tiled entrance hall was still as grand as ever it had been, with its great yellow and black star surmounted by dark red and white small stars, but the wide marble flight of stairs leading to the presidential offices were no longer gleaming; the bleached white marble steps were now dull and brown-gray.

Sotho's private secretary, Ilbrahim Otanga, met Appleby at the top of the stairs. "You are welcome, Doctor," he said and extended his hand.

Appleby took Otanga's hand and shook it. "It's good to see you, Ilbrahim. How are you?"

"I am well. As well as one can be in troubled times. The president is expecting you."

"And he is well?"

"He is in good health. You bring him news? Good news?"

Appleby nodded. "I think so. At least it's not bad news."

Otanga's smile was wry. "Absence of bad news is good news. Come, Doctor, the president is in his suite and the coffee is hot. At least Angwana has coffee. And, Doctor—Colonel Magasi wishes to take you to lunch after you have seen the president."

"I've no wish to see him. He hardly spoke a word on our flight to the capital."

"Perhaps he has much on his mind."

"A guilty conscience?"

"One would have to assume that the colonel has a conscience, Dr. Appleby."

President Sotho was a surprisingly small man, gnomelike as he rose from the great chair behind the massive desk, his hand outstretched in welcome. Neither man stood on ceremony. Appleby walked forward and took Sotho's outstretched hand and shook it warmly, feeling the strength in Sotho's grasp.

"Three months," Sotho said. "It has been three months since you went out into the wilderness with Dr. Blohm. Three months since we have sat together and talked. Come—sit down. Otanga, coffee for Dr. Appleby, and anything else he wishes."

"I think I have good news, Mr. President," Appleby said.

Sotho held up a restraining hand. "Not yet. Bad news I hear immediately. Good news can wait until we have renewed our friendship."

"Our friendship has never been in doubt," Appleby said.

"Good," said Sotho. "We will talk as friends."

Otanga handed Appleby a cup of black, sweet coffee, then served Sotho.

"Now," said Sotho, "how is your friend, Ernst Blohm?"

"He's well and somewhat excited. As a matter of fact, I am too. Good news can't wait—here." Appleby took the paper packet from his pocket and gave it to the president. "I think we've found it. At least my instincts backed by the survey Ernst and I have done suggest a good find."

Sotho opened the packet and spilled the diamonds onto his blotter pad. For a while he was quite still, both hands against his cheeks, gazing at the cluster of stones that ranged in color from clear white to pale yellow.

"They're alluvial," said Appleby, "but they haven't travelled far, if at all."

"They are good stones?" asked Sotho.

"The best. Mostly flawless. Of good value. Mr. President—it's difficult for me to restrain my enthusiasm."

"Then please do not. There is little enough of it in Angwana."

"I want a full-scale mining operation," said Appleby. "It will be long-term as far as I can see, and we'll need equipment—expensive equipment."

"What do you suggest?"

"One way is to bring in the Consolidated Diamond Mining Corporation. It works well in Tanzania and other countries. Grant them the concession and Angwana will profit without spending a penny."

Still looking at the diamonds, Sotho said, "Is that your wish? Is it the ideal situation? Remember, Doctor, certain Angwanans are against outside interference and cooperation." He lifted his gaze from the diamonds. "Old wars die hard with some, and I have to run with the hare and hunt with the hounds."

"We could go it alone," said Appleby, "with the help of an expert mining engineer. How's the treasury?"

Sotho hunched his shoulders. "Emaciated."

"We'd need heavy plant to work the site," said Appleby. "Expensive machinery, and we'd have to import men who know their job."

Sotho returned his gaze to the diamonds. "How long did it take you to find these?"

"A few hours—and there are many more. Blohm is surveying the area now."

Sotho fingered the diamonds. "Can you estimate the worth of these?"

"There's thirty carats there. I'd say round about sixty thousand U.S. dollars. That's a very rough guess."

"As much as that?" Sotho's face expressed disbelief. "And you just picked them up?"

"Yes."

"How long will it take to thoroughly search the area?"

"You mean for surface finds? Years probably. I'll need at least a hundred workers, Mr. President, and naturally, Colonel Magasi will bring in a large body of his security guards."

"Are you not being overoptimistic, Doctor?"

"Where the colonel is concerned, I am pessimistic."

Sotho laughed. "I did not mean Magasi, Doctor. I meant your expectations of this site and its possible yield."

"Both Blohm and I are convinced that we should start large-scale mining."

"Which will take much money." Sotho thought for a while, then said, "Workers will be no problem, and Magasi will, as you say, take care of security. I suggest that you find out what machinery can be spared from the Kundi Mine. Give Otanga your list, and he will see that it is transported to the site."

"Eventually we'll have to bring in experienced miners," Appleby said. "It's true that surface work can go ahead, but I'm anxious to get to the heart of the site, the core of diamond-bearing blue ground—the pipe itself. I need expert miners headed by a specialist."

"Which you will have." Sotho nodded his head several times. "If I share your optimism, Doctor, my reaction is that with regular finds such as these"—he fingered the small pile of crystals—"in a matter of a few months we will be in a position to buy all that you need. Meanwhile"—Sotho fingertipped the diamonds into the packet—"I will channel these through the Diamond Trading Company as from the Kundi."

"I have a suggestion to make," Appleby said. "Would it be possible for someone other than Colonel Magasi to take them to Freetown?"

"You feel their carat value might lessen between here and Sierra Leone if the colonel takes them?"

"Little diamonds are easily lost."

Sotho smiled and shook his head. "Colonel Magasi never *loses* diamonds, Doctor."

Appleby left Colonel Magasi and a lunch he had not enjoyed, and walked back to his hotel. Any savor he might have found in a civilized meal after months of camp food had been lost in the sight and sound of the man facing him across the table.

It was over coffee that his conversation with Magasi had shown the two faces of Angwana: the one out for power and self-interest; and the other equally searching for power, but as a tool for the improvement and well-being of the Angwanan people.

Magasi, lighting a thin black cigar, had said, "Our president is a good and liberal man, don't you agree, Doctor? By liberal I mean in his handling of the affairs of the nation."

"He has patience," Appleby replied. "Not a common attribute in Africa's emergent states."

"Those states were patient for hundreds of years." Twin jets of cigar smoke emerged from Magasi's nostrils. "Can you blame them for wanting and demanding as their right the way of life enjoyed by the white races?"

"It takes time—evolution."

"Time!" Magasi brushed Appleby's comment aside with a dismissive gesture of his hand. "There *is no* time. A man has only one life. The president seems to think that he will live to see the result of his long-term policies of live-in-peace and hope-for-the-best."

"The president isn't passive, Colonel," said Appleby. "Due entirely to his efforts and policies, Angwana has received aid from both Britain and America."

"He could have got more by expressing interest in Russia."

"That kind of diplomatic game isn't the president's cup of tea." Appleby paused, holding Magasi's gaze. "Would it be yours, Colonel?"

"Perhaps. . . . I take the cynical view of Angwana. We have coffee and little else. A few diamonds and other gems to sell. Elitism is the political and economic future for Angwana. The country will never be rich enough to give Mr. Average Angwanan a Western standard of living. The president knows this but smokes his pipe dream of a rich Angwana."

"It may not be a pipe dream," Appleby said.

Magasi raised his eyebrows. "So?"

"It's early days, yet. Both Ernst Blohm and I believe Angwana moderately rich in minerals. It's simply a question of finding them."

"A guarded statement," said Magasi. "When I was a child I was taught by Christians. Seek and ye shall find. When you find Angwana's riches, let me be the first to know."

"Why?"

Magasi did not reply for a few seconds, then he said, "It is right that those responsible should profit first. Dr. Blohm and yourself would be near, very near, the top of the list of beneficiaries. I would ensure that."

"Wouldn't that be in the president's gift?"

"Certainly." Magasi's mouth twitched into a semblance of a smile. "Get in touch with Angwanan politics, Doctor. Presidents come and presidents go. I repeat, should you find what we seek, I will ensure that you will be rewarded."

Appleby wiped his mouth with his table napkin and got to his feet. "You've a taste for ambiguity, Colonel. The president will ensure that I shall profit by the find—Colonel Magasi will ensure that I'll profit. Sounds like Magasi for president."

Magasi, still seated at table, smiled up at Appleby, the thick lips parting to reveal large close-set teeth. "They change presidents every four years in America," he said. "The Angwanan constitution does not contain the clause allowing for a lifetime president."

It was true, Appleby thought as he entered the hotel. I am naive when it comes to African politics, but, he added to his thoughts, it is better by far to remain outside the Angwanan political scene; concentrate on the job in hand and leave behind-the-scenes wheeling and dealing to men like Magasi and to better men like Sotho.

Appleby's hotel room was white and comfortably cool. He showered away dust and fatigue, then lay on the bed. On impulse he picked up the telephone and booked a call through to Sierra Leone. When the call came through, Appleby had already dozed off into shallow sleep. He awoke and reached for the telephone.

"Mac?"

"Who else, Arthur? You called me. How goes the amateur digging?"

"It goes well."

"Are you phoning from Angwana?"

"From the capital."

Mackenzie's deep chuckle came over the line. "Is that what it's called? A stink-lily by any other name would smell as badly."

"I've found a pipe, Mac—a rich one, I think. Surface finds are unbelievable."

"You mean alluvial? Washed down from miles upriver?"

"Oh, no. It's a pipe, Mac, and overburden's practically nonexistent. I'll know more when plant arrives from the Kundi Mine, but I'd know a damn sight more if you were here. I need your advice."

"I'm not looking for a job, Arthur."

"What about a visit, then?"

"Not yet, laddie. I'm extending the Komalu by another shaft—a very delicate operation. I might manage a visit in six or eight weeks. What's the best you've found on this pimple of a pipe?"

"An eight-carat stone. My foot found it the day after we arrived at the site. Mac—the stone's just short of Cape quality, so Ernst tells me, and so I believe."

"That'd be Ernst Blohm? The chap with every *-ologist* after his name except *gyne-?*"

"That's Ernst. Look, Mac, in a few days I'll have an auger drill on the site, sorting gear, too. And I want to start boring a tunnel. That's where your advice would be useful."

"Then don't do anything I wouldn't do. How's security in your neck of the woods?"

"In peculiar hands, Mac. Colonel Magasi and his guards."

"Well, that's good news."

"Good news? Do you know that he filches from our Kundi Mine?"

"It's protection money well spent, Arthur. Magasi will see that no other hands steal diamonds."

CHAPTER 4.

ARNOLD Mackenzie, engineer in charge at the Komalu Mine, woke very early, dressed, and walked away from the mine. It was his custom to catch the early hours of the morning and watch the newly risen sun shafting through the mists of the swampland that lay beyond the mine. It was then, and only then, that Sierra Leone suggested a kind of beauty to the hard gaze of Mackenzie. But with sunup, the mists cleared and the sharp glare of the sun beating down on the land, the harsh reality of that land depressed him into a kind of hate.

Living conditions strictly for the peasants, Mackenzie thought, and meant it. Good enough for the Koidu crouchers whose eyes never left the ground, permanently searching for diamonds scattered on the surface of the ground; good enough for the diamond company's night watchman whose hands were ready to receive bribes; good enough for the illicits who took their little packets of stones to shady men who arrived in mud-spattered Mercedes in the middle of the night and paid the illicits chicken-feed prices.

Dash. Dash was what you paid for the illegal transaction in Sierra Leone, and Mackenzie could think of no one, including himself, who had not used this form of currency. A pocketful of dash could work wonders with the security police, of both high and low status. The Portuguese had brought in the word: das meaning "bribe."

A mile from the mine Mackenzie stopped and looked through the shifting veils of mist to the dank swampland and fields of tall elephant grass spaced out between the swamps. This was diamond country, he thought, steaming heat, vultures, and corruption; hardly the place for Beauty to lie waiting to be kissed into life by a cutter in Antwerp or Tel Aviv.

"Unbelievable," Mackenzie said aloud, hating what he saw and loving what it gave, and, as he looked, he translated the Sierra Leone landscape into the shape of his ambition, changing the swampland smell on the light, humid breeze into the sharp, sweet smell of conifers and heather brought by the wind in the Scottish Highlands. No swamps, no elephant grass, but mountains, pale mauve, rising up into a fresh sky, and crystal-clear streams fast-running with trout and salmon, and deer silhouetted on the skyline.

He looked again at the reality stretching out before him. Muck. Miles and miles of muck containing unbelievable riches. "God snatched handfuls of stars and threw them on the land called Sierra Leone"— that was how a pious missionary with more than one eye on the interests of the government-controlled Diamond Mining Company had called the land on which the native workers toiled.

"Good old God!" Mackenzie murmured, and turned his back on both Scottish dream and the land that was rapidly making him a rich man.

Mackenzie hated Africa, hated it for what it was and what it would be in the dangerously near future. He saw the continent as a cow giving rich milk as long as the right hands pulled its udders. When those hands left, inept fingers would tug at its teats and the milk would dry up. He looked at his own hands swinging with military precision as he walked; those hands would soon be quitting Africa. One really big milk yield from the old cow and that would be it.

He thought of Arthur Appleby, a man who was giving his life for a worthless cause like so many whites who had made Africa their homeland. Like Britain's descent into the Dark Ages after the Roman occupation, the mindless hordes were gathering in uncrushable strength for their drive against the weakening control of white-dominated countries.

And liberal, decent-minded Arthur Appleby would continue to love his black brothers like an indulgent, myopic elder brother and excuse their excesses on grounds that were rapidly becoming unsupportable.

Arthur Appleby. As Mackenzie passed through the mine's security gate he remembered Appleby's enthusiastic telephone call and invitation. It might be interesting to hop across to Angwana and renew his years-old friendship with him, but not until the last milking operation was over and done with and Mackenzie could say "Goodbye, Africa, and we'll never meet again!"

After breakfast he sat in his office scrutinizing yet again plans for extending the mine's operational strength. He raised his eyes from the specifications and looked through the window at the sprawl of the rich Komalu Mine and the hole abandoned in favor of underground mining now that open-cast diamond recovery had come to an end.

East of the hole and some two hundred and fifty yards from its edge the main shaft ran seven hundred feet down into the earth; and branching out of the shaft, eight tunnels led into the diamond-bearing rock, kimberlite. Below the eight tunnels a new excavation, Tunnel 9, was within sixty yards of its strike into the blue rock.

To the west of the hole, work had begun on a new shaft. Here, rocky rising ground had to be levelled, blasted out of existence, and work was scheduled to begin in a few weeks' time.

Mackenzie's justification for a new shaft had been that it would speed up production. With two shafts and tunnels boring deeper and deeper until they reached the limit of the volcanic pipe containing kimberlite, diamond recovery would be doubled. Overproduction was no trouble. The De Beers–instigated Central Selling Organization control of supplies and price maintenance took care of that. Glut and scarcity were two factors balanced to a nicety by the CSO. In the case of glut, supplies were stockpiled and issue controlled; in times of scarcity the stockpiles were milked so that sparse production was unnoticed. An organization dreamed into existence by Sir Ernest Oppenheimer, a man of vision.

Like me, thought Mackenzie. I, too, am a man of vision, and also one-minded and ambitious.

Mackenzie was a big man with the shrewd face of a Scot. A healthy tan covered a freckled face surmounted by short-cropped wiry hair once sandy-red but now bleached by the African sun to the color of pale hay. His eyes were deep-set, gray, their corners fan-wrinkled, so that his face suggested kindliness and humor. The face of a man to be respected and trusted; a man of solid determination and justifiably proud of his part in the development of the Komalu Mine. Apart from South Africa, in the Kimberley area and the Transvaal, there were no other diamond mines in Africa with underground workings, and he could take full credit for the sophisticated Komalu. The fact that he took another form of credit was his secret.

This credit, when weighed against the profits made by him for the government-controlled Komalu Mine, was nothing—pennies pinched from millions. He had never been greedy, had never overreached himself. Over the years he had regularly siphoned off small quantities of high-grade diamonds, low in carats but high in value, through trusted men—Jacob Zuncasi, a licensed digger in Sierra Leone, and James Drake Turner, a vice president of Gem International in New York. And two bank accounts had steadily increased their deposits: Mr. Angus Arnold's account at the Bank of Liberia in Monrovia; and the Mackenzie-Turner joint account in the Banque d'Helvétie in Geneva, a bank whose safety-deposit vaults held a Mackenzie-Turner box containing a small stockpile of diamonds.

By ordinary standards, Mackenzie was a rich man, but Mackenzie ambitioned beyond his assets in Monrovia and Geneva. He was now forty-seven, and two years past the time he had set for the realization of his dream to quit Africa. It was time for a big killing, and he had spent many months in its preparation.

This was to be the big one, as Jamie Turner would have put it, and it dwarfed the deals he had made through Zuncasi and Turner. The term *big killing* was apt, regrettable but apt, and the killing itself much too big for Zuncasi to handle. Two thousand or so carats offered to the CSO in Freetown by Zuncasi would cause a sensation, and questions would be asked. Zuncasi meant pin money; the Mackenzie-Turner partnership, plus Dr. Rikel's ever-reliable aid, meant millions.

Mackenzie looked at his watch; it was time for a tour of inspection. Today or tomorrow he'd phone Jamie Turner and give the lad a report on progress and ask about the Mexico collection. Then he remembered that Jamie might be in London attending a sight at the Central Selling Organization and buying, legally, many thousands of dollars' worth of diamonds for Gem International.

CHAPTER 5.

FOUR thousand five hundred miles northwest of Sierra Leone James Drake Turner abandoned his struggle against sleeplessness and looked at his watch; glowing in the dark, the figures told him that it was 2:30 A.M. in New York and 7:30 in London; in Sierra Leone, which was in the same longitude of time, it would be 7:30, and Mackenzie would be up and about.

In London Carol might still be asleep or just about to wake. Just two more days and he'd be with her again, like the last time, when he had seen her come out of sleep smiling and ready to accept his encircling arms.

Now Mackenzie entered his mental imagery. Mackenzie and Carol Grantham had become the catalysts that were to change his life, and both were welcome. C for diamond/carbon; C for Carol; the four C's of the diamond world, Clarity, Color, Carat, and Cut. Carol had all of those qualities; clear in beauty, of perfect color, worth her carat weight in gold, and certainly a cut above any woman he had known.

And the C's were building up in Sierra Leone under Mac's decisive, capable hands. Over two thousand carats, he'd said, and soon to be shipped. The very thought of so much diamond was a sleep-robber.

A bedside table, lamp and telephone away—his wife lay sleeping in what she called "her scallop shell of quiet," the shell into which, aided by sleep-inducers, she had crept over the last year, emerging now and then to beg for the intimacy of argument, some clash that would cut through his absorption in a world from which she was excluded.

Turner had arrived back from Mexico at midnight thanking God that she had taken her sleep capsule, the threatened talk averted. Talk at a difficult level was the last thing he wanted; how could a man speak truth when so much had to be hidden?

Carol had been the final catalyst to widen the estrangement of himself and Joanie. Where, before he had met Carol, marriage could

20

have gone on in its negative way with neither partner finding an alternative, now there was only one solution, and he wished to God Joanie had found it and not him, and knew that it was a cowardly wish.

Carol, Mackenzie, Sierra Leone, diamonds—he'd had enough of vivid mental images and needed the feel of something real and tangible.

He climbed out of bed, donned dressing gown, and left the bedroom, closing the door behind him. The living room with its wide west window through which moon-cold light streamed contained all that a man or woman with conventional expensive tastes could buy: two giant facing chesterfields, Duncan Phyffe and Louis Quinze furniture, a huge carpet reputed to be Aubusson, and, occupying an entire wall, a collection of Turner reproductions dominated by a finely executed copy of that painter's self-portrait. The painting was the only item in the room that in Jamie Turner's opinion was not junk. To have as a direct forebear the great English painter was a damn sight bigger honor than owning an Aubusson carpet over which he now walked.

For a while he stood by the window looking down at the street below. He could see little beyond the reach of the hard road lighting on Riverside Drive and the Henry Hudson Parkway, and nothing of the Hudson River or the lights of Jersey City away to the left.

He turned away from the window and sat on the window seat, hands folded in lap, playing the waiting game until sleep came. Mackenzie and the diamonds came into his mind again, superseding the lingering image of Carol. Mackenzie hadn't actually used the word; he had said, "A serious accident might well be involved." Sending a mule to Mexico with twenty carats was a minor-league deal, but carrying two thousand carats was big and dangerous enough to suggest real trouble.

"It has to be the last operation," Mac had said, "so let it be a big one."

Over two thousand carats, and Turner didn't know how Mackenzie planned to get them out of Sierra Leone. All he knew was that at some near-future date he'd fly down to South America and pick up the diamonds and get them to Geneva. There would be no trouble at the Geneva end; the danger began at the beginning of the operation and in Mac's choice of carrier, and he, Turner, would be clean up to the moment he collected from the mule.

Over two thousand carats of high-quality stones and split down the middle. Added to his share of the three million dollars' worth in the Swiss bank, it meant that he could leave Joanie everything he possessed in the States, even his personal and much-loved collection of diamonds. On the thought, he got up from the window seat and went to the wall safe, dialled a combination of five numbers, swung open the door, and took out a leather wallet.

He returned to the window seat and sat down and carefully opened the wallet; it contained six white paper packets and a twelve-inch square of black velvet. He brought his knees together and spread the velvet on his lap, then selected a packet and unfolded it, gently spilling its contents onto the velvet. The twelve variously cut diamonds sparkled like stars in a frosty, clear night, flashing sharp, prismatic colors as they caught the cold sodium glare of the street lights.

Turner fingered the crystals into patterns, first into a cross and then into a circle, adding the contents from other packets. The polished diamonds glittered with life, and Turner named them: Blue-White, Top Silver Cape, Top Wesselton, Top Crystal, Jager, River—like runners in a high-class race and all born out of magma and cut into Briolette, Marquise, Emerald, Antwerp Rose, Brabant, Perruzzi. . . .

It was 3:30 when he returned the last of the diamonds to its packet and placed the wallet in the safe.

He settled down on one of the chesterfields, the images in his mind now dulled. He could sleep now that the beauty and reality of diamond had replaced disturbing conjecture.

Turner slept round to 7:30, when he awoke, showered, and dressed. He went quietly into the bedroom and looked at Joanie curled up in her shell, breakfasted on scrambled eggs and fiercely black coffee, then took the elevator down to the ground floor.

Despite his lack of sleep he felt fit, fit enough to enjoy the good air of a fine morning and walk the blocks to the offices of Gem International Corporation of America.

He glanced at his watch—8:45. Sometime during the morning, he'd look in on Dr. Heit and Emilio Canzetti, the former for his psycho-analytical/medical help, and the latter for the transfer of twenty carats he'd taken off the mule in Mexico.

CHAPTER **6.**

TWO-FIFTEEN P.M., London, and employees of the Diamond Corporation had resumed work after the lunchtime break.

Security, as always, was as tight in the day as it was at night, since eighty percent of the world's diamond production found its way into the vaults and sorting rooms of the Corporation's solid six-columned building with its bronze doors and burly, authoritative commanding-officerlike Corps of Commissioners ready to block the path of anyone unknown entering the diamond-hard Fort Knox of London.

By 2:30 all three hundred employees engaged in the sorting and valuation of rough diamonds were hard at it, the sorters with tweezers and sharp eyes examining structure and color of crystals—little mounds of rough diamonds on six-inch squares of white paper—and sorting the sheep from the goats.

No gigantic Cullinan would be sorted here. A solid, incredible diamond weighing over three thousand carats, quite accidentally discovered in 1905, would command attention far beyond the powers of the employee and directorate army stationed in the City of London; it would be a world event likely to eclipse any sporting or political upheaval, deserving banner headlines throughout the world. The little heaps of diamonds are low in carat value, down or up according to color and structure, shape and size.

In the upper sorting room the elite sorters were quietly working at their light desks ranged along the north side of the long room. Few of the young trainee sorters on the lowest sorting floor would attain the expertise needed to graduate to this room; it required talent of an unusual nature and in no way dependent on academic qualifications for entry to the elitist group now making final judgment on stones that had slowly ascended from the lower floors.

Carol Grantham had both academic qualifications and that indefinable talent for accurate judgment of diamond quality. She had taken her degree in geology, an overall study that had led her to a passion for gemstones: zircon, amethyst, tourmaline, topaz, ruby—the names conjured up concepts of magical events millions of years ago. It was this fascination she had for gemstones that had compelled her to abandon all thoughts of using her degree in teaching, or setting about the hopeless search for a post in an overcrowded profession. She had applied to the Diamond Corporation and rapidly climbed to the top, where she now sorted through the cluster of high-quality diamonds on her table.

Carol's tweezers separated a one-and-a-half-carat crystal from the mound. This was a good one, an icositetrahedron, and only the second she had found in her eighteen months in the Corporation's employment. And its color was first class—Top Cape or Wesselton.

She picked up a loupe, the magnifying glass used by sorters, and examined the crystal more closely. There was no fracture, no imperfection. Even in its rough state it sent back its message of hidden fire waiting to be released by the cutter's art. It was worth confirmation, and she turned in her chair and beckoned to Roger Bruckland, quality supervisor on her floor. He came over and said, "What've you got, Carol —an Orloff?"

"Not quite," she said, and quoted from the library of her mind. "One and a half carats as opposed to one hundred and eighty-nine point sixty carats isn't likely to cause confusion even in the mind of a beginner."

"So what *have* you got?" asked Bruckland.

"A good one. I want confirmation, that's all."

"Go ahead."

"One and a half carats, Blue-White, icositetrahedron."

Bruckland produced his own loupe and focused on the stone. "A good one," he agreed. "Flawless—perfect color. Want an on-the-spot evaluation?"

"No. Apart from its market value, it happens to be beautiful."

"If you've seen one, you've seen 'em all," Bruckland said.

"I disagree."

"It's like workers in a sweet factory. Once they've been given their fill, sweeties lose their attraction."

"In this case, not very apt. I neither eat nor covet diamonds."

"You just love them for their own sake?"

"Yes."

"We are touchy today, aren't we?" Bruckland did not wait for an answer but moved away to the central tables where sorted mounds of diamonds were heaped.

It was true, Carol thought as she resumed work, I am edgy and without humor; Bruckland is a good man, knowledgeable and helpful, the best of the floor directors. Then Bruckland, the sorters ranged along the north window wall, and the subdued murmur in the long sorting and valuation room faded from her mind as she concentrated on the diamonds glittering on the six-inch-square frosted glass desk light. But other distracting thoughts came to her. She had been unprepared for the American who had entered her life and threatened to stay in it. Life had seemed complete and satisfying before the agency party at which she had met him.

Diamond cut diamond. It was as if the abrasive quality of herself and James Drake Turner had been the factor to bring them together, that each had precisely the same cutting power but equally the power to live together in a setting. They were alike in the qualities demanded by those who assessed the value of diamonds.

Halting her thoughts for a moment, she inspected a small pale-yellow crystal; turning it round over the bright light, she detected a small dark spot on the tiny octahedron, a mark against its clarity.

The morning after the night before had been without regrets— memory of what had happened between them not recalled with embarrassment but remembered with a kind of stunned wonder. And there had been no protestations of undying love. He had said, "It doesn't end here, Carol," and she had replied, "Of course not."

They had left her flat, he to catch a plane to Geneva, she to take a taxi to the Diamond Corporation and the CSO. Two days later a postcard had arrived from Geneva with the message "Remember me?" and signed "James DT."

Carol tweezered out two yellow shapes—irregular unbroken crystals—and placed them on the table beyond the top right corner of the desk light. The remaining three corners were reserved for stones, cleavages, and macles; flats—diamonds with flat parallel sides like pieces of broken glass—had their own ignoble place at the top of the table, between the cleavages and stones.

The trouble with this drake, Carol thought, is that there's a duck attached to him. A paraphrase of an old song ran through her head: "Ducks do it,/Drakes do it,/Idiots living in Bucks do it,/Let's do it,/Let's fall in love."

Poor Mrs. Duck, Carol thought. If I say yes and we do, what will Mrs. Duck do?

She examined a crystal shape for flaws, found none, and transferred it to the growing cluster in the top right-hand corner. She worked with diamonds, she loved diamonds, James was a diamond man and loved diamonds; it was a diamond world. Even her father, Norman

Grantham, was up to his neck in diamonds in the hope that his advertising agency would one day handle a chunk of the CSO's publicity and promotional material.

Regret came to her as she thought of David Brook. Poor David, poor Mrs. Duck. J. D. Turner's appearance had put an end to what had seemed a growing response to David's patient and strong love. Three weeks ago, with Turner on his way to Geneva, she had lunched with David, had been unusually silent and withdrawn, and in answer to his quietly spoken question, "If there's something wrong, Carol, tell me. There is, isn't there?" She had told him.

On the strength of one night with a man she had known for two days, she had used her ability to tell the hard truth despite a warning voice that said, "Hold your counsel, wait until you've really tested your attraction to this American." She had told David the hard truth and watched the hurt enter his face.

Damn! She had put a macle in with the flats. She must clear her mind of distracting thoughts and images. Refocus her eyes on the sparkling cluster of diamonds; allow them to occupy every compartment in her mind: a macle . . . a shape . . . small, irregular . . . another macle of good color. . . . He had written:

> I shall be in London for the next sight—diamonds and you, Carol—and I can't think of two better reasons for getting on a plane and winging over. I can't ask you to cancel any dates you might have made during the days of the sight, but if you wanted to see me as much as I want to see you, you'd put off dinner with the Queen!
>
> Things haven't changed domestically—they never will, I guess. It's a fact not without sadness but there it is. I've told you how things stand, so if we take up where we left off, you won't be the "thief" you thought you were.
>
> There's much happening—most of it good, I think. I'm hoping you'll find it good, too. You're very much part of my life, Carol. It's odd, isn't it? Strangers meet and, in a flash, cease to be strangers. Did it happen to us or have I imagined it?
>
> I'll be hitting London next Friday—will you give me the evening? I'll contact you when I arrive at the CSO. . . .

Another macle . . . a shape . . . a stone . . . another stone . . . soon he would be in London. At 7:30 Friday evening she would see him again.

CHAPTER 7.

IN their various capacities the top executives of Gem International covered every aspect of the diamond and precious gem world. Its investments were, for the most part, safely lodged in mining corporations, but if the prospects seemed good, a gamble was made now and then. Western Australia was a case in point; recently a surface discovery of high-quality stones had been made there.

From this starting point Gem International's interests were spread over a wide field. The purchase of rough diamonds from legitimate sources, mainly from the Central Selling Organization—the CSO—in London, and occasionally from sources less legitimate was the start of a process that ran through the offices and workshops of GI. It was a tight little, right little island, with its own cutters, polishers, and designers. The luxury buyer entering its showrooms on Fifth Avenue would imagine that he was entering another Tiffany's, and know nothing of the activity above the ground floor. Here the process of converting rough stones into ornaments to be worn, or hidden away in safety-deposit boxes and taken out once or twice a year to be worn to impress, was begun and finished in the various floors occupied by the corporation.

In the old days, fifteen years ago by the estimate of the corporation's president, Randolph Stuyvver, the company had bought the rough and then contracted out the cutting, polishing, and setting to craftsmen and designers in Europe and Israel. It was an unnecessarily complicated system, and Stuyvver had simplified it by recruiting his own team of men, a heavy initial investment but one that had brought a quick return in profits. Stuyvver had his buyers—men of undoubted perception— cutters as expert as the world's best, and, in Stuyvver's opinion, a chief designer as good as Fabergé.

The important men were the buyers, those men who flew the world circuits seeing and buying, each year attending the ten sights at the CSO in London, as well as the sights in the Central African Republic, and—Stuyvver was proud of the honesty and discretion of his men, vice presidents all—acquiring packets of high-quality gems from unnamed sources.

James Drake Turner was typical of the buyers. He had a nose and an eye, a real taste for diamonds; and he had "flair"—talent a buyer must be born with and a talent sharpened by experience. If Stuyvver had set down a list of his buyers in order of excellence, Turner would head that list. It never crossed Stuyvver's mind that Jamie Turner's activity was not concerned solely with Gem International's sacred interests. And there was no reason why Stuyvver should doubt any one of his top men and employees. In his fifteen years as president there had not been the slightest hint of sticky fingers at Gem International, no gossipy rumor that any man or woman had stepped outside the rules of honesty and loyalty according to the Book of Stuyvver.

Sitting in his presidential office, Randolph Stuyvver buzzed his first secretary and ordered coffee. Life felt extraordinarily good. In two weeks prices of cut diamonds had rocketed, thanks to the Israelis who, in their wisdom, had suddenly closed shop, holding back the release of cut and polished diamonds and creating a shortage. Stuyvver's own personal cache of polished stones had increased in value by twenty-five percent, and the corporation's reserve collection was selling like hot cakes. Astonishingly quick money. A diamond worth a hundred grand two weeks ago was now worth a hundred and twenty-five. Sometime soon, with the market about to burst the top thermometer, the Israelis would start to unload, collecting top prices while the going was good. A cunning move, Stuyvver thought; Israel's cash holdings throughout the world would swell and make that country's future as secure as that of any state in its troubled part of the world.

And it had been Jamie Turner who had brought the intelligence to Stuyvver. "A hunch," Jamie had called it after his return from London with the million-dollar packet he had bought from the CSO; an "informed hunch" culled from a conversation he had with a diamond man over lunch.

A good man, Jamie Turner. In his middle thirties, with a long way to go—and the only way was up.

Stuyvver buzzed his secretary again. "When Mr. Turner arrives, ask him to come and see me. Soon as."

"Yes, Mr. Stuyvver."

Turner left Randolph Stuyvver's benevolent presence with the great man's parting message: "Find me a really good packet at the CSO's sight, Jamie—have a good trip and enjoy yourself."

Back in his office, Turner told his secretary to expect him to return after lunch, then took the elevator down and walked the few blocks to the tall apartment building containing Dr. Heit's consulting room and, on the floor below, the apartment and office of Emilio Canzetti.

The elevator man recognized Turner. "Dr. Heit, sir?"

"Right. How's the doctor?"

"One of the finest guys ever lived. I tell him my problems and he gives me good answers and for free. A regular guy, Dr. Heit."

"The best," Turner said.

He left the elevator and walked along the corridor to Dr. Heit's door, then, hearing the elevator's doors close, turned on his heel and walked back to the stairs leading to the lower floor and Canzetti's apartment.

Ten minutes later he left Canzetti, twenty thousand dollars in his pocket, mounted the staircase, and walked the corridor to Dr. Heit's consulting rooms.

Turner pulled back his shirt cuffs and showed Dr. Heit his wrists. "There's no sign yet, but I recognize that damned tingling sensation. I don't fancy another dose of lichen planus."

"You did have a bad time," Heit said. "Just over two years ago, if I remember accurately."

"And you pumped me full of some cortisone derivative, and I put on twenty pounds in four days. My stomach looked like Buddha's."

"It won't happen again. At least with nothing like the same severity." Heit looked closely at Turner's wrists. "You're very lucky, James. Lucky that your psychic problems find an outlet in lichen planus. Others might lose their memory or foam at the mouth and run. Medication and a little psychic probing—what do you think?"

"My head's yours."

"Any dreams worth mentioning?"

"Just the old repetitive malarkey."

"Mm. . . ." Heit looked away from Turner and through the surgery window; from his consulting rooms he could see a fine view across the park. "Tell me about this old malarkey."

"You've heard it before, and it's still crazy." It was time he changed the story, gave it a new twist. "I'm with Joanie and we've parked the car someplace and I can't find it. Neither can Joanie. One minute it's night, next minute it's day. We go up steps, we go down steps. Through one parking lot, then another." Turner rubbed his forehead with the fingertips of his right hand; now for something new: "One thing's different, though. I see something on the ground. It's glinting either in the moonlight or sunshine."

"Oh?"

"It's a diamond—a big one. Flawless and beautiful."

"And then?"

"End of dream." Turner leaned forward and looked earnestly into Heit's face. "Does it mean anything?"

"Only that we are getting near to a breakthrough, James." Heit was pleased. "You are still looking for yourself—your real self. The diamond is, perhaps, the sign. You can remember no continuation of the dream?"

"No. In the last frame I'm about to pick it up."

"Excellent." Heit considered the man facing him across the desk: a cooperative patient, open and ready to talk. "Any erotic dreams or day thoughts along the same lines?"

"There was one," Turner said.

"Were you passive or aggressive?"

"Aggressive, at first. It began with a girl I knew years back—before I met Joanie. In the dream we were making it like—"

"Wait," Heit said "You said 'we.' Do you mean you were both equally demanding from the beginning?"

"Oh, no—I started it. Then it became mutual. Well, everything was going along fine, and then Joanie took over. It wasn't the same after that."

"Interesting." Heit nodded his appreciation. "Metamorphosis. The wish that your wife could be the girl you once knew. This girl—did you have a full sexual relationship with her?"

Turner shook his head. "Not in the way you mean. Pretty damn close, though. Everything but. We were going full steam when she found some other guy. She said it was love and not what we had. That's fifteen years ago." He didn't have to fool Heit on this one. "I guess it still rankles," he added.

Heit took shorthand notes in his case notebook. "We'll think about that one, James. You should have told me about her earlier."

Turner shrugged. "I'm thirty-five. That's no age to be a lovesick freshman."

"There is no age limit. Well, now—how is the business life and the world of diamonds?"

"Pretty good. Never better. As a matter of fact—" Turner paused, an inner voice telling him that some things are best left hidden "—something big is coming up. Risky, but good."

"Moneywise or sane-makingwise?"

Turned smiled. "In my book, Doctor, they're one and the same thing. I remember the lack of money, debts, and the corresponding anxiety too well to separate money from mental health."

"But you're solvent, secure in your position in Gem International, a vice president with every chance of getting to the top. And you love that pure carbon you buy and sell. So why must you pursue the dollar?"

"I want fallback security. Be my own man. A rich dropout, if the term doesn't offend your professional ears."

Heit smiled tolerantly. "Nothing offends my professional ear. So— you wish to indulge in all your fantasies. To abandon responsibility for others. To be selfish. Quite natural, of course." Heit cradled his hands and leaned forward. "James, by nature man is prodigal, predatory, and selfish. Woman, on the other hand, while equally a predator, is not prodigal. Instead, she uses her skills to trap the male for a certain purpose, that of using his seed to fertilize her egg. After that, her only need of the male is that he should supply her with food while she nurtures and, later, suckles her young."

"Man the hunter," said Turner.

"On the contrary," Heit said. "Man the fetcher and carrier, James. Man the slave to woman. Man deceives himself when he imagines himself a member of the dominant sex. He is simply a useful tool."

"You're doing my psyche one hell of a lot of good," Turner said. "Why don't we men go to Times Square and publicly burn our Jockey shorts?"

"I've been speaking your mind, James. Or didn't you hear me?"

"I heard."

"So what is the message?"

"Make money and screw whoever I like, when, where, and how I like."

Heit beamed. "Excellent! I suggest you start with your wife. You have the right, you have her permission. You are aggressive in business, reasonably wealthy, so siphon off some of that aggression into your sex life. Laughing philosopher stuff. Primitive but good."

Turner got up from his chair. "So, instead of giving Joanie diamonds, I give her the family jewels?"

"Family jewels?"

Turner smiled. "That's a euphemism, Doctor."

"I take it the term refers to male genitalia?"

"Right."

"There seem to be more euphemistic terms for things sexual than for any other physical or emotional characteristic. Now"—Heit leaned back in his chair and considered Turner very seriously—"this little disorder of yours—I suggest we use cortisone again, one of its milder derivatives."

"I'd rather rely on relief from nervous tension," Turner said. "No injections."

"As you wish. I will prescribe a mild sedative. Mogadon, I think. This nervous tension, James, would it be due to the big deal you mentioned?"

"That, plus Joanie."

"Then I wish you early success to both ventures." Heit opened his appointment book. "Shall we say same time next week?"

Turner shook his head. "I'm off on a trip."

"Anywhere interesting?"

"London. I'm buying diamonds for the corporation."

Heit smiled. "Perhaps you will find your monster diamond and yourself at the same time."

"You're a perceptive guy," Turner said.

He left Heit's consulting room and took the elevator down to the ground floor. It was good for the nerves and lichen planus to let out just so much and sport with sexy old Heit. It was convenient to have a father confessor to whom you told lies that barely covered the truth; it also supplied excellent cover for occasional visits to Emilio Canzetti.

CHAPTER **8.**

T H E sky was still dark but graying as dawn approached, and Turner stood looking out of the window, out across Riverside Drive, the Henry Hudson Parkway, and the river. England was three thousand five hundred miles away, and London had already started its day's work. Carol would be seated at her sorter's table. Not long now, although the waiting seemed interminable. His bags were packed. With sunup he'd get a cab to take him to the airport. No sense or purpose in saying "Bye, now" to Joanie—she'd be deep in drugged oblivion. Thank God she'd taken her sedative and the threatened talk had been avoided yet again. She would have asked for truth, and that was something he couldn't reveal. Even the trip to Mexico to collect twenty carats of high-quality mixed rough from one of Mackenzie's mules to be sold the following day to Emilio Canzetti, had to be masked by his Gem International cover. Still, it wasn't easy to live a double life; deception, like courage, was exhaustible.

The coward in him rose as he heard the door behind him open and close and Joan's quiet voice "Jamie? . . . You said we'd talk when you got back from Mexico."

He turned away from the window, irritation replacing fear. "Leave it, Joanie, leave it."

"We've left it far too long. I want answers, Jamie."

"Who doesn't?"

"Is it just sex that's gone? Was it only sex held us together?"

"Maybe. It was a damned useful ingredient."

"I did try, Jamie."

"We both tried. It stopped working for you, and it partly worked for me because a crowing cock knows no conscience or where it's put."

"Is that all it meant?"

"It meant nothing more to both of us. It was two years ago, Joanie —two years. I felt ashamed that I'd taken advantage of your altruism.

33

You didn't want it—there was no love in it. You let me use you. I was a
louse to grind away until I'd finished. You let me use you. You went
through the motions and you weren't moved—not one little bit. What
did you think? That it would do me good because I had that lousy
lichen planus?"

"That hurts."

"So does the memory. I could have wept afterwards—for both of us.
Sex is a traitor, it solves nothing. It leads us into a relationship, then
takes off."

"We'd gone off on different tracks, Jamie. I wanted us back on."

"I wanted it, too."

"Where did kindliness and liking go?" Her voice was even-pitched,
cool, and rational. "When you're here, we sleep in the same bedroom.
Sometimes we eat a meal together—alone. But do we ever really talk to
each other?"

"We talk."

"On the surface. We have people in and you tell your stories of
faraway places and I laugh at your jokes." She paused, then said very
quietly, "When they've gone, we've nothing to say to each other. There's
a kind of silence which one of us breaks by saying, 'It went well, I
think.' "

"I'm sorry."

"So what do you want to do—about us, I mean?"

"I don't know."

"I think you do know, Jamie. You're just scared. You want out and
you're too scared to do anything about it."

He heard her come farther into the room and stand close behind
him. "I want you to know, Jamie, that if that's what you want, tell me.
This is no life for either of us. I could walk out, but I can't. This is a
nothing world. I doubt if we're even friends. When did we last laugh
together—when we were alone, I mean? Or tell each other confidences?
You went away from me first, I think. Something closed up in you. You
gathered secrets—things you couldn't tell me, or wouldn't. Was it because you couldn't trust me, or you thought I wouldn't understand? I'm
trying to understand, Jamie. I care enough to want back what we once
had. But if it isn't possible, tell me. I hate this nothing world, Jamie—
it frightens me."

He formed himself to turn and face her, fighting back his revulsion
for the pathetic. Managing an expression of concern, he reached out
and placed his hand against her cheek, and she recoiled.

"I don't want pretend sympathy! Love me or leave me—do you
hear?"

"Perhaps—" Turner hesitated, knowing it was the wrong approach. "Go on, Jamie."

"If we didn't see each other for a while. Do our own thing—whatever that is—"

"That's the coward's way. Soften the blow. Take separate vacations —wonderfully refreshing for tired marital relations. Get invigorated by getting screwed or screwing someone else. Isn't that how you get an old, old man to live another year?"

"For God's sake!" Turner flashed to anger, exasperated. "Now, look —I want to leave you and I don't want to leave you. I don't know what the hell I want until I see it—what we both want. For some reason I can't give it to you and you can't give it to me."

As if she had not heard him, she said, "Three years ago, was it? Maybe it was four. You came back from London or Africa or South America—it could have been anywhere. You talked to me as if I wasn't really there, you know? As if I was a half-person or someone you weren't really focusing on. You looked at me or through me, unless I came close and demanded your attention. You changed the pattern of our lives, Jamie. You'd say you'd be back in three days and it would be two weeks and I'd ask why and you'd say 'I got held up.' Then I'd say, 'What happened?' and you'd say, 'You know how it is.' I never knew how it was."

"Stuyvver stepped up my buying. I had more on my mind," Turner said. "Responsibility was greater. Mistakes easier to make."

"You've spent your life buying diamonds," Joan said.

It was difficult for him to return her searching gaze without lowering his eyes.

"Why should you have so much on your mind when you were doing what you love doing? It's not only diamonds, is it, Jamie?"

Here at least he could speak the truth and cover the lie. "It is diamonds, Joanie—and all that goes with diamonds."

"Like your friend Mackenzie? He's loomed large in your life. Hardly a week goes by without his laughing voice chuckling over the line all the way from Africa."

"He happens to be important to GI."

"And to you?"

"If it's important to GI, it's important to me."

"In what way?"

"In every way."

"You see?" she said. "You tell me nothing."

"There's nothing I can tell you. If I can't see you it's because I'm blind. If I can't hear you, it's because I'm deaf."

"It's as simple as that?"

"No. As complicated as that. I'm negative, Joanie, strictly negative. Ask old Heit—he's head-shrunk me, or thinks he has. Talks about the prodigal male and Man the hunter."

"Do you tell him the truth?"

"It's his job to find the truth. He wants both fantasy and reality. I give him both."

And am I covering up? he thought. I'm giving her nothing because the truth about Mackenzie and what was going to happen would shock her and endanger him. And Carol, he'd yet to find out how deep their relationship would be; if it turned out to be all that he hoped for, the success of Mackenzie's plan was all-important to his future with Carol. Self-protection, that's all it was. Joanie had no part in the life he had taken up; she was too honest. With less honesty on her part, they might have made it together.

"What do you give me?" Joan asked. "Reality?"

"I can't give you any answers—I'm sorry."

"You really have closed the door, haven't you, Jamie?"

"The door closed by itself. Somebody else had a hand on the latch."

"Whose, I wonder?"

She left the room as quietly as she had entered, and Turner looked out the window at the light of dawn on the river and the New Jersey Palisades. In a moment of self-deprecation he told himself that he was a lousy bet-hedger; that if Carol wasn't available and the Mackenzie op failed, where would he be? At least Joanie represented a background against which he could look around for another catalyst.

And now she'd be swallowing sleeping pills and curling up in that scallop shell, where she'd sleep like the dead until the daily help, following standard orders, would enter the bedroom at eleven o'clock and deliver the morning orison "Rise and greet God's kindly light, ma'am."

Flight departure was two hours off, and he was sick of waiting. He put on his topcoat, collected his baggage, and left the apartment.

As the cab bore him to Kennedy he remembered with discomfort the night—two years ago—when they'd tried to get back on course. The Adirondacks; the house by the lake and the scene set for the new coming-together; the starting-all-over-again, when Joanie had played the seductress and he'd responded as if he'd visited a whore, knowing all the time that she was getting nothing, *but nothing* out of it, just the uncertain pleasure of offering a service to sustain a marriage that had lost its enchantment, and her poor husband who wasn't well because of nervous tension. Sex had died that night, and the burial service had been quiet, and until today, this early morning it had been tacitly understood that neither would mention the loss but would let it live at the back of their minds, mourned but not forgotten.

The cabdriver entered the expressway to cover the last few miles to the airport, and Turner felt relief and anticipation taking over from self-examination. He wondered if the excitement he felt when flying from Kennedy or LaGuardia had anything to do with his desire to get away from the apartment on Riverside Drive. The old euphoria was mounting; he said to the cabbie, "Hey, do you like getting away from home?"

"You mean do I like getting away from the broad I married and who I wish to God would jump in the East River? Oh, boy!"

Turner checked in at the airport and made his way to the departure lounge. As he entered a familiar face caught his eye. He raised a hand in greeting: "Going to the sight?" he asked.

"Such a sight and with such a request," Sol Grunwald said.

Such a sight and such a request, Solomon David Grunwald said to himself as he obeyed the sign that told him he could now unfasten his seat belt. Two days ago he had obeyed a summons no reasonable diamond dealer could ignore. He had taken a flight to Denver, Colorado, where he had transferred to a chauffeur-driven car owned by *the* Robert Randall, and had been taken to a real piece of movie country. A flat plain, near desert, stretched away to the horizon; to the west a ridge of high, eroded rock towered into a sky streaked with high cirrus. At the base of the ridge he had found Robert Randall's all-the-comforts-of-home trailer parked on the edge of a cluster of location-unit portable huts, generator vans, a couple of huge wind machines, a Panavision camera mounted on a dolly and covered by a jumbo-size umbrella, and, to judge by a group of men drinking out of beer cans, a motorized chuck wagon. Beyond the cluster soldiers, whose uniforms Grunwald could not identify, lounged in the shade cast by a row of bell tents.

Grunwald was disappointed that the barren landscape was bereft of a one-horse main street with saloons, cathouses, corrals, and gunfighters with holsters tied to their thighs, and there wasn't a horse in sight. The famous actor he'd come to see had won his spurs in classic Westerns, so why weren't they making with guys falling off roofs?

Randall, sitting in the trailer, was not even dressed like a gunfighter; instead he wore outmoded empire-builder tropical gear—breeches, riding boots, epauletted shirt. On a table stood a solar topee, circa 1900. Two years ago, in exactly the same spot, he had worn a black Stetson, black shirt with a white scarf, black pants tucked into high-heeled Mexican boots, gun belt with two holsters carrying Navy

Colt .45s—waiting for the call to act, once again, the decent tin-star man near dry-gulched by rustlers. It was a fake old world, and Randall alternated between love and hate for it. What else could a good-looking man do if he couldn't paint or write best sellers, make money in real estate, or run for president, or if he hadn't the acumen to turn rubbish into gold?

Lean-faced, tall, broad-shouldered, narrow-hipped, with eyes that could look hurt or pleased, in love or in hate, with hair that curled at the nape of his neck and no trace of baldness, Robert Randall had two Oscars behind him and no broken marriages because he had never married, a fact that intrigued gossip writers who speculated whether RR was a fag.

Randall was not a fag; he was heterosexual and did not give a damn for those who doubted his masculinity. Whenever he felt the need to release sexual compulsion, he obeyed it with discretion. In any case, as he often told himself, "I'm too damned exhausted with filming to screw every dame that wants to."

Kay was different. She wasn't in the movie business, never had been, and didn't want to be. As far as she was concerned, movies came and movies went. Great stars glittered in the firmament, then died; and fans wept over graves and said, "Movies like that will never be made again," and she thanked Metro-Goldwyn-Mayer they never would be made again.

Randall looked at the sweating, blue-jowled Grunwald and said, "I want something unique, Grunwald—you understand? Something that doesn't yet exist. Secondhand goods, you can keep."

"Sure, Mr. Randall, but it'll cost you plenty."

"To hell with the cost. I've looked at diamonds. I know the difference between a stone, an irregular, a cleavage, macle, and flat. You think you can shop around and buy something that's been worn and chased around somebody's last will and testament and tell me that's what I want?"

"You do me an injustice, Mr. Randall."

"I want a diamond taken straight from the mine, you understand? In its natural rough state. I want it cut into two types—a Brilliant with fifty-eight facets, and an Antwerp Rose. That's what I want, Grunwald, and I want it quick."

Grunwald said, "So I hightail it back to New York or wherever and pick up an eighty-carat octahedron rough and get it cut in a shake of a rabbi's beard? Mister—you don't find an eighty-carat rough overnight."

"Go see my producer and look at schedules," Randall said. "Sometime ahead, we go on location for three weeks in Africa. When I get back, I marry the girl. I want those diamonds set and ready when I get back."

"Sure," Grunwald said. "Sure, Mr. Randall. Do I get a guarantee? I mean—that stone's going to cost a heap."

"No guarantees." Randall's voice was firm. "Don't believe in 'em— weakens a man's efforts. You take it or leave it, Grunwald."

"I'll take it," said Grunwald. He looked at Randall's riding boots, breeches, and tunic shirt, then at the sun helmet. "I don't get it. Is this some kinda unkosher Western? I mean, this is cowboy country, but you look like some throwback to Ronald Colman in *Beau Geste* or something."

Randall's manner softened. "I'm a white hunter, Grunwald, carrying the white man's burden before the First World War." A smile warmed his face. "And it isn't even a remake."

Grunwald's cigar had gone out. He took it from his mouth and looked at it, ruefully obeying the good cigar smoker's rule, Never relight a smoke. The money he was wasting by throwing away the long stub reminded him of the cash commitment he'd have to take on to fulfil Randall's commission.

"It'll take every buck I've got," he said. "An eighty-carat pure-white flawless! It'll mean trips God-knows-where."

"So take trips God-knows-where," Randall said.

"Sadie, my wife, already calls herself a diamond widow. I tell her, 'So you want to be a widow made of common glass?' "

"Profit is a great comforter, Grunwald." Randall looked at his watch, then got to his feet. "Stick around if you've the time. I'm due to spend the whole damned day acting a stiff-upper-lipped Brit covering the last of a hundred miles trek on foot through the desert, alone and unafraid. You might get a laugh watching."

Grunwald shook his head. "I should want my illusions ruined, Mr. Randall? When I go to a movie, you think I pay good money not to weep tears or laugh like a hyena?" He went to the door of the caravan. "This walk through the desert—they give you water or let you thirst to make it for real?"

Randall smiled. "Just behind the camera dolly, there's an ice bucket stacked with bottles of champagne."

Grunwald shook his head sadly. "Is nothing sacred?"

One hour out of Kennedy, Grunwald followed a bladder-twinge instruction and heaved himself from his seat and made his way down the Boeing's aisle. Jamie Turner saw his limping approach and held out a restraining hand: "There's a rumor floating around, Grunwald. I hear you're buying for movie stars."

"Singular," Grunwald said, "not plural. One movie star. I hear rumors, too. Like a guy named J. D. Turner using a high-style dame with a hairdo looking like an exploding meringue."

Turner looked puzzled.

"So this dame has diamonds stuck to her scalp under the meringue," Grunwald said. "You get it, Mr. Turner?"

"More hygienic than the old method, Grunwald." Turner smiled. "Where'd you hear this?"

"I didn't. It's a Grunwald variation on an old theme, Mr. Turner. Use it sometime—you should take up smuggling." Grunwald winced. "I wish to urinate. You will excuse me?"

"Hit the target," Turner said. "See you at the CSO."

CHAPTER **9**.

THE Old Lady of Threadneedle Street—the Bank of England—
is London's first Fort Knox; the Central Selling Organization in Charterhouse Street, its second. In its vaults, well underground and protected
by every security device dreamed up by man, lies over eighty percent of
the world's production of gem diamonds. Industrial diamonds, the dull,
undistinguished brothers of gem-quality stones, are sold direct to buyers who do not have to have the backing of three brokers who will claim
one percent of the value of the gem-quality buyer's packet. A buyer
needs more than cash to become an accredited buyer from the CSO. He
must have unimpeachable references and be free from any taint of
double-dealing and illicit diamond buying.

Ask how many carats are stored down in those vaults; no answer
will be forthcoming. Ask for details of the largest crystals stored down
there; again there will be no answer. The information is guarded more
sacredly than a Swiss bank account or a confession to a priest.

Ten times a year accredited buyers come to London to attend a
sight. The buyers have already submitted their request and the amount
of money they wish to spend. The packets of crystals are stacked in
what appear to be old envelope boxes, and the CSO does the buyer
proud, for the boxes contain anything from fifty to a hundred packets.
The buyer will spend days opening and closing each diamond paper,
magnifying glass held just so far from eye to crystal.

Sol Grunwald reckoned it would take him three days to inspect the
packets offered him before he could say "Okay, I'll take this one." And
as he had said over his years of trading with the CSO, he would say
again, knowing the answer, "How about taking a peep at the vaults,
huh?"

"Sorry, Mr. Grunwald. Out of the question."

Many years ago a hammertoe, a long-neglected hammertoe, had
given Sol Grunwald a permanent limp. It was not pain but the memory

of the years of unnecessary pain that caused his deformed foot to be light in touch and his other sound foot heavy. This tolerance of pain, of inconvenience, was paralleled by other habits, notably his inability to cope successfully with the lighting of the cigars that he smoked incessantly. A heavy smoker of Grunwald's character would have invested long ago in an efficient means of lighting up, but Sol Grunwald relied on matches. Sadie, his wife, had given him three gas lighters, but these had been mislaid in a matter of days, in one case in a matter of hours.

But where diamond was concerned, Grunwald was totally efficient; he could smell out a bad one, an imperfect, almost by instinct and even before he brought his magnifying loupe to bear on the stone. Both his feet in this respect were planted firmly and evenly balanced on the ground, and he needed no gas lighter to see the fire in the diamond—or its lack of flame.

"Know what I'd like to do?" he said to Mr. Dalmon. "I'd like to spend a coupla weeks in the vaults picking out the stones I want."

Mr. Dalmon shook his head. "Just not on, Mr. Grunwald. Sorry."

"A guy can dream." Grunwald took the jeweller's loupe out of his right eye socket, revealing the violet-stained ring under the pouch. "Okay. I take the packet."

"All for cutting?"

"Fifty percent, and if I make a buck I'll be lucky."

"Come now, Mr. Grunwald. Once the stones are cut and polished, you know as well as I you'll get double the price you paid for the rough."

"With pain-in-the-ass double-dealers fouling the sidewalks? I tell you, Mr. Dalmon, when Grunwald walks out of Charterhouse Street he feels koshered. My face—you would say it is a face filled with rich Jewish blood? My blood left me with my check. You should have a transfusion unit standing by already!"

Mr. Dalmon laughed; it was always a pleasure to do business with Solomon Grunwald. "You are larger than life, Mr. Grunwald," he said.

And Grunwald knew it; he traded on it. He could have become smooth-spoken, urbane, but a streak of honesty, or obstinacy, compelled him to retain his American-Yiddisher speech form and its vernacular. To become a smooth talker would be to betray his father and mother, sisters and brothers, their friends and relations. His style, whether used in Cartier's, Tiffany's, or the Diamond Corporation, was the same one he used in haggling over the price of a chicken or a cabbage in a Brooklyn market. Once you met Grunwald, you never forgot Grunwald. He made a hole in the atmosphere.

"Now I wish you to make me happy," Grunwald said. "Something so special my voice falters."

"What is it, Mr. Grunwald?"

"I want a single stone and just about the purest white God ever made."

"Oh, yes," said Mr. Dalmon.

"An octahedron of eighty carats. Not less—more if necessary."

"Put in your request, Mr. Grunwald, and we'll see what we can do. It's an unusual request, however."

"So I got to ask for the stone and state the price?"

"It's usual."

Grunwald stroked his chin that was blueing from four-o'clock stubble. "That's the hell of it. I've never dealt with a stone that size before. You want to hear the story? I tell you the story. . . . I give thanks to my brother, Dave, who is in the movie business—such a brother! When he hears that Robert Randall, the movie star, wants diamonds for his bride-to-be, my brother tells him there is only one man can find the best and his name is Solomon Grunwald. My brother, David, does not lie, Mr. Dalmon. You respect me at the CSO?"

"With very great respect."

"So I buy the best that money can buy."

"The CSO has *only* the best."

Grunwald smiled. "Yeah, eighty-five percent of the world market. So I ask you, Mr. Dalmon, find me such a stone and let me know how much so I can put in a request."

Mr. Dalmon nodded. "I think that could be arranged."

"I got to know soon. Cable me soon as. And no competition, right? If some buyer wants the same deal, I have first call—you know what I mean?"

"I know exactly what you mean," Mr. Dalmon said, and a note of correction entered his voice. "I must remind you, Mr. Grunwald, such a stone would be valued according to demand and supply. We would assess its value by that standard of judgment and decide on a price. Give me four or five days, and you will hear from me."

"Make it loud and clear."

"Rest assured, Mr. Grunwald."

Grunwald left the office with Mr. Dalmon, the packets he had bought tucked away in the lining pockets of his waistcoat. At the same time James Drake Turner emerged from another room and hailed Grunwald.

"How's the rough diamond, Grunwald?"

"Mr. Turner, this rough diamond has facets so polished you could see your face in them. And Gem International—it still struggles?"

"We stay afloat, Grunwald, despite the loners in the business."

"Shall I tell you a secret of success, Mr. Turner? I will tell you anyway. Cut down on overheads and vice presidents, and from a little office, industry, and a reputation—such a reputation!—for honesty, it is pure profit."

"You should have come into GI when Stuyvver asked you."

Grunwald looked upwards. "Give me liberty or give me death! Have I done badly, Turner? And does a famous movie star go to Gem International when he wants something special for his intended?"

"I heard about it, Grunwald. I guess he wants something untouched by human hand. *Shalom*, Grunwald."

"*Mazel un b'rochah*, Turner."

"What does that mean?" Mr. Dalmon asked. "Is it Hebrew?"

"Yiddish. Means 'Good luck and blessings.' "

Watching Turner stride briskly down the corridor, Grunwald said, "He's a funny guy—one of the best in the business."

"Extremely good," said Mr. Dalmon.

"He makes cracks about loners when he's got what it takes to step out on his own. He's got nose—the instinct. Should I take a partner it would be J. D. Turner, Mr. Dalmon."

"A formidable partnership, Mr. Grunwald."

At the first of the bronze doors Mr. Dalmon shook hands with Grunwald. "I'll not forget your request. I'll see what I can do in the next few days."

"Cable me, huh?"

"I'll do that."

"I mean this is not only for real, but urgent. A stone like that can't be cut in a couple of days."

As he stepped out into Charterhouse Street Sol Grunwald thought about the disturbing, though profitable, change in what had been the normally worrying business of buying stones in the rough, having them cut, then haggling in a diamond bourse, or taking the rough to a diamond club and selling to a buyer not credited at the CSO. This last made a few useful dollars in a quick turnover.

But an eighty-carat pure-white; it made him sweat to think of the cost, and he'd sweat until the stone had been cut, delivered, and paid for by Robert Randall. Months of anxiety loomed ahead unless he could find the stone within the next few days.

He stumped up Hatton Garden, a stout and sturdy middle-aged man in a dark-blue suit, dark-blue raincoat, and gray trilby. He looked at his watch—four hours yet to kill before the concert at the Festival Hall and a chunk of his favorite music, Brahms's Violin Concerto.

The dignified facade of Hatton Garden's Diamond Club came up on his left, and he entered, reaching for the plastic folder containing his membership card. With luck someone from Antwerp, Tel Aviv, or

45

Africa might be in the club; someone who might have, or know about, an eighty-carat pure-white octahedron. A man should have such luck!

The largest stone offered him in the Diamond Club was a thirteen-carat octahedron. Grunwald's reaction was immediate: "You think I am buying for midgets? Offer me a stone above eighty carats—one that's as pure as the driven snow, and we might talk business."

Grunwald was a man with troubles that were skin-deep, Turner thought as he left the CSO building and hailed a taxi to take him to the Hilton Hotel; he could see why he hadn't taken up Randolph Stuyvver's offer to join Gem International. As Grunwald had put it, "Me with all those smooth guys in executive gray? You want to lower the tone of GI? I would lose character, Turner, and that I do not want." Which, translated, meant "I get along very well. I am my own boss. My reputation is as high as any diamond man's. Why should I become something I am not?"

Good for you, Grunwald, Turner thought; maybe I'll be joining your ranks pretty soon.

It was Friday, and in three hours' time he'd call for Carol. The thought stimulated him into a state of high expectancy, and he told himself to take it easy. He had five days in London before cutting across to Geneva to add Canzetti's dollars to the growing pile of cash and diamonds in the Swiss bank. Play it gently, and don't rush the scene you have in mind, James Drake Turner. Play it as if you're certain what you want to happen will happen tonight, tomorrow night, or the night after. As he paid off the cabbie he felt lightheaded and confident. He was three and a half thousand miles away from New York and Joanie, and both might have been three and a half thousand light-years away. He felt so damned confident and happy, he played the dumb American and gave the cabbie a five-pound note, saying, "Will a pound note cover the tab?"

The cabbie was no fool. "That's right, guv. What about the change?"

"Keep it, my friend."

They dined at a restaurant of Carol's choosing, eating Italian, but drinking French. Night had fallen when they left the restaurant and walked hand in hand up the King's Road until they caught a taxi, which Carol directed to her address. As the taxi turned into Sloane Street each obeyed an impulse and kissed, lightly at first, then urgently, oblivious to the grin on the driver's face as he watched in his passenger mirror.

At the door of her flat Turner said, "Your place or mine, Carol?"

She understood immediately. "Mine," she said, and inserted the key into the lock.

Carol leaned on one arm and watched Turner come out of sleep. Returning his smile, she said, "You were twitching in your sleep, Jamie."

"Was I? I don't remember dreaming a twitch or anything likely to cause me to twitch."

"Who is Mac?"

"Why?"

"Sometime during the night I woke up to hear you mumbling. It sounded like a conversation. Now and then you said, 'Good old Mac.' That's all I could make out."

"Must be Arnold Mackenzie. He's a mining engineer in Africa. A big feller, Carol." He took her face in his hands. "Any regrets, Carol?"

She shook her head. "Not for lovemaking with you. Like last time, I feel a bit like a thief."

"You haven't stolen anything, Carol. There's been no sex in my marriage for two years—mutually, that is."

"Is that why you were so hungry?"

"You were every bit as ravenous as me, Carol. God knows what your neighbors thought. Shall we make it again—now?"

"No. I've got to go to work, Jamie. What will you do today?"

"Back to the Hilton and change, then to the CSO and look at more packets and try not to see you in every diamond."

"That's nice."

"Distracting. Can I see you this evening—tonight? Tomorrow morning too?"

"I'm free at lunchtime, Jamie."

"I'm not. Richard Walker's feeding me. You know him?"

"I've met him. They say he's a hawk in dove's clothing."

"He's in love with my wife, Carol."

"What!"

"It's true, but it has nothing to do with the failure of our marriage. When it happens—I mean, when I leave her, she'll have a strong shoulder to lean on. He's a good guy—I like him."

Carol went into thought, silent.

"Carol?" he said.

"I was thinking. Making love is one thing—a permanent relationship is another. I'm very cautious, Jamie. I'm liberated enough to go to bed with you, but—I don't want to be the only reason why you leave your wife. That doesn't make awfully good sense, does it? I could say, if you leave her here and now, we'll live together as from now, but I can't, Jamie. I want time with you without living with you. I'm leaving the future out for the present, you see. When you're no longer married, that's when we can plan for the future."

"Some speech," Turner said. "Okay. It makes sense—good sense. It wouldn't, though, if it kept us out of bed. It would make no sense at all."

"We'd only get frustrated—hung up."

"Like now?"

She got out of bed, beautiful and naked. "Not like now. I want a bath."

"I'll join you," Turner said.

A shadow crossed his mind; he'd said the same thing to Joanie after their wedding night.

The unit had finished filming for the day, and the hot Colorado sun had served them well; set in a fine blue sky, it had shone as if following the script—a bonus to a budget-conscious director.

As Randall wearily made his way to his caravan, assistant director Colly Shaw said, "A great day, Bob—a great day! We jumped a day ahead of schedule."

"It was okay," Randall said. "Very okay." He was tired, and his back ached; since eight o'clock that morning he'd made twenty-five runs over ground strewn with explosive charges representing bullet strikes.

"We got some fine shots," Colly said. "Very, very fine shots. Tomorrow we do the scene where you get wounded—*zim-bang!* Bullet strike . . . blood flow . . . then the old Randall close-ups showing pain, resignation—boy! You're always so goddamned reliable!"

"So when do we get back to the studio for interior shots?"

"See how things go tomorrow, huh?"

"I reckon on four weeks for the shots."

"Could be."

"No longer," Randall said, "and I mean that. Fill-ins when Kay and I get back. I want that understood."

"It's understood, Bob—understood. There's something else that won't take long—" Colly hesitated, and Randall said, "What the hell now?"

"Rosa Collins is waiting, Bob. She's important, and she's a fan. Give her a few minutes."

"Hell!" Randall said. "I've been dodging those bloody charges all day and now you want me to dodge the charges of a damned gossip writer?"

"Just see her, Bob. She's okay and good for you."

What did it matter? Randall thought. He'd always put the job first, privacy second. Hard work and privacy. He'd earned his fifteen years of success by giving himself to work in working hours and then, with the day over, the sixty-mile drive to peace and solitude deep in the hills and away from the studios and the rats.

He entered his caravan and slumped down into an armchair. "Okay, Colly—bring her in."

Rosa Collins was fat and dumpy with small feet but with a reputation that could sink a rising star overnight.

As she entered the caravan Randall got to his feet and held out his hand. "Good to see you, Rosa."

Rosa Collins peered up into his face. "I'm nearsighted, Randall, but I can see you're tired."

"Age does not wither me, but location shooting slays me, Collins. Light an' set, pilgrim."

"Won't waste time," Rosa said. "About your marriage to Kay Summers. Any date yet?"

"When we've finished shooting."

"Where's it to be?"

"It's private, Collins—very private."

"Fair enough. You're one movie actor I grant the privilege of privacy—in some matters. You're a rich man, Randall, a movie multimillionaire. You've never paid alimony because you never married, right?"

"Right."

"You know what they've said about you in the past?"

"Yup."

"It doesn't bother you?"

"Ask my twenty-four bastard kids scattered over the country." Randall smiled. "Maybe I just waited for the real thing, Collins."

Rosa thought for a moment, then said, "It could be true. It's unusual, and it's the kind of thing that's dying out. I like it, though. It's old-fashioned but fits in with your image—the one I've got, that is. You love this girl?"

"Very much, Collins. I've waited a long time for Kay to appear on the scene."

"You're doing me proud, Randall. Can I ask for more?"

"Ask."

"What are you going to give the girl—apart from the obvious, I mean? My crap readers like gold-plated Cadillacs and expensive shim-sham. So what will you give the girl as a wedding present?"

"Diamonds."

"You're not buying from the ex-Burtons?"

"I don't buy secondhand, Collins. I've got a funny fat man, one of the best diamond buyers, looking for a high-carat rough diamond—a big one to be cut into two stones and set into a ring and a pendant."

"Cost a heap?"

"Well over the million."

"Who's your buyer?"

"Sol Grunwald."

"And who'll cut the diamond?"

"Heinert of Antwerp. The best, I'm told. Norman Teufel will design and do the setting."

"Why not an American designer, Randall?"

"Teufel *is* an American. Works in New York."

"When do I get to see them?"

"After I've given them to Kay. Do you want an exclusive?"

"I'd like that. Just one thing—why not go to Tiffany's? They've got some of the best geegaws in the world."

"I told you—I want nothing secondhand for Kay. A stone in its natural state, cut and polished to my order, set the way I want it. I figure that's better than diamonds pushed around by other hands. More personal, you understand?"

Rosa reached out a hand and laid it on Randall's arm. "You're a nice guy, Randall. You've given me a lot—I'm obliged. You know what?"

"What?"

"If I were you, I'd tell movies to go to hell, and soak in a hot bath."

"That's what I intend to do—until tomorrow when they do a thousand takes of me getting a bullet."

At the door Rosa Collins paused. "I take it the girl knows about the diamonds?"

"She knows."

"I wouldn't write it up if she didn't. I like you, Randall. Wish you the best for the new movie. I'll see you again."

Tony Klein, head of Klein Enterprises, New York, sat at the desk in his one-office organization and looked at his right-hand man, Swede Petersen, sprawling his large frame in the swivel chair on the other side of the desk.

"So what's the grouse, Tony?" Swede asked.

"The grouse is expansion," said Klein, "which we have not got. Look at it this way, Swede—we play it safe all along the line, getting out if the going's bad and the policy's paid dividends."

"Just friendly persuasion." Petersen grinned and flexed his biceps. "And being a big guy helps."

"Up to a point," Klein said, "but it sticks in my gullet, all those guys getting cuts until we get the merchandise. A third here and a third there. We get the last third, maybe less."

"We don't take the risks the guys take, Tony."

"So we don't expand." Klein looked round the office. "We are small but not beautiful." The telephone bleeped, and Klein reached for it, cradling the receiver between ear and shoulder. "Yeah?"

A delicate, precise voice came over the line: "This is Emilio Canzetti."

"Hi, Milly."

"An idea for an assignment, Klein, since you have not been unhelpful in the past. The movie actor, Robert Randall, is giving diamonds to his best-beloved. This you would know if you have read the Rosa Collins gossip column."

"I should read it, Milly?"

"It might keep you in touch, Klein. Listen. The column tells those capable of reading the printed word that a dealer named Grunwald has been commissioned by Randall to buy a diamond in the rough and then to get it cut. I understand that the resulting diamond or diamonds will be worth in excess of one million dollars."

"That is something," Klein said.

"The column mentions that the rough stone will be unusually large. What does that suggest to you, Klein?"

"You're in diamonds, Milly, you tell me."

"That Grunwald will go to Europe to buy the rough. Regularly, he goes to London to buy. Klein—you and the excellent Swede have served me well in the past. You may not know diamond, but you know how to steal. I want the Randall diamonds, Klein."

"So would lots of guys."

"Get it or them, and we will split down the middle."

"If we got them, sixty-forty in my favor's a better scene. I'll think about it, Milly."

"You'll do more than that, Klein, otherwise I will bring in other more capable hands."

Klein grinned at Petersen. "Yeah, Milly—guys with fingerprints in police records."

"Perhaps that is why I approach you, Klein. Both you and Swede are comparatively clean."

"Compliments, Milly?"

"And small-time. That may be to our advantage. Neither you nor Swede have known diamond faces—that is, well-known."

"I'll talk to Swede. You hear any more, Milly, you tell me."

"Of course. My hearing is very acute. Klein. One other thing—keep it in the family, with no contracting out."

Klein hung up and looked thoughtfully at Swede. "That was opportunity knocking. Canzetti with something big."

"How big?"

"Diamond worth over a million."

"Whose?"

"Nobody's yet. I'm interested, Swede. Just so far I'm interested. Could be expansion. There's a diamond dealer, name of Grunwald. Check him out. I want you where he is. Canzetti says Grunwald will go to Europe—London, maybe. Tail him, Swede."

"To London?"

"Anywhere if the prospect's good."

Petersen was silent for a space, then he said, "It gets rougher near the top, Tony."

"Expansion means you take risks. Get moving, Swede. Find Grunwald. We take it from here—play it as it comes. And get me a copy of the paper that does the Rosa Collins column. I can read as well as that fink Canzetti."

CHAPTER **10.**

s I x days after he returned from London and the CSO's sight,
Solomon Grunwald received a telegram from Mr. Dalmon suggesting
that he put in a request for an eighty-carat pure-white diamond costing
seven hundred and fifty thousand dollars. On receipt of his reply, a
special sight would be arranged forthwith.

Grunwald cabled his request and took the first flight out of Kennedy. Sadie, his wife, drove him to the airport. "For diamonds, Sol, I
sometimes think you would sell your wife and risk your life."

"That rhymes," Grunwald said. "You should be a poet, Sadie."

"And will you come straight back for your grandson's bar mitzvah?
Oh, no—you go to Antwerp and drink beer and talk diamonds at the
bourse and worry yourself sick—"

"Sadie, do you want for clothes or a nice house that is detached and
sons who are set up in business and doing very well? And do you want
for money to buy food? You are clicking your teeth, Sadie. And if I
should die, who would be the wealthiest widow in Queens on account of
insurance?"

"I speak as your wife, Sol."

"Who weighs many more carats than the size of a house and is
worth as much to me? So shut up, Sadie, and give love to your husband
who works only for his wife and family."

Sadie fingered the necklace she wore—carob seeds taken from the
locust bean, interspersed with garnets. It was nice of Sol, thoughtful, to
have the seeds, originally used as carat weights, strung together with
garnets. "This deal you have with Robert Randall, Sol—when you have
done, you will give me a present?"

"I'll give you a present, Sadie."

"What will it be, Sol?"

"A husband who has lost weight due to anxiety."

*   *   *

Anxiety rested lightly on Swede Petersen's shoulders as the Boeing lifted off Kennedy Airport and headed east. Tailing Grunwald was a pleasure when it involved jetting to Europe and keeping a quiet eye on the fat cigar smoker in seat sixty up the aisle.

"Just a hunch," Swede had told Klein. "Grunwald went to a diamond sight in London six days ago—one of the yearly ten, right?"

"So?"

"So why does he book a flight to London only six days later?"

"You tell me."

"Maybe he's got what he wants for Randall."

Klein thought for a moment, then said, "Get on that flight, Swede."

"I booked it already, Tony."

Grunwald held the crystal up to the light. Through the loupe he could see the fire burning in the octahedron. It was perfect, flawless, a Blue-White.

Sol knew he had found the Randall diamond. The beautiful octahedron had sent out a message that was almost sexual. It had said "Take me" long before he had used objective judgment to assess its value and weigh the price he had to pay against that assessment.

"Okay," he said. "I like it, I like it fine."

"I thought you would," said Mr. Dalmon.

"Such a stone should rest on velvet surrounded by security guards with guns. My life is in that diamond, Mr. Dalmon, my very life."

"I'm sure your life is worth more than seven hundred and fifty thousand dollars, Mr. Grunwald." Mr. Dalmon smiled and, as Grunwald took out his cigar case, produced his lighter and waited for Grunwald to fumble for a matchbook before thumbing the lighter into flame.

Grunwald kindled his cigar, then said, "Seven hundred and fifty thousand bucks. . . . Is it right a man's life should be held by an eight-sided stone?"

Dalmon smiled. "That is up to you, Mr. Grunwald."

"If Sadie, my wife, knew what I have paid, she would see ruin staring her in the face. So—I take my ruin with me, and the CSO takes my check for three quarters of a million dollars."

Mr. Dalmon looked at his gas lighter, a Christmas present from a CSO client. "If it would help, Mr. Grunwald, accept this lighter as a present. I imagine you will smoke many cigars in the next few weeks."

"Then you look for matchbooks, huh?"

"I don't smoke," Mr. Dalmon said. "I never have. An odd habit."

"Not smoking?"

"Oh, no—*smoking* is a very odd habit."

"So's tap-dancing," Grunwald said. "Hard on the feet."

Transaction completed, Mr. Dalmon saw Grunwald to the bronze doors. "So, the next stop is Antwerp, Mr. Grunwald. Give my respects to Pieter Heinert—a very fine craftsman."

"The best," Grunwald said. "Thanks for the lighter."

He caught an evening flight to Antwerp, booked in at a hotel, drank four Belgian beers which he did not like, and went to bed early, the diamond in his pajama coat pocket and near to his heart.

He was at Pieter Heinert's workshop early and spent the best part of the morning watching and worrying as Heinert prepared the stone for slitting, and he smoked incessantly, lighting his cigars from the Bunsen burner on Heinert's workbench.

Heinert had inserted the diamond in the holder; it was now set hard in a mixture of plaster of paris and glue. "I hope you appreciate the method I am using to saw the stone, Mr. Grunwald," he said. "I could use a diamond-impregnated disc, but I am going to use a more traditional method. Oddly enough, it should work out less expensive."

"Suits me," Grunwald said.

"In cutting the stone, I shall wear out many sawing discs and, of course, many days."

"Sure. I know."

"Regular applications of diamond powder mixed with olive oil—" Heinert indicated a dish containing gray paste: "That was made up in anticipation of your visit. The sawing disc will be fed with the paste and slowly, slowly, we will cut this beautiful stone."

"Seven hundred and fifty thousand dollars," Grunwald said. "If that damned saw goes *mechulah* on me—"

Heinert raised an eyebrow. "So why do you come to Belgium's best cutter, Mr. Grunwald? If you expect mistakes, you go elsewhere. What is seven hundred and fifty thousand dollars? When I have finished, you will have two stones with a value of twice that amount."

"I get nervous."

"Then go away."

"I got to stay. This diamond's my baby, Heinert, my sweet, sweet baby. If I had tits and that stone could suck, I would feed it with my life."

Heinert made a sound of disgust. "No diamond is worth such love."

"Three quarters of a million dollars is. You ever raise money like that on a single stone? Let me tell you, all I got is in that stone—every goddam cent!"

Dryly Heinert said, "You have nothing to lose, Mr. Grunwald. You

Grunwald and ordered a large Scotch.

Grunwald said, "Hiya."

"Hi."

"The beer's lousy."

"That's why I ordered Scotch."

Swede Petersen looked at Grunwald's worried face. "You on vacation?"

Grunwald looked sour. "I'm wearing a camera, sunglasses, and Bermuda shorts?"

"You're not on vacation?"

"Then what gives with vacations if a guy's on business in Antwerp and drinking lousy Belgian beer?"

"No offense. Take it easy. It's just good to hear an honest-to-goodness American voice straight out of New York."

Grunwald's face softened. "I'm sorry. Normally I'm a happy, friendly guy. I stroke cats and pat heads of dogs and do not put stupid questions to friendly fellow Yankees. I also do not like Belgian beer."

"Leave the beer. I'll buy you a Scotch." Petersen caught the barman's eye. "Scotch *pour mon ami.*" He smiled at Grunwald. "That's French. I don't know Belgian lingo."

"Who does?" Grunwald said.

"What business you in?" asked Petersen.

"Diamonds."

"Is that so? I import and export. Charlie Anderson's the name. Friends call me Chuck."

"So what do you export and import?"

"Whatever's worth exporting and importing."

Grunwald nodded his approval. "Eggs in many baskets, that's safe. Mine are in one goddamned basket for the first time in my life, and I'm losing weight faster than an ice cube in the Sahara." He pushed the half-empty beer glass away from him. "Cow's urine." He picked up the glass of Scotch.

Petersen said, "Drink hearty. You got a name?"

"Grunwald. Solomon Grunwald. Home's in Queens, office on Forty-seventh Street." Grunwald took a cigar from his pocket case and stuck it in his mouth, fumbling for matches. "Hell!" he said. "You got a light, Anderson?"

"Sure." Petersen snapped his lighter under Grunwald's cigar.

Between drags Grunwald said, "I lose matches and lighters like kids lose their virginities these days."

"Like there's no decency left," said Petersen. "What's this egg you got in one basket?"

"Like I told you, my business is diamonds. I should correct myself

—my business is in *one* diamond. For a famous movie star I enter into a contract that I love and hate."

"Hey!" Petersen said. "Didn't I read about it? Robert Randall buying big for his bride to the melody of a million bucks?"

Grunwald nodded. "I saw the piece."

"Now I remember," Petersen said. "The column named you. Grunwald. Well—whad'ya know?"

"That I am a very worried man, Anderson."

"The higher you get, Sol, the more worried. Am I right?"

"I guess so." Grunwald heaved himself off the barstool. "I'll return the drink sometime, Anderson. I leave my baby in Antwerp and go back to New York. In two weeks, maybe, I fly back to Antwerp like I am a jet-set person."

"Be careful now, huh? Nice talking to you, Sol."

"Mutual," Grunwald said. "See you."

CHAPTER 11.

THE weeks dragged by slowly for Sol Grunwald and James Drake Turner. In Grunwald's case, he thought constantly of the diamond being processed by Heinert in Antwerp, the saw spinning its way through the octahedron eight hours a day, five days a week. And each day Grunwald phoned Heinert to receive the same calm assurance that all went well and that Mr. Grunwald *must* be patient.

In Turner's case, he waited for two major events: the final call from Mackenzie that the countdown had begun, and reunion with Carol in Geneva. While the two were unrelated and always had been, a future with Carol and the start of a new life was certainly dependent on the success of his partnership with Mackenzie.

Turner had spent little time at the apartment on Riverside Drive. After his confrontation with Joan in the early hours of the morning, she had retired back into her shell, emerging when the occasion demanded it and acting out the part of Mrs. James Drake Turner, hostess to her husband's business friends.

Turner had also missed out on a sight at the CSO. At the last minute Randolph Stuyvver had taken it into his head to attend the sight himself, and Turner had no alternative but to occupy Stuyvver's chair, and he had fretted and fumed with frustration during Stuyvver's ten days' absence. Each day he had phoned Carol, telling her of his anger, to be calmed, momentarily, by her assurance that they had all the time in the world.

Tension was building up as he waited on Mackenzie's call and the escape to freedom, and he doubled the dose of tranquilizers prescribed by Dr. Heit. It was now six weeks since he had seen Carol in London. Six weeks in which he had sat in Stuyvver's chair, taken trips on GI business to Los Angeles and, it seemed, every damned point on the compass except London. There had not even been a chance of a week-end pleasure trip to London and Carol; each time he had found a two-day gap in his schedules, something would come up and he would angrily tell his secretary to cancel his flight booking. And Mackenzie's calls had been too infrequent; two telephone conversations, guarded and cryptic, and the same number of airmail letters assuring him that plans were nearing completion and now needed only confirmation that the mule had arrived and was ready to carry.

Mackenzie's choice of a mule worried Turner. The carrier had had no previous experience of carrying illicit diamonds and therefore was not known to diamond security men. Mackenzie called it a plus, for the man would not be under suspicion; but his inexperience worried Turner. Turner was reassured when Mackenzie told him that the mule would not be carrying when he left Sierra Leone but would collect in South America, but Turner still did not know exactly how the operation would work.

"Over two thousand carats, Jamie," Mackenzie had told him over the telephone. "Just bear that in mind. When the time comes, I'll tell how, when, and where. I'm waiting on a bit of news from London. When that comes you'll hear from me. This will be the big one, Jamie— worth waiting for."

How, when, and where? And who was the mule?

Three houses away from the Diamond Club in Hatton Garden a four-story building contained a shop on the ground floor and, on the second and third, the office and workshops of Leonard Snow, diamond cutter and dealer.

The man mounting the stairs to the second floor was bespectacled and middle-aged, and his face was pallid, a yellowish tinge to that pallor suggesting that malaria had made him its host.

Five large uncut emeralds were in his inside jacket pocket and wrapped in tissue paper. Until eight o'clock that morning and during clearance through customs at Heathrow Airport, those stones had been distributed about his clothing. The end of his journey was in sight, but the terrors that had pursued him for weeks still nagged at his mind. One day soon, he told himself, the fear of violent death or imprisonment would go, but not before he had forgotten the days spent with the Quaqueros, Colombia's illicit miners, and had paid out nearly all the money he possessed. And then the foul journey up the Magdalena River to Santa Marta and eventually to Panama where he had flown to London.

This for a man who might extend a hand in friendship and coop- eration or stab him in the back. Reward or punishment according to the laws of the devil who'd found him out and had offered the return of his soul for services rendered. The devil had said, "Do this and I'll consider whether you're worth saving. Do this and you'll not only have freedom but money to last you the rest of your worthless life."

And there seemed little of life left. He halted for a moment until his breathing eased, then trod the last of the stairs. On the landing he faced a door that might have belonged to a seedy private investigator. A lensed eyehole was set two feet below the lintel of the door; under the lens a small plaque bore the inscription "L. Snow."

He pressed the door buzzer and waited, aware of, but not seeing, an eye scanning him from the eyehole.

A voice spoke, apparently from nowhere: "Yes?"

He spoke to the door: "My name is Partridge. Mr. Snow is expecting me."

"One moment, please."

The door opened to reveal a pink-faced, balding man in his sixties smiling his welcome. "Please come in, Mr. Partridge. I am Leonard Snow."

Partridge entered, and Snow closed the door behind him. Across the sparsely furnished room a door was partly opened; through the space came the sound of motors whirring softly and a hissing sound that came and went.

"My workrooms are through there," Mr. Snow said. "Do please sit down. Emeralds, I believe?"

Partridge sat down and took the tissue-wrapped package from his pocket. "The best I could buy. I have to ask for your opinion." Carefully he peeled away the layers of tissue and gently pushed the exposed emeralds across the table.

Screwing a jeweller's loupe into his left eye, Mr. Snow examined the stones. "Oh, yes," he said. "Really first-class. South American, of course. Colombian?"

"Yes."

Head still bent over the emeralds, Mr. Snow said, "I take it you were recommended?"

"Yes."

"May I ask by whom?"

"A mutual friend at the Komalu Mine."

"Ah, yes—he is known to me. A man to be trusted, Mr. Partridge." Mr. Snow picked up the largest of the emeralds and held it up against the east light entering the window of the room. "Truly rare and precious. A many-faceted cut, I think. No common Step or Trap for this one." Taking the loupe from his eye, he looked at Partridge. "Did you have a comfortable journey?"

"No—it was hell."

"I am sorry to hear that. Foreign travel can be distressing." Mr. Snow returned to the table and carefully folded the tissue paper round the emeralds. "You may safely leave these with me, Mr. Partridge."

Partridge got to his feet. "I've very little money," he said. "He told me—"

"That I would help?" Mr. Snow said. "Our mutual friend is a thoughtful man, Mr. Partridge." He took an envelope from his pocket. "You will find enough here to cover you between London and South America. I understand you will be contacted by our mutual friend when you arrive."

Partridge took the envelope. "If I survive."

"Come now, a good night's sleep will work wonders. A good meal with wine, and an early night. A good prescription, Mr. Partridge."

Partridge descended the stairs with part of his burden shed. If only he could feel energy motivating his movements instead of sheer will-power forcing him to put one foot forward, then to bring it back as the other foot took his weight. And if only he could feel relief that the first part of his punishment was over, a relief that would give him strength to face the second and last part of the devil's assignment.

The hotel room was small, neatly furnished, but without personality, and Partridge loathed it. He longed for it to contain something with which he could identify, a picture, maybe, or an ornament that sent out the message "I am here to comfort and please you." Even the Gideon Bible on the bedside table was as impersonal as the hotel rules posted on the door.

His forehead was damp with sweat, yet his whole body shuddered. He reckoned the room temperature touched the high sixties, warm enough to warrant the hotel's standard equipment of a feather-light eiderdown, two thin blankets, and the sheet that he now pulled up to his chin, sweating as he shook with cold.

He had ignored Mr. Snow's advice and had gone straight to his room and crawled into bed still partly dressed. My blood must be running thin as water, he thought, and lively with malaria—and this despite the tablets he had regularly, religiously taken since the mild attack in Colombia. Temperature should be taken, he told himself; but he'd broken the thermometer in the cockroach-infested hotel in Bogotá and, in his panic flight to England, hadn't replaced it.

The shivering increased, and Partridge willed his body to stop, clenching his fists, eyes tight-closed, and his body reacted with an attack of nausea that abated as he began to climb out of bed to be sick in the hand basin. He sat on the edge of the bed, head in hands, until the bitter taste of bile left his mouth, then he crawled back under the blankets and eiderdown. Somehow he must create order out of the chaos racking his body. Mind over matter . . . psychosomatic control of mind and brain over rebellious body, over the shuddering jumble of nerves, muscles, and viscera. Take the advice of Mackenzie— big, reliable Mackenzie of the iron will: *"Stop snivelling, Partridge. If you want peace of mind, earn the bloody thing!"*

Peace of mind. Nirvana. The attainable promised by Mackenzie. Remembered words and scenes. The beginning of it all when Jacob Zuncasi had approached him at the Komalu and spoken persuasive words. Mackenzie had known, of course; right from the start he'd known; how else could the ease with which he'd stolen from the mine be explained? He had asked Mackenzie why this task? Why not some- one with experience, a mule accustomed to carrying illicit out of the country? *"Because you don't look like a mule, Partridge, and I'd like to see if you've guts enough to face up to risks thieves take."*

My body has been desecrated, Partridge thought. Did you consider that, Mr. Mackenzie? I was always a fastidious man, Mr. Mackenzie, and now my body is teeming with malevolent hosts excreting dirt and filth into my bloodstream.

Mackenzie's words again, searing into his brain: *"Cut and run if you wish, Partridge. Flog the emeralds if you get them, but I'll block every road you take. You'll be finished. You're not man enough or young enough to risk losing what you've stolen for. What do you call your little house overlooking the dancing sea—The Covey? I can take it from you at the drop of a hat!"*

So much to lose, so much he wanted. The house overlooking the Atlantic. Sitting on the veranda, long drink in hand, watching the sun go down and listening to whatever music he had chosen to match the mood of the sunset. Dramatic sunsets—stormy, purple, black, and red —called for Wagner. Soft, pearly colors called for Debussy.

Loneliness, like a heavy pall of black, pressed down on Partridge, and he pulled the blankets up and over his head, feeling the heat of his breath fanning the shivering cold of his shoulder. Now the dark was of his own making and not that of the small, functional hotel room and the Cromwell Road and the city that had been his birthplace but was now as alien as a distant planet.

Weeks ago . . . Sunday morning and the rainy season over and the earth scent rising sweetly from a garden bursting with new life. . . . Mackenzie, huge with authority, striding up the stepped path. . . . *"Well, Partridge, how does your stolen garden grow?"*. . . Tomorrow and the long flight to Rio, then upcoast to Aracaju where he'd collect and deliver. A simple task, Mackenzie had said. Nothing like dicing with death in Bogotá—just getting acquainted with that which is dead and gone. . . .

Partridge noted that his body had quieted down. He spoke into the dark umbrella of blankets and sheet: "I can't cut and run—I can't!"

Thoughts dulled, smothering anxiety, the shivering. The drugs he had taken forced his body and mind into quiescence. Sleep came, like death-slumber. Later, toward dawn, his subconscious broke through, charged him with monsters ever pursuing him down endless corridors of unspeakable horrors. And, as always, when there seemed to be a glimmer of light at the end of a corridor, it turned out to be the glowing, genial, strong face of Mackenzie.

It was late when Mr. Snow left his office and workshop. Before collecting his car from the parking lot, he called in at a late-closing post office and sent a telegram: *"The bird arrived safely stop very green and good stop will advise treatment and disposal stop best wishes stop Lion in Winter stop."*

The telegram was addressed to Mackenzie at Komalu Mining Company, Komalu, Sierra Leone.

Arnold Mackenzie picked up Leonard Snow's telegram and read it again. He'd taken a chance with Partridge, but the man had completed his first task. Mackenzie was surprised that Partridge's stamina had been able to stand the trip to Colombia. It had been in the cards that the Quaqueros, smelling free money, would have quickly disposed of Partridge.

Poor Partridge, Mackenzie thought; a bird without the mental agility or nerve to get away unaided with thefts of little diamonds. Partridge might have wondered why he'd got through strict, routine inspection so many times, or why it had been so simple to visit Jacob Zuncasi and dispose of his little but valuable hauls. But there was an element of innocence, a lack of guile in Partridge that would forever make him a puppet, a sick little creature made to dance this way or that according to the whims of its master.

In two years as a sorter at the Komalu Mine Partridge had collected and converted enough stones to buy a small house and garden. Mackenzie had seen it and photographed it and included the photographs in the dossier he had compiled on Felix Partridge.

Mackenzie had accurately assessed how the man would react when privately confronted with the evidence he had collected. Partridge had not blustered or protested his innocence. He had simply looked at the future Mackenzie outlined for him, and wept. Mackenzie hated tears, and he had spoken roughly, brutally, to Partridge and offered two alternatives: a long term of imprisonment and confiscation of all that he owned, or the chance to wipe the slate clean with punishment and reward. And Partridge had gratefully accepted, ignorant of the dangers and terrors involved.

"The bird arrived safely . . . very green and good—" So Partridge had bought and delivered the goods; he'd survived Bogotá and the Quaqueros, spending the last of his money, and that was good. The trial by fire had been a wise decision, and it hadn't cost Mackenzie a penny. Snow would see the emeralds cut and polished and a substantial sum deposited in one of Mackenzie's numerous bank accounts.

Mackenzie allowed himself a moment's pity for Partridge; the man's second and last task was not one Mackenzie fancied himself. Then he thought, Damn it! When he gets back to Freetown and gets his reward, he can live in peace and security for the rest of his life.

Franz Rikel, Komalu's resident doctor, entered Mackenzie's office without knocking on the door. Thin and stooped, looking older than his forty years, Rikel was tanned yellow-brown from years under the Sierra Leone sun. His small pointed black beard, which Mackenzie disliked, tapered his face into a narrow triangle.

Mackenzie smiled his welcome. "How am I, Doctor?"

"No doubt fitter than I will ever be."

"Physician, heal thyself," Mackenzie said. "Cheer up. A few more days—a couple of weeks, and you'll be in Switzerland. Isn't that where doctors sent ailing patients in the good old days?"

"It is where I am sending this one. I've had too many years in the land of the white man's grave." Rikel sat down heavily in the chair on the visitor's side of Mackenzie's desk. "Mandragez is prepared," he said. "At least he thinks he is prepared." He paused, then said, "I never thought I could do what I am doing."

"Men have done worse," Mackenzie said blandly. "In any case, it's my finger on the button. Take comfort from the fact that you're an accessory, and that's all. You've profited in the past and you'll profit in the near future. When you're in Geneva looking at the sun glinting on Mont Blanc, you'll thank your lucky stars and forget Mandragez. And I'll do the same in Scotland."

"I try to focus my mind on such a picture," said Rikel. "Mandragez will soon be in the tunnel?"

Mackenzie nodded. "And happy as a sandboy. That's a good way to go out, Rikel. When I shuffle off my mortal coil, I'd like to be fooled that I'm about to enter the good life."

"Not being a Christian," Rikel said. "Your friend, Turner—what manner of man is he?"

"Likeable, good-looking chap. Sense of humor, and loves diamonds. What I'd call a borderline crook. We get on well. Like me, Jamie's prepared to step outside the law to get what he wants. We're not congenital criminals, Rikel. Once we've got what we want, there'll be no deviation from the straight and narrow. Upright citizens, both."

"Then I wish you luck. Both of you. You appear to be equally blessed with radiant health and optimism, and depression is apparently unknown to you."

"Except when you come to see me with a grim face that seldom smiles."

"Then what?"

Mackenzie opened a drawer in his desk and took out a bottle of Scotch and two glasses. Pouring two measures, he said, "Then I take a dram and depress the slight hint of depression I feel after counselling a Swiss doctor to take life easy." He pushed one of the glasses toward Rikel and raised his own. "Your good health, Doctor. Leave crime to the Scots and the Americans."

Rikel did not return the toast. For a moment he stared at his glass, then picked it up and drained it in one swallow.

Mackenzie watched Rikel in silence; lines of strain showed in the doctor's face—anxiety or ill health, it was hard to tell, but both states were dangerous to the smooth-running of the next few days.

"Have another, Rikel?" Mackenzie said.

Rikel shook his head and got to his feet. "So now we wait," he said.

"Not for long. When the blasting starts. And, Doctor—you won't be needed for a day or two, maybe more."

"I understand. They only die who only sit and wait." Rikel made for the door and opened it, letting in a brazen shaft of sunlight. "You'll call me as soon as it's over?"

Mackenzie nodded. "As regulations demand." A moment of pity struck him. "I wish I could let you off this last bit, Rikel. I can't, you know? You're essential—you always have been."

"I accepted the terms. There is no need for expressions of regret."

"Keep your mind on the Swiss Alps and the good life."

"Of course."

"Then go well—stay well."

You do that, Doctor, Mackenzie thought as the door closed behind

Rikel. Think of jolly, yoiking yodelling, and weigh gain against guilt. You once told me that death is a trifle, a drop in the ocean of the life that had been and will be. And then Mackenzie weighed his own life in the balance, and it was worth more than he would gain by the death of a Brazilian diamond miner.

He was thinking too much, and he poured another measure of whisky into his glass. Thousands of miles away, Jamie Turner would be thinking, too, thinking of the trip from New York down to Aracaju. They were two of a kind, he and Jamie; two of a special kind, capable of love and devotion, of loyalty and patriotism, of liking quite ordinary things—spring and fair women, and heather and mountains, and that incredible prehistoric wonder made of pure carbon, diamond.

Mackenzie emptied his glass and returned bottle and glasses to the desk drawer. No more drinking until the emergency was over. A totally clear head for the next few days; drink depressed worry and could make a man overconfident.

The tiny red eye above the toggle marked "Personal" glowed, synchronizing with a low buzz. He depressed the switch, and the voice of his secretary, Sara, came through the speaker grid: "Your call to New York, sir."

"Thank you, Sara. . . . Jamie?"

"About time you called." Turner's voice came clear over the line.

"Sweating, Jamie?" Mackenzie asked.

"Not exactly. Just don't like waiting on a call. What's the latest?"

"Market is good. Production as anticipated. Rikel doesn't look too well but is expected to survive. No worker problems and Tunnel Nine is well under way. How are things with you?"

"Okay. I may be flying down to Rio in a few days. I'm waiting for the go-ahead."

"If you get it, I'd like you to contact an agent of mine. His name's Partridge—Felix Partridge. Stubborn as a mule, but reliable—if you get what I mean. Should be in Aracaju next day or so. There's a letter in the post for you. I've addressed it to your home."

"With details, Mac? You've kept me damn short of details."

"With full details. Have a large brandy before you read it. How's life in New York?"

"Cheap. You should hear the screams in the night. What's the price in Sierra?"

"Considerably cheaper than in New York. A funeral costs more than a killing in this neck of the woods. Tell you this, Jamie, if one of our miners cops it, and if he's a foreign worker, South American, say, the cost of putting him in a casket and transporting him back to his native

land is as much as he'd earn in six months. Add compensation to his
dependents, if he had any, and the bill tots up to more than he'd earn
in a lifetime. Still, that's a contingency the company is prepared for."

"What does that mean, Mac?"

"Read my letter, Jamie. Read the letter and wait on my call."

"When will that be?"

"Tomorrow. Start waiting at nine o'clock."

"I'll be at GI."

"I'll call you there, Jamie—whether it's on or not. Give my love to
your wife."

"You'll have to do that personally. You know how it is, Mac."

"I've never been in that position. We'll meet up in Switzerland, and
you can tell your uncle where you went wrong."

"Maybe I'll do that. If everything pans out okay, I'll have to talk to
her."

"Sum up the situation briefly, Jamie."

"*Finito.*"

"Thank God I've never had to face up to a failed marriage. Goodbye,
Jamie—and read my letter."

Mackenzie snapped the box toggle to "off." Turner's marital problems struck Mackenzie as trivial. A relationship lasted as long as the
food contained in it. When the larder was emptied, you went in search
of a new cache, and if you didn't find it, you went hungry, or changed
your diet.

Mackenzie swivelled in his chair and looked out across Komalu
Mine. Turner now had all the latest information but none of the visual
details. He could not see the towering machinery surmounting the entrance to the main shaft, its eight tunnels and Number 9 slowly boring
its way into the pipe.

Arnold Mackenzie's mental vision panned down the shaft to Tunnel 9; in half an hour a change of shift would bring Juan Mandragez
and his team of five miners down the shaft to take over the drilling. And
sometime after that, blasting operations would begin on the high
ground to the west, when the Komalu area would be noisy with the
sound of high explosives detonating, a perfect cover sound to conceal
the softer thumps that would collapse Tunnel 9.

It would take days to reach the entombed men. Round-the-clock
rescue teams would work feverishly hacking their way through fallen
rock in the futureless hope that Mandragez and his fellows would be
found alive. Mackenzie had no doubt that Mandragez would die; it was
planned and inevitable, but uncertainties existed. It had taken months
to persuade the company to begin work on a new shaft with a system of
tunnel similar to the existing shaft. There was the economic factor—

production was high and satisfactory; there was also the danger that blasting operations might weaken the shaft with its system of tunnels. Mackenzie brushed aside objections by the logic of his argument, experience, and reputation. The uncertainty in his own mind was the accuracy of his judgment. Mackenzie reckoned his chances at fifty-fifty. Geological faults existed in the land surrounding the mine, and the scale of the blasting operation should cause severe enough tremors to disturb the hole and main shaft, bringing about the collapse and flooding of all the tunnels, including Tunnel 9. But it was still a gamble.

He leaned back in his chair, his relaxed body and calm, good-humored face suggesting nothing of his mental activity. Through the window he could see teams of miners assembling at the top of the shaft, awaiting the change of shift. Faithful, trusting Mandragez was there with his team of five men, and as Mackenzie watched he saw Mandragez turn and look up at his master.

Mackenzie looked at his watch. Any moment now and the change-of-shift siren would howl, and Mandragez would take his last look at the sky, then enter the caged lift to the first of his graves.

A spark of anger touched Mackenzie, and quite suddenly he wanted to grip Jamie Turner's shoulders and shake them. A fleabite marital problem, that was Jamie's only problem; that, plus searching for a non-existent Holy Grail called love. It was high time he learned that the world was a jungle, and a man survived by resisting threats of invasion and possession. The only way to live was to hold on to a vision of your own life and not that of others. A jungle, that's all it is, Jamie, Mackenzie thought. Get wise to the fact and aim to be a top predator. Take the choicest bits of your kill, and leave the offal to vultures and scavengers.

Steady, Mackenzie told himself. Unclench your hands, relax your shoulders. Listen—there goes the siren. In two hours' time it will happen; a touch of the index finger on your left hand, and the result of months of planning will show its two-thousand-carat face.

Two, three days to reach the trapped miners. Dr. Franz Rikel's statement of cause of death and the dispatch of Mandragez's body home to Aracaju.

Just two hours to go, and Mackenzie's finger would jab down on the firing button of the small radio transmitter in the left-hand drawer of his desk and send out a signal that would start a series of explosions in Tunnel 9.

They were the longest two hours in Mackenzie's life.

Juan Mandragez swallowed the last of the diamonds, surprised that a total intake of sixteen ounces had acted in the same way as its equivalent in digestible food. The hunger pangs he usually felt after an hour or so's work in Tunnel 9 had gone.

Some distance away from him he could hear the other five members of his shift drilling into the rock and edging nearer to the kimberlite. He glanced at his gaudy digital watch; not long to go before a section of the tunnel would collapse and entomb both him and the five men; then hours waiting in the cold tunnel while rescue workers hacked their way through the fallen rock.

Senhor Mackenzie was a man of brain, thought Mandragez, a thorough man; the oxygen pack was a thoughtful act, for rescue might take longer than Senhor Mackenzie had calculated.

There was no doubt in Mandragez's mind. He *knew* Senhor Mackenzie and Dr. Rikel were imaginative and meticulous men, and generous too. Everything would go according to plan. A few hours in the tomb, and rescue workers would break through and find the Brazilian, Juan Mandragez, in a state of severe shock. And the other workers in the tunnel? Their fate was in the lap of the gods and not in the hands of Juan's Catholic God.

He could see future events as clearly as if they had happened before. The little capsule Dr. Rikel had given him, which he must swallow in five minutes' time, would induce all the symptoms of shock. He would be taken away on a stretcher and rushed to the company's little hospital, there tended by Dr. Rikel. After that a few days recovering from his experience, with the doctor making sure that his natural functions were behaving normally, and then—Mandragez smiled—the bedpan he would use would never again know such a rich evacuation.

Recovered but still shaken, with his nerve gone, he would tell his employers that he could never again enter a tunnel, that his work as a diamond miner was over and that he wished to return to his native land, Brazil, and the home of his parents in the village ten kilometers outside Aracaju. Senhor Mackenzie had guaranteed his passage home would be paid, as well as compensation for his terrible experience in the tunnel.

He looked at his watch: another two minutes before swallowing Dr. Rikel's capsule.

The sum paid in compensation was, of course, not very much, but the fortune in cruzeiros awaiting his arrival in Aracaju would make him the richest man in the village.

He took the capsule from the vest pocket of his miner's suit and put it in his mouth, allowed it to rest for a moment on his tongue, then gulped it down to join his last, indigestible meal.

Not long to go now. He sat down on the floor of the tunnel, his back against the rough wall, exactly in the position ordered by Senhor Mackenzie, and waited. The noise from the drilling had been very loud, but now it had lessened, and was lessening still as he became drowsy and a little cold. Before he slipped into unconsciousness, he imagined banners stretched across the little village main street. There were many banners, each proclaiming Welcome Home, Juan.

CHAPTER 12.

APPLEBY'S decision to cut a tunnel through from the bottom terrace of the cliff was based not on solid reasoning but on sheer impatience to get to the heart of the pipe bearing the diamondiferous blue ground—kimberlite.

Surface work would take many months of careful shifting and sorting through the layers of sand and gravel that lay above the spread of yellow ground, the weathered kimberlite. Not that the surface yield had been sparse; on the contrary, the ratio between gem-quality and industrial diamond had been exceptionally good and of high quality.

But it was the blue ground of the pipe itself that Appleby wanted to penetrate. He had estimated that the tunnel would have to bore two hundred and eighty feet from the terrace to reach the kimberlite pipe; drilling from the summit of the mound had established where the yellow ground ended and the blue ground began.

Two months had passed since he had stood on the bank of the extinct river and found the garnets and the diamond; now his work force had increased to a hundred men, and Magasi's security force had, by ratio, also increased.

Insufficient machinery, insufficient means to buy sophisticated methods of extraction, constantly nagged at Appleby, yet he could see the reasons for Sotho's determination to hold one hundred percent of the new mine. Concessions were easy enough to grant to De Beers and the Consolidated Diamond Mining Corporation; concessions that would cause the immediate arrival of an army of technicians, workers, and equipment that would increase production prodigiously. But Sotho had said no, Angwana must go it alone, for it pleased the Angwanans; it showed an independence of spirit that echoed the words spoken on Independence Day.

It would take many, many months more for surface work to reach the yellow ground that lay above the kimberlite. Sotho had said, "But,

72

my dear Doctor, we are doing well. The treasury is showing signs of recovery by the yield. The CSO are paying good prices for our consignments. Be patient, Doctor. Don't the Scots have a saying, Many a mickle makes a muckle?"

And Sotho could tell Magasi that, thought Appleby. Magasi was mickling and muckling every week, filching not only from the regular consignments but also by private sorties along the terraces.

Light was fading from the evening sky, any moment now the siren Magasi had installed would signal the end of the workday. The site had changed since that memorable dawn when Appleby's heels had scuffed back the sand and gravel. The area was now encircled by wire fencing and patrolled by armed guards with trigger-happy fingers. Appleby likened it to a prison camp; himself, Blohm, and Magasi were the only inhabitants with the right to come and go as they pleased.

Appleby stood at the mouth of the tunnel that was boring into the heart of the terraced mound, and he could hear the sound of miners drilling their way forward. Progress was so slow, Appleby thought. Surface workers had only scratched the skin covering what he hoped was rich ground, truly rich ground, and the men now drilling in the tunnel were using near obsolete machinery. Eventually they would reach the diamond-rich pipe. Eventually. With Sotho's treasury showing signs of recovery, it would be possible to buy equipment that would halve recovery time. Eventually.

Magasi's siren split the early evening air, and Appleby entered the tunnel. The drillers would not have heard the siren over the sound of the compressor activating the drill.

They saw him coming toward them, and Appleby's hand raised in the signal they had come to know. The worker standing by the diesel-driven compressor thumbed the ignition off, and the motor ground into silence.

"End of shift," Appleby said.

"Yes, sah."

The tunnel was lit by a single two-hundred-watt lamp, and Appleby stood alone as the last of the workers left the tunnel. Appleby stood six feet four, and the roof of the tunnel barely touched five feet six, so that he had to stoop. It should be higher, he thought, but you had to cut down on height if you wanted to forge ahead. A workable tunnel should be ten feet high and as wide, with a rail track and rolling stock to remove the debris, debris that contained recoverable diamonds. As it was, the mounds were building up on the bank of the extinct river, awaiting removal to crushers and sorters, recovery and washing plant, equipment that would eventually come. Eventually; as soon as Angwana could afford the capital investment.

Appleby left the tunnel and climbed the metal-runged ladder up the terraced cliff and walked slowly back to the mining encampment. It was time for a further session with Sotho. The week's yield had been surprisingly good—small stuff but of high quality.

He walked to the work huts, hands behind his back, the evening breeze wisping out the wings of hair above his ears. Tomorrow he would get Magasi's pilot to fly him to the capital, and insist that the president take a long-term view and pledge all future production to the acquisition of essential machinery. And a word with Magasi would help if he were told that production could be doubled, trebled even, if only Sotho would agree. Sometimes it helped to have the devil on one's side, even at the cost of increasing Magasi's pickings.

Appleby spoke his thoughts as he entered his hut where Blohm was bent over a petrological microscope: "He can take ten percent of the whole damn production if I can get the equipment."

Blohm looked up. "Who can?"

"Mm? . . . Oh—I was thinking of Magasi." Appleby walked to his locker, opened it, and withdrew an unopened bottle of whisky. "Besides, I find an unholy delight in seducing a Muslim into bad ways." Appleby slipped the bottle into the side pocket of his tunic. "I'm off for a chat. Back later."

Miles distant, a dark line on the horizon marked the beginning of Angwana's only green and fertile belt, an area fed by the country's main river. The sky above the horizon, and through which the Piper Aztec was flying, was milky-blue and cloudless.

Appleby sat in the copilot's seat and saw not sky and horizon but a vision of a heavy media separator. At the Consolidated Mining Company plant in South-West Africa he had seen the efficient separators with their cone-shaped tanks, twelve feet across, filled with ferrosilicon slurry in which broken blue ground and gravels were fed. A simple, clever process, Appleby thought; light, worthless material floats on top of the heavy liquid slurry, while heavier material, including diamonds, sinks to the bottom to be extracted, then to be transferred to grease surface concentrators.

As things stood at the site, loss potential was high, ridiculously high. It had neither separator nor grease surface concentrators—plant that would cost more money than Sotho's treasury could afford.

In his mind's eye Appleby saw the concentrator in action; the grease belt, tilted sideways and constantly fed by a strong flow of water, at right angles to the belt, washing away dross to leave diamonds adhering to the grease—further evidence of the magical properties of diamond.

Totally resistant to water—and the only mineral with that talent—it had an affinity with grease. Zircon, ruby, sapphire, tourmaline—any gem you could put a name to, with the exception of diamond, ran with water and away from grease.

Angwana's green and pleasant region now spread out under the Aztec, and Appleby came out of his diamond reverie. "How much longer?" he asked the pilot.

"Seven minutes, sah. I have radioed for a car to take you to the president."

"Thank you."

The devil of it is, Appleby thought, I am not a mining engineer. Mineralogist, geologist, gemmologist, I am all of those, but I am not a mining engineer, nor is Blohm. The new site needed a man, the best that money could buy. So who was the man? Appleby could name many, but they were under contract in the major mining areas, South Africa, Zaire, Ghana, Angola, Sierra Leone; the USSR would gladly step in with massive aid—with a tiger-smile on its face.

Sierra Leone had Arnold Mackenzie; a man typical of Scotland's contribution to technology, he was the type needed by Angwana. A man of rugged honesty, authoritative and decisive, and more concerned with diamond extraction than their worth.

It had been more than a year since Appleby had visited the Komalu Mine and spent five days in the company of Mackenzie learning much that had been useful. He remembered Mackenzie's words at the end of his visit: "You'll need more than your chemistry set, Arthur. Old Sotho had better sell out to De Beers if he wants a wee bit of money in his sporran. What's the Kundi Mine's annual production—ten thousand metric carats, isn't it? Want me to lend you a few spades?"

Appleby thought of a confrontation between Mackenzie and Magasi and inwardly groaned. Scottish granite meeting an equally hard mineral. But Mackenzie would have little time for Magasi; sooner or later Mackenzie would express his dislike by ramming his fist into Magasi's face, which, Appleby had to admit would be worth seeing.

"We are landing now, sah," the pilot said.

"So Colonel Magasi thinks well of the idea," President Sotho said, and sipped at the black, sweet coffee to which he was addicted. "And if I agree, we are at one."

"Politically desirable," Appleby said. "Wouldn't you think?"

"Perhaps, Doctor—what you have done by discovering this new mine has meant much to Angwana—and to me personally. You saw the new hospital slowly growing up from its foundations?"

"I saw it on my way from the airfield."

"There is housing, too," Sotho said. "If I had my way both the housing development and the hospital would bear your name."

"Unnecessary," Appleby said.

"It would express my personal thanks." Sotho opened a black leather-bound file. "Angwana has obtained credit, Doctor. That, plus earnings from the Appleby Mine—"

"Appleby Mine?"

"The title was passed with unanimous approval yesterday."

"Does Magasi know?"

"Not yet. You think he will object?"

"I don't know. I wouldn't have advised it."

Sotho smiled. "Then, should he attempt a coup and succeed, he will change it to the Magasi Mine. As I was saying, with the earnings from the Appleby Mine and the credit I have been able to get, the hospital grows, as does the housing development. Now you want me to halt the work and funnel every penny into the new mine?"

"Just for a short time," Appleby said.

"How short?"

Appleby spread his hands. "I couldn't say with any degree of accuracy. Three months—six. Who knows? We need the best equipment and a man, an engineer experienced in mining. Mr. President, you will pay interest on credit—that's getting in hock—"

"In hock? What does that mean?"

"Getting into debt. Oh—I know it's not too hard to ward off collectors, but independence is lost when money's borrowed."

"That's true." Sotho fingered his tie, and Appleby noticed that it bore the colors of Oxford. "When I was an undergraduate, I borrowed and read Polonius's words of wisdom, 'Neither a borrower nor a lender be, for borrowing dulls the edge of husbandry.' Why do scholars consider Polonius a bore, Doctor? He spoke words of wisdom."

"There's another way, of course," Appleby said.

"Bring in De Beers?" Sotho shook his head. "Out of the question. I am not at war with De Beers or South Africa, but I am black and an African, Doctor. I must follow the color of my skin and be at peace with my more militant neighbors. Do you understand?"

"I've always understood," Appleby replied. "And you know my attitude. Neither black nor white is particularly beautiful. One can be as good or as ugly as the other."

"And that is my view." Sotho looked down at the open file. "A terrible decision to make, Doctor. Can you give me guarantees?"

"Only those based on experience and intuition."

"Intuition is always suspect."

"Then rely on experience, Mr. President. Call in an expert—a mining expert. Get his appraisal. If I've proved it's a rich site, let an engineer assess the prospect and the cost of bringing in the equipment we need."

"A breathing space," Sotho said. "Again I'm in your hands, Doctor. Who shall we call in?"

"Arnold Mackenzie. I doubt if you could find a better mining engineer in Africa. I've known him for years, Mr. President. He's under contract with the Sierra Leone Diamond Mining Company."

"But would he come to Angwana?"

"Nothing is lost by asking. I did speak with him two months ago. He said he'd like to see the mine."

Sotho nodded. "As you say, Doctor, nothing is lost by asking. Tell Mr. Mackenzie that I personally would appreciate his expert advice." He indicated the telephone on his desk. "Call him now. In case unworthy ears listen, I will scramble the line."

It took thirty minutes for contact to be established between Angwana and Sierra Leone, and the line was noisy with static. Appleby said, "Can you speak a little louder, Mac? This is a terrible line."

"This is a devil of a time to call! We've got an emergency on. What d'you want, Arthur?"

"I want you to come to Angwana—I need your advice. Mac, I'm speaking from the palace. The president is with me. He, too, would appreciate your help."

"I can't come yet."

"What's wrong?"

"Blasting tremors caused the collapse of a new tunnel. We've dead to cope with. Of all the times to call!"

"I'm sorry, Mac."

"It was my blasted fault!"

"I can't believe that."

"It's true, nevertheless. I've had it, Arthur. What the hell! My contract expires in a few weeks, anyway. I'm finished with the Komalu and Africa."

"That doesn't sound like you, Mac. Will you come to Angwana?"

"Maybe—in a few weeks' time. When I've cleared up this mess."

"I'll fly to Freetown and pick you up. President Sotho's anxious to meet you."

"I might be impressed if you make it President Carter. Tin-pot African dictators are two a penny. Get off the line, Arthur—wait on my call."

"But you'll come?"

"All right. Wait till you hear from me. Now get the hell off the line!"

Appleby hung up and turned to Sotho. "He'll come."

"Good. What was the trouble?"

"An accident in one of the tunnels. If I were cold-blooded—which I am not—I'd see the accident as fortuitous. He intends leaving Africa. With luck, we might persuade him to stay with us."

"He is leaving because of the accident?"

"So I gather. His contract is running out, and he feels responsible for the tunnel collapse." Appleby shook his head. "That's Mackenzie—always takes responsibility for both success and failure. Mac is a very big man, Mr. President."

"A perfect separation," Heinert said, and laid the bishop's head and smaller stone on the fluorescent light box. "Tomorrow we start the bruting. I suppose you will be present?"

"Maybe. If I can bear the pain when I see those carats being lathed off."

Grunwald had flown in from New York, regretting that he'd miss the sight of the CSO and that he dared not spend more cash on a packet. He had taxied from Antwerp Airport in time to witness the last few minutes of the sawing disc's progress through his baby.

"Thirty-percent loss," Grunwald said. "Now I face the bruting of my baby and a loss of thirty-percent carat value!"

Heinert could understand Grunwald's sense of loss. The bishop's head would be set in a bruting lathe and rounded by a diamond cemented at the end of a long stick and used like a turning chisel against wood to round the bishop's head into a circular outline.

"Diamond cut diamond, Mr. Grunwald," Heinert said. "A principle we must accept. Nothing else, as you know, will make the slightest impression on a diamond. We lose carats but gain when we finally polish the facets."

"And you gain the carats I lose."

"Invent an alternative, then, and you'll be a rich man." Heinert frowned irritation. "Why don't you go home, Mr. Grunwald? It will be weeks before the stones are ready."

"Maybe."

"Go to your film star and tell him that all goes well. Perhaps he might advance you the money you have staked; that, surely, will lessen your worries."

Grunwald shook his head. "I don't do business that way. Work on an advance and you cripple your bargaining legs. So I tell him the rough stone cost X number of bucks—you want me to tell him my profit margin? No, sir! When those two beauties are ready, I get an appraisal from the diamond graders and tell Randall how much he owes me."

"Which will be considerable."

"Randall can afford it. For anxiety and danger, I charge him nothing."

"I'm sure the final price will cover the damage to your mental health," Heinert said. "It will not cover the damage to mine by having you watch every revolution of the lathe. Don't you trust me or my judgment, Mr. Grunwald?"

"You've too much to lose by dealing crooked," Grunwald said. "I trust every one of your facets. Trouble is, I don't trust every one of mine."

"Tomorrow morning, then. Bruting will begin at nine o'clock precisely. I take it you will be here to see precious carats taken off the diamond?"

"If I can stand it. If not—if I find the pain too much, I'll drown my sorrows in the lousy beer you Belgians make."

"I will have a doctor standing by, Mr. Grunwald. As in the case of Asscher cleaving the giant Cullinan in 1905, we must be prepared for a sudden decline in your health."

"Such solicitude," Grunwald said. "How long for the bruting?"

"Between two and three days."

"Then you make the first facet?"

Heinert nodded.

"Then, if my heart, which has served me well, continues to pump, I'll stay and watch the first facet cut."

"And you will then fly home and leave me in peace, Mr. Grunwald?"

"Sure—but I'll phone you every day."

Heinert smiled. "I will arrange for a special recorded message to answer your call."

Grunwald limped away from Heinert's workshop, the loss of thirty percent of the diamond's weight resting heavily on his shoulders. Thirty percent into thin air—*thirty percent*. It was almost unbearable, but think of the profit, Grunwald told himself; the bucks mount as the carats are ground away on the scaife. Think on that and be comforted.

From the cafe across the road from Heinert's workshop, Swede Petersen watched Grunwald's limping figure make its way toward the center of Antwerp. He waited two minutes, then left the cafe, crossed the road, and entered Heinert's premises.

A discussion with Pieter Heinert over the best type of cut for the nine-carat rough diamond Klein had wheedled out of Canzetti led to Swede's request for a conducted tour of the workshop. Thirty minutes later, as Mr. Larsen of Pittsburgh, he left Heinert's with more than a fair notion of the time when Grunwald would take possession of the Randall diamonds. Even though the intro to the workshop had cost sixteen thousand dollars—the value of the Canzetti stone—gentle persuasion was still the order of the day. Better still, he could report back to Tony that he'd actually *seen* the Randall diamonds. He could now take it easy as Grunwald's shadow. D Day—Diamond Day—was only a few weeks ahead.

CHAPTER 13.

TURNER looked at his desk clock: 8:30 A.M. He had slept little, dozing the night away in troubled dreams. He had left Riverside Drive breakfastless at 7:30 and taken a cab to Gem International, the rain falling from a leaden sky matching his mood.

In thirty minutes Mackenzie's call would come through. Turner looked at the sweep hand of the desk clock wiping away the seconds. Mackenzie's letter had disturbed him, adding mental images, nightmarish in content, to his already troubled mind. Now he understood Mackenzie's references to an unsuspected mule carrying out of Sierra Leone and the method sickened him. And then the second mule and his task; Turner thanked God that it would not be *his* job to recover the diamonds.

Think of those glittering stones, Turner told himself. Concentrate on the colors he would see—colors ranging from blue-whites through to the pinks, and ambers and blues and yellows flashing with the fire of life; concentrate and cut through the monochrome vision of death in the tunnel.

He glanced at his watch, then at the desk clock: 9:05. "Come on, Mac!" he said aloud. "Come on!"

His secretary was late. She entered his office apologizing. Seeing his anxious face, she said, "You look tired—shall I make you coffee?"

"Yes."

At 9:50 the call hadn't come. He left his desk and went to the liquor cabinet and poured a three-finger measure of whisky. He downed it swiftly, gagging at the shock to his throat and stomach.

In five minutes he felt better, anxiety depressed by the alcohol. He drank his third cup of black coffee and watched the minute hand creep round the face of the desk clock.

Mackenzie's call came at 10:30.

"Jamie?"

"What the devil kept you?"

"The devil himself. Sweating on the top line, Jamie?"

"You know damn well I'm sweating."

"Easy, easy." Mackenzie's voice was calm. "The marriage has been arranged, Jamie. The bridegroom's sorry to keep you waiting at the altar. He's now fit and ready to promise faithfulness in sickness and in health—and certainly for the richer."

"There's no hitch?"

"None so far. The schedule stands. Just you be in Aracaju when the parcel arrives. The poor wee bridegroom will arrive dead on time."

"I don't like your sense of humor at this moment, Mac."

"I don't like it either, but it helps. Now, look, Jamie. The groom goes to the altar in style—my agent will see to that. Everyone will have been paid. In Aracaju take delivery and hotfoot it to Geneva. Just follow the schedule, and all will go well. All right?"

"It's this bloody waiting, Mac."

"I know, laddie. Just a little longer. I'll phone through an ETA when I know it—okay?"

"Yes."

"Want me to wish the bridegroom every happiness?"

"Don't be so damned cynical!"

The condition of the bodies recovered from the collapsed tunnel did not warrant an autopsy—asphyxia and multiple injuries sustained through crushing were obvious causes of death—but Rikel insisted on one.

He was now working on the sixth and last body, that of Juan Mandragez. Rikel's scalpel made an incision from the peak of the epigastrium down to the umbilicus, the sharp blade cutting through skin and fatty tissue in one confident slice. Rikel then clamped open the lips of the gash, baring the liver behind the arc of the rib cage, the stomach, and the omentum covering the intestines. There had been slight compression of the organs, Rikel noted, and no doubt ribs had been fractured; these facts he would enter in his report including spinal damage and asphyxia.

He picked up the scalpel and now made a cut across the stomach. Again he clamped the incision open. Mandragez had obeyed instructions to take no food. The bowl of the stomach was clean, the diamonds clotted together by the viscous juices contained in the bowl.

As he reached in to scoop out the diamonds Rikel observed that the stones had obeyed their unique quality of adhering to greasy substances. Now there was nothing left in Mandragez's stomach, and Rikel released the clamps, then those retaining the lips of his first incision. This he carefully stitched with fine nylon thread, leaving an opening immediately above the slit bag of the stomach.

He left the table on which the body lay, and carried the bowl containing the diamonds to the sink, where he poured solvent onto the greasy cluster of diamonds. When they were clean and separated, he packed them into a waterproof wallet and securely sealed it.

He went back to the body and inserted the wallet into the opening he left; then, taking up needle and nylon thread, he completed the task of resealing the upper part of the abdomen.

Rikel went back to the sink, peeled off his rubber gloves, and feeling like Pontius Pilate, washed his hands. He telephoned Mackenzie.

"The postmortem is completed," he said.

"Good."

"Cause of death is as I expected—internal injuries and asphyxia. I shall complete my report in the next hour and send it to the directorate."

"I see. Well, Doctor, the directorate will accept your findings, so I suggest we get on with burial proceedings. I've already made arrangements for Mandragez to be shipped to Aracaju. Will you get him coffined immediately?"

"I will see that it is done."

"Just one thing, Doctor. Mandragez. . . . I take it his body is fit to be seen? Everything in its place?"

"Everything. My job is at an end, Mackenzie. No more—nothing."

"Of course. That was the agreement. You'll find your expectation in Geneva." Mackenzie chuckled. "When you get to Switzerland, Doctor, don't nip across the border to Divonne and spend your money on the gambling tables."

"I wish you to hell," Rikel said.

"It's as good a place for villains as any I know," Mackenzie said. "See you there, Rikel."

Had he witnessed his departure from Freetown, Juan Mandragez would have been impressed. In the first place, his coffin was the best that money could buy—black ebonized wood with ornate, highly polished brass handles and decoration—and was reverently carried from the mine in a black Mercedes followed by a cortege of fellow miners. In the second place, Senhor Mackenzie and top-ranking staff had joined the cortege on the journey from Komalu to the dock in Kroo Bay.

As the bearers slowly mounted the ramp from the quayside and into the ship, Mackenzie, hat held against his heart, felt relief swamp the guilt he had experienced since his finger had depressed the button and set off the explosions that had caused the tunnel collapse.

At the investigation he had stated, "I should have considered the effect of nearby blasting operations not only on Tunnel 9 but on the rest of the tunnels. I did not consider it and hold myself to blame." He had announced to the company that he did not wish to renew his contract and used as an excuse responsibility for the accident. It was both truth and untruth, and the investigators had declared him quite innocent of blame, but Mackenzie had stuck to his guns, had tendered his resignation, and resisted all attempts at changing his mind.

The bearers and coffin had disappeared into the bowels of the ship and down to the refrigeration hold, where Mandragez would rest until the ship docked at Aracaju in four days. The hearse followers stood in groups, chatting, and Mackenzie put on his hat. What next? he thought. A call to Jamie Turner giving him the go-ahead and the ETA, and another to Partridge holed up in Aracaju; a few more days at the Komalu clearing up before clearing out, and waiting for Jamie to call and tell him that collection had been made. But before anything, a very stiff Scotch—he hadn't touched a drop since his finger had stabbed down the button.

He was walking away from the dock when he was hailed from a parked Ford.

"Mac?"

Mackenzie turned and saw Jason Meadows of International Diamond Security leaning out of his car window. "Can an IDSO man give you a lift?"

Mackenzie hesitated for a moment, then said, "I want a drink. The Bintumani. It's outside this stinking city."

"Hop in, then."

Meadows said, "Have another, Mac?"

"Why not? I feel like turning it into a wake with everyone pissed and happy."

They sat in the bar whose window looked over Aberdeen Hill to the Lumley Beach and the blue Atlantic beyond. Just past the bar, swimmers and dippers splashed in the pool.

"Can guarantee getting pissed," Meadows said. "Don't know about the happy part. You're off, then, Mac?"

"Aye. Few more days. I'm finished here."

"So it's one for the road, then." Meadows signalled to the bar steward to bring refills.

"What road?" Mackenzie asked.

"Scotland?"

"I'll drink to that." Mackenzie watched the bar steward put two glasses of Scotch on the table.

"You didn't have to leave the Komalu," Meadows said. "You were exonerated from all blame."

"My contract's come to an end. I've had enough, and I want for Scotland and the pure air."

"Having made your pile, of course."

"I've done well. I didn't sweat years in Africa for love or fun."

"I hear you've done *very* well," Meadows said.

Mackenzie sipped at the cold whisky, then fingered out the ice and let it fall on the table. "What's that supposed to mean?"

"You hear this and you hear that. You know how it is, Mac. Trickles from London and all points west, south, east, and north. There's sweet damn all we can do about it. Sierra's a good escape route, don't you think, Mac?"

"I wouldn't know. I dig out the diamonds, that's all."

"You certainly do that, Mac. You command a great deal of respect."

"From you?"

Meadows nodded. "From me, especially, but I let liking overcome suspicion. Bernard Manston, now, he's different, keeps his nose to the ground like a bloodhound. I'm glad you're leaving Africa, Mac."

"I am, too. Why your concern?"

"Call it a feeling based on the trickles I mentioned. I get used to hearing Bernard talking names of illicits and buyers. When he mentions the name of Arnold Mackenzie, I get really concerned." Meadows tapped the side of his glass. "Bell's make a good whisky."

Mackenzie picked up Meadows's glass and looked at the ice cubes in the amber whisky. "Aye, it's blasphemy to put ice in it. Next time tell the steward no ice," Mackenzie said. "What other names does Manston mention?"

"That bastard Magasi. You know, he comes to Freetown with packets pinched from the Kundi Mine. He's covered by diplomatic privilege and all that cock."

"Who says they're stolen packets?"

"You hear things. I know he delivers regularly to the trading office on behalf of his government, and that's all nice and legal. It's just that rumor has it he also deals on the side."

"Not my concern," Mackenzie said.

"Bernard's seen you drinking with him."

"I'm interested in Angwana."

"Do you think Magasi peddles on the side?"

"I know damn well he does. Manston knows, too."

"Bernard has the notion he sells to Jacob Zuncasi. You know him, don't you, Mac?"

"And you know him and Manston knows him and everyone knows him. He's a licensed digger and a good one."

"Just another name, Mac. Bernard likes names and plays a link game. He selects a few names and weaves plots round them." Meadows smiled. "Still, you're leaving, so yours won't be a name to the game. You're off soon?"

"Few more days."

"And bonnie Scotland?"

"Angwana first," said Mackenzie, and drained his glass.

Meadows's face expressed surprise: "Angwana? There's nothing in that poor country for you, Mac. There's rumors, of course—a rich find. That's funny ha-ha."

"I've been invited to give a professional opinion. When you see Manston you can tell him that Arthur Appleby and President Sotho begged me to come."

"Appleby's that white Angwanan, isn't he? Partner's a German named Blohm. Looking for a pot of gold where there ain't none."

"Appleby thinks he's found it. He's an old friend—I don't mind spending a few weeks helping him out on development plans."

"Where's the site?"

Mackenzie grinned. "Ask Magasi next time you see him."

"Saves time asking you, Mac. Will you keep in touch? I mean the CSO handles Angwana's poverty-stricken production of gem and industrial. They'd like to know if something big turns up."

"So would the IDBs and Magasi." Mackenzie got to his feet. "I've things to do."

"I'll drive you back," Meadows said.

He dropped Mackenzie off in the center of Freetown. "I'll say good-bye, then, Mac. I'm glad you're going—I mean that sincerely. I'll tell Bernard when he gets back. Just a chat over drinks. Take care, Mac."

"I always do," Mackenzie said.

She sat by the window, silent and withdrawn, gazing out across the Hudson River.

Turner said again, "What will you do, Joanie?"

"I don't know. I've no exciting plans like flying down to Rio and then to Switzerland."

"I really am sorry."

"I suppose you are, in a way."

"In many ways, Joanie. It's not easy to pull down the curtain and that's it, folks—hope you enjoyed the show. I do remember the good times, you know?"

"What was is now a might-have-been. Feeling guilty, Jamie?"

"That—plus responsibility."

"You'll bear one and shrug off the other. I know you, Jamie. Guilt won't be too much of a problem. And responsibility? I'll have my pound of flesh, if that's what you mean by responsibility."

Turner drank from his third glass of Bourbon. "I care enough to think about your future."

"Maybe it'll be a happy release." She turned and smiled at him without humor. "The marriage passed away peacefully during the night. No flowers by request. Why can't you be honest and tell me how excited you are at the prospect of freedom? The world's your oyster. Why not be glad, Jamie? An exhausting party's over, and the guests have gone. No need to worry about who will play Santa Claus at Christmas because we've no children. That's a pity, don't you think, Jamie? Two or three kids might have kept me company through the lonely years."

"I'm sorry. At least we're young enough to start new relationships."

"Which you intend doing forthwith. Who is she, Jamie?"

"There isn't anyone yet."

"Yet," she said. "I like that 'yet.' You're as transparent as glass sometimes, Jamie." She watched him go toward the liquor cabinet. "Don't have any more—you've built up enough courage to face me and I'm cold sober."

"Yes," Turner said. "I guess I've built up enough guts to meet you on equal ground." He put down his empty glass and faced her. "We're both guilty of a failed marriage, and I don't give a damn about percentages of blame. I'll take seventy, and you can take thirty, if it does any good. We've had no kind of life together for a long time."

"You mentioned the death of sex when we last talked."

"If there was a chance, do you think I wouldn't stay?"

"So who's protesting? Perhaps I care enough about you to worry about *your* future."

Turner said, "I'll make out." Then, because it had sounded lame and stupid, he added, "I don't know if there is someone else for me. It's not why we've come to a dead end. That's true, you know—and you've admitted it. Why can't we act without bitterness?"

"All right—without malice or bitterness, Jamie. What's next—the financial arrangement? Fifty-fifty, isn't it?"

"I want you to have more."

"All donations gratefully received."

"I want you to have everything," he said. "There's a hundred and thirty thousand dollars' worth of diamonds in the safe. They're yours,

Joanie. They're good security. Use them if you have to. Diamond is good collateral."

"Diamond didn't act as good collateral for us. It's been diamonds, diamonds, diamonds, and table talk about diamonds. There's been too much diamond in our lives."

"If I'd been in real estate, you'd have said the same about houses."

"Only if you'd become obsessed. What is it with you, Jamie—love of diamonds for their own sake or their cash value?"

"Both. I like them for their own sake and sell them because we've lived rich on the proceeds."

"Rich!"

"I'm leaving our joint account as it is. I won't be using it. I've enough to see me through."

"You'll put this in writing, of course."

"If you wish."

They were silent for a while, she staring out of the window and Turner, his back to the liquor cabinet, resisting the impulse to reach for the bottle.

She said, "So it's tomorrow, then?"

"Afternoon flight to Rio. I'm not sure how long I'll be there before flying to Geneva. Do you want me to let you know?"

"Would there be any point, Jamie? You carry insurance, so if you have a fatal accident, I'll collect. There's no outstanding bills, and you're leaving me well provided for." She got up from the window seat, arms clasped, hugging herself. "There's the night to get through, Jamie. Difficult, isn't it?"

"Yes—it's difficult." He covered his face with his hands. "God!" he said, "I'm so sorry."

"I am too, Jamie. I truly am."

At the door she paused and looked at him, her face composed and calm. "We can either be lovers or acquaintances who don't particularly like each other. The first category's out, so we're not left with much, are we?"

"Perhaps—" he said, but the door had closed behind her.

A few seconds later he said, "What the hell!" and reached for the Bourbon.

Turner took his seat on Flight 519, a Pan Am 747 bound for Rio de Janeiro. A six-hour journey lay ahead of him and another flight in a chartered plane upcoast to Aracaju, a further nine hundred miles to add to the mileage from Kennedy Airport.

Turner slotted together the buckles of his seat belt and settled back in his seat. He hated takeoff; the angle at which a 747 left the ground seemed impossibly dangerous, unlike the angle at which a light aircraft took to the air with nose pointed and the rest of the aircraft following; the big aircraft thundered into the sky belly forward. That reminded him of Stuyvver, good old Randolph Stuyvver, president of Gem International, who had, as the Mafia might put it, a big belly, meaning strength and power. When Turner had been called to his presence, Stuyvver had given him fatherly advice: "Take no chances, James. You've good standing in our world—don't let it down. Speaking for the corporation, I'll be happy to welcome you in the future as a client—your credit is good, James."

"That's good of you, sir. I'll be in touch, of course."

"One other thing, James—the stock you hold with this company, I take it you intend leaving things as they stand?"

"I'm sorry, sir. I'll need every cent."

"Not to worry, James—not to worry. Just don't use the open market."

"It depends on the price, sir."

"Of course. Find out what price you can get, and I will add ten percent above that price. Keep things in the family, James."

The rising whine of the Boeing's engines cut into his thoughts, and he felt pressure forcing him back into his seat as the pilot released the aircraft's brakes and began his takeoff run.

Eyes closed, Turner waited until the rumbling sound had ceased and the Boeing was airborne. Already the plane had reached two thousand feet and was climbing. Turner looked through his side window and saw New York spread out below and rapidly receding as the plane took up a bearing south.

He unbuckled his seat belt and relaxed. Maybe he had been rash to resign from GI and convert his stock into cash; maybe it would have been wiser to carry the packet to Geneva under the flag of GI and then, with the caper over and done with, cut loose from the corporation. But everything had called for a decisive ending; after that final talk with Joanie there was nothing for it but to cut moorings. The caper could go wrong, of course, but that was a natural hazard and nothing more; once the packet was in his hands there was no apparent danger. The mule was the shaky part of the operation. If he chose to run, South America was a grand place to get lost in.

So what? He and Mac had two million stashed away in the Swiss bank; if things went wrong, they'd have ample funds to start all over again.

A stewardess appeared and asked, "Can I get you a drink, sir?"

"Sure," he said. "Gin and tonic. You have Gordon's gin?"

"Yes, sir."

"A big one, then."

Three seats away from Turner, Bernard Manston, IDSO investigator, studied the passenger list given him on authorization issued by the U.S. Treasury Department. Rapidly scanning the list, he recognized only one diamond name, that of James Drake Turner, in seat 5. Manston beckoned to a stewardess and returned the list, then left his seat and made his way forward to seat 5.

"Mr. Turner?"

"Yes?"

"I'm Bernard Manston, IDSO. May I join you?"

A flicker of suspicion crossed Turner's face, then he said, "I'd be delighted, Mr. Manston."

Manston took the seat beside Turner. "Six hours flying is a long time to kill if you're not an aviation buff—and I'm not. The glamour went years ago. Are you for Rio?"

"Yes."

"You're Gem International, if my memory serves me right."

"Uh-huh."

"I know your name. GI's a good firm. Randolph Stuyvver still president and the big man?"

"Bigger than ever," Turner replied. "How do you know my name?"

"You're a regular buyer in London, Mr. Turner. I'm IDSO's memory man." Manston tapped the side of his head. "My chief's Richard Walker —do you know him?"

"He's an old friend."

"Well—Dick Walker says I've no brain, just file boxes."

"Probably better than brains."

"Dick thinks so."

The stewardess appeared with Turner's gin and tonic, and Manston asked for the same. "Another drink," he said, "on yet another plane. Then dinner, breakfast, lunch, tea, more drinks, and then it's dinnertime again. It's the story of my life. I'm based in Freetown, but I do practically a world circuit every year. Months of snooping, listening to whispers. I get the feeling that Mother Earth is shrinking. Sometimes I think the only way of getting the globe back to its true size is to walk the circumference."

"Hard on the feet," Turner said, and held his glass against the light. "The color of a finest white diamond. Dick Walker told me that. The gin has to be Gordon's and the tonic Schweppes."

Manston took his drink from the stewardess. "I wouldn't know that. As I was saying, this shrinking earth. Perhaps longer stopovers would help or slower aircraft with bunks. Flying boats—you know the sort?

Top speed ninety miles an hour and a dining lounge with wine waiters and folded napkins in glasses."

"Few of us have time to kill," Turner said.

"A man can dream," said Manston. "Are you on business or pleasure?"

"Business." There was a questioning look on Manston's face, and Turner added, "Pleasure thrown in, maybe. And you?"

"More or less routine, then I'm off to Sierra Leone and Freetown. Thought I'd look in on the trouble at the Komalu. Did you hear about it?"

"The news came through at the corporation."

"Nasty business. Shouldn't have happened. I mean, the mine's got a first-class engineer named Mackenzie. He could dynamite a penny off Nelson's hat in Trafalgar Square without taking a chip off Nelson's mug. Anyway, I'll get a report and the investigation's findings, listen to whispers if any, plus a few names to add to my list of baddies. What are you buying?"

The question was so sudden Turner had no answer. "This and that."

"If you're after emeralds, steer clear of Rio. Go up the coast to Aracaju. There's a dealer called Gilberto Noni. He's worth seeing and more honest than most dealers in Brazil. Not exactly honest, but just inside the law, not that there's much law in Brazil. Anyway, I couldn't care less about illicit emerald—I'm a diamond man. Gilberto Noni's your man. He sells good Colombian stuff—straight from Bogotá, Murder City. Another thing—be prepared to spend a long time looking at what he offers. When he tells you that's all he has, say you're not buying and make as if you're leaving. It's then he'll show you the good stuff." Manston smiled apologetically. "I'm talking too much and probably teaching you to suck eggs."

The sweat was running down Turner's back. He loosened his collar and tie. "You've been helpful," he said. "I'll take your advice about Noni."

"Mention my name. That'll tell him you know the right people."

Turner glanced through the cabin window. "Bermuda down below and a hell of a way yet. I wonder what movie Pan Am's showing?"

Manston grinned. "There's lots of kids on board, so it's probably *Lassie, Come Home.* One day, Pan Am will get around to showing blue films. That'll be the day!"

"For whom?" asked Turner.

"It'd make a change. Can I buy you another gin?" Manston had noticed the loosening of Turner's collar and tie. "With plenty of ice," he added. "Might cool you down, Mr. Turner."

Turner accepted and silently wished the man to hell.

* * *

The chartered Boeing 707 roared off the runway at Dakar Airport on the last leg of its journey from Colorado to Freetown.

The flight from Denver to Dakar had been long and tiring after weeks of location shooting. "Seven thousand miles," Randall complained to the producer, Archie Strauss. "How much farther?"

"An hour's flying time, Bob."

"Refuelling stops or for God knows what at New York and Dakar. Too damn long to be in the air. The way I feel, the movie isn't worth it."

"We're running out of budget," Strauss said, "and this is one movie that's going to hit the original budget bang on the nose. A few weeks' location work in and around Freetown and the movie's in the can. It's worth it, Bob." He looked at Randall's tired face; the only time fans liked Randall looking bushed was when he was acting bushed. "Just a few weeks, Bob, then it's home and honeymoon."

"I'll be so goddamned tired the bride will think she's married a eunuch."

"A rest-up in Freetown and you'll feel different."

"A bed in an air-conditioned room, that's all I want." Remembering past location trips, Randall added, "Post a guard at the bedroom door. Lovesick matrons and father-fixated kids and reporters I can do without."

"Sure, Bob, you won't be disturbed. Two days' rest-up and we start shooting. No sound—we can dub that in later. You got the routine?"

"By heart. Just press the button and the dummy does what it's told."

"That's my boy!"

Randall closed his eyes against the glare of the early morning sun streaming through the cabin window. He felt more than middle-aged, he felt old, old. Twenty-five years in the movie business was a hundred years too long. You finished shooting one and began another before the previous film had been edited, and you dreamed a mixed salad of movies: riding a horse through a one-horse town and next minute you'd be burning up a city road in a fast Cadillac screwing a girl under a close-up lens and a thousand eyes. Maybe it would all change living quietly with Kay in the miles-from-nowhere house he'd built. Dreams of peace. Dreams maybe happy as their day. And no more movies, no more.

Yeah, thought Strauss as he looked at Randall's face, maybe it is time you crossed the age barrier. Older parts; the way Fred March had to change and managed it after years of spiritual torment. There was that script came in the other day about an ageing senator still hankering after the presidency without a hope in hell of getting it. Randall would look good with his hair bleached white and grown a little longer. A shock to the fans, maybe, but Randall would put on one hell of a performance, an Oscar performance.

Strauss resisted the impulse to break into Randall's closed-eyes solitude and tell him about the new film. Hold it, Strauss said to himself; get this one in the can first; get the guy married and refreshed, then tell him, "Bob—I've got the greatest part any actor's ever been offered. There's an Oscar in it as sure as God made Laurel and Hardy. . . ."

CHAPTER 14.

EIGHT miles from the center of Freetown, Mackenzie sat in the bar of the Bintumani Hotel and waited for telephone calls from South America; one from Jamie Turner to announce his arrival in Rio, and the second from Partridge to tell him that Mandragez had arrived at Aracaju. Jamie and the corpse were to be trusted absolutely, but Partridge remained the uncertain factor. Then Mackenzie mentally shrugged away the importance of Partridge; if the man balked at the final muling, other hands could do the dirty work; if Jamie couldn't or wouldn't, other hands could be bought. Another day—two, perhaps— and the operation would be over, with Jamie flying to Geneva as safe as the Bank of Scotland.

Doubts wiped from his mind, Mackenzie summoned the bar steward and ordered a double Scotch, specifying Bell's. An hour later he was called to the telephone.

"Mac?"

"Hello, Jamie."

"I'm here in Rio."

"Fine. When do you leave for Aracaju?"

"In two hours."

"If you want me, you'll find me here at the Bintumani or at the Komalu. Don't phone unless something goes wrong. I'll contact you at the Sergipe Hotel in Aracaju—understand?"

"Okay, Mac."

Mackenzie went back to the bar and waited for Partridge's call.

The ship from Freetown stood at its quayside mooring, and the ramp from ship to quay was being lowered. A small group of men and women, like black, hooded crows, watched and waited a few yards away from where the ramp touched the quay.

94

Partridge nodded to four sober-suited men standing by the first of three limousines, and they moved toward the ramp and mounted its slope into the ship.

It was early morning, misty, and the port of Aracaju was a monotone of grays, and Partridge shivered.

Movement at the top of the ramp caught his attention. He watched the bearers tread carefully down the ramp, the coffin on their shoulders. The group of mourners broke into a low, keening sound, half song, half undulating moan of anguish.

The coffin bearers reached the end of the ramp and moved toward the first limousine, the group of mourners falling in behind. Partridge supposed that the leading figures—the old man with bald head bent low, the woman heavily veiled—were the dead man's parents. The rest would be relatives, and Partridge thanked God there were no children present; he could assume that Mandragez was unmarried or without children.

Partridge walked to his hired car and climbed into the driver's seat. When the hearse began to move off, he switched on the ignition and started the car, then slipped into gear as the three limousine hearses moved away from the quay for the ten-mile journey to Dantos and the service and interment.

Not long now and the nightmare would be over. The sickness and the recurrent high temperatures, the blood he'd found in his stool the night before, would be in the past and forgotten. He'd see a doctor, kick this malaria for good, and rest in his house outside Freetown on that beautiful hill overlooking the white-gold beaches and the blue Atlantic. Peace and serenity of mind.

The hearse was travelling at ten miles an hour, passing pedestrians who reverently doffed their hats or made the sign of the cross. He'd stop at the first pay phone and make the call to Mackenzie; there would be plenty of time to catch up with the hearse, attend the service for the dead, and watch the burial.

He made the call to the Bintumani and returned to his car. One mile from Aracaju the sickness came on him again. He stopped the car and vomited at the side of the road, using every escapist avenue in his mind to avoid seeing the blackish tinge to his vomit.

He got back into the car, a headache beating his brain with hammer blows.

The two men with Felix Partridge were short and stocky, the width of their shoulders suggesting that they were used to heavy work, perhaps digging or hauling. Each held a spade and waited in the darkness, which grew deeper as the last light from the sun left the sky.

Partridge looked at his watch as if to gain comfort from the sweep hand that denoted the passing of seconds, the minutes, before what he had to do and get done with would be over.

One of the men said, "Senhor, when can we start?"

"Soon," Partridge said. "There are still drinkers in the bar. We must wait until they leave."

The man gave a short laugh. "They are not likely to bring their drinks into a cemetery at night, Senhor. There are two sorts of spirits—those that come from the dead and those that come from bottles."

"Soon," Partridge said again.

The air was rapidly cooling, and Partridge wished that he had put on a warm coat; the chill struck through his thin shirt, penetrating his skin until it reached his bones.

From where they stood, the street sloped down past the cantina and through the close-huddled houses until it met a maze of tiny streets where it was lost as the land rose, and the pantiled roofs of Dantos revealed the whole of the village.

To the east, three miles from Dantos, the Atlantic lapped the coast. A westerly breeze now brought a damp sea chill inland, and Partridge shuddered.

"The senhor is cold, perhaps?" asked one of the men.

"I should have brought a coat."

"The digging will make *us* warm."

Men emerged from the cantina and walked down the street, their hard boots clicking on the rough stone chips that metalled the street. Partridge waited; already lights were winking out over Dantos. He looked up the street to the high-walled cemetery with its ornate wrought-iron gates depicting the wings of an angel.

"Now, I think," Partridge said. "And we will have no trouble."

"Trouble, senhor?"

"What I have to do, I do alone. Then when I have done, you will leave everything as we found it."

"Everything, senhor?"

"As far as you are concerned, everything."

The man with questions shrugged and shouldered his spade. "Should not the senhor learn to trust men who are well paid?"

They moved up the street and toward the angel gates dimly etched against the last vestige of light in the sky. As if to comfort Partridge, one of the men said quietly, "It will not be difficult—the earth will not have settled. Fifteen minutes will see it done, and then, if the senhor does not object, Pedron and I will look the other way by taking a drink in the cantina."

"I've no objection," Partridge said. "But no more than ten minutes."

"We will then drive back to Aracaju?" the man with questions asked.

"Yes."

"Where we will be paid?"

"As arranged."

The angel gates opened on hinges that had been well oiled, and Partridge supposed that constant use of the cemetery warranted their care; the death rate in Dantos was high, and respect for the dead amounted to adoration.

They picked their way through the close-packed graves, skirting round ornate and towering structures that marked the resting place of deceased wealthy inhabitants, and edging along foot-wide paths through the simple peasant graves.

"Here," Partridge said.

Mandragez lay under a six-by-four-foot mound of flowers and wreaths; at its head an iron cross had been placed.

"Your relative had a good funeral, senhor," Pedron said. "Enough flowers for a wedding."

"If it is my relative."

"I would not wish to look on the face of one that has been buried."

"I have to make sure—and there is no time to lose."

The men worked with care, removing the wreaths and bunches of flowers and remembering the order in which they had been placed on the grave.

When the first spade stabbed into the earth, Partridge turned away so that he gazed down the hill to the huddle of Dantos's roofs. A thin sickle moon hung over the village, and the stars were now bright in the dark sky. The breeze blowing in from the sea had died, but a shiver ran down Partridge's spine; he could feel its shuddering descent from the nape of his neck to his coccyx. He folded his arms, hands tucked under his armpits.

The spades stabbed and stabbed again, the pile of removed earth growing on the left side of the grave, and Partridge still looked silently out toward the village. Then he heard a change in the sounds coming from the grave, the sound of steel striking against wood.

"Senhor? . . . We have reached it." The man's voice was quiet, a whisper that cut into Partridge's consciousness as if the man had shouted. "Senhor? . . . Pedron will unscrew the lid now?"

"Yes."

"Good—and then we will go to the cantina?"

"You will go to the cantina." Partridge repeated the words like an automaton. "Yes . . . yes." He turned and looked down at the opened grave, at Pedron brushing away loose soil from the first of the screws. Not long now before the last of the horrors would be over. He watched in silence as Pedron worked his way round the coffin, and prayed that he would not faint or be sick when the razor-sharp scalpel made its first incision. His shudders were uncontrollable, and he guessed that the fever was mounting in his bloodstream. He slipped on the rubber gloves he had bought, and took the encased scalpel from his shirt pocket.

Pedron said, "The last of the screws, senhor. Shall we now leave?"

"Yes," Partridge said. "Leave now. When you return, wait for me by the gates. Then you can finish your work."

The refrigeration hold of the ship from Freetown had not been efficient; the smell that rose from the opened coffin made Partridge gag. He closed his nostrils against the smell and breathed heavily through open mouth.

The scalpel cut through the nylon stitching above and below the marks Rikel had made, and Partridge, fighting revulsion, inserted his hand into the incision. He closed his eyes and forced his fingers to touch substances that yielded until they closed round the wallet. With the action came a wave of nausea that blacked him out as he retched into the grave. He recovered slowly, saliva cleansing his mouth of the sour taste of bile, sight and sound returning so that, once again, he became aware of the wallet in his hand.

He came away from the grave and stood near the gates clutching at their intricate ironwork for support and breathing in the sea-scented night air.

Light flashed from the door of the cantina, and two silhouettes were momentarily etched against the light. The sound of footsteps came toward him up the hill, and he heard the voice of the man with questions: "Senhor—is it time?"

"It's time," Partridge said. "Leave everything as you found it."

"It is your relative?"

"Yes."

"Such sadness," the other man said. Partridge heard irony in the voice.

If Partridge had slept, then sleep had been as nightmarish as wakefulness, interspersed with bouts of nausea and bowel movements having nothing to expel. At some time during the long night he had been racked by an attack of shivering that made his teeth chatter.

The sun had just risen, casting a sultry light through the bedroom window, and he looked at his watch. Another three hours before his rendezvous with Mackenzie's man.

The headache had softened its blows; it was now, by comparison, a gentle pulse pain and bearable—a reminder, almost, that his heart was still beating. He felt so utterly weak, and he wished he could sleep and sleep without dreams, without the memory of the nocturnal obscenity he had directed and in which he had acted the leading part. It seemed, too, that his body had given up its attack of diarrhoea and nausea and was sleeping but keeping watch by its sentinel in his head.

He slipped into a doze from which he awoke two hours later, surprised that so much time had passed without agony. He washed and shaved at the hand basin, forcing himself to perform a normal task that had become almost Herculean, noting with revulsion that his eyes were bloodshot and his face malaria-yellow. He swallowed antimalarial tablets, gagging as he washed them down with lukewarm water from the tap.

Weakened by his efforts at the hand basin, he sat for a while looking out the window and down at the narrow street. Only another two thousand miles to go and he'd put himself into the hands of the best medical care he could find. The thought cheered him and gave him energy to dress.

A short walk to the bar where he would meet Mackenzie's man, and then two thousand miles to Freetown; after all he'd been through, it was no distance at all.

The waterproof wallet he had taken from the grave was out of sight in his old briefcase bearing his initials, F.O.P.—Felix Oswald Partridge; the letters and the word they spelt had never occurred to him as being funny. He knew what was in the wallet and had no desire to open it. He had known what it would contain when Mackenzie had given him details of this last assignment; he had also known that he could have cut and run with the wallet, but he was too exhausted to think he could elude Mackenzie. The peace that awaited him in Sierra Leone was payment and reward enough.

Jamie Turner had breakfasted well on the balcony of his hotel room. He now drank his second cup of coffee and watched the sunlight dancing on the Atlantic as it rolled into the harbor of Aracaju.

He had arrived a little before nightfall. In Rio he had hired a private aircraft to fly him up the coast to Aracaju, where he had booked in at the Sergipe Hotel, dined, and then located the bar designated by Mackenzie for his rendezvous with the mule.

Returning to the hotel, he had waited for Mackenzie's call before going to bed. The conversation had been short and cryptic.

"Tonight's the night, Jamie."

"Right."

"Found a decent bar yet?"

"The one you suggested."

"Good. Drink to absent friends at ten-thirty. If you meet a bird, tell it something about the Emerald Isles. It'll expect it."

"Understood, Mac."

"Give it enough food to fly back to Freetown, and tell it it can roost happily for the rest of its life. That's on the level, Jamie—there's no double cross. But if it lays an egg, let me know right away. I'll be at the Komalu."

The Jaquito Bar on the west side of São Paulo Square looked out across a small garden to a baroque church that gleamed creamy-pink in the harsh sunlight. Eyes squinted against the glare, Turner entered the bar and stood in the doorway until his eyes adjusted to the dark of the bar.

Along the left side of the long narrow room tables and chairs were arranged. At the last table a man sat, hunched over a cup of coffee.

The barman looked at Turner: *"Senhor?"*

"Coffee."

"Sim, senhor."

Turner walked down the room and sat at the last but one table. As he did so the man raised his head, a question in his eyes. Turner nodded a greeting and said, *"Bom día."*

The man replied in English: "Good morning."

The barman came with Turner's coffee and a glass of water. Turner spoke to the seated man: "Mind if I join you?"

"No."

"That's a fine church across the square. Looks more like an elegant fun palace than a church."

"It's one way of glorifying Jesus Christ."

The man's face was not that of a mule, Turner thought. Usually you saw cunning and a certain cockiness of manner, shiftiness too; but the face opposite was that of an ordinary man who had suffered and was suffering. The unhealthy pallor, yellowish, the sunken cheeks and eyes veined, and thin, bony fingers that twitched.

"The garden in the square looks as green as the Emerald Isles," Turner said.

The man exhaled a sigh of relief. "Thank God you've come. My name is Partridge, like the bird."

"Good." Turner nodded. "How did things go?"

"They went. He can't ask for anything more. If he does—I've reached the end. After last night—"

"You've my assurance there's nothing more to do—after you've given me the package."

The briefcase was on the chair beside Partridge. He reached over, unlatched it, and took out the wallet. "I washed it," he said, "in disinfectant. My hands too."

"That was sensible." Turner took the wallet and slipped it in his jacket pocket. "You don't look well," he said.

· "I'm not. Malaria, mostly, and some other bug is infecting me. I didn't open the wallet. I know what's in it, but I didn't open it. I promised Mackenzie I wouldn't open it."

"No names," Turner said.

"I'm sorry. He stands over me like God or the devil."

"You've had a bad time?"

"I've seen hell, and it's worse than any biblical description."

"You've left it now," Turner said. "You can start forgetting. You'll need some money. Our friend suggested it when I spoke to him." Turner took out his billfold and extracted ten bills. "A thousand dollars. They'll see you back to Freetown. Go soon—you need treatment. See a doctor."

"Do you care that much? Does our—friend?"

"I sincerely do. He would too if he could see you."

Partridge took the money and looked at it. "He said everything would be as promised when I got back to Freetown. Will it be?"

"Yes. I spoke to him last night. He's a man of his word. I'll phone him this morning and give him the okay."

"After you've inspected the wallet?"

"Of course."

"Are you like him?"

"I don't think so. I haven't got his guts."

"Is that what he's got?"

"I know he's a hard man too. Perhaps his years in Africa have made him hard. I know him as a rock-steady friend."

"You don't look crooked," Partridge said. "Why is that?"

"I'm a master of disguise." Turner stirred sugar into his coffee. "Maybe I've got virtues I don't know about that shine through. When will you leave Aracaju?"

"Tomorrow if I'm well enough. I'll rest up at the Estancia."

"See a doctor first."

"Do you care if I live or die?"

"Yes, I do. I know why and how you got in this spot, and I'm glad you've got your release. It was hard-earned, and our friend needn't have gone so far. But you've got through. Take care now."

"I've no one to turn to. For two months I've lived in my head. Last night, in the cemetery, I was sick in the grave—when my hand touched the wallet. It was like stealing a heart." Partridge leaned his elbows on the table and covered his face with his hands, muffling his voice. "I'll stop talking soon and you can go. It helps—talking. I've had no one to talk to."

"I'm listening," Turner said. "If it helps, I'll sit with you as long as it takes you to unload."

"You're nothing like I imagined you to be. You're an American, aren't you?"

"Yes."

"I've never been to America. I was a Londoner. I came out to Sierra Leone when I was twenty. I'm forty-five now, and I've aged twenty years in two months."

"Rest and medical care will make you years younger. Keep your mind on that. When you get back, there'll be no more troubles. Everything will be taken care of—you can rely on that. Do you believe me?"

Partridge uncovered his face. "I believe you." The knife of pain was lancing into his intestines again, and he clasped his stomach. "Perhaps you'd better go and tell him that I followed his orders to the letter."

Sweat had broken out on Partridge's forehead, and Turner said, "A brandy might help."

Partridge shook his head. "I couldn't hold it down. I'd be sick again. Can I ask for one last assurance?"

"Yes."

"After you've phoned him—can I get in touch with you? Just to make sure?"

"I'll be at the Sergipe Hotel until tomorrow."

"If I ring you, who should I ask for?"

"I'm sorry—no names. Ask for the American—describe me."

"Thank you," Partridge said. "You've been kind."

"Would you like me to see you back to your hotel?"

Partridge shook his head. "Just leave me here. It's helped—talking to you."

Turner held out his hand, resisting revulsion when Partridge clasped it and he felt the damp contact of his hand. "Phone me tonight," Turner said. "Please take care."

"I'm glad it was you at the end of the road," Partridge said.

Turner opened the wallet. Queasiness touched his excitement as his fingers peeled back the layers of lint. He came to the last layer and paused, remembering Partridge's words: "*I didn't open the wallet.* . . . *I promised Mackenzie I wouldn't open it.*" For my hands only, Turner thought, and unfolded the last layer.

What he saw cut through the lingering image of Partridge and the dead mule from Freetown. The stones lying on the white lint were incredible in their color and quantity. Two thousand one hundred and seven carats, Mac had said. Sixteen ounces!

Under the concentrated light of the desk lamp, fire leapt from the stones. Pure-whites, pale-blues and greens, amber and champagne—the colors were impossibly beautiful, and Turner's hands trembled as they gripped the edge of the desk. Mac had been so goddamned selective, not a single macle or flat among them—octahedrons and irregular shapes in a brilliant heaped cluster.

He was staring at millions of dollars. Even allowing for spotted and flawed crystals in the cluster, their value was immense. The current price for a flawless diamond was in the neighborhood of eight thousand dollars per carat; at that rate, he was looking at a fortune worth over sixteen million dollars in the *rough* state. Cut and polished, they would double in value. Double!

Turner got up and went to the drinks table. He poured a large measure of Bourbon and drank it straight, then went back to the writing desk. As he sat down a ghost image of Partridge's face flitted across his mind and then was gone to be replaced by Mackenzie's rugged, good-humored face. "Oh, Mac!" Turner said aloud. "You've done well. You've got your thousands of Scottish acres!"

Away with childish, unsophisticated wonder, he told himself; get out your 10X lens and examine every stone one by one. Gaze into the heart of each crystal and bring objective, expert judgment to bear. Use tweezers and do the job professionally. This one . . . an irregular Blue-White . . . examine for spotting . . . two carats? Just about. There's its heart, firing its prismatic beauty at me. An octahedron . . . pale-champagne and must be four carats at least. . . .

Time passed, and minutes lengthened into hours as he tweezered crystals out of the pile and held them under the magnifying loupe, his mind totally concentrated on the task.

Three hours after he had opened the wallet, the telephone rang and he reached for the receiver, eyes still fixed on the pale-blue diamond held in the tweezers.

Mackenzie's voice, loud and angry, came over the line: "What the hell do you think you're doing? I've waited by this damn phone for two hours!"

"Mac?"

"Who the blazes do you think it is? Two bloody hours I've waited."

"I'm sorry."

"Sorry be damned! If anything's gone wrong—"

"Nothing's gone wrong, Mac—nothing! I've got them. Mac—they're out of this world."

"I don't give a tinker's fart which world they're out of!"

"Cool it, Mac. Please cool it. I got involved, that's all, and time passed. They're beautiful and incredible. There's color range and quality. There's a Pale-Blue—eight carats, I think. You should see it, Mac!"

"I've seen them. I've spent years getting them together. I told you this would be the big one. I know they're good. They're just pure carbon and harder than women, so stop fucking them. Get down to business, Jamie. I've finished sounding off, so talk details."

"I've given Partridge his passage home. I assured him you'd keep your promise."

"I always do. What next?"

"He's ill, I think—very ill."

"So?"

"I thought I'd tell you."

"You've told me. Next?"

"Mac, I'm sorry I kept you waiting."

Mackenzie's chuckle came over the phone. "All right, Jamie—I've cooled down. You like the pebbles?"

"Like them? I'm in a state of shock. Do you know how much they're worth?"

"I can do sums, Jamie. The world's your oyster—mine too. Now, what's your next move?"

"I'd planned to go to Geneva from here, but I don't like the idea of carrying the packet. If you have no objection, I'll mail them to the Swiss bank—to await my arrival."

"Do what you think best, Jamie."

"Carrying that amount would increase my sweat and blink rate. I'd be searched as soon as I reached customs control."

"So when will you get to Geneva?"

"After the packet. I'm getting the next flight back to New York, sleep for a few hours, then hop across to Geneva. I'll be staying at the usual place, Mac—the Hôtel des Bergues. When will I see you?"

"In a few weeks' time. I'm doing a bit of charity work in Angwana for an old friend. Nothing like behaving like the honest, decent man I am. There's no hurry—except when you're waiting on a lazy, good-for-nothing Yank."

"I was staggered by the sheer size and beauty, Mac."

"So stop staggering and get those stones to Geneva. I'll contact you there in a few days. Don't try to reach me, Jamie. From now on I make all contacts, unless the packet gets lost in the post. Understood?"

"Understood."

"We've done it, Jamie."

"We've done it, Mac."

"Is there anything else worth mentioning, Jamie?"

"I don't know. On the flight from New York I was talked at by an IDSO man, name of Manston. He mentioned your name and the Komalu accident."

"Did you let on that you knew me?"

"I'm not that stupid, Mac."

"Just as well. He and his underling, Meadows, are bloody pests."

"Then it's lucky their top man is a personal friend of mine, Dick Walker—do you know him?"

"I know about him, that's all. Steer clear of IDSO men for a time, Jamie."

"Don't worry, I will. I don't like sweating or blinking out Morse-coded messages that I'm an illicit."

"Better than telling 'em you're illegitimate and a bastard. Okay, Jamie—that's it. No further contact until you hear from me."

CHAPTER 15.

MIDNIGHT. Jamie Turner was asleep when the urgent ringing of the telephone brought him awake. He reached out, found the receiver, and mumbled into it: "Yes?"

"*Senhor americano?*"

"Who?"

"I was told to ask for the *americano.*"

"Who told you?"

"The Englishman in the Estancia Hotel."

"What do you want?"

"Will you come to the Englishman, senhor? He is ill and asks for you."

"It's late. Tell him I'll come in the morning."

"Senhor." The man's voice was quiet, insistent. "Perhaps there will be no morning for the Englishman."

It could be a trick, Turner thought. In the desk drawer lay sixteen million dollars' worth of diamonds. Did the caller know about them?

"I'm sorry," he said. "I can't come now. Who are you?"

"My name is Pedron. I went to Dantos with the Englishman and did work for him in the place of the dead. He told me to tell you this."

"Tell him I'll be with him first thing in the morning."

"He asks for you to come now. His room is numbered by a five. He said you would come because you cared. I have done what I was asked to do. *Adeus, senhor.*"

"Hold it," Turner said. "He told you where to find me?"

"*Americanos* stay in rich hotels, and the Sergipe is for the rich. I ask to speak to the *americano*, that is all. If you have any pity, you will go to him."

The line went dead, and Turner replaced the receiver. For a while he lay on his back, pity for the man he had seen in the morning fighting with mistrust of the quiet Brazilian voice he had just heard. Sleep halted the fight, then left him at first light and the fight was on again.

It was difficult to read between the lines spoken by a Brazilian in good English; the politeness and elegance of the man's speech could hide much. And what could he give to Partridge if, indeed, Partridge had asked for him?

Damn Partridge and the soft-spoken Brazilian; he'd gone to bed thinking of the diamonds and Carol. Everything had gone smoothly and exactly to plan—now this, whatever it was.

He showered and dressed, pocketed the wallet, then went down to the reception foyer and asked the night clerk for directions to the Estancia Hotel. He was about to go through the swinging doors leading to the street when he returned and asked the clerk for use of the hotel safe.

"We have a visitors' safe, senhor," the clerk said.

The wallet interred in the safe, Turner requested paper and an envelope. He wrote a brief message in which he stated that the bearer of the letter had the authority to take the wallet from the safe. He folded the letter and placed it in the envelope and addressed it to A. Mackenzie at Komalu Mining Company, Komalu, Sierra Leone. He sealed the envelope and handed it to the clerk. "I want this posted not later than this afternoon."

"There is a collection in one hour, senhor."

"Post it this afternoon. It may not have to be sent."

The Estancia was little more than a boardinghouse, small and seedy, lying in a huddle of houses in a back street. There was no one in the fly-blown lobby, and obeying a sign which bore the legend "*Quartos* 1–5," he climbed a steep, narrow staircase.

There was no reply when he knocked on the door marked "5" and he knocked again. He waited for a while, then tried the door, which yielded under pressure, and he stepped into the darkened room.

In the dim light he could see the cheap furnishings: a wardrobe, two wooden chairs, a table under the small window, and the bed. Turner's nose wrinkled in disgust; the air was dirty, humid, and oppressive. Somewhere in the room a mosquito whined. Dawn light seeping through a chink in the curtains covering the window cast a pale shaft on the bed where Partridge lay, his eyes open and glinting in the pale light.

"Partridge?" Turner said. "I'm sorry I couldn't come before. . . . Partridge?"

He went close to the bed and looked at the eyes that glared at something or nothing beyond his gaze. Between the eyes and low on

Partridge's forehead, a dark-red caste mark stood out livid on the pale skin.

"You asked me to come," Turner said. "What did you want?"

He knew there would be no answer, yet he persisted, trying to break through the impossible barrier he faced. "Wake up—wake up, Partridge!"

Sunlight joined the light from the chink in the curtains, and the caste mark was a brighter red now. Then the caste mark moved, and Turner saw that it was a bedbug fat with the blood of the man who had died.

A wave of nausea rose up in Turner, and he turned away from the eyes and the bloated bug. The mosquito whine came nearer; when it seemed about to penetrate his ear, Turner jerked his head and made an ineffective swipe at the insect. Noises from the street sounded, isolated sounds: a shop shutter being rattled up, a moped spluttering down the street.

The room was impregnated with the presence of death and the sour smell of vomit, and Turner moved to the window intending to open it, to let in what remained of the dawn's cool air and the sounds of life in the streets—anything to kill the smell and death-presence in the room. On the table by the window there was a small clear-plastic bottle and a writing pad.

Turner picked up the pad and read what was written in words that trailed as if tired:

> I wanted you to come—to talk. No one to ask. It is two o'clock and I have been very sick. Pedron said he would again ask you to come. Corruption is in me—like the man in the coffin and the smell. Tell Mackenzie—devil—devil—devil! Mackenzie devil. You said you cared—you have not come. Please help me. . . .

Turner ripped the sheet off the pad and put it in his pocket. He picked up the plastic bottle and saw that it contained three capsules; he recognized them as Nembutal—Joanie had used them at one time. If Partridge had used them for his last supper they had not caused his death—no one died from an overdose with his eyes open; the seed of death must have been planted in Partridge long before he arrived in Aracaju.

Questions, conjecture, analysis of cause of death—there was no time for probing the secrets of the room and the dead man. Turner began to leave the room, treading quietly; then he stopped as he saw Partridge's eyes glinting as thin, dawn sunlight shafted through the chink in the curtains. The caste mark had gone; perhaps it had sought a sleeping berth in the hair of its host or had begun its slow, blood-bloated journey back to its nest in the bed or a crack in the wall.

Turner forced his fingertips to close the lids over the eyes, then left the room, shutting the door gently behind him.

Back in the Sergipe Hotel, he retrieved his wallet and the letter he had addressed to Mackenzie. Later, after a breakfast consisting solely of coffee—he had no stomach for food—he bought packing materials and wrapped the diamonds into a neat package which he addressed to J. D. Turner at Banque d'Helvétie, Place Genève, Geneva, Switzerland. He posted it in Rio, one hour before his flight to New York.

CHAPTER 16.

TURNER came out of Kennedy Airport depressed and tired. Added to the depression was the vivid memory of Partridge, and the smell of the room still lingered in his nostrils. Night had fallen, and resisting the instinct to tell the cabdriver "198 Riverside Drive," he said, "The Waldorf-Astoria."

He checked in, showered, and changed, then ate a lonely, depressing meal, trying, but failing, to concentrate his mind on Carol, Geneva, and the diamonds he had mailed to Switzerland.

He was asleep by midnight. At one o'clock he tore himself out of a dream in which he was crawling with bedbugs and drowning in a sea of vomit, and reached for the telephone.

His wife's sleepy voice mumbled a response, and he said, "Joanie?"

"Mmmm?"

"It's me, Joanie!"

"Jamie?"

"I had to speak to someone."

"I don't understand. You're in Geneva."

"No—I'm here—in New York. The Waldorf."

"Why are you calling? I don't understand."

"I had a dream, Joanie—a bad dream. I had to hear your voice."

"So now you've heard it. Is there something wrong?"

"I don't know. I woke up and called you. Wait, Joanie—wait."

He controlled his breathing until it was quiet, then he spoke to her again: "I woke up from the dream. I called you. I guess it was an automatic call for help. I just don't know."

"A mechanical response, Jamie? So what do we talk about?"

"I don't know. I'm sorry—you were asleep."

"Aren't you going to Geneva?"

"Tomorrow—no, today, of course. I'm sorry it's so late."

"Well—have a good trip. What time are you leaving?"

"Afternoon flight—three-thirty. I'm sorry I called you. I was having a bad time."

"Well—"

"Goodbye, Joanie. Thanks for listening."

"Goodbye, Jamie. Pleasant dreams."

"I think I'll stay awake."

In ten minutes he was asleep again. This time no dreams or nightmarish monsters disturbed his rest. He slept round to half-past nine and breakfasted late. At twelve-thirty he walked the distance to the White Bear restaurant, aware that his choice of eating place was sentimental.

Because of happier past times in the restaurant, he was not surprised to find Joan sitting at the bar drinking a Negroni.

"Hello," he said.

She looked at his reflection in the bar mirror. "You look as if you've had a rough trip."

"You don't. You look as good as I'd like to feel." Turner nodded to the barman: "I'll have the same as this lady."

"That's no lady, that's your wife," she said. "To crack an old joke."

"Why?" Turner asked. "Why are you here, Joanie?"

"Your call worried me."

"You could have told me to go to hell."

"Wasn't that where you'd just been? What was the dream, Jamie?"

"It's too obscene to talk about." He looked at the Negroni and smiled. "We came to the White Bear after we were married. We drank Negronis then, too. Is that why you came here?"

"Why not? Much can be swamped in sentiment. Will you lunch with me?"

"Sure."

"No previous appointment?"

"No."

"I thought maybe you brought *her* here."

Turner finished his drink before replying. "Some questions don't need answers," he said. "That's one of them."

"Consider it unsaid." She spoke to his mirror reflection. "I'm glad and sad about us all at the same time. If I let sadness take over, I say bitchy things, so pardon the cattiness."

"And if you're feeling glad?"

"I'll wish you well, Jamie, and hope we have a good time in the future."

During the meal, conversation skated over thin ice. She thought she would take a vacation somewhere; New York wasn't the happiest place, what with humidity, that good old, bad old discomfort index, and all that, and what did he think? He thought it was a good idea. She thought, too, it was a good idea to leave Gem International and go it alone in Europe; and thank you, Jamie, for being so generous—if you need money you've only to ask, you know that. Isn't it true that if feet itch it's time to move on? Geneva sounds marvellous and so near France and Italy and Germany. It is good to behave like two civilized, sensible people with the best years of their lives yet to come—oh, yes, they are yet to come. Who knows? Life might turn out so good they could meet as friends.

Then the ice cracked, and she said, "What happened, Jamie? It was something bad, wasn't it? In Rio?"

"Upcoast from Rio. I saw death at close quarters. The dream I had —before I called you—I think I was that dead man dying again. I'd rather not talk about it."

"Talking helps. Isn't that why you called me?"

"You said I was acting on a mechanical response. Let's leave it that I needed you at that moment."

"That's vaguely flattering, Jamie. Am I to take it as a compliment?"

"You were the only one I thought of turning to."

"Next time you have a bad dream, make sure there's someone in bed with you."

He didn't reply but reached for the bottle of wine and filled his glass.

"I'm sorry," she said. "That was catty. I'd made up my mind that if we met again, I'd be sensible and kind and think only of the good times. It's difficult to stop caring, and if you care, you're either malicious or loving, or both."

"End it, Joanie," he said. He could see deep water coming up— waters that were treacherous and too deep for survival. "If we're to talk, go over the good times and keep it at that level."

She looked into his face; there were shadows in it she hadn't seen before. It was a mask, a good-looking mask covering much that she would never know. She pushed coffee cup and saucer away from her. "I think I'll go now, Jamie."

He stayed seated and said, "If I've no one in bed with me when I'm dying again—"

"Call me," she said. "Just reach for the phone again."

He watched her leave the restaurant and felt like a heel. She had nothing to hide but disappointment; nothing dirty or underhand to cover; no dead men and the smell of vomit and a bedbug crawling. Why the hell couldn't she have left it as things stood—even after his 1:00 A.M. call—instead of turning up at the White Bear looking years younger and giving him permission to go East, young man, and see the world?

There was some wine left in the bottle, and he emptied it into his glass, observing as he did so that it was the exact color of a ruby—or the color of a blood-bloated bedbug.

He put down the glass, called for his check, paid it, and left the restaurant.

Bernard Manston sat with Gilberto Noni in the room behind the shop and drank coffee. "The American certainly arrived in Aracaju," he said. "His name's in the hotel register—J. D. Turner."

Noni shook his head. "No American came here."

"He said he was buying stones—I gave him your name. I recommended you, Noni."

"I thank you, Mr. Manston. Perhaps he went elsewhere."

"He came and he went," Manston said. "Back to Rio after a couple of days. Who else peddles emerald in Aracaju?"

Noni shrugged. "Who knows? There are many in the back streets. Mine is the only good emerald house in Aracaju."

"Pity. I thought I'd put some good business your way, Noni."

"It is of no consequence. I have enough trouble without wondering whether an American buys or buys not. I am a man of property, Mr. Manston, and property can mean trouble. I have inherited a dead man, and it seems I must bear the cost of giving him decent burial."

Manston smiled. "You're a religious chap, Noni—you should consider it a pleasure."

"I have thought of requesting the Komalu Mining Company in Sierra Leone to take responsibility."

Manston looked sharply at Noni. "Why?"

"The dead man was an employee of that company."

"What was he doing here?"

"Dying." Noni sighed. "It is very inconvenient."

"Does he have a name?"

"Partridge, and he dies in my hotel, the Estancia. There was more than enough money to pay for his funeral, and a mass—the police took the money."

"Had he been here long?"

"Three days."

"Do you have any dates?"

"As far as can be determined, he died three days ago. The police have his papers." Noni poured more coffee and said, "This is of interest to you—this dead man?"

"Anyone, dead or alive, connected with diamonds is interesting.

I'll call on the police, see what I can find out."

"Mention of my name might influence them, Mr. Manston." Noni looked sour. "I contribute handsomely to their funds."

An hour later Manston was on the telephone and talking to Jason Meadows in Freetown. "Chase this, Jasey. A Komalu sorter named Partridge. Found stone-cold dead in Aracaju."

"Aracaju?"

"That's right. I'm phoning from there."

"A good place for the dead, Bernard. The Komalu shipped a corpse to Aracaju a week or so ago. One of the miners killed in the tunnel collapse. Do you want his name?"

"Might as well."

"Mandragez—Juan Mandragez, a Brazilian. I watched the sendoff. All the top brass turned out, including Mackenzie. I had drinks and a chat with Mac afterwards. He's leaving the Komalu in a few weeks' time, then nipping across to Angwana—he's been asked to look at what promises to be a rich find. Appleby's the man there."

"Why is Mackenzie leaving?"

"He's taken responsibility for the accident. He's also fed up with Africa and says he's done well enough to laird it in Scotland. Are you on to something, Bernard?"

"Just adding two and two together. I'm making it five at the moment. Look, Jasey—if you see Mac, ask him about Partridge. I'd like to know why he dies in Aracaju after a brief trip to London. I looked at his passport. Freetown to Bogotá, Bogotá to London, London to Rio, then up to Aracaju and death from natural causes. That's a long trip to the grave, Jasey. Just nose around, will you? I'll be back in Freetown in two, three days. Anything happening?"

"A film unit's arrived—American. They're doing location work. Robert Randall's the star. A bit of diamond news—got it from an assistant to an assistant producer. A buyer named Grunwald should be arriving in a couple of weeks' time with diamonds worth over the million-dollar mark. They're for Randall."

Manston's memory flashed recognition data. "Grunwald—Solomon. American. CSO buyer . . . Jasey—keep your eyes open. See if Grunwald has a tail."

"Haven't seen any villains of that calibre in Freetown."

"When I get back, we'll get our noses to the ground."

Manston rang off and sat for a while in the hotel lobby. He had the corner pieces of the jigsaw puzzle and few bearing portions of faces and fragments of background, and he had no idea of the size of the puzzle; it could contain a thousand pieces or only a hundred. He looked across the lobby to the reception desk; the night clerk was replacing the day clerk; perhaps the night man might have a little information regarding the movements of J. D. Turner during his brief stay in the Sergipe Hotel.

Manston got to his feet and strolled across the lobby to the desk, fingering a cruzeiro note high enough in value to loosen discreet tongues.

CHAPTER 17.

T H E airport buildings and hangars, drab when the skies were clear and bathed in sunshine, looked even more drab in the rain. Three DC-9s, the total number of aircraft comprising Angwana's airline, were ranged on the concrete apron. No flight departures were booked for this day, nor were there to be any for the next two days. At the eastern end of the airport the Angwanan Air Force Base was lost in the misty rain, its squadron of old HS Buccaneers ranged in takeoff position for an alert that had not been sounded for seven months.

The TriStar descended through the mist and rain and touched down with spumes of spray as the wheels hit the runway. Waiting by Sotho's presidential car, Appleby heard the scream of reverse jets and saw the TriStar's landing speed slowly lessen. At the end of its run it turned and rumbled to the apron where the landing stairs waited to be driven to the TriStar's doors.

The burly figure of Mackenzie appeared in the exit door at the front of the TriStar, and Appleby said, "That's Mr. Mackenzie. About to come down the stairs."

"If you will wait here, Doctor," said an airport official standing with him, "I will go to the plane and collect his luggage."

"Thank you."

"You are cleared to leave the airport without formalities."

"Again, thank you."

Mackenzie's handshake was in keeping with his large frame; it enveloped Appleby's bony hand in a warm, strong grip. "Well, Arthur, you old devil, where'd you get this bloody rain from?"

"You brought it with you, Mac," Appleby replied. "Or call it Highland mist—laid on to make you feel at home." He indicated the waiting palace Mercedes. "You see, Mac? The presidential car, complete with bonnet flag and in your honor. We're due at the palace. Don't let protocol worry you."

"It never does," Mackenzie said. "I just don't follow it. I don't bow or curtsey. Kings and presidents take me as I am or not at all. I'm a mining engineer, not a court hanger-on."

"I've told Sotho to expect a wild Scottish savage," said Appleby, "but go easy, Mac. Those around the president like to see respect paid to a man who's doing his best for a poor country."

"Then I won't spit in his eye and call him 'laddie.' " Mackenzie looked about him. "I didn't expect glamour in Angwana, but this—"

"Better times will change it, Mac. I believe those times have come."

The airport official returned and said, "Sirs? Mr. Mackenzie's luggage is now in the car. You are free to go."

"Free to go," Mackenzie said as he climbed into the Mercedes. "Straight out of a dictator's phrase book."

"It wasn't meant in that way, Mac. You've been given VIP clearance."

"It's what I'm used to. Tell me about the new mine."

"It's rich. I don't know what the long-term prospects are, but, Mac, we've only scratched the surface and the yield so far, in what—two months?—has exceeded Angwana's other mine's yearly production. And the gem quality is high. I want machinery and skilled men, Mac. I think I've convinced Sotho that every penny the mine earns should be poured back into it. That's why you're here. With your advice I can prove that production can be trebled."

The car sped past the two-acre site on which the new hospital had begun to rise. Appleby pointed it out and said, "It will mean work must stop on Sotho's pride and joy. The housing development, too. It's difficult in an emergent country to put over the long-term view. They want it now, and I can understand it. With patience, they'd get something better."

"So what do I tell Sotho?"

"When you've seen the site and can honestly say it, tell him that, given the tools, he'll see a handsome return on Angwana's money in a few months."

"And you believe that, Arthur?"

"With all my heart."

"I was told Scotland bred large men," Sotho said, his small figure dwarfed by Mackenzie's six-feet-four.

"Only in the Highlands," Mackenzie said. "The Lowlands breed little men with stumpy legs."

"Angwanans are small with thin legs," said Sotho, "and we have no highlands. A tall Angwanan is a rarity, Mr. Mackenzie."

Ilbrahim Otanga appeared with coffee and began pouring it out into little cups. A bottle of whisky stood on the tray, and seeing the surprised look on Appleby's face, Sotho said, "To honor Mr. Mackenzie's visit, Doctor. As a Muslim, I will forgo the pleasure but bend the rules. Ilbrahim, whisky for Dr. Appleby and Mr. Mackenzie."

"Yes, Mr. President."

They were seated round a low table away from the presidential desk with its background of draped Angwanan flags. Through the window Mackenzie could see guards armed with M-16 rifles posted at strategic points round the lawn that stretched its length two hundred feet to the high wall surrounding the palace.

"In the old days," Mackenzie said, "there wouldn't have been a wall. Just a sentry box at the entrance marked by two white-painted boulders, and a Union Jack flying in the middle of a lawn as green and smooth as a billiard table."

"Much has happened since then," Sotho replied. "The wall became essential." Then he laughed. "There was nothing to stop the black man from coming in except the sentry's gun. Now I have to keep the black man out with armed guards and a high wall. One day the wall will come down."

Appleby said, "Mr. Mackenzie has agreed to give us his expert opinion on the new mine, Mr. President."

"The Appleby Mine," Sotho corrected.

"As you wish," Appleby said. "I have given him only the barest details. When he has seen it, he will be able to tell us what we need."

Watching Mackenzie drain the last of the whisky from the tiny glasses Otanga had filled, Sotho said, "And when will that be?"

"Two or three weeks." Mackenzie put down his glass and looked across the room to Otanga.

Sotho interpreted his glance and called out, "Ilbrahim—Mr. Mackenzie's glass is empty."

"Thank you," said Mackenzie. "A nod's evidently as good as a wink to a blind horse."

"Ilbrahim has very good eyesight, Mr. Mackenzie."

"I'd no intention of appearing rude."

"And I saw no such intention in the look or the words of a thirsty man."

Appleby shifted in his seat; Mackenzie was putting his damned foot in it. "Mr. Mackenzie," he said, "has offered his services free of charge, Mr. President."

"Why, Mr. Mackenzie?" Sotho asked. "Angwana is not so poor that it cannot pay a man for his services."

"It's possible I wish Angwana well," Mackenzie said. "Your administration is one of the few in Africa with policies that might save Africa. In any case, Arthur Appleby loves Angwana. On that recommendation alone, I'm prepared to wave the flag of Angwana."

"An honest sentiment, Mr. Mackenzie. Dr. Appleby warned me that you spoke your mind without fear or favor and that you would not use diplomatic language."

Mackenzie looked at Appleby and grinned. "I don't like wasting time," he said. "If my words offend and I'm asked to leave, I go. I like things understood without elegant trimmings, Mr. President. If I think you haven't a hope in hell I'll tell you and I'll exchange prejudice for prejudice. If a West Indian calls me a honky, I'll use my right to call him a nigger."

"Please, Mac," Appleby said.

Mackenzie ignored him. "Equality to me means that I can call a colored man a black bastard just as he can call me a white, pink, or putty-colored bastard of an imperialistic pig."

"Marvellous!" Sotho clapped his hands together. "Mr. Mackenzie, you are the best white bastard I have met."

Mackenzie smiled. "You're not bad yourself for a thieving black politician."

"For heaven's sake, Mac!" Appleby said.

Sotho gave his attention to Appleby. "Are you worried, Doctor? Are you afraid Mr. Mackenzie will make me feel like poor Gunga Din? On the contrary, your friend has made me feel equal to the superior white race. . . . Ilbrahim?"

"Sir?"

"Did you hear what has passed between Dr. Appleby, Mr. Mackenzie, and myself?"

"No, sir."

"I must get you a hearing aid, Ilbrahim." Sotho smiled at Mackenzie. "Now—that is diplomatic, Mr. Mackenzie. . . . Ilbrahim, please to take notes. You will record that following discussion with Mr. Mackenzie, it is agreed that he will visit the Appleby Mine and assess its value and whether it is desirable to invest every possible cent of our currency into its development. As from this moment, treasury funds will be frozen pending Mr. Mackenzie's report, which will be on my desk in—when, Mr. Mackenzie?"

"Give me three weeks."

"In three weeks, Ilbrahim. Copies to my cabinet—and include Colonel Magasi." Sotho turned to Mackenzie: "Will you be able to determine the productivity of the mine for the next ten years?"

"Until the pipe's reached, there's no way of telling, but I'll make a calculated guess. Just give me three weeks with Appleby and Blohm, and you'll have my opinion—for what it's worth."

Sotho dipped his head in acknowledgment. "Just prove that diamonds are Angwana's best friend, Mr. Mackenzie. That is all I ask."

"No man could ask for more," Mackenzie replied.

It seemed that the meeting had come to an end, and Appleby began to rise from his chair. Mackenzie remained seated, and Sotho asked, "You have a question, Mr. Mackenzie?"

"There're political corns I might tread on." Mackenzie's brows lowered. "Back in Freetown Colonel Magasi's name isn't unknown. I'll tell you now, I've a low opinion of him. If he gets in my way, I'll tread on his corn."

"Then please wear soft shoes, Mr. Mackenzie. In your bluff Scottish way Colonel Magasi could be called a necessary evil. His ability to keep law and order is essential to a government emerging from conflict. I would ask you to bear in mind that the colonel desires a rich Angwana every bit as much as I, and he will go along with any plan that will speed my country's rise from rags to riches."

"And when that time comes—what then?"

Sotho hunched his shoulders. "We shall see. Colonel Joseph Magasi is not the only ambitious Angwanan. Try not to be too outspoken in your dealings with him. With me, you can say anything you wish. Magasi is quick to anger, and that is a sight I do not recommend."

"So I've heard," Mackenzie said. "All right, Mr. President. I'll speak honeyed words and wear velvet gloves."

"It's the best way. Flattery goes a long distance—even with presidents of emergent countries."

"I'll remember that, too," Mackenzie said.

The Piper Aztec was flying at two thousand feet, and Mackenzie, looking down at the barren landscape, said, "Godforsaken place. Wasted land that could be made productive. A bit of Israeli know-how would help."

"It's mainly lack of water, Mac, despite that rain," Appleby said. "Angwana has only one river worth mentioning."

"There's plenty upcountry. Sotho could siphon some off or get Magasi's guns to go off on a spree."

"It just isn't on, Mac. When we—I mean, when the British were here, they tried groundnuts and mining for bauxite and copper. It all ended in failure. Things have got worse since independence. Sotho's predecessor soaked up foreign aid like the Sahara in a shower of rain.

He left virtually nothing in the treasury, an unflyable air force, and thirty new Mercedes with neither petrol nor oil to run them. An appalling waste of money."

"The price of corruption," Mackenzie said. "Your little man, Sotho —he's different?"

"I know so. He doesn't like filling his pockets with easy money from foreign governments. Sotho has a dream."

"And what's that?"

"A United States of Africa."

Mackenzie burst into laughter. "That's rich! That's the biggest bloody joke of the century! A united Africa? Man, in Europe they've only just started after centuries emerging from the Dark Ages, and they're still bickering and buggering up every damn scheme that might unite them. A United States of Africa? That's not a dream—that's a sick joke."

"It has to happen, therefore it will." Appleby pointed ahead as the Aztec began to lose height. "We're nearly there. Welcome to the Appleby Mine, Mac."

CHAPTER **18.**

T W O weeks had passed since Mackenzie's arrival at the mine, and he was impressed. The Appleby Mine was the smallest area find he had come across in his experience, but its diamond yield per surface acre was the richest he had ever seen. And Appleby's decision to bore through the terraced cliff to the blue ground was unexpectedly wise; the composition of the strata through which the tunnel ran was solid enough not to warrant pit-propping.

But while Mackenzie was impressed, he was also appalled by the shambles representing security. The site was a sitting duck for the guns of Magasi and his corrupt guards. It was damned amateur and naive. If the find had been in Sierra Leone or South Africa, the place would have been ringed by double security fences, and plant and mine workers brought up in a matter of days. Appleby had stumbled on the site months ago, and they were still scratching like hens on the surface.

In the weeks Mackenzie had spent with Appleby and Blohm visions of an early return to Europe and Scotland had faded, become less urgent, now that Jamie Turner was safe and sound in Geneva. There was a further oddity, he reflected; he had no wish to keep the diamonds he had picked up during his inspection of the site. Even the largest he had found, a 1.2-carat irregular, he had handed over to Appleby and Blohm.

Standing at the entrance to Appleby's tunnel, he listened to the sound of a pneumatic drill boring through the rock seventy-five feet away. A six feet high and wide chamber was too small; it should be widened, made higher, then two drills could work and make faster progress.

Mackenzie looked at the mounds of rubble heaped along the bottom terrace. Not to have plant capable of sifting through the mounds was criminal. They were probably rich in diamonds, spotted like currants in a plum duff.

He turned away from the tunnel and mounted the rungs of the steel ladder, up the terraced cliff. He had seen all he wanted to see, and could confirm Appleby's enthusiastic expectations. A trip to the capital and a talk with the little president was in order, a call to Jamie in Geneva to tell him that he'd be delayed in Angwana for a few weeks —but first, a talk with Magasi and a none too gentle persuasion regarding the colonel's future.

"Come now, Magasi," Mackenzie said. "We're alike in many respects. You've profited in much the same way as I have, but you did it with my help. Why spend years getting what you want when you can get it in less?"

Magasi sipped at the forbidden whisky. "I am not sure what you mean, Mackenzie."

"I'm not concerned with your political ambitions—I don't give a damn for them. How much have you salted away in Freetown and Monrovia?"

"A useful amount."

"Peanuts. I want to talk real money. The sort of money Jacob Zuncasi can't handle. He was fine for the stones you've filched from the Kundi, but something a thousand times bigger is about to happen."

"I cannot understand you."

"Suppose I tell the president there's no alternative but to bring in De Beers and the CDM, do you know what that would mean?"

"No."

"You could say goodbye to rich pickings. No more trips to Freetown and a ten-percent filch from the Kundi packets you're supposed to sell to the government trading office. You'll never be honest, Magasi, but you'd lose your thieving hands."

Magasi frowned. "You do not chop words, Mackenzie."

"You mean 'mince.' Why the hell should I? This is a very rich mine, Magasi. If I advise Angwana going it alone, you'll have a free hand and you'll need an outlet. Zuncasi's no good. The stones you'll steal will be too good and too many for friend Jacob."

"You would be the outlet?"

Mackenzie nodded. "A European outlet. You've diplomatic privilege, though, God knows, you've never earned it. It's foolproof, Magasi, so you're capable of seeing it through."

"So what is your proposition, Mackenzie?"

"Back my advice not to bring in outside help except mine. If Sotho can't or won't raise the wind, I can."

"Are you so rich?" Magasi asked. He drank the last of the whisky in his glass and watched Mackenzie refill it.

"Rich enough," Mackenzie said. "You've a strong Magasi faction in Angwana, I gather."

"I have my supporters."

"And they'll back you on Angwana going it alone?"

"If I tell them."

"Then tell them, Magasi. Tell them good and strong." Mackenzie got to his feet. "One other thing, I come and go when and where I please. I also want transport, by land or air, when I please and to go where I please."

The whisky had gone to Magasi's head. Mackenzie's figure had a second outline, and Magasi shook his head to clear his vision. When it had cleared, he said, "Treat me with respect, Mackenzie."

"Earn it and I will."

Mackenzie left Magasi's control hut and walked to Appleby's section. It would be easy to persuade Appleby that with or without his help, Angwana should go it alone; Blohm might prove difficult. It was hard to put a finger on Blohm's attitude; a reserve, mistrust, perhaps a combination of both. He had a habit of asking silent questions and expressing doubt by a look, and it disturbed Mackenzie. Where Appleby was naive and trusting, Blohm was singularly unimpressionable and skeptical.

Ernst Blohm was bent over his binocular microscope when Mackenzie entered the hut, and Appleby was at the drawing desk working on yet another sectional plan of the site.

Mackenzie said, "I'd like a word with you both."

Appleby came away from the drawing desk. "Of course, Mac."

"Blohm, too."

Without raising his head, Blohm said, "I am listening, Mr. Mackenzie."

"It's time we reported to Sotho," Mackenzie said. "I agree with your estimation of the site's potential, and your basic plan, Arthur, is the right one. You've both been damned brilliant or lucky—both, I expect. It's the next move that's important—its development."

"That was never in doubt," Blohm said quietly.

"You'll need plant and masses of it," said Mackenzie. "Experienced miners, and all that goes with them. You're scratching the surface at the moment and piling up stuff from the tunnel that's too precious to be left standing like rubbish dumps. An immediate investment plus a long-term diet of money. Put in a few million pounds sterling, you'll get back thousands of millions."

"How can Sotho get the millions, Mac?" Appleby asked. "He wouldn't let De Beers near the Kundi."

"There's three alternatives and you've anticipated the first. Bring in De Beers and the CDM, call in private investors, or get Angwana's treasury to pour into the mine every cent it earns, begs, borrows, or steals."

"You've talked to Magasi, of course," Blohm said.

"I have—he's too important to be the last to be consulted."

"And you have told him your views?"

"Yes. Whichever alternative is used, you'll need the support of the Magasi gang—and don't remind me that he'll have to be paid by the turning of blind eyes, Blohm. I know Magasi."

"I'm sure you do." Blohm took his eyes away from the microscope. "The president will not allow De Beers to run the mine—of that I am sure. And money from the treasury? Doubtful, because he is concentrating all the money he can spare on the hospital and housing development. This private investor, Mr. Mackenzie, does he have a name?"

"A small syndicate—two men."

"Of whom you are one?"

"As it happens, yes, Dr. Blohm."

Appleby said, "Can you really raise such money, Mac?"

"More, if necessary. I can arrange it overnight. Point is, if that's the answer, I'll not go ahead without full acceptance by both you and Blohm."

"Full acceptance can only come when we have full details, Mr. Mackenzie," Blohm said. "For example, what return would you expect from such an investment?"

"A reasonable return. That can be discussed with Sotho and whoever runs Angwana's economy. I'm asking you to agree with the principle. Argument can come later."

Blohm shrugged. "If Arthur agrees with the principle, then I am with him."

"Don't be *too* reluctant," Mackenzie said. "What do you say, Arthur?"

"I think you've guessed my reaction, Mac. It's a good plan, and it solves many problems."

"So how soon do we get to see Sotho?"

"I'll radio in and request an appointment."

Mackenzie chuckled. "You treat the wee man like a king."

It took three days of discussion before Sotho arrived at a decision. Mackenzie had presented his three alternatives and had refrained from stating his preference. The first, as Blohm had predicted, did not appeal to Sotho; he made it clear that he rejected it entirely on political grounds, although he could see the immediate advantages in purely financial terms.

"I would like to talk about your second alternative, Mr. Mackenzie," the president said. "Private investment. This is possible?"

"There are individuals far-seeing, perceptive, and rich enough to invest in the Appleby. It's difficult to predict its long-term yield, but on a short-term basis it's a gilt-edged investment."

"You are a financier as well as a mining engineer, Mr. Mackenzie. These individuals—are they black or white?"

"White."

"A pity," said Sotho. "Why are there no black multimillionaires?" Mackenzie grinned. "There's Muhammad Ali."

"These white investors," Sotho asked, "what kind of return would they expect on their investment?"

"At a rough guess, twenty percent of the mine's production."

"As high as that?"

Mackenzie stretched his legs and folded his arms. "Negotiation goes a long way," he said. "I don't want to offend you, Mr. President, but the African states aren't exactly stable countries. Too many damn coups to warrant an investor risking good money without ensuring a quick and profitable return. Think of Ghana. Hell, think of Uganda."

Sotho made a mental calculation. "If the Appleby when it is in full production yields twenty thousand carats per year—"

"It's unwise to deal in exact figures at this stage."

"A hypothetical figure, Mr. Mackenzie—it helps me understand the economics. At eight thousand dollars per carat—that is the going price for rough gem-quality diamond?"

"Round about."

"Then twenty thousand carats would be valued at one hundred and sixty million dollars. At twenty percent, the investor would take thirty-two million. Shylock rates, Mr. Mackenzie."

"You're assuming the twenty thousand carats are of the highest quality."

"Also, the investor would, no doubt, insist on a hard-and-fast withdrawal clause. The thought of thirty-two million dollars leaving Angwana in the pocket of a white investor pains me, Mr. Mackenzie." Sotho shook his head. "Much too much."

"It's reasonable in my view. De Beers might ask for more," Mackenzie said. "You've heard about the Jwaneng Mine in Botswana? De Beers Consolidated are backing it to the tune of a hundred and twenty million pounds. Pounds—not U.S. dollars. In a few years—four, maybe —annual production's likely to be in the neighborhood of four million carats. De Beers Consolidated aren't pouring in that cash without a high return. I'm not saying the Appleby is as rich as the Jwaneng, but you never know."

"We developed the Kundi without De Beers and foreign investors."

"The Kundi's a scrap heap," Mackenzie said contemptuously. "Compared with the Appleby, it's a rubbish dump. What's its yield—five percent gem and ninety-five industrial?"

"It has brought a steady but useful income to Angwana, Mr. Mackenzie."

"The Appleby will make the country rich."

"Richer if I do not bring in investors."

Mackenzie's temper was rising. "Then guarantee your people subsistence level and a halt to all public spending. God Almighty, most Angwanans are on the poverty line; filling their bellies won't cost much. Your army's as dim as a candle, and any one of your air force planes would find it hard to get off the ground, let alone fight. Put the whole damn lot on emergency rations and pour every penny you've got in the treasury into the Appleby. In a year's time you'll be rich enough to build hospitals and housing estates, and send your soldiers to Sandhurst."

"Stop it, Mac!" Appleby said.

Mackenzie was angry. "I'm damned if I will! I'll talk to President Sotho as man to man. If he doesn't like it, he can kick me out of the country."

"I want Mr. Mackenzie to continue, Doctor," Sotho said.

"And I'll do it. This housing and hospital development—what's it worth? Your people will starve in their brand-new houses, then get carted off to the new hospital to be treated for pellagra, beriberi, or any other illness caused by starvation. As soon as they're fed and brought back to health, they can go back to their new houses and starve once again!"

"I apologize for my friend," Appleby said. "He does not have to use such words."

Sotho held up a restraining hand. "Peace, Doctor. Mr. Mackenzie is speaking plain, unvarnished truth. It is unpalatable and I vaguely resent what he has said, but it is too near the truth to be ignored." Sotho folded his hands and rested them on the desk. "I will have to talk to my cabinet, gentlemen. I will test their reactions on two alternatives: private investment as you, Mr. Mackenzie, suggest, or drain the treasury."

"Men get less angry when their stomachs are full," Mackenzie said. "Even the Magasis of this world tread softly when profits speak loud."

"How well you know the colonel, Mr. Mackenzie." Sotho got to his feet and held out his hand. "I must ask you to stay in the capital until a decision is reached. Another day, perhaps two."

It was the first of many discussions. On the third day Appleby and Mackenzie were called to the palace.

"First of all," Sotho said, "I wish to thank you, Mr. Mackenzie, for your offer of financial aid on the terms we finally agreed upon. Seven and a half percent was very reasonable indeed."

"I told you it was negotiable, Mr. President."

"I understood that, of course. Let me tell you how I arrived at a decision. Angwana is surrounded by unrest. Soviet and Cuban infiltration, guerilla fighters and terrorists, and the CIA moving in mysterious ways. So much of the trouble is senseless and based on the magical properties of communism, anarchy, and the dream of Western capitalist standards of living. I thank God that Angwana is strategically unimportant. Troubles, real troubles, will start when and if it becomes a rich state. But I cannot wish Angwana to remain poor." Sotho picked up his coffee cup and drank; Mackenzie and Appleby followed his action as if to fill a gap.

"You are basically correct, Mr. Mackenzie," Sotho continued, "in your theory that full stomachs dull anger, and when we last talked, you made a thinly disguised reference to the fact that opposition can be lessened with the use of bribes. I knew precisely whom you meant by— and I quote your exact words—'Looking the other way will guarantee first-class security and cooperation.' Full stomachs and a quiet opposition. These factors were very much in my mind in reaching a decision." Sotho accepted another cup of coffee from Otanga. "Mr. Mackenzie, you suggested that the Central Selling Organization should set up a trading office here in Angwana."

"It would be sensible. There's no point in going through their Sierra Leone office as you have done with the Kundi production." Mackenzie smiled. "You could always mail 'em direct to South Africa, but I don't think you would."

"You know I would not."

"That's a damn silly attitude, if you'll pardon me. South Africa's a stabilizing influence in this continent. Take it away and Africa will degenerate into the Dark Ages. I'd rather see a thousand Vorsters than one Amin." Mackenzie's face had darkened, and Appleby looked away, embarrassed.

"Many would take your criticisms as racist, Mr. Mackenzie," Sotho said.

"I'm not. White or black, Irish or French, Cuban, Russian, or American—each is as good or as bad as the other."

" 'A man's a man for all that,' to quote your national bard, Mr. Mackenzie."

"Or a louse."

Tentatively Appleby said, "Haven't we strayed away a little? I mean from the object of this meeting?"

"An interesting side issue, Doctor." Sotho leaned back in his chair. "Yesterday I spoke to a CSO representative in London. Naturally, I was guarded in what I said."

"Who was it?" Mackenzie asked.

"One of the board directors. Speaking to him confirmed what I had in mind. You'll approve, I think, Mr. Mackenzie. You called the Kundi a scrap heap when compared with the potential of the Appleby. I agree with you. This is my decision, and I have full cabinet backing. Plant and men will be removed from the Kundi and transferred to the Appleby. A skeleton production team will remain at the Kundi. For six months all funds will be channelled into the Appleby Mine, and work on hospitals and housing will stop—for six months. And, Mr. Mackenzie, bellies will be filled. One other thing, Colonel Magasi enthusiastically backed the idea of Angwana staying independent of outside help. At some future date I will invite the CSO to set up office in Angwana. Meanwhile we will continue to sell through Sierra Leone." Sotho smiled. "Colonel Magasi was *very* pleased."

You cunning black bastard, Mackenzie thought. You've taken the best of my thinking and turned it to your own advantage. Aloud he said, "I congratulate you, Mr. President. I hope it's a wise decision."

Sotho turned to Appleby: "Doctor?"

"I'm very glad—very glad, indeed."

Sotho spread his hands wide in an expansive gesture. "So no outside help whatsoever. Your kind proposition, Mr. Mackenzie, I turn down with my grateful thanks, and I insist on calling you a friend of Angwana."

"Thank you," said Mackenzie.

They had two hours to kill before flying back to the mine, and Appleby steered a silent Mackenzie into the bar of the Palace Hotel. He ordered two large whiskies, specifying Bell's, and waited until Mackenzie had drunk half of his before saying, "Well, Mac?"

"The cunning little black bastard!"

"I don't understand. You were in favor of Angwana going it alone. Sotho's been wise, not cunning."

"I've been outsmarted, Arthur. I wanted that holding in the mine.

I saw a good return for the money I was ready to put into it—and that's honest. I've not an ounce of altruism in me, so don't cast me in the role of a man who does things out of pure Christian charity. The idea of raping your mine and stealing its virginity appealed to me." He drained his glass. "Get me another, Arthur."

His glass refilled, Mackenzie cradled it in his hands and stared into it. "I suppose I've got to take my hat off to Sotho—he's small in stature but bloody big in brain. Jamie would laugh his teeth out."

"Jamie?"

"He'd have been my coinvestor. American. We're two of a kind, Arthur. We like money. It's damned useful stuff to have. I'm rich, Arthur, bloody rich, but I couldn't resist the chance of getting richer. Cunning little bastard!" Good humor was returning to Mackenzie, and he chuckled. "What the hell! I've made my pile, and I can buy what I want. Tell you one thing, when Blohm hears about it, he'll dance with joy. Mackenzie outsmarted. *Hoch—hoch—hoch und heil!*"

Appleby's first whisky was still half full. He said, "What Ernst doesn't care for about you is your worldly cynicism, Mac. I'm not particularly fond of it, either."

"Dreamers all," Mackenzie said. "Blohm, you, Sotho up to a point —where would you be without men like me to keep your feet on the ground and your heads out of the clouds? Even Sotho admits the necessity of animals like Magasi."

"And I do not. Police, yes. Sadistic brutes, no!"

"In the context of this troubled continent, Magasi's far from being unique. Think of my ancestors if you want a comparison. Cruel, kilted savages with red hair, massive bollocks, and no brains. And that goes for Angwanan natives at their present stage. Magasi's typical."

"I'm an Angwanan," Appleby said. "I'm of this world."

Mackenzie uttered a sound of disgust. "You're damn well not! You're white and you're English. You've no real place in Africa. Face up to it, Arthur. Africa's getting blacker every day. You're only welcome because you're needed. If you live long enough in this country, you'll be Angwana's Uncle Tom. Be like me, get out what you can, then scarper back to civilization and your own kind."

"I've always considered you an optimist," Appleby said.

"Just the opinion of a man full of hope for his own future." Mackenzie looked beyond Appleby, beyond Angwana. "In Sierra, at the Komalu, I'd watch the vultures perching. They were waiting for death, Arthur. I used to take potshots at them. Real sitting ducks, but no matter how many I shot, they'd be replaced in no time at all. Point is, I was one of the carcasses they were waiting for. I got this mad feeling that since white meat was getting scarce, I was marked down as the chef's special dish. Soon there'll be no white meat, only black."

"You're corroding my hope for the future," Appleby said.

"Live for another hundred years and you *might* see Sotho's dream of a United States of Africa come true." Mackenzie finished his whisky. "I'll be away soon. I'll see you under way, then it's Scotland and the memory of vultures replaced by golden eagles in the Highlands." He got to his feet. "Come on. Let's get out of this tarnished memory of the British Empire and back to the famous Appleby discovery."

Mackenzie looked out the Aztec's cabin window; Angwana's green-belt, fed only by one river and an immature delta, was thinning out to the arid, scrub-covered flatland extending to the mine. "How many miles from the river to the mine?" he asked the pilot.

"About ninety miles, sir."

"You'll need to tap that water," Mackenzie said to Appleby. "Ninety miles of pipeline plus a pumping station. Will the river stand it?"

"It's more or less constant throughout the year. Rains upcountry feed it during the rainy season. After that, it straggles. This is dry country, Mac. It catches the fringe of the wet season most years. In a good year—the last was three years ago—we enjoyed as much rain as Sierra Leone, and Angwana rejoiced."

"Sometime you might try drilling. Could be there's an underground supply, but get that pipeline started right away. It'll cost old Sotho a packet—that's his and your problem now."

"We still need your advice."

"A few weeks, maybe. I'll draw up a few specifications, make recommendations, and list equipment you'll need, then it's farewell, Africa. Tell Blohm exactly what happened. Knowing my moneymaking plan failed might make him dislike me less. Another thing—when the CSO sets up office in Angwana, make sure Magasi still gets his pickings. He'll have no more trips to Freetown with the Appleby or Kundi packets."

The Aztec began its descent to the landing strip. As the wheels touched down, Mackenzie said, "I'll tell Magasi that his criminal future is assured, if you've no objection—he can take it from me. I've dealt with his kind for the last twenty years or so."

CHAPTER **19.**

SOL GRUNWALD'S one comfort during the weeks of wait-
ing had been contemplation of the diamond's price escalation from the
rough octahedron—itself a thing of beauty—to cut and polished stones,
the Brilliant and the Antwerp Rose. The beginning and the end, such a
beautiful curtain raiser, such a beautiful last-act curtain! Seven hundred
and fifty thousand dollars for the rough; $1,500,000 for the two polished
stones. In between those two sums came deductions for expenses:
$7,000 to Heinert ($1,000 more than his normal charge, but for such a
stone you pay a premium). Travel and subsistence: $6,000, or there-
abouts. Interest on borrowed money: ten percent on $300,000 for a six-
month loan, $30,000. Apart from the incalculable cost of nervous wear
and tear, Sol had to set $43,000 against the $1,500,000 he would receive
from Randall—a profit of $707,000! It was a great comfort to set it
against the paucity of the balance figure he saw on his bank state-
ments, and against his missing two sights at the Central Selling Organization, although he called in on Mr. Dalmon to give him a *shalom*
during his shuttle trips between New York and Antwerp.

The weeks of waiting were more bearable for Klein and Petersen,
for the profit/loss ratio indicated high potential gain with a ridiculously
low loss. Klein reckoned that Swede's expenses would touch the $8,000
mark, and that was peanuts compared with $1,000,000 even after
Canzetti had taken his percentage, so what an investment! For an ex-
penditure of $8,000, a profit of $600,000, give or take a few dollars,
assuming he could get Canzetti to agree to a sixty-forty deal in Klein Enterprises' favor.

Profit for Grunwald and Klein was a great comforter, yet over both
men hung uncertainties. For Grunwald, an increase in blood pressure
gave him thoughts of mortality. For Klein, it was the fear that desire

for the immense profit might force him outside his rule of nonviolence in a lethal sense. While he personally could never kill for gain, there was a hidden violence in Swede, violence held in check so far by the reasonable profits they had enjoyed. But the Randall diamond killing was big, and Klein knew that Swede had to play it as it came, come what may.

Few more days, that's all, Klein thought; Swede had it all figured out. A right-hand man like that deserved a full partnership.

Swede Petersen's departure from New York en route to Antwerp preceded Grunwald's by four hours. Now that he was known to Grunwald, Swede had to resemble the invisible man. From now on he had to tread carefully, as he neared the high point of the operation, and danger was escalating; it wasn't easy to keep to the rule of gentle persuasion when you could almost feel the prize in your hands. "You may *have* to get a little tough," Klein had said, but had not specified how tough. "Play it as it comes," Tony had also said, and that was the way of it. Buy one or two insurance policies in Antwerp; figure out contingencies, should difficult circumstances arise. A million bucks had a strange effect on a guy's morality.

Sol Grunwald took his seat on Sabena Flight 209 out of Antwerp to Freetown, the two cut diamonds he had collected from Heinert the previous day nestling in his buyer's waistcoat.

It had been murder watching the cast-iron scaife, impregnated with oil and diamond dust, grinding away at the last facets on the Brilliant and the Antwerp Rose, with Heinert's eye the only gauge measuring depth and angle of cut. Like an expectant father, Grunwald had fretted and worried Heinert during the last few hours, and as if Grunwald were an expectant father, Heinert had suggested lunch, leaving the final polishing to his number-one craftsman. It had been a prolonged lunch, and Grunwald was slightly drunk when Heinert brought him back to the workshop and showed him the two completed diamonds resting brilliantly on a black-velvet square.

Grunwald had reacted with all the wonder of a father who had expected a malformed child but had, in fact, sired a genius of a baby, *two* beautiful babies!

Heinert had left him gazing at the stones. An hour later he returned and told Grunwald to go—after writing out a check for seven thousand dollars.

Grunwald, eyes still fixed on the diamonds, silently handed Heinert his checkbook. "Just write the words," he said. "I'll sign it."

Heinert had done a first-class job, and in record time the stones had been graded and certificated, identiprinted, measured, spectrometered, and weighed, their characteristics described in greater detail than those of a master criminal, but it was hell having to trip down to Africa on the whim of a movie star. Sol wanted back home with Sadie and Sadie's cooking and Randall's check cleared. The setting of the stones wasn't his concern; he'd hand them over to Randall's lawyer who'd give them to the designer, and that would be that.

At the back of the plane Swede Petersen hid behind sunglasses and the previous edition of the *New York Times*. As the Sabena Boeing began its takeoff run Petersen felt closer to the diamonds he knew were tucked away somewhere on the body of the fat New Yorker strapped in his seat way up the aisle. Freetown, Petersen thought; you couldn't wish for a better place for a gentle heist; there was more graft in that city than in any other he could name, and graft meant ease of operation. Who needed guns and blackjacks, kidnaps and knives? He and Tony Klein had done well by *gentle* persuasion.

The panel above Petersen's head announced that he could smoke if he wished and that he could now unfasten his seat belt. Grunwald also saw the announcement and stuck a cigar in his mouth, at the same time reaching for a matchbook, one of six he'd got at the airport. He'd lost the lighter Dalmon had given him.

The air-conditioning system in the hotel was faulty. From time to time the cool in Randall's bedroom would give way to a humid stillness that made him sweat, and then, as the system pulled itself together and pumped cold air into the room, the sweat cooled on Randall's body, so that he shivered and pulled the sheet and blankets over his head.

He slept off and on for five hours and felt that he had not slept at all. He got out of bed and showered, then, clad only in a short terry-cloth robe, sat on the balcony of his bedroom looking out across Freetown. Strauss had promised him protection and solitude until tomorrow morning and had kept his promise, but its value lay only in the abstract. Randall wanted company, but company of his own choosing, and Kay was that choice, and Kay was seven or eight thousand miles away in Los Angeles.

He rang room service and ordered ice-cold orange juice; it was too early for liquor; at that time of day you felt lousy after the effects had worn off, and your acting showed it.

Freetown. The place shimmered in heat, the haze coming in from the Atlantic cotton-wooling that heat and settling down over the sprawl of the city like the mist that periodically settled over San Francisco and sweated the life out of its residents.

Johnny Downs, stationed outside his door, entered with the orange juice. He put the tray down on the balcony table and said, "There's a fat, impatient guy sitting in the lobby. Says he wants to see you."

"Did he give a name?"

"Grunwald—Sol Grunwald. Says he has stones that stick in his gall bladder. I tell him go see a doctor, but he says, 'Tell Mr. Randall, the stones hurt.' That make sense?"

"It makes sense, Johnny. Tell him to come up."

"Strauss said you're not to be disturbed."

"I am disturbed, so send Grunwald up."

"Okay—if you say so."

When Sol Grunwald came out on the balcony, he was perspiring. Randall indicated a chair. "Take a seat, Mr. Grunwald—you're hot."

Grunwald collapsed into the chair. "I've been hot since I left London with your diamond two months ago—or maybe it was two years. I sweated in Antwerp, and the weight Sadie said I should lose, I've lost sitting downstairs in that lousy lobby."

"What about my stones?"

"I've got 'em."

Randall looked at Sol's dark suit and the waistcoat. "Why don't you get out of that gear, Grunwald? You're in the tropics. Take a shower. Have orange juice."

"Diamonds first. All my life, diamonds come first." Grunwald peeled off his jacket and then his waistcoat, which he turned inside out. "I got 'em here." He unbuttoned the flap covering a small pocket and withdrew a wad of cotton wool held together by two thin rubber bands. Keeping the wad in his left hand, he reached his right hand into the inside pocket of his jacket and took out a square of black velvet. "You gotta see them on black velvet."

Sol smoothed out the velvet square on the tabletop, then carefully removed the rubber bands from the cotton wool. From where Randall sat, the operation seemed trivial; even when Grunwald placed the diamonds on the velvet, there seemed to be no significance in the performance.

Sol now reached into a waistcoat pocket and took out a loupe, which he held out to Randall. "The best stones money can buy, Mr. Randall. Heinert is a genius, you know that? You got the best Brilliant and the best Antwerp Rose. Look into 'em—live in 'em, Mr. Randall!"

Randall pulled the velvet square toward him and focused the loupe on the Brilliant.

"What d'you see?" asked Grunwald.

The sun, now overhead and filtering through the haze, lanced back from the diamond, the fifty-eight facets glittering in tiny planes of prismatic color, from red to orange, to yellow, green and blue and a vibrant, intense violet; and interspersed with the colors were dazzling spots of pure white light.

Lethargy and disenchantment left Randall. Ten times larger than life under the power of the loupe, an incredible world of celestial light existed.

"So what d'you say?" asked Grunwald.

Still gazing at the Brilliant, Randall said, "I didn't think it was possible. You hear talk about diamonds. You read ads, and you don't believe either the stories you hear or the ads you read, but this—"

"Where diamond is concerned, believe everything you read," Grunwald said. "Can I tell a lie about diamonds? No, sir. So I can lie about price—who doesn't. But when Grunwald says diamonds are beautiful, Grunwald tells the truth."

The smaller stone, the Antwerp Rose, was equally beautiful in its different way. As it rested on its flat base the twelve facets seemed to throw out the diamond's fire in a gentler manner, almost soothing in its quiet reception and refraction of light.

And Randall thought of them worn by Kay who equalled the diamonds' capacity to excite and then to soothe.

"They're fine, Grunwald," he said. "Just fine. If you want bigger words, you know them better than me. If I had a script, maybe I could rhapsodize over them. Take it that I think they're beautiful."

"What I want is for you to take 'em," Grunwald said. "I get the feeling there's a dog at my heels and I don't like it. So you take the diamonds, okay? Me—I don't want the responsibility."

Randall shook his head. "I'm back in America three weeks from now. I want these set and ready when I land in New York." Looking at Grunwald's gray, tired face, he added, "Why not rest up for a couple of days, Grunwald?"

"Rest, I need."

"Leave the diamonds with me. Eat well and sleep well, then hop a flight and get the stones to New York."

"You got to put them somewhere safe." Grunwald took a cigar from his jacket pocket, fumbled for a matchbook, and lit the cigar with a hand that trembled. "My goddamned nerves!" he said.

Randall smiled. "You'll feel better when you get my check, Mr. Grunwald. See my lawyer after you've delivered the diamonds. I'm not going to question your price. Tell him the figure and you can rest easy with—Sadie, isn't it?"

"Sadie." Grunwald sighed. "When I left Kennedy, I thought she was fat and maybe we'd known each other too long. Now, all I want is Sadie and all my married kids and the bar mitzvahs and sabbaths in Queens. I'll take the two days, Mr. Randall."

"Be my guest, Grunwald."

Grunwald looked at the diamonds glittering on the black velvet. "Keep 'em someplace safe," he said again. "Lose 'em and Grunwald's lost more than weight."

"They'll be safe," Randall said.

Joan Turner looked at the small, but beautiful collection of diamonds she had taken from the wall safe. Jamie had called them his "security against a dull old age," and now they were hers, to sell or keep. He had been too generous, too concerned. To sell his stock back to Gem International, and give her the whole of the amount, was madness. And he did not intend using their joint account; she knew his private account stood somewhere in the neighborhood of forty thousand dollars—nowhere near enough to start up alone in the diamond buying and selling world. Jamie was either naive or covering up, and she rejected the former. So she was left with one reason for Jamie's generosity, and that wasn't simply another woman. Why had he returned from South America looking as if he'd seen a ghost when he could have gone straight to Geneva as he had planned?

A telephone call eased her problem. In the past few years she had met Richard Walker many times and liked him, but less than he liked her, which meant that her liking did not include sex, and when his voice came over the line after she had accepted a person-to-person call from London, she felt a wave of relief.

"Joan?"

"I'm here, Richard." It was good to hear him say her proper name; no one else called her "Joan"; it was always the diminutive, which she had come to hate. "Well—" she said.

"I thought I'd ring you and declare my undying love."

"That's a very nice thought, Richard."

"Any chance of you telling me the same sort of thing?"

"Will undying liking do?"

"It's all I have to live for . . . Joan? You suddenly dropped into my mind—well, suddenly's not true—you're always there coming and going. Now tell me how you are and how Jamie is."

"Things aren't too good, Richard. I'm left high and dry. No"—she corrected herself—"not high and dry. That sounds safe and happy and I'm neither."

"Do you want a shoulder to cry on?"

"I could do with one."

"Right away?"

She laughed. "It's good to hear you say that, Richard. You probably mean it."

"With all my heart, Joan. What's the trouble?"

"Jamie's left me."

"I see. . . ."

He was silent for a space, and she said, "Richard?"

"I'm still here. Look, Joan, I had an ulterior motive in phoning you. One of the advantages of my job is that I can take off for exotic places at the drop of a hat. I'm about due for a trip to Freetown. I could travel via New York even though it's the long way round. Will tomorrow do?"

"What for?"

"A walk through the zoo, a tear-soaked shoulder now and then, a good dinner at La Grenouille—that's still my favorite restaurant—and after, you might invite me up for coffee."

"No coffee, Richard. But I do want to see you. Need to, actually. I won't tell you why just now."

"Right. Expect me at Riverside Drive round about two-thirty your time."

"Do you really mean that?"

"Of course. I haven't clocked up my yearly mileage half enough yet, and Joan—I do want to see you—very much. This thing about Jamie—is it really bad?"

"I don't know, but I want to know."

"Tell me what to do and I'll do it. I'd be a willing corespondent, of course—as long as it's on the level. The real thing, you know?"

"At this moment I'm so glad to hear your voice, I'd hop into bed with you."

"Then hold on to that moment like grim death, Joan. If only I could be radio-transmitted to you right now. . . . Two-thirty or so tomorrow, Joan?"

"Thank you, Richard. Thank you very, very much."

"You're welcome, as they say in your benighted country."

She replaced the phone, in a state of near happiness, illogically feeling relief and love for the man who would arrive tomorrow and on whose shoulder she would certainly lean and try not to weep.

". . . And I've realized just how much I cut myself off from Jamie's world. I was never interested—not really interested—in his trips abroad. Maybe it was jealousy on my part because the world of diamonds satisfied ninety percent of his life and I supplied the remaining ten. Not much for a wife, Richard."

"If that's how it was, it's not how I see marriage." Walker beckoned to the waiter. "We'll take coffee now."

They had dined at La Grenouille after walking through Central Park where Joan had talked about her parting from Jamie. Walker had listened with the pleasure, partly reluctant, of a man hoping to step into another man's shoes. On another level, the events leading up to the separation interested him professionally.

"Tell me about Jamie's association with Mackenzie and Sierra Leone," he said. "This afternoon Mackenzie's name kept coming up."

"About two years ago, perhaps a little longer, Jamie came back from Sierra Leone, and this man, Arnold Mackenzie, called the apartment. Jamie wasn't in so we talked. He sounded like a large, good-humored man."

"He is," Walker said. "Six feet four and big in every way. Did you speak with him again?"

"Now and then over the last two years—if Jamie wasn't immediately available when he called."

"How do you mean 'immediately available'?"

"He might have been in the bath—you know? Tell me about Sierra Leone, Richard."

Walker thought for a moment, then said, "Freetown's a strange place. It's hot and mostly humid and has a wet and dry season. But I know it and Monrovia, in Liberia, as escape routes for illicit diamond peddling. Freetown's only a hundred miles or so from Monrovia, and the border between the two countries is loosely guarded. If you're ready to pay dash, anything goes."

"Dash?"

"Bribes—graft. Liberia's one great flag of convenience. If you've the dash, there's nothing you can't buy—diamonds *and* police protection."

"Jamie's been to Freetown several times."

"All diamond men get there sooner or later," Walker said. "Sierra mines high-quality gems—the Komalu Mine especially, and that brings us back to Mackenzie. The Komalu was his baby. He developed it into top efficiency. He's left now, of course. He was offered the world to stay when his contract came to an end, but he refused. I don't know whether I feel sorry for him or not."

"Why?"

"He took responsibility for the accident—a mining engineer's worst dream."

"What accident?"

"Didn't Jamie tell you, Joan? It was headline news on diamond ticker tape, and Mackenzie figured large."

Joan cast her mind back. "Three or four weeks ago Mackenzie called Jamie," she said. "It was in the evening."

"Do you remember anything of their conversation."

"Not much. Jamie said something like 'If there's anything big coming out the mine, let me know'—something like that. Is it important, Richard? It's as if you're interrogating me."

"I've a sharp assistant based in Freetown," Walker said. "His name's Manston. He comes up with theories and puts them on my plate. I follow them up because Manston's damned good at his job. His latest theory is entitled 'Mackenzie.' Now Jamie's name is linked with his. I expect it's innocent. Can I be your potential lover and security man at the same time, Joan?"

"It's an odd mixture. Since it's good to be wanted by another man who also is a kind of cop, I think I can take it. What do you want to know?"

"Dates, et cetera. Today's the twenty-sixth, and the Komalu accident happened on the tenth. You say Mackenzie called three weeks ago?"

"It could have been a month, I can't remember exactly."

" 'If there's anything big coming out of the mine, let me know.' You heard Jamie say that?"

"That's right."

"What else did he say?"

"I don't know. He listened without saying much, then asked Mackenzie to hold the line while he went to the study to look at some notes. The rest of the call he took from there."

"What was Jamie's state of mind at the time—and after?"

"Tense, preoccupied—thousands of miles away from me. Then it all came to a head. I called for a showdown—I wish I hadn't in some ways. It was the night before he left for South America—Rio de Janeiro. He'd resigned from GI, and he told me he intended settling in Geneva. But he came back to New York. He called me at one o'clock in the morning— from the Waldorf. I didn't understand. We met the following day. No" —she corrected herself—"the same day. At the White Bear. He looked terrible, Richard—as though he'd seen a ghost or worse. He didn't tell me much. Something had happened in South America—it was all vague and cryptic. Jamie said he'd seen a man die—upcoast or somewhere. He'd a dream the night before—that's when he called me. He'd dreamt that *he* was the dead man dying again."

"Why did he want to see you?"

"He didn't. We'd both obeyed a morbid impulse to revisit the scene of our love-and-marriage crime. And that was that. Jamie was booked on an afternoon flight to Geneva. I went back to the apartment, then you called and rescued me from very unhappy introspection."

"Jamie's a bloody fool," Walker said angrily. "I don't know why the hell I still think of him as a friend when I should be saying 'Good riddance to bad rubbish.' "

"Jamie isn't bad rubbish, Richard. Is he in trouble?"

Walker shook his head. "As far as I'm concerned, he isn't, but Manston poses a question and I have to take it seriously. Joan, I'll keep my enquiries very private."

"I want more than that," she said very deliberately. "I want to know about Jamie. I want to know if there is another woman, Richard. I want to know why he was damned generous in handing over so much to me. I've got his diamond collection, every cent realized on the stock he held with GI—more, much more than a divorce lawyer would ask for. Our joint account is entirely mine—he told me so. Why so generous?"

"Obviously he has a private account."

"But I've seen a statement of his account with Chase. He'd left it lying around. It stood at forty thousand dollars, Richard. He can't operate as a buyer with so little."

Walker nodded slowly. "You want me to really dig into Jamie's past and future, Joan? I don't like snooping on friends."

"Even if it's to save them—or to save me?"

"I'll do it to save you, not Jamie." Walker gripped her hand. "I don't feel much loyalty for Jamie. He's also your husband, and I'm not. If I uncover anything shady and punishable by law, I'll act without fear or favor."

"Would you really do that?"

"If it enters my life professionally, yes."

"Then you'd have no choice," she said. "I understand that. But if you prevented him from—oh, I don't know what."

"Prevention's part of my job, Joan. Anyway, we've probably talked him into a situation that doesn't exist. It'll be difficult playing the man of honor when I'm in love with the suspect's wife."

"Why do you, Richard? Love me, I mean. I've given you nothing."

"Love is like that. You don't have a real choice." With his eyes he indicated a table across the aisle. "You see that bejewelled old trout over there with her gigolo? If I had a choice, I'd fall madly in love with her so that I wouldn't love you."

"You couldn't possibly want to make love to her."

"I would if I loved her. Let's leave it at that and I'll accept your invitation to come up to your apartment for coffee, and hope that the coffee is a euphemism."

"The coffee will be Blue Mountain and filtered, not percolated. And it won't interfere with your sleep when you return to your hotel."

They walked to Riverside Drive. Turning down West Ninety-first Street, he took her hand. The action seemed natural, and she returned his grip. At the entrance to the apartment building, she stopped and looked into his face. "Richard," she said. "I'd like to be in love with you. If I had the choice, I'd choose you now—this minute. The borderline between liking you and loving you is very thin."

"Just that little bit of the chemical formula is missing," he said. "I was always bad at chemistry, otherwise I'd rush to the nearest drugstore and get the missing chemical made up and slip it into the coffee you're about to make."

CHAPTER **20.**

THE peak of Mont Blanc glittered in the late afternoon sunlight, and the Trident banked and began the descent to Geneva Airport. Carol Grantham looked out the window of the Trident and saw the suburb of Chambésy and, beyond that, the airport complex with its runways and control tower. Jamie Turner would be waiting somewhere in the terminal building, and she wondered how she would react when she emerged from customs and saw him. Would her heart sink or rise, or simply beat on an even plane and register neither pleasure nor disappointment? Again she reassured herself that there was nothing to lose. It was not an assignation in the true dramatic and romantic sense of the word. She was taking a two-week holiday in Switzerland, and someone she knew quite well happened to be in the country at the same time—a friend with whom she could share the holiday.

The Trident touched down, its engines whining as the pilot reversed thrust. Reaching the end of its landing run, the plane turned slowly and began its run to the disembarkation point.

From the observation window in the terminal Turner watched the Trident come to a halt and the ramp move into position. The doors of the aircraft opened, and stewardesses appeared wearing Miss BA smiles, and Turner counted the passengers as they descended.

Even at two hundred meters he recognized her as she appeared at the top of the stairway, and it was not entirely visual recognition. The magnetism he had felt at their first meeting was still there. As if responding to the attraction, Carol halted at the foot of the ramp and looked up at the observation window.

They said little to each other as the taxi took them to the Hôtel des Bergues. They spoke small stuff. Was it a smooth flight? A half-clouded sky all the way from Heathrow. No holdups, thank God; no strikes at all—imagine that. Geneva is sunny, and how did the Alps look? Marvellous, fantastic—it is good to get away from London.

It was later, after she had gone to her room and changed, then joined Turner in the bar, that their talk became intimate.

He said, "I've burned my boats, Carol. My wife understands, although she doesn't know about you. I've quit Gem International, and it's not the seven-year itch. It's for real. I knew it when you stepped down from the plane."

"You want me to tell you the same thing, Jamie?"

"I'd like it—you know that."

"Let's wait a bit, shall we?"

"There's no hurry. We've places to visit—people to see over at Cologny. Some of them are okay, some are punk. Those, we don't visit. Carol? . . . I'm going to enjoy your company. If you can say the same about mine—well—you know what I mean."

"Take the two ingredients and blend slowly," Carol said, "and allow to mature in a temperate heat until they become one. That's a good recipe."

"You know what I want to say, Carol—the way I feel about you."

"That's not in the recipe, but I'll take it as read or spoken. If you want any subliminal message from me, I've come to Geneva at your invitation—for two weeks' holiday, Jamie." She took her drink and walked over to the window, and Turner followed her.

A breeze ruffled the lake, and the sun glinted on the ripples. "Golden oysters," Carol said. "There's no life in that lake, Jamie—did you know that?"

"We've got polluted lakes in America."

"Golden oysters," Carol repeated. "Like gold in a corrupt world."

Her words touched Turner's sense of guilt. "In the jungle people survive as best they can. They do things they don't particularly like—kill to live—kill to eat."

Carol smiled. "Have you killed anyone lately, Jamie?"

The dead face of Felix Partridge came into Turner's mind, and the price paid to further an ambition reckoned in millions of dollars. "Not recently," he said, and his voice was without humor.

"How serious we are," Carol said, and smiled at him. "Anyone would think the ace of diamonds is the ace of spades."

"The death card," Turner said. "Hell! We need another drink." He forced a smile to his face. "Anyway, who says I'm the ace of diamonds?"

Bernard Manston found Robert Randall sitting at a table on the balcony of the hotel.

"Mr. Randall? May I have a word with you?"

Randall indicated a chair. "Sure. Light an' set."

"I've heard you say that on the screen. *The Californios* and *Kiowa Trail*—adapted from novels by Louis L'Amour. Light an' set."

"It's a lousy habit but fans expect it." Randall smiled. "I'm no fast gun, and I don't like horses. If you're a fan, mister, be disillusioned."

"I'm not disillusioned, and I like your pictures. I'm Bernard Manston."

"Glad to know you, Mr. Manston. What's on your mind? You don't look like an autograph hunter."

"I'm concerned about the diamonds I gather Sol Grunwald brought to you."

Manston fished in his wallet and drew out his card of identity. "I'm an IDSO investigator, Mr. Randall. I see, or try to see, where diamonds are coming and going. The lines are buzzing. Have been for weeks. Grunwald got his stone from the CSO—since then, we've kept an eye on progress, making sure they're safe. Information's been passed along the line. It caught up with me in Freetown, so it's on my plate."

Randall handed the card back to Manston. "There's no trouble," he said. "Grunwald got what I asked for. When the poor guy's recovered from weeks of worry, he'll take them back to New York for setting."

"Who has them now?"

"Now that's asking for a lot, Mr. Manston."

"I want to help make sure Grunwald gets them to New York."

"Any reason why he shouldn't?"

"A man named Petersen," Manston replied. "He's known. Works for a crooked countryman of yours, Tony Klein. When gems are nicked, some thoughts turn to Klein and Petersen. Lock up your daughter, lock up your diamonds, the iceman cometh. In other words, they're interested in the Randall diamonds, and Petersen has trailed Grunwald from Antwerp. I'll say this for Klein and Petersen, they don't use much force. I mean, they don't use rubber hoses and guns. Petersen's in Freetown, Mr. Randall—waiting."

"What's this Petersen like?"

"Height six one, weighs fifteen stone—you'd say two hundred and ten pounds—ash-blond hair cut short, jaw like a battleship, pale-gray eyes, and small feet for a man that height and weight. A good-looking chap."

"Sounds like a movie star," Randall said. "Okay, Mr. Manston, what's your advice?"

"Mail the stones to New York—it's quick and it's safe. See it from Grunwald's point of view. He's thought well of in London. He's the CSO's favorite rough diamond."

"You know him?"

Manston shook his head. "I keep in the shadows. I see but am not seen. But I remember all I see and read." He tapped his head. "I boast about being IDSO's memory man, and it's true. I never forget a fact or a name. Some people collect diamonds, I collect diamond faces."

"Interesting," said Randall.

"Saw you were in Freetown, Mr. Randall, and thought I'd offer a bit of advice—free, gratis, and for nothing. Look, those two diamonds are worth one hell of a lot, something over a million dollars I'm told. They're worth stealing. The chances of Grunwald getting them back to New York are the sort of chance a three-legged horse has of winning the Grand National. That's my opinion, Mr. Randall—with Petersen wearing the winning colors."

"Maybe a jock named Manston will pass the finish line before Petersen," Randall said. "I'm in the fake business, Manston. I could do a freefall from twenty thousand feet and I wouldn't have to leave the studio to do it. Your script is one of the lousiest I've seen. You produce credentials that don't mean a thing, warn me against a guy named Petersen—if you want to impress me, Manston, prove that you're not after the diamonds."

Offended, Manston said, "You can check up here in Sierra Leone. Go to the IDSO office here in Freetown. Better still, come with me and do an identity check." Manston got to his feet. "I came here to give you a friendly warning, that's all—and to offer help if needed. It's obvious you don't need it."

"All right, Mr. Manston—please sit down. I'll buy you a drink and tell you sorry. I've spent the best part of my life with shysters with advice, and I'm sick to death of it. Please—I'd like you to stay and drink with me. I've had a son of a bitch of a day."

"Well—" Manston sat down and rested his arms on the table. "Perhaps I presumed a bit. I'm no diplomat. But I am on the level, Mr. Randall."

"Sure." Randall snapped his fingers at the waiter collecting glasses from tables along the balcony. "What's your poison, Manston?"

"Lime juice and soda."

"With what?"

"Just lime juice and soda."

Randall smiled. "That makes you a real Limey, Manston. I'll join you, and you can tell me how to protect that stage Jew Grunwald." He gave the drinks order, then said, "After you've told me your idea of a strategy, I'll get Grunwald along. Just a further precaution, Mr. Manston. If Grunwald says you're one of the good guys, then I'll accept his okay."

"Fair enough," Manston said.

* * *

The sun was dipping rapidly in the western sky when Sol Grunwald limped onto the balcony. He had slept a solid ten hours, felt refreshed, and needed a drink.

Randall said, "Glad you could join us, Grunwald."

Grunwald eased himself down into a chair. "Such luxury. I sleep ten hours, then drink a long, cool beer with a famous movie star. I give a couple of diamonds to the famous movie star, and I walk as light as a fairy in Columbus Circle." He looked questioningly at Manston.

"Bernard Manston," Randall said, "meet Sol Grunwald."

"Regular buyer CSO," said Manston. "'Usually deals with a CSO man named Dalmon. Knows my chief, Richard Walker. Solomon David Grunwald: office on Forty-seventh Street, New York; has three brokers behind him, Marchant, Alvin, and Tucker. Purchase of packet prior to eighty-carat pure stone, one hundred thousand dollars. Seldom misses a sight at the CSO. Walks with limp and smokes cigars. How am I doing, Mr. Grunwald?"

Grunwald's face was creased in bewilderment. "How the hell do you know all that?"

"Mr. Manston tells me he's an IDSO investigator," said Randall. "He's concerned about your safety."

"Now he's concerned," Grunwald said. "Unless I pick up a bug in this sweatshop called Freetown, I feel good and safe."

"Sure you do," Randall said. "Mr. Manston wants you to stay that way. I offended him by questioning his motives. I thought maybe you'd ask him one or two questions—you know what I mean?"

"Like is he or isn't he?"

"That's the idea."

"Okay."

The waiter appeared with Grunwald's beer. He drank half, then put down the glass and took Manston through five minutes of questioning. When he had finished, Grunwald said, "He's an IDSO eye, all right. Glad to know you, Mr. Manston. I like guys who care for Sol Grunwald's life and happiness. I should like more guys to feel that way. If we'd met up in Antwerp, maybe I wouldn't have lost weight."

"I'd like to ask you a question or two," Manston said.

"Shoot."

"Did you meet up with anyone in Antwerp?"

"Only Heinert."

"What about casuals—strangers."

Grunwald shrugged. "Maybe one or two in bars."

"Belgians?"

"Waiters and barkeeps. Hold it—there was one guy, an American."

"Can you describe him?"

"A big guy. I wasn't feeling so good. I acted like a slob."

"What did you talk about?"

"Me," said Grunwald.

"This man. Over six feet tall, blond, gray eyes—big jaw?"

Grunwald cast his mind back. "Could be. Yeah—that fits, name of Anderson."

Manston shook his head. "Petersen—not Anderson."

"So who's this Petersen?" Grunwald asked.

Randall answered: "According to Mr. Manston, Grunwald, he's interested in my diamonds."

"The hell you say."

"I'm surprised Mr. Grunwald got this far," said Manston. "Let me put you in the picture, Mr. Grunwald. The IDSO grapevine sent out the message that a certain party in New York would like to lay his hands on the Randall diamonds. Ever hear of Tony Klein?"

"That jerk!" Grunwald looked away in disgust. "Why should I worry about a small-time crook like Klein?"

"Petersen's his action man," said Manston, "and rumor has it Klein's aiming to be big-time."

"So?"

"If you met up with Petersen in Antwerp, he's tailed you, Mr. Grunwald. All the way to Freetown. He's here now."

Grunwald absorbed the news in silence. He finished his beer, and Randall beckoned to the waiter for a refill.

"So how come I get this far and give Mr. Randall the stones, huh?"

"You're an old hand," Manston said. "Perhaps you didn't give him the chance."

"I take precautions."

"Perhaps Petersen intends taking them from Mr. Randall," Manston said. "I thought I'd warn you both. That's the least I can do. Mail the diamonds to New York, Mr. Randall—it's common practice. You might even get them through customs without paying duty."

"In my case, that's not a factor," Randall said. "Maybe I prefer the hard way. Call it cussed if you like, but there's no character in mailing a couple of diamonds. No drama. I'd rather let Grunwald battle his way through to my lawyer's office after fighting off hoodlums. What do you say, Grunwald?"

Grunwald spoke to Manston: "You hear this celebrated movie actor? He dreams up a Bogart script that should've been koshered at birth, and gets a hammertoed Jewish diamond dealer to play the lead.

My life! But does he offer me a million dollars to feature in this film? No, sir!"

"I could always raise your percentage profit, Grunwald," said Randall.

"So make me an offer," Grunwald replied.

Manston frowned. "You're both taking this matter too lightly. It's not a comedy act. I've seen men who've been killed for a fraction of the value of your diamonds, Mr. Randall. I've seen men broken through the theft of a few stones in which they'd invested the whole of their financial security."

Randall folded his hands in an attitude of prayer: "So endeth the first lesson," he said. "I don't think you need to worry, Mr. Manston. Movie actors aren't all that dumb. I've got a few ideas of my own."

"I got one or two as well," Grunwald said. "You know what? This beer's okay."

Manston looked at the label on the bottle. "That's because it's British."

Manston dredged up further information from his memory banks. "Have you traded with Gem International, Mr. Grunwald?" he asked.

"Sure. Many times."

"Turner," Manston said. "James Drake Turner. Does that name ring a bell?"

"I know the guy," Grunwald said. "So what?"

"You hear stories," said Manston.

"I hear stories?"

"I mean one hears stories, Mr. Grunwald."

"There's one about a frog turns into a prince," said Grunwald, "and another about a dame who stuffed a hundred carats up her fanny so every time she took the weight off her feet she sat on a fortune."

"The story I heard concerns deals on the side."

Grunwald chuckled. "Tell me the name of one dealer who'd absolutely never pay bucks for the odd illicit."

"Difficult," Manston said. "They don't let on. It's when there's a big escape people like me get worried."

"You should have such worries." Grunwald looked at Randall. "You like your diamonds, Mr. Randall?"

"I like them fine."

"I got a bill of sale from the CSO." Grunwald looked at Manston under lowered brows. "I put in a request and got what I want. You want to check?"

"I know Mr. Dalmon, Mr. Grunwald. I don't have to check."

"So what's with Turner and Gem International?"

"I thought you might have heard something. Turner's upped and left GI, apparently without enough capital to start a newsstand. One or two other factors join the story to make an interesting jigsaw puzzle."

"You think maybe Grunwald's one of the pieces?" Randall asked.

"Perish the thought," said Manston. "Mr. Grunwald's a respected buyer at the CSO, accredited and backed by the right people. I was wondering if he'd heard anything that might help me."

"No," Grunwald said, "not a thing. I tell you. I've been so worried these weeks I haven't noticed a thing. Except that I like this beer."

Randall snapped his fingers at the waiter and pointed to Grunwald's empty glass.

Robert Randall surfaced from sleep at 6:00 A.M. with a throbbing headache, cursing the day that lay ahead, and cursing a film unit that had insisted on location shooting in Africa when the scenes could have been shot in the USA. Budget respect was the nigger in the woodpile, and the metaphor eased Randall's resentment. In the States a crowd scene involving hundreds of murderous, black-as-night, spear-waving natives, plus a few dozen specimens of African wildlife, would have pushed the budget way over the danger mark.

Randall looked at the blotches on his legs, and the Elastoplast patches covering the worst of the bites.

He had slept heavily after retiring early and taking a double dose of sleeping pills to combat disenchantment and physical discomfort. He now washed away the last of the drug's effect by taking a cold shower, surprised that the water was actually cold.

The headache was still pulsing in his head, and he went into the sitting room; somewhere in his baggage he'd put aspirin. As he entered the room he frowned, then stood for a moment scanning the room, relating what he saw to the previous night's memory of the position of furniture, pictures, and ornaments.

Something was different; the placing of objects was not the same. A drawer in the writing desk was partly open, and one of the framed paintings of a glamourized Freetown was slightly askew. What else? Randall walked slowly round the room, noting each article hanging or standing.

"Bastards!" he said, remembering Manston's warning, then sat down and peeled off an Elastoplast patch from his right shin. He picked the diamonds off the patch and clutched them in his hand.

The partly opened drawer in the writing desk: Kay's letters were in there, and he got to his feet and pulled out the drawer. The letters, previously held together by a rubber band, had been taken out of their envelopes and left scattered. Randall felt a wave of anger. Petersen? Had

Petersen entered the suite during the night and padded around searching for the diamonds? "You filthy bastard!" Randall said aloud.

As he put the letters back into the envelopes his mind firmed. All right, he'd show Petersen and Klein what clumsy shits they were. He didn't quite know how he'd do it, but it would be done.

He closed the desk drawer, then went to the window and looked out across Freetown to the sea. He stayed there for five minutes waiting for an idea to take shape, then he went to the telephone and asked the operator for Manston's number.

His conversation with Manston was brief and to the point. He explained his idea, and Manston immediately supported it with practical advice and help.

"You're a friend in need, Mr. Manston," Randall said.

"It seems we've both the same sense of humor," Manston replied. "I can be with you in one hour. I've got the carat weights. Would you like me to shop around?"

"I can manage that."

"Try a shop called Tangi's. I think I've seen 'em there. It's not far from your hotel. Turn left outside, and it's about five hundred yards."

"See you in an hour, then."

Swede Petersen was tired and frustrated. His 2:00 A.M. visit to Randall's suite, and his inability to sleep, had brought him out into the streets and to an early-morning breakfast in a cafe-bar. He now gazed moodily out the cafe window waiting for some inspiration, some plan of action to enter a head that was not unusually dumb but was certainly numb at the moment. Then he saw Randall on the opposite side of the street striding away from the hotel.

Petersen got up, slapped more than enough money on the counter, and left the cafe. He followed at a distance of fifty yards, then stopped as Randall stopped and peered up at a fascia board. Petersen could see the gaudy lettering: *Tangi*. Randall entered the shop, and Petersen waited. Two minutes later Randall emerged and began to walk back the way he had come.

Petersen watched his receding figure, then he crossed the road and looked through the shop window at the collection of goods displayed: souvenirs, pottery, cheap African carvings fresh from Hong Kong, T-shirts bearing the names of American universities, an assortment of pipes ranging from meerschaum to briar, desk lighters in imitation onyx and alabaster.

Petersen went into the shop. From behind the counter Mr. Tangi nodded good morning and Petersen pointed to the shelves stacked with cigarette packets. "Marlboro," he said. "Two packs. You know who just came in?"

"No, sah."

"One of the world's great movie stars, that's all. What did he buy?" Tangi told him.

"Is that so?" Petersen said. "Well, what's good enough for Robert Randall is good enough for me. I'll take one."

Minds thinking alike are not necessarily great, but certain truths, courses of action—even backing a winning horse—can occur at roughly the same time to utterly disparate minds. Petersen knew that Randall did not smoke, so why should he buy a cheap tin lighter?

Randall took his seat at the balcony table and ordered breakfast. The sun was well up in a clear sky and promised a good shooting schedule. The laterite roads glowed pink in the morning light, and as Randall looked out across Freetown he saw a flight of vultures wheel down and settle on the galvanized-iron roof of a warehouse half a mile distant.

He was drinking his second cup of coffee when Grunwald appeared, an unlit cigar in his mouth.

"You are a very funny man, Grunwald," Randall said. "You prove the axiom that none of us is perfect. You're a man of diamond—hard, brilliant, and methodical. I was told that if I wanted a stone that no one else had owned, Sol Grunwald would get it where others couldn't. That you were a man who never missed a trick. So why the hell can't you get your cigars lit in an organized way?"

"Like you said," Grunwald replied. "We're none of us perfect. You seen me limp?"

"I have."

"Hammertoe. Let it go too far for successful surgery. So I limp and I lose lighters and buy matches. You perfect, Mr. Randall?"

Randall smiled and showed his perfect teeth. "You think these choppers are the teeth I was born with? And I wear lifts in my shoes. Here"—Randall reached into his pocket and took out the lighter he had bought—"a gift, Grunwald. It's the cheapest money can buy." From another pocket he took three lighter-fuel capsules. "Lighter gasoline," he said. "When you get no flame, you unscrew the end of the lighter and squirt fuel into the lint."

"I had one of those when I was a kid," Grunwald said. "You know something? I've still got it somewhere back home."

"So take it and don't lose it."

Grunwald took the lighter and the capsules. "This ain't disposable," he said. "It could last a guy his lifetime."

"Just make sure it lasts you to New York."

It was a simple tube, sheet-tin, topped by a thumb-wheel set against flint and surmounted by a wind guard. The screw cap at the bottom bore the stamped inscription *Made in Belgium.*

Grunwald thumbed the lighter into flame. "It's great," he said. "I'll treasure this. A new leaf I'll turn over." He struck flame again. "Just like I was a kid on the Fourth of July lighting up firecrackers and rockets."

"You're off today, then," Randall said. "You're to be envied. I've a couple more weeks in this hellhole. When do you leave?"

"Flying up to Dakar by the afternoon flight. Night in Dakar, then first flight to New York in the morning. So, as from this minute, I think of Palestinian bombs and hijackers, engine failure and maybe I should have been born with wings. You still want me to take the diamonds?"

Randall nodded. "Just take off, Grunwald. See my lawyer in New York, and the deal's complete. He'll give you my check. Just tell him how much, that's all."

"So you give me the stones."

"You've got them," Randall said.

For a while Grunwald was silent, sipping the coffee Randall had poured for him. Eventually he said, "Okay, Mr. Randall. So I got the diamonds—but where the hell are they?"

"Just unscrew the cap at the bottom of the lighter."

"Huh?"

"You heard me, Grunwald."

"Is that where they are?"

"Could be. Just don't lose it."

Grunwald was silent for a count of ten. "And all for kicks," he said, and passed a hand over his sweating forehead. "Okay. Some of us wear a kinda vest, with inside pockets a sleight-of-hand merchant can't reach. And some of us stick the stones in our pants pocket. But you put them in a lighter and I lose lighters and there's a hood named Petersen on my trail. I'll tell you this, Mr. Randall. If Petersen or any other guy tells me this is a stickup, he gets the lighter. You got to accept the condition."

"It's accepted."

"I mean, I'm no hero, you understand? I kept to contract when I handed the diamonds to you, right?"

"Right."

"Holy cow!" Grunwald said. "That guy I met in Antwerp—Petersen

—I told him I lose lighters like kids lose their virginities these days, you know that? Like there's no decency left. Petersen I tell this to! What are you in, mister, the risk business?"

"You could call it that, Grunwald."

"So now I am a high-risk mule," Grunwald said. "My life I risk at the whim of a movie star. I have a hood on my tail and I can count my last living hours. This I shall not tell Sadie, my wife, should she be so lucky as to see me again."

"Think of your profit and stop breaking my heart," Randall said. "This rough-diamond-Jewish act, Grunwald—how deep does it go?"

Grunwald thought for a moment, then smiled. "I guess it's like a bulletproof vest. It's no good being a half-Jew. I went the whole hog— excuse the mention of pork—and you know what? People like me. I'm a funny man. They laugh their asses off and say, 'That Grunwald— did you ever meet a guy like that except in a book or *Abie's Irish Rose*? When he says, "Do I need a hole in my head?" you believe every Yiddish joke you ever heard. . . .' You play poker with me, Mr. Randall. I guarantee you won't read a single thought in my head—in which there is no hole, Mr. Randall. I'm needle sharp, an expert in my business, and have all the attributes of my people—intellect, foresight, patience, and an armor thicker than a rhinoceros. I love and understand music— good music—like many Jews. I am also proud to be a Jew . . . I forgive but never forget. I mourn but I do not shed useless tears for what has happened to my people. . . ."

The stage Yiddisher had vanished from Grunwald's manner and speech. He spoke with the dignity of a rabbi and in the poetry of the Talmud. When he had finished, Randall said, "You put my acting ability to shame, Mr. Grunwald. So which do I take as the real Solomon David Grunwald?"

"A diamond peddler named Grunwald who speaks in questions that need no answers." Grunwald's style suddenly changed. "You would want for me to walk like a fairy and talk like the Queen of England? Sadie, my wife, she would say, 'What has happened to you, Sol? Is caviar better than bagels and chicken soup with barley?' "

"Which is better, Grunwald?"

"Bagels and chicken soup."

CHAPTER 21.

A s Richard Walker entered the hotel lobby Manston's stocky, aggressive figure came to meet him.

"Welcome back, Dick. The delights of Freetown have missed you."

"I haven't missed them. It was cooler in New York. I'll book in, and we'll have a drink. Better still, find a quiet spot in the bar and get two really good ones set up. I'll join you there."

Five minutes later he joined Manston and picked up his gin and tonic. "The right time and the right drink," he said. "You've a good memory."

"That's what I told a fellow gin-and-tonic drinker not long ago. I'm the CSO's memory man. I tell everyone that."

"Don't they get bored?"

Manston grinned. "Some of 'em look scared."

"Do you have any news?"

"A regular CSO buyer named Grunwald's in Freetown. Brought a couple of super cut stones for Robert Randall, the film star. He's here doing location shooting. Natives are cheaper to hire in Sierra than in the States. I gave Randall a bit of advice re safety precautions, and he listened to me—wise man. The stones are worth one and a half million dollars."

"Chitchat," Walker said. "I want whispers. Bits from your suspicious mind. Who's in town, apart from film stars and Solomon Grunwald."

"Swede Petersen's in Freetown."

"And who is Petersen?"

"A crook. American. I think he's after Randall's diamonds."

Tired after his flight from New York, Walker said, "I'm not interested in that kind of criminal. Stop nattering. Grunwald's diamonds were bought legally and cut in the same way. I want Mackenzie information."

"Ah!" Manston's face lit up. "More bits and pieces. I'm on to some-thing, Dick. I can feel it in my bones."

"Don't wait to see an osteopath, just tell me."

Five minutes later Walker interrupted Manston's enthusiastic nar-rative and said, "When you talked to Turner on the plane, how did he seem?"

"On his guard. Are you on to something?"

"I don't know. At the moment it's personal."

"He's on my mind too," Manston said, "and it's not personal. I chased him up to Aracaju and back again—he's out of this hemisphere now."

"And Mackenzie?"

"Angwana—doing charity work, or so he says. . . . Dick? If there is something going on—"

"I'm on an errand of mercy." Walker smiled without humor. "It goes against the grain because of the people involved. Keep me in touch with every move, everything you come up with."

Manston frowned. "I don't get it," he said.

"You wouldn't want it," said Walker. He emptied his glass and got to his feet. "A bath and a change, then dinner and an early night. Are you eating with me?"

"If you pick up the bill."

"As your chief, it's my burden and privilege." Using both hands, he pressed tiredness from his face. "You can pay for the drinks. If I don't flake out, I'll see you at the bar seven-thirty."

"Your word is law, chief."

It was after their meal that Walker defined his interest in Macken-zie and Turner: "I'm hoping there's no wrong-side-of-the-fence diamond dealing between Jamie Turner and Mackenzie. Turner's a personal friend. To stop you ferreting, I'll tell you now—I'm interested in his wife. Two days ago I was with her in New York." Seeing the half-smile on Manston's face, Walker said, "There's nothing on, if that's what you're thinking. I'd like to say otherwise, but that's not the way it is. So I'm serving two masters. Because of your damned jigsaw puzzle I'm serving IDSO. On the other hand, I'm trying to help a friend, and the two conflict."

"Do you know where Turner is?" asked Manston. "Because if you don't, I do. Geneva."

"The Hôtel des Bergues on the Quai des Bergues."

Manston looked disappointed. "I was saving up that bit of news. I've even got his flight number from New York."

"I shall be going to Geneva in a couple of days. I'll see Jamie Turner. Perhaps he'll enlighten me. It's odd, Bernard. A man holding down a top-salaried directorship in an international company suddenly throws in his hand, leaves his wife with double the settlement the sharpest divorce lawyer would demand, and goes off into the blue to go it alone as a free-lance buyer." Walker paused, frowning. "Unless he's got cash tucked away, I don't see, and neither can Joan, where he'll get the money to walk tall through the CSO's bronze doors."

"Doesn't his wife know how much he's got?"

"Not enough to go it alone. Chicken feed if he intends free-lance buying."

"Know what I'd do in your place?" Manston said. "I'd do my level best to put the skids under J. D. Turner."

"But then, you're not a nice man, Bernard."

"What about *cherchez la femme*?"

"That's another possibility. Perhaps I'll find out when I get to Geneva."

In its rising the sun broke free of the alpine barrier and sent shafts of light flooding across Geneva. It pierced the windows of the Hôtel des Bergues and slanted across the floor of Suite 20 to touch the sleeping faces of Carol and Turner. It failed to disturb him out of sleep, but Carol's eyelids opened to receive the full force of the sun's light. She turned her head on the pillow and looked at Turner's face, bringing it into sharp focus as she came fully awake.

No regrets. No sadness following the fulfillment she had shared with him. Pure pleasure looking and seeing together during the day, and high, sensual joy in each other's bodies during the night. Liking and loving; the two emotions had become one, so that when the loving was done, liking took over and sustained them until it changed to the act of loving.

And the shadows had gone from his face, those odd memories that had suddenly struck at him in the first week of her stay. His gaiety, and sense of fun and the ridiculous, had had a brittle feel during those first days; it had been too self-conscious and lacking in the spontaneity to which she had responded at their first meeting.

She reached out and ran fingertips over his lips, seeing them curve into a sleep-smile as if he knew the fingers touching him were hers. From across the lake a church clock chimed the hour, and Carol counted the chimes to six o'clock. In six hours' time she would board the plane for England, home, and diamonds in the CSO, leaving Jamie alone and loveless in Geneva. "Not for long, Jamie," she said. "Just a month—is that so very long?"

Her words, spoken quietly, broke into his sleep, and he came awake.

"Carol?"

"I'm here, Jamie." She came close and into his encircling arm.

"Today's the day, isn't it?"

"I'm afraid so."

"What do you say, Carol?"

"About what?"

"Us."

"Yes."

"Forever?"

"Just like diamonds. A month, that's all."

"There's weekends."

"Perhaps. We'll see."

"Why the uncertainty?"

"It's not uncertainty—about us, I mean. What's left of my family is pretty well knit. I've got to tell my father—I've two brothers as well. It's a big step for me, Jamie. It's one I'm going to take, but not by dropping out."

"And when the month's out?"

"I'll come to Geneva."

"I'll find a house, a good house. Remember that valley at the foot of the Jura? Maybe there's something I can buy there."

For a while she did not answer, then she said, "I'm not going to live with you, Jamie. I'll see you, make love to you, but we're not setting up house till you're divorced. You can find me a flat in Geneva—for which I'll pay. I'm an old-fashioned girl, Jamie."

"A man in love wants guarantees," Turner said. "This one does, anyway. I've changed my whole life for you, Carol, and I want it settled and secure."

The world held so many uncertainties, so many dangers; the image of Partridge, dead in a sordid hotel in Aracaju, came into his mind. Carol saw the darkness in his face. "What is it?" she asked.

He released part of the truth. "A poor dead man I once saw."

The Swissair TriStar reached the end of its takeoff run and climbed steeply. Turner watched it take up course for London until it was lost in the high cloud. As he left the airport and got into a taxi the thought came to him that things were back to normal, and the thought discomforted him. What did "back to normal" mean? A return to memories of Aracaju? To thoughts of Joanie? He had lost himself in Carol; the all-blanketing sensuality and the pure joy of being with her and looking at her and listening to her voice and responses were a thing of the immediate past. Now he had to live without that intoxication and return to the world of practicality, and the thought was depressing.

He thought of Mackenzie now in Angwana and wished that Mac would finally quit Africa and join him in Geneva. The truth is, he told himself, I want an end to the association; Mackenzie *must* belong to the past if there was to be a future. The slate had to be wiped clean. Once the split had been made—the fifty-fifty share-out—with the Scotsman striding his thousands of Argyllshire acres, life would really begin again.

Turner paid the taxi driver and entered the hotel; at least the necessity of a drink followed by a good lunch was something that could not be denied. As he entered the bar with its wide window over the lake he could see Carol's golden oysters dancing on the water. As he stood by the window a voice intruded on his thoughts: "Can I get you a drink, sir?"

Without turning his head, Turner said, "An Americano." Then the voice with its English accent made him look round.

"How are you, Jamie?" Richard Walker asked.

They lunched together at the Chat d'Noire, a small restaurant on the outskirts of Geneva, Turner not responding to Richard Walker's diamond talk. Eventually, as Turner guessed it would, Walker began to talk about Joanie. "Saw her in New York a few days ago, Jamie," he said.

"How was she?"

"Sensible."

"What does that mean?"

"She's faced up to the situation, but she's worried about you. There's much she doesn't understand. You were too generous, Jamie."

"I think that's my business, don't you?"

"I didn't ask Joan to make it mine. If you want me to put my cards on the table—I'm in love with her. Have been for a long time. Anything that concerns her, concerns me. Sorry."

"Who called for an apology?" Turner reached for the wine and refilled their glasses. "You've a clear field, Dick. I'm out of the running. Didn't Joanie tell you?"

"Just that you'd both agreed to part. Old habits die hard—you're still a habit. End of hopeless love story." Casually he said, "Spent a few days in Freetown after seeing Joan. I had to contact Bernard Manston. He said he met you on a flight from New York to Rio. Did you get your emeralds?"

"I didn't like what I saw."

"I'm not surprised. I thought you were strictly a diamond man."

Turner shrugged. "I bought stones other than diamond for Gem International."

"Talking of GI," Walker said, "that's one of the things bothering Joan. She reckons you haven't the capital to branch out alone. You sold your stock to GI and gave every cent to Joan. Your diamond collection, too. That's a lot of capital, Jamie. Joan has an idea how much you've got—you can't trade on that—it's too small."

"I know men who've started on less."

"You're not a beginner, Jamie. Look, I am prying and not only for Joan's sake. I've enough liking and respect for you to act as a friend. In need, if necessary."

"I'm not in need. I've credit and three brokers behind me." Turner smiled. "What do you want, Dick? Apart from my wife?"

"You know my job, Jamie. Only once in my life have I had to shop a friend. I didn't like the process. I heard enough from Manston to share Joan's concern."

"So?"

"You're respected at the CSO. I'd hate to see that respect go."

"That sounds like a warning," Turner said. "Put it into real words."

"Be careful whom you choose as a friend."

"Maybe I'll ask you to check." Turner beckoned to the waiter. "Coffee—black. Do you want brandy, Dick?"

"Armagnac."

"Make it two, waiter." Turner drained his wineglass, then said, "What else bothers Joanie?"

"The usual."

"What's that?"

"Another woman, naturally."

"There are thousands of other women. I don't intend to live a celibate life." Turner watched the waiter pour the coffee and then the brandy. When the waiter had left their table, he said, "You can tell Joanie there will be another woman."

"Does she have a name?"

"She will have—mine."

"So it's as final as that between you and Joan?"

"Joan accepted the fact when we talked and parted."

"It's also a fact that she cares enough to worry about you."

"I can't help that. I care, too, if you want to know. You don't forget a body immediately after it's under six feet of earth."

Walker frowned and looked at Turner. "That's a morbid observation. Are you so acquainted with death?"

"It's a fact of life—if it isn't too paradoxical for you."

Walker held his brandy glass in both hands and looked into its bowl. Turner watched him rotate the glass so that the brandy made a vortex. "What else is on your mind, Dick, apart from love of my estranged wife and fears for my future?"

Walker said, "I've hinted so far, Jamie. Do you want me to lay it on the line?"

"Lay what on the line?"

"Exactly what's going on."

"What is going on?"

"Bernard Manston's in Freetown. He follows a scent like a blood-hound. He's interested in you—and Arnold Mackenzie. He won't give up, Jamie. Manston doesn't believe in coincidences. He mixes up place names like Komalu and Aracaju, then throws in names of persons—the names of two dead men and those of James Drake Turner and Arnold Mackenzie—and finds that the mixture promises to make a tasty dish."

"If he eats it he'll be sick."

"I doubt it." Walker sipped his brandy and looked at Turner over the glass.

"It's no secret that I know Mackenzie. I've bought from Sierra Leone, so it's natural I should meet up with him. I've known him for years."

"It's what happened in Aracaju that bothers Manston. You know as well as I do that Noni has the best emeralds in South America. According to Manston, you were in South America to buy and you didn't. Yet you go to Aracaju, stay a couple of days, then leave for the States like a bat out of hell."

"Aracaju's no place for a rest."

"A good place to die, though. Incidentally, Gilberto Noni owns the hotel where one of the men died. A man called Partridge—used to work at the Komalu as a sorter. Mackenzie knew him."

Turner was silent. The bedbug on Partridge's dead forehead came clearly into his mental vision, a brown-red spot above eyes that stared but did not see, and the hands, stiff in rigor mortis, clutching the blanket.

"There's more if you want to hear it," Walker said.

"If you want to tell it."

"I know how Manston works, you see? It's also my job and I don't like it when it raises mixed loyalties. Manston has no such problem. He'll ferret out the truth if it's there, and he'll act without fear or favor."

"You can do the same," Turner said. "I've nothing to fear. So I've bought now and then from the illicits. What buyer hasn't with the per-centage not controlled by the CSO floating around? I've caught a few bargains that way via Monrovia. Again, who hasn't taken a drink with a peddler coming across the border from Sierra Leone? Do you think the illicits are going to walk into the CSO office and say, "Look what I found. Can I have the regulation price'?"

"That side of your business doesn't worry me," Walker said. "I know it goes on, the CSO knows it goes on. It's this magic name, Aracaju. A body is shipped from Freetown, the body of a miner killed in the Komalu tunnel collapse. And where does the body land up? In a small village a few miles out of Aracaju, and a couple of days later Partridge dies in a shabby hotel round about the time you pay the town a visit."

"Coincidence," Turner said. "Unrelated events and nothing more. If you've got a message for me, Dick, let me have it."

"Your standing with the CSO, Jamie. I'd hate to see you lose that. It's hard to become an accredited buyer but damned easy to lose the privilege."

"A fate worse than death," Turner said. "What you're saying, Dick, and saying it loud and clear, is that suspicion, founded or unfounded, could make me an unwelcome visitor at Two Charterhouse Street."

"Depending on Mahston's report."

"Not on yours, Dick?"

"If I couldn't knock holes in it, I'd have no alternative but to put it to the board."

"Any idea what I'm supposed to have done?"

"No. I've told you all I know."

"Good old British honor and duty before love, old boy," Turner said. "Go ahead, Dick. Discredit me—win your spurs and carry off the woman you love."

Nettled, Walker said, "I might even do that, Jamie. Just don't force my hand." He looked at Turner, his face serious. "If it means anything to you, I've no intention of telling Joan about Carol."

Angry, his face flushed, Turner said, "You *have* kept your eyes open, haven't you? Was it part of your brief? You tell Joanie what you damn well like. You'd make a bloody good divorce snooper!"

"That wasn't and isn't part of my brief, Jamie. I came here in good faith and to warn you."

"Okay. So you've warned me. End of conversation and future contact." Turner got up from the table. "Tell my wife that I shall continue to live in a manner to which I have become accustomed. You can also tell the CSO they'll receive essential documents and credentials to guarantee my acceptance as an accredited buyer, and my first request will be in the neighborhood of a million dollars."

"As much as that, Jamie?" Walker said calmly. "It wouldn't have made any difference if you'd said five million. I've no intention of telling the CSO—that's your business. If you're accepted, you're accepted. I'll tell Joan she's not to worry and that everything's going according to plan. Wish you luck, Jamie."

CHAPTER **22.**

GRUNWALD boarded the link flight to Dakar refreshed and ready for the long flight home. At Dakar he'd have just thirty minutes' wait in the transit lounge before catching the flight to New York. As he fastened his seat belt, and the Boeing rumbled to its takeoff run, he thought of the long hauls to Antwerp, from London and the CSO, to watch the stages of the cutting of the Randall diamonds, then back to New York and back again to Antwerp, and the flight to Freetown and Robert Randall—and all the time he'd been followed and watched by an itchy-fingered hood with a taste for diamonds.

Randall's notion was crazy, of course; at the same time, it wasn't a bad way to mule a couple of diamonds all the way to the States, if you'd a yen for doing it the hard way like you were acting in a movie entitled *The Diamond Mule* or *Grunwald the Diamond Jerk.*

Panels flashed their message that smoking was now permitted, and Grunwald took out a cigar and kindled it using Randall's lighter.

From his window on the right-hand side of the plane he saw the coastline running up from Freetown to Dakar. Some country, he thought; from its earth, from its troubled and dangerous earth, came forth diamonds, and he had done well by them. That such beauty came from such a continent seemed anomalous; glaucoma, yellow fever, typhoid, elephantiasis—you name the diseases and that was Africa if you cared to think of the place in those terms.

In the observation tower at Freetown Airport, Petersen watched until the plane was out of sight, then checked in with baggage and entered the transit lounge to wait for his flight number to be called. In a little less than an hour he, too, would take off for Dakar; by that time Fats Grunwald would have made transit in Dakar Airport and heard the message over the speakers: *"Mr. Grunwald—Mr. Solomon Grunwald. . . . Here is a message for Mr. Solomon Grunwald. Would Mr. Grun-*

wald please go to Receptions where an important message awaits him?
Mr. Grunwald—Mr. Solomon Grunwald. . . ."

The message telephoned through from Freetown was simple and imperative: *"Change of plans. Mr. Randall wishes Mr. Grunwald to book in at the International Hotel and await Mr. Randall's arrival."*

So what the hell now? thought Grunwald. He collected his baggage and took a taxi to the International. He growled his request for a room and, on giving his name, was told that Mr. Randall had already made the reservation.

"Did he say anything else?" Grunwald asked.

"Only that he was sorry to delay you and that he would be arriving this evening from Freetown."

Grunwald swore in Yiddish and followed the porter to the lift. The porter, a black man with dark gingery hair, was chatty. "Would you be Jewish, Mr. Grunwald?"

"They don't come more Jewish."

"I am Jewish also."

Grunwald looked at the black face with its gingery hair. "So's Sammy Davis, Junior," he growled. *"Mizzeltof."*

"Shalom, Mr. Grunwald."

It seemed that he had only just finished the glass of the wine sent up to him with Mr. Randall's compliments when he woke up feeling dizzy, a headache thumping at his temples. It was some time before he could focus his vision, and when it cleared, he took in the sight of his disordered room.

His suitcase had been ripped to pieces, its contents scattered. He found it odd, too, that although he had sat fully dressed, he was now stripped down to his underpants, the clothes he had worn cut to rags and strewn round the chair on which he slumped, and he himself not quite able to comprehend what had happened. Sol looked at his watch, trying to remember the time at which he'd accepted the wine and had that glass. Four hours. He'd slept for four hours and right through a hurricane.

He rose shakily to his feet and looked about him, feeling naked. He found his billfold and passport; his money hadn't been touched, neither had his credit cards, American Express and other pieces of plastic money. Then, through the mists of his clouded mind, came the image of two diamonds resting on a black-velvet square, and he clutched his

·

stomach as a violent bowel movement racked him.

When he staggered out of the bathroom weakened by the sudden bout of diarrhoea, he stood for several minutes looking at the rags and ruins that had been his possessions. Someone once said, "Hammer your thoughts into unity." That's what he had to do, hammer his chaotic, ruinous thoughts into some kind of unity. He couldn't walk about a hotel room clad only in underpants.

He couldn't believe the diamonds had gone, and he couldn't think how something at the back of his mind told him they hadn't gone. So where was the lighter? It came to him suddenly. He had poured a glass of wine, set it down on the low table, settled into a deep armchair, taken a Havana out of his cigar case, and fumbled for the lighter—jacket pockets, then pants pockets. He couldn't believe he'd done it again— not another lighter, and such a special lighter. To steady a rising panic, he'd downed the glass of wine in two deep drafts, then refilled the glass and drank that. A bowl on the table contained a dozen hotel match-books, and he remembered taking one and striking flame to his cigar, then a third glass of the wine before—before what?

"Before I wake up stripped to my underpants," Grunwald said aloud.

Instinct led him to the armchair. He'd sat down pretty heavily be-fore pouring the wine and sticking a cigar in his mouth, so what hap-pens to a stout guy who sits in deep armchairs? Nickels and dimes fall out of his pants pockets and slip down the sides of armchairs. He'd last used the lighter in the taxi from Dakar Airport when the coffee-colored driver had said, "You give me a light, sah?" Oh, my God! Grunwald thought, it could be in that buggy.

Chair first. Grunwald rubbed his hands together nervously, then advanced on the chair and slipped his hands down either side of the seat. A sharp pain pierced one of the fingers on his left hand and he withdrew it hurriedly—a pin was stuck to his middle finger. His right hand continued to grope, then a sweat of pure relief broke out on his forehead. He straightened up, the lighter clutched in both hands and close to his heart.

He went to the window, and in the sunlight slanting through it he unscrewed the bottom of the lighter and picked out the lint until the first of the gems glinted in the sunlight. A second and much larger wave of relief swept over him, and his eyes filled with tears, then he replaced the lint. He felt fine and to hell with the headache and trots—is it not good for a man to have a clearing out now and again?

He reached for the telephone and asked to speak to the man in charge. The girl on the switchboard said, "Perhaps I can help you, sir."

"Look, miss," said Grunwald. "I want a man who knows what a

man wears. I want to buy a suit. I want to buy a shirt. My shoes? My shoes are fine—they are without soles or heels. . . ."

An hour later Grunwald surveyed himself in the mirror. A light-blue casual jacket, navy-blue trousers, white shirt, and psychedelic tie weren't his usual attire, and the pants were tight. The assistant manager, Moroccan by birth and polite, said, "You look very fine, sir."

"Like an American tourist, is that what you mean?"

"I am sorry, sir. You will tell me the extent of your loss, and the hotel will replace every article."

"To hell with that. Just find out who came to my room, or maybe you think a hurricane visited me."

"It cannot be anyone employed here, sir. Every man and woman is honest."

"Like Al Capone! What kind of joint is this? You see that wine— it's doped. So who sends me doped wine that sends me to sleep for four hours so I miss my flight to New York?"

The assistant manager spread his hands wide. "It is a mystery, sir."

"Yeah, I know. You ask who brought the wine and you find nobody brought it, so forget it. You can do two things: send up a bottle of champagne—unopened, you understand—and book a call to Freetown. I want to speak to a Mr. Robert Randall."

The assistant manager's gaze flickered down at the broken fragments of Grunwald's cigars. "You would like a cigar, also, Mr. Grunwald?"

"A whole damn box!"

The call to Randall came through at 6:30, and Randall sounded irritable: "What now, Grunwald. Where the devil are you?"

"In Dakar. You want to know where the devil I am or was? I was in hell, Mr. Randall, you should want to know. I got your message and book in at the hotel, then I drink the wine you send up with Mr. Randall's compliments, and wake up four hours later wearing my underpants only. My custom-built suit is ripped to pieces, my baggage torn apart, and I empty my bowels. That's where the devil I was, you should care."

"Take it easy, Grunwald. Take it easy. . . . What about the lighter?"

"You can thank Grunwald's ability to lose things. This time down the side of a chair."

"And the diamonds?"

"I had me a quick look, they're okay. My health and my life I'm not sure of."

"You sound fit enough, Grunwald. Look, I sent no message or

doped wine. Have you seen Petersen?"

"I have not. You guess that's who it was set me up?"

"It's a reasonable guess. Look, Grunwald, give the bastard a run for his money. Get a gun, hire a bodyguard. Do anything you like, but get the hell out of Dakar and head for New York. Remember one thing —whatever happens, you'll be paid in full and not lose a cent."

"Do I get that in writing?"

"Just take my word. See my lawyer, tell him the cost, and he'll give you a check. Now get off the line—I've spent the best part of today trudging through swamp. I got five leeches up my legs and a million bug bites and all for the sake of movie realism. Get on that flight to New York and *shalom,* Grunwald. And stop beating that stage Yiddisher head of yours."

"*Shalom,* Mr. Randall," Grunwald said, and shook his head at the lack of sympathy the great had for the humble.

The squeak had been as narrow and thin as a dying mosquito's last gasp, thought Grunwald. If he hadn't mislaid the lighter—he closed his eyes at the thought, the consequences were unthinkable. The lighter hadn't been taken this time, but what about the next time, and the next?

You have brains, Grunwald told himself; as a man of diamonds you have learned every trick played in the game. You know the economics of the trade inside and out. You have an unerring instinct for telling the good from the bad; you are an authority on diamond and every gem in the sparkler calendar, so use those brains and instincts and take out insurance against loss of pride and spiritual hurt.

He left the hotel and wandered through the streets, antennae at the back of his head probing like radar for a tail over six feet in height. Now and again he paused to look into shop windows that reflected back his image and those of passersby. No Petersen; or if there was, he was keeping well hidden. He stopped and looked into a jeweller's window; rings, necklaces, pendants, and clasps glittered back at him, and suddenly he knew what he had to do.

It took him five minutes to find what he wanted: two rings set with the finest paste stones, a Brilliant and an Antwerp Rose. A further five minutes convinced the dealer that Grunwald knew the difference between paste and gems and that an amalgam of zinc and copper wasn't gold, and Grunwald's haggled price was accepted.

Grunwald now had to search for the third article to implement the caper he had in mind. He tried three tobacconists before he struck lucky in a mean side street and matched the Randall lighter.

Back in the hotel, he paid a visit to the men's toilet and dropped coins into a contraceptive-vending machine, shamefaced as he put the packet of three into his inside jacket pocket.

In the privacy of his room, and with one eye on the clock, he pried the stones out of their settings and inserted them into the lighter he'd bought from the shop in the side street, and he hoped he wouldn't get them mixed up in the preliminaries. He opened the pack of contraceptives. As he unrolled a condom he thought, That this should be put to such a use! He inserted the Randall lighter and twisted the unoccupied length of the condom into a knot.

Then he got to his feet and limped to the bathroom, remembering a Christian hymn he'd heard in London's Saint Andrew's (God forgive a Hebrew remembering a Christian hymn!). "God be in my head and in my ———"

Grunwald was flying presidential class; it was worth extra bucks to lounge in comparative comfort on a banquette near the bar. His thirst and palate longed for many cool beers, but a buildup of carbon dioxide made a man pass wind, and that Grunwald did not want to do; so he was drinking a dry Martini when Petersen came up the three stairs and into the lounge. Grunwald beckoned him over: "Hey! Anderson, isn't it? I want to buy you a drink—I guess I behaved like a slob in Antwerp. I was worried, okay?"

"No offense," Petersen said. "I'll have what you're drinking."

Grunwald signalled the steward, then took a cigar out of his pocket and stuck it in his mouth. "Have I had troubles," he said. "You want to hear about my troubles?"

"Sure."

Grunwald struck flame with his lighter. He blew two smoke rings, perfectly formed. "Now I feel good," he said. "Troubles? Such troubles. In Dakar I'm Mickey-Finned. Out like a light. When I wake—and such a pain in my head and like I got arsenic in my bowels—I'm stripped to my underpants, my suit torn to shreds, and the hotel room like a hurricane hit it. Even my cigars, which I love, were broken. So what did they want, whoever it was?"

Petersen sipped his Martini, eyeing Grunwald's lighter. "Money?" he said.

"No, sir!" Grunwald shook his head. "My money is okay, my passport is okay. I tell you, Anderson, in my business it's understood we run risks, right? So whoever put me out didn't get what guys like me carry. I should be such a schmuck to let some heister take what is my business to carry on my person?"

Grunwald put the lighter down on the low table and picked up his

Martini. "I am definitely not a schmuck, Anderson, and I feel good. I take home a present, which my wife, Sadie, will treasure, and Sol Grunwald, who has done good business."

"Yeah?"

Grunwald tapped the lighter with a forefinger. "That's the present. What d'ya think, Anderson? How much is that lighter worth?"

"One-fifty?"

"Mister, that lighter was given me by Robert Randall. To me, it is worth over a million bucks. And when I say Robert Randall, I mean *the* Robert Randall, who is my friend."

Petersen had finished his drink. "You need another," Grunwald said. "I could buy drinks for the whole planeload, I feel so good. In six hours New York and mission accomplished, as John Wayne said when he captured Iwo Jima."

Grunwald heaved himself off the banquette, picked up Petersen's glass, and went to the bar. For a few seconds his back was turned to Petersen, and Petersen acted—a lightning switch of lighters that made him break out into a sweat. The action barely completed, Grunwald turned round, beaming. "I'm just guessing it was John Wayne. Could've been Gregory Peck or some other guy." He carried the Martinis back to the table and sat down. "I can't buy drinks, you know that? In presidential they're for free."

"It was John Wayne said it." Petersen smiled. "Or some other guy."

The lighter was still on the table and Grunwald picked it up, vaguely disappointed. He pressed his dumb-cluck act: "I love this lighter, Anderson. It means more to me than—" Words seemed to fail him.

"I know how it is," Petersen said. "A guy can get sentimental about the craziest things." He drained his glass.

"Boy, can you drink Martinis!" Grunwald said.

Petersen got to his feet. "I've got some paperwork to do, okay? Take an hour or so, then we drink our way to New York."

"Sure." Grunwald gave his head a quick sideways jerk in approval. "See you later. You got a first name?"

"Didn't I tell you in Antwerp? It's Charlie, but I'm called Chuck."

"We'll drink the bar dry, Chuck."

Grunwald waited until Petersen had taken the steps down and out of the bar, then he picked up the lighter. Flipping back the hinged cap, he thumbed the wheel. There was a bright spark but no flame. He tried again. Still no flame, and he raised the lighter to his nose and sniffed.

A smile spread across Grunwald's face, and he unscrewed the bottom of the lighter. He picked out the wad of lint and looked into the barrel. Grunwald's smile grew bigger. He had to hand it to Petersen, the guy had a keen wit and nerve.

Grunwald replaced the screw cap and closed the hinged cap. Maybe he'd get the chance to make Petersen sweat a little before the plane touched down at Kennedy.

Petersen closed the toilet door behind him and locked it, then he unscrewed the bottom of the lighter. He picked at the lint and took out the first wad, holding the barrel of the lighter upward; he looked down at the faceted stone glinting up at him. "Oh, Jesus! Oh, sweet Jesus! I've got them," he said. "Tony, I've got them. I've got them!" He spilled out the large Brilliant and then the Antwerp Rose. A million dollars' worth!

Knuckles rapped on the door, and Petersen called out, "Hold it!" He put the stones back in the lighter, then the wad of lint, and screwed back the bottom cap. He looked at his watch: another five hours before they touched down at Kennedy. Five hours of hoping that Grunwald wouldn't inspect the dud lighter. "We'll drink the bar dry," Grunwald had said. Okay, that's just what they'd do. He'd got many guys drunk before; he'd get Grunwald stoned out of his mind.

He unzipped his fly and urinated, the marksman in him directing the stream so that it hit the drain flap dead center. He flushed the bowl, zipped his fly, and opened the door.

"Sorry," he said to the anxious woman waiting outside. "My zipper stuck."

Grunwald was surprised when Petersen returned. "Some paperwork," he said.

"What the hell!" Petersen said. "A guy can be too conscientious. You want to drink that bar dry? Then let's get started."

Grunwald had an unlighted cigar in his mouth. He picked up the lighter and toyed with it. "I love this lighter, Anderson," he said.

"So you said. Martinis okay?"

Grunwald thumbed the lighter; the spark was bright, but no flame sprang up. He tried again, and Petersen suddenly felt cold; of all the goddamned stupid mistakes, he'd forgotten to fill it!

At his fifth unsuccessful try, Grunwald said, "Must be outa fuel. I got some in my hand luggage back in my seat." He began to ease up from the banquette, and Petersen reached out a restraining hand.

"Save it, Sol," he said, and snapped his Ronson under Grunwald's cigar. "You don't use high-octane gas in a pressurized plane flying at thirty-five thousand feet."

"You tell me something new," said Grunwald. "That is a fact?"

"Air-safety rules."

"My life!" said Grunwald. "I carry a bomb in my hand luggage."

"Can't be too careful, Sol. Let's drink. You've done well, and Chuck Anderson's export and import business has thrived. Let's drink to success on all fronts, huh?"

Grunwald's bowels rumbled, and he tightened his sphincter muscles. "Back and front," he said.

"Huh?"

"My bowels do not, definitely do not, like travel and time differences and crazy foreign foods and mornings that should be nights. Sadie, my wife, will give me roughage."

The bar steward handed them massive dry Martinis.

"You worry too much," Petersen said. "Drink hearty. These are what I call dry Martinis—big, cold, and free. Say, there's something I've wanted to ask you. Are diamonds a good investment? I mean, could I make a packet by investing a few grand?"

Grunwald shook his head. "You're not in the business. You'd be a re-tail buyer, unless you know a few illicits or you're a jewel thief. Okay, let's say you buy a new Cadillac and at the same time you buy a diamond for the same amount—you with me?"

Petersen nodded. "I buy a Caddie and a diamond costing the same."

"Five years pass. You got inflation, rising prices. Now you want a new Caddie and you don't have the bucks. So you sell the diamond, and the price you'll get will buy a new Cadillac at the new price. Point is, Chuck, you won't be able to buy two new Caddies. You've kept up with rising prices is all."

"I think I got it," said Petersen.

"What you got is defense, Chuck. Your old Caddie is crapped out. It's got rust, and the fender's hanging off. It's a heap with two hundred thousand miles on the clock, and not worth a dime. But your diamond's kept pace with rising prices."

"So diamonds are safe?"

"As houses," Grunwald said. "What diamond can buy you today buys the same thing five, ten, twenty years ahead. Chuck, listen to me. Take a ten-dollar bill and think what it can buy now. You think that ten-spot's going to buy you the same thing five years from now?"

"Boy!" Petersen said. "You sure know economics."

It was time to make Petersen sweat a little. Grunwald lowered his voice: "Tell you this, Chuck. I know guys who work on the fringe, guys handling hot ice. You heard of Klein?"

"Klein?"

"Runs his business from New York. Handles anything stolen, from chastity belts to diamond. You're a nice guy, Chuck, but you could be a diamond heister—forgive the assumption, plainly you are not a crook—but you could be sussing me for a heist. Chuck, by dispossessing me of what I carry, you would be a very rich man." Grunwald looked earnestly into Petersen's face. "That is one way of making bucks out of diamonds. The other way is to be a dealer like me. You hot, Chuck? You got sweat on your forehead."

Weakly Petersen said, "You can't open windows in Boeings flying at thirty-five thousand feet."

"When I sweat, Chuck, I sweat blood." Grunwald drank deeply of his Martini. "Or I sweat Martini. Time for another, Chuck."

"Sure, time for a coupla dozen."

Grunwald stuck a cigar into his mouth; before his lips had clamped down on the cigar, Petersen's Ronson was in flame and held under its tip.

"You're mighty quick on the draw," Grunwald said.

Sol Grunwald felt terrible. He looked out the cabin window and down at Martha's Vineyard, twenty thousand feet below the plane, tired eyes focused on the coastline running down to New York. Not long now before the plane touched down at Kennedy Airport, and the relief that place held for him. Across the aisle Petersen sat in his seat apparently at one with his world despite his intake of liquor. He glanced at Grunwald and smiled. "How're you feeling, Sol?"

"Lousy. Soon as I get to Randall's lawyer and finish my business, I shall give my body and soul up to Sadie, my wife. I am not well, Chuck."

"You're hung over, that's all."

"That is all? I have road-mending equipment in my head and you tell me that is all? I do not even wish to smoke. So you look good and took drink for drink with me. If you have a secret, then tell me."

"I'm six one and my legs are hollow. Maybe that's where it goes. Too long a circuit for it to get to my head."

"And I'm five eight and a horizontal six one viewed sideways." Grunwald clasped his stomach with both hands. "I filled this damn thing with too much."

"We must do it again sometime," Petersen said. "I'll call you."

Grunwald shook his head. "Never again will I drink with you, Chuck." He lifted his hands and held his head. "The road menders have now dug a hole and are boring down into the cables of my mind." A spark of humor pierced the dark pain in his head, and he added, "You'll have yours later, Chuck—kinda delayed action, know what I mean?"

"Maybe," said Petersen.

It was agonizing getting through customs, despite the ease with which Grunwald was passed through—that is, with minimum inspection. He collected his baggage and dumped it, then found a toilet. There he spent an anxious and painful ten minutes, his every effort energizing the thumping in his head. When he emerged from the toilet, he went to the hand basins and carefully washed, finally holding his face under cold water. When he had finished, he stood very still, hands holding onto the rim of the basin. The pain in his head had lessened after the agony of the toilet and the sweet cold of the water on his face. He adjusted the set of his tie, pulled his stomach in as far as it would go, collected his baggage, and walked out of the airport. The first taxi rush was over, and he climbed into a yellow cab and rapped out, "Park Avenue, Four-two-two."

Randall's lawyer was affable and welcoming. "You look tired, Mr. Grunwald," he said.

"I drank with a crook. For the sake of Robert Randall and his diamonds I suffer in my head and my ass and drink hard liquor with a hood I wish never to see again."

Walter Mattinger nodded. "Mr. Randall telephoned me. He said there was some kind of trouble. But you're safe and sound, Mr. Grunwald. Your check is ready. Just tell me the amount."

Grunwald reached into his pocket and took out the lighter. "The goods first. Never again will I be a mule."

"A mule?"

"A guy that carries diamonds and don't want others to see them's called a mule."

"Of course. It was a necessary precaution, Mr. Grunwald. The diamonds are extremely valuable."

"Sure. All I got to do now is deliver, then I tell you the price and you give me Randall's check." Grunwald smiled his confidence and tapped the lighter on the desk. "They're in this lighter, Mattinger. Randall's got the grading certificate."

Mattinger shook his head. "On the contrary, the diamonds arrived yesterday afternoon and are now safely lodged where no thieving hand can touch them."

Grunwald frowned. "You said what?"

"The grading certificate also. Mr. Randall asked me to offer you his apologies with the message that 'Whatever Grunwald charges it was worth giving those bums a ride.' I take it he was referring to thieves trying to steal the diamonds." Grunwald was silent. Mattinger added, "The package came by airmail, Mr. Grunwald. Hardly the safest method of transport."

Grunwald held Mattinger's gaze for a count of ten, then unscrewed the lighter cap, picked out the lint, and spilled out the diamonds. Mattinger watched the forefinger of Grunwald's right hand stir the two stones.

"Paste," Grunwald said. "A couple of bits of lousy strass!" He could see how worthless they were, how unlike the real thing, and he felt shame. "Of all the schmucks. Why the hell didn't I see they were fakes when I opened that damned lighter in Dakar?"

"Worry can blind a man," Mattinger said.

"I was stupid!" Grunwald hit his forehead with the palm of his hand. "Stupid!"

"Perhaps you were very tired," suggested Mattinger.

"I was sick as a dog. I played an old-time trick that's covered in corns." Grunwald breathed heavily, and Mattinger waited. "Some trick," Grunwald continued. "After the tornado hit me in Dakar, and with this guy Petersen tailing me, I stuffed the lighter up my ass."

Mattinger frowned and looked at the lighter with distaste. "How unpleasant."

"It was also painful." Anger cut into Grunwald's tiredness. "That son of a bitch Randall!"

"He's willing to pay for your discomfort, Mr. Grunwald. It's said that a good profit is a great comforter."

"If this story gets around—"

"It's safe with me, Mr. Grunwald."

"Then don't tell Randall."

"You have my word."

"Okay, then." Grunwald did a rapid mental calculation, adding travel expenses plus the amount he had spent in the contraceptive-vending machine to one and a half million dollars.

Mattinger picked up his pen and wrote the figures on the check. "There," he said. "Mission completed—as John Wayne said."

"It was some other guy." Grunwald took the check from Mattinger's hand and heaved himself to his feet. "Maybe one day I'll see the joke."

"I'm sure you will. Mr. Randall said that you had a great sense of humor."

Grunwald was on his way out when Mattinger said, "Your lighter, Mr. Grunwald."

Grunwald turned. Mattinger had not touched the lighter. It rested on the desk, lying on its side, the paste diamonds glittering. "Give it to Randall and tell him he knows where he can put it."

Grunwald called at his bank and deposited Randall's check, then hailed a cab and directed it to his home in Queens. As he sat back in the cab he took out Petersen's lighter and unscrewed the end, then opened his hand luggage and recovered one of the fuel capsules Randall had given him. Biting off the sealed nipple end, he squirted fuel into the lint padding, then replaced the bottom cap. He waited until the fuel had seeped through to the wick, then struck flame and lighted his cigar.

Grunwald's sense of humor slowly returned; he had to be grateful for small mercies. Suppose he'd picked out the stones in that hotel room in Dakar—how would he have felt? That was easy to answer. He'd have felt a bigger bum than Petersen gloating over the cheap paste he'd stolen on the flight to New York. Maybe Petersen alias Chuck Anderson's shoulders were broad enough to carry the burden of disappointment and the knowledge that he'd been conned, to say nothing of a delayed-action hangover.

Grunwald began to grin, and the grin spread to a chuckle. Somewhere in New York Tony Klein would have taken the lighter from Petersen's hand, tipped out the Brilliant and the Antwerp Rose and— Grunwald wondered how long it would take Klein and Petersen to realize what a couple of bums they'd been.

CHAPTER 23.

THE afterglow of sunset was fading as Mackenzie, Appleby, and Blohm drank sundowners under the corrugated iron veranda of the work hut. From where they sat they could see the spread of the site and the result of weeks of intense activity.

Appleby refilled Mackenzie's glass and said, "You've done us proud, Mac."

Mackenzie nodded. "I advised. You consented. Easy."

Reluctantly Blohm said, "I would like to add my appreciation to that of Arthur's, Mackenzie."

"Praise indeed." Mackenzie grinned. *"Danke schön, Herr Doktor.* There's a long way to go yet, but things seem to have changed for the better."

It was true. What had been an untidy sprawl of huts surrounded by a wire fence and nothing more than a token security gesture was now an orderly, regimented pattern of prefabricated huts, segregated into three areas on the eastern perimeter; workers' quarters, security, and Appleby's HQ.

Magasi's section comprised four long huts arranged to form a quadrangle in which was set a pole rising fifty feet and bearing the flag of Angwana. As a parade ground, the quadrangle's seventy-feet-square area was adequate for Magasi's twenty security guards; it was also private—ideal as a punishment area. Mackenzie called it "Terror Square."

The site was virtually a prison. The fence surrounding the Appleby was now twenty feet high and topped with barbed wire. There were only two gates: one providing entry and exit for the trucks and tankers that came daily, and another giving access to that part of the cliff whose descent led to the tunnel. By day the perimeter of the fenced enclosure was guarded by Magasi's men armed with M-16 automatic weapons and nightsticks.

177

Workers numbered a hundred: of these, twenty were experienced miners brought from the Kundi Mine, and the rest were hard-working beasts of burden and treated as such by Magasi.

Appleby's headquarters consisted of four huts, a large one for his and Blohm's equipment, and three smaller ones bearing metal plaques on which names had been stamped—*Appleby, Blohm, Mackenzie*—huts for sleeping or for times of privacy.

Fifty yards away work had begun on a separating and sorting shed. When finished, it would rise to a height of fifty feet and extend to a length of one hundred feet. A few more weeks would see the structure finished and ready to house equipment stripped from the Kundi and new plant now on its way from the coast.

Water had been the greatest problem. Daily, tankers brought water to the Appleby for both human and industrial consumption. A further three weeks would see the last length of pipe laid to connect the mine with the river, ninety miles distant.

Beyond the main gate, and two hundred yards away, what had once been a cleared stretch of land had now been smoothed and rolled into a length of hard-packed broken rock and earth: a landing strip. From this strip Magasi flew his Piper Aztec to the capital with recoveries of diamond and associated gemstones—trips that included extra mileage to Freetown after he had registered the estimated weight and value of the recovery at the palace. In Freetown the stones were taken to the trading office for valuation and the price of purchase accredited to the Angwanan government. Magasi also visited Jacob Zuncasi on his own behalf for a small-packet evaluation and payment accredited to an account in a Liberian bank.

There were times when Mackenzie wondered why he stayed, for there was no profit in his stay. Helping Appleby seemed to be an excuse rather than a reason. And Jamie Turner was impatient for him to come to Geneva to finalize their partnership and divide profits. Another two or three weeks at the Appleby, certainly not more. Dear old gentle Arthur would need his support while Blohm took his annual leave in Germany. The thought of Blohm's holiday made Mackenzie angry; it was typical of the calm, everything-in-its-place German to stick to routine and take a holiday—the very word *holiday* stuck in Mackenzie's gullet. He visualized Blohm clad in lederhosen and singing *"Trink, trink, brüderlein, trink"*—and felt a rise of anger. Did Blohm think the mounds of precious diamondiferous rubble were sand castles to be washed away by an uncaring tide while he drank cholly Cherman beer with an equally cholly Cherman *Mutter und Vater*?

There was every reason for leaving Angwana and none that he could see or understand for staying, yet he planned, inspected, and advised as if his living depended upon it. He alternated between annoyance and amusement at the doctors' unworldly attitude to their work; Appleby and Blohm's contracts with Sotho's government, based on an early assessment, were obviously well below, impossibly below, their worth now that they had found the Appleby.

Mackenzie watched the last of the sunset leave the sky, and panned his gaze round the darkened site. He felt an odd contentment resting on the turbulence that had motivated him throughout his years in Africa. It was like oil on troubled water, and he found it disturbing; the time wasn't ripe for taking it easy, earning Blohm's praise, and smugly contemplating the result of his expertise.

Lights were glowing in the windows of the workers' huts and from Magasi's compound. Transistor-radio sound, strangely Western, came faintly over the night air.

"Pop music from another world," Appleby said. "It's at moments like this you feel at home—at peace."

Mackenzie expelled air from his lungs in a noisy explosion. "Speak for yourself, Arthur. Where's the haggis and bagpipes and a crisp night frost? You're talking balls."

"No I'm not, Mac. This is my country, and it's good to feel we've helped it toward a decent independence."

"What about your own independence?" Mackenzie asked. "If I'd done what you've been doing over the years for Angwana, I'd have called for a new arrangement with Sotho. If the mine's yield continues to improve—and it looks damn well like it—you'll be diamond millionaires. You've grown used to feeding off crumbs—time you looked at the state of your own cash box."

"We are under contract," said Blohm. "The terms were, and are, adequate. I can see no reason to alter or break the agreement."

"A laborer's worthy of his hire, but you're both good fools," Mackenzie replied. "Some might say you're morally right. I say you're both damn fools when Angwanans like Sotho and his government, Magasi and his faction, will benefit. They'll be riding around in gold-plated Mercedes while you're scratching around in a beat-up Land-Rover eating out of cans."

"You're jumping the gun, Mac," Appleby said. "Both our contracts run out in a few months—three, to be precise. New contracts will be drawn up—Sotho has already mentioned it. I think the terms will reflect his gratitude."

"Ask for ten percent of the yield and no salary," Mackenzie said. "Or five percent each. You'll be rich men and getting only what you deserve. You could, of course, ask for danger money. A man needs insurance in this neck of the woods."

Blohm looked at Appleby: "Arthur, are you a geologist entirely for the money?"

"You know the answer to that, Ernst."

"Mackenzie does not." Blohm transferred his gaze to Mackenzie. "As a mining engineer, you have my respect, Mackenzie. It would be difficult to find a better man in that field. I have believed that you respect and love your profession. Is that true?"

"I believe in it as a means to an end."

"And that is?"

Mackenzie smiled. "To get what I want. I'm middle-aged with good years ahead of me. I came to this godforsaken continent for one reason —to make money. I don't know if you were born with a silver spoon in your mouth or one that was nickel-plated. When I came to Africa it was with one ambition—to buy a piece of Scotland, a big piece. Point about the spoon is, the one I was born with was made of base metal. No Groves of Academe for me—just the hard way. I had no time for academic standards of morality, and I still haven't. I came to Africa to make money, and I made it. Are you shocked, Blohm?"

"You have only confirmed my opinion of you."

Appleby said, "Stop this, Mac! Why must you paint yourself so black?"

"So that I can't be seen in the dark. On the other hand, it enables me to deal with the Magasis of this world. Both of you treat them as missionaries would. I give as good or bad as I get."

"And look the other way when the Magasis take their pleasure," said Blohm.

"Those two men flogged for hiding a couple of itsy-bitsy diamonds up their rectums, Doctor? That's jungle law, nothing more, and to be expected. Hunt with the hounds and run with the hare. Why does Sotho tolerate Magasi? Why does he allow Magasi all those perquisites? Regular pinching from both this mine and the Kundi, plus the occasional killing, flogging, torture, and you name it, Magasi can have it. Keep the beast happy and you can survive in this jungle. It's the African version of the protection racket."

"One of the men flogged by Magasi died," Blohm said.

Mackenzie's face hardened. "So what are *you* going to do about it, Doctor? Apart from taking your annual holiday in Krautland?"

"You mean 'Germany,' of course, Mackenzie."

"Depends which bit, East or West."

"I do not have to reply to that." Blohm got to his feet. "My father, who fought in the 1914–1918 war, called the Scots 'Ladies from Hell.' He was correct in every detail."

"What did he mean by that?" Mackenzie asked as Blohm left the hut.

"Perhaps he was doubting your masculinity, Mac," Appleby said. "Why do you antagonize him?"

"He antagonizes me."

"You don't give him a chance. You flaunt your cynicism."

"I am what I am," Mackenzie said. "And if he doesn't like what I am, he can ignore the fact that I exist. Perhaps"—Mackenzie thought for a moment—"it may be that he holds up a mirror to show me my faults, and I hit back to kill what I see. I wouldn't say this to anyone but you, Arthur. I've guilts, but I try to keep faith with Mackenzie's law and keep them hidden. End of confession—and forget what I've said. I've nearly finished here. I'll be going soon."

"When, Mac?"

"I don't know. Would you like me to stay while Blohm takes his stupid holiday?"

"I'd prefer it."

"All right, then. The day he gets back, I pack my bags. The pipeline will be finished and working. It's the Western Isles for me, Arthur. It's about time a Mackenzie became laird of all he surveys."

Mackenzie could not sleep. Light from the moon shafted through the small window of the hut, a cold light at variance with the warm humidity of the night. He sat up and rested an elbow on the sill; dim lights were glowing round the perimeter of the camp, and as usual the gates and terrace end of the site were unguarded. He looked at his watch: 2:00.

He was unusually wide awake, as if an undefined presentiment were pressing on his mind, so that he was alert, his senses tingling with an anticipation that was neither pleasant nor fearful but an amalgam of both.

He climbed out of bed and dressed, obeying the force that kept him awake, and habit, which told him to take his miner's helmet off its peg and the satchel containing a cold, sharp chisel and a geologist's hammer. The question "Why?" was strong in his mind, yet he opened the door of his hut, stepped out into the night, and closed the door quietly behind him.

The full moon had begun its descent as he trod softly past Appleby's and Blohm's huts; another two and a half hours and the sun would rise, killing the moon and the stars glittering in the moon-pale night.

He took up a bearing directly toward the cliff gate, as if homing on a signal, and he could see no reason why he should walk in a moonlit landscape unlikely to bring peace of mind and inducement to sleep.

Once he stopped on the decision to turn back; it was stupid, irrational, to abandon rest, even if sleep escaped him; better to have taken a large tot of whisky. The decision was weak; he moved on again, mistrusting the compulsion but unable to resist it.

The steel rungs of the ladder running down the terraced cliff gleamed like black ice in the moonlight, and Mackenzie made his way down them, reluctant still to follow the illogical beckoning from bed to tunnel.

For a while he stood looking at the dark mouth of the tunnel, then he put on his helmet and switched on the headlamp. He moved into the tunnel, head bent to clear the roof. After seventy-five feet he straightened his back; enlargement of the tunnel to ten feet by ten had been wise—the pair of drills now working had extended the tunnel by forty feet. The skip rails running through the tunnel had speeded up operations, too; the wheeled skip, loaded with precious rubble, winched out, and manually pushed back, had cut out hours of sweated and wasted labor.

Mackenzie reached the end of the tunnel, and the beam from the headlamp struck the craggy wall that marked the end of the day's work. He moved his head from side to side and then up so that the light touched the point where the roof met the wall. He panned his gaze slowly downward; three feet down from the roof a bright sparkle, like a tiny star, winked at him, and Mackenzie moved closer, the helmet lamp concentrating its beam on the sparkle of light.

"Twinkle, twinkle, little star," Mackenzie said. "I know damn well what you are."

He unslung the satchel and took out the chisel and hammer. At first he gently probed at the melaphyre surrounding the crystal; then, as the chisel was resisted, he began to tap it with the hammer, aware of a growing excitement. The diamond was extending its size. From what it had first been, a tiny sparkle of bright prismatic light, it was now projecting half an inch from its bed of melaphyre, with each of its facets running out at acute angles and into the rock.

Mackenzie resumed his probe, attacking the melaphyre six inches away from the crystal and describing a circular cut with the diamond as a radial center, the sharp taps from the hammer and chisel echoing down the tunnel.

And then he had to stop as the magnitude of the imbedded crystal struck his incredulous mind. Within the twelve-inch diameter of the area he had probed, the outer limits of the crystal were now revealed. Three inches projected the rock amalgam; three inches of an irregular stone. Mackenzie touched the diamond and brushed away fragments of melaphyre, then tried to move it from its bed. There was no movement, and Mackenzie felt a weakness in his stomach that spread to his legs, so that he had to lean against the rough wall of the tunnel, his eyes fixed on the diamond projecting from the rock.

The trembling in his legs ceased. Now he was impatient, and his hammering less careful, the chisel biting into the crystal's bed, eating its way into the last of the holding rock.

Arthur Appleby had come out of sleep at the sound of footsteps quietly padding the gravel path outside his hut. He had vaguely wondered who would be walking in the night, and then slipped back into shallow sleep. One hour later he came fully awake, remembering the sound, and he climbed out of bed and opened the door of the hut.

The moon was yellowing as it set. Somewhere in the darkness an insect was sending out a warning or a mating message, and Appleby listened, trying to identify the species. It was neither locust nor cicada, and night birds were nonexistent in the region. The sound was faint and distant, undiverted by breezes, for the night was still. Now and then the clicking or tapping ceased for a few minutes—as if the bird or insect were resting before resuming its call.

Unable to identify the source, Appleby frowned, then dressed quickly and left the hut, walking quietly and slowly toward the sound. Clear of the encampment, the sound was louder but still distant, its direction apparent; it came from the terraced cliff or near it.

Reaching the edge of the cliff, he looked down at its acutely sloped angle and recognized the sound. It was one he had known most of his adult life: hammer on chisel.

Magasi, he thought. Magasi moonlighting and doing his own prospecting?

Appleby descended the steel ladder, his desert boots making no sound on the metal rungs.

Mackenzie had pried the diamond out of its bed, and he held it in hands that trembled. "Dear God," he said aloud. "Oh, my dear God!" The crystal was small, easily contained in the palm of his hand, yet it was massive in its potential—its cold, glittering potential.

His mind and senses were blocked to everything but the irregular crystal. It was as if he had given birth to the stone, which had taken millions of years in its gestation and delivery.

He turned the diamond over and over in his hands, the beam from his helmet lamp touching off fire from the crystal, sharp prismatic lances hitting the retinas of his eyes, so that he blinked against their brilliance.

Carbon. A lump of pure carbon, that's all it is, Mackenzie thought; yet worth more than anything he could imagine. It was smaller than the Cullinan, but now, seventy-three years since Wells happened on that stone quite by chance, the crystal Mackenzie held in his hands seemed beyond price. It rendered the Cullinan's value a pittance.

He turned it over in his hands, its internal fire flashing through its grained, greasy surfaces. Was it flawless? How many carats? Carbon. A lump of pure carbon that rested in his slightly cupped hand, its length measured by the distance between the base of his palm and the middle of his third finger. And the diameter? He reckoned it to be three inches at its widest point.

As he stared at it, it assumed the volume and weight of a massive boulder, a monolith; the very magnitude of its value made his hand seem like the hand of a gigantic god.

A pulse thumped in his temples. How long had he been in the tunnel? In a strange sense he had been chipping at the diamond's bedrock from the moment he had stepped onto African soil. The moment now was the undefined, unknown reason why he had suffered life in a despised continent for so many years. All had led to this—this incredible wonder lying in the palm of his hand.

Rational thought crept slowly back. He was behaving like a diamond romantic. Carbon, that's all it is. Coal is carbon—vegetable matter made solid by pressure. Diamond is pure carbon, spewed up out of volcanic fire under enormous pressure. That's all, yet he was holding a crystal of unbelievable value. He examined it closely; frosting gave way to characteristic greasy graining. It was impossible to see any discoloration in the light from his helmet lamp. Perhaps it was flawed with an ugly heart. Even so, it was still unique and as unprecedented as the intuition that had brought him out of the hut and into the tunnel. A secret process born of ambition and dedication had moved his feet through the night and down the steel ladder.

His ears picked up a distant sound, and he jerked his head around. Rockfall? Some insect, with no desire for diamond, eating a fellow insect? Mackenzie grinned. Let dog eat bloody dog, this night was his, the diamond was his.

The sound, its remembrance, was lost as he looked again at the crystal. A few more moments savoring his destiny mark. He was alone with one of the greatest prizes to be found on earth, and he had to act as if he'd found a common mineral, which he would slip into his pocket, then casually walk away out of the tunnel and back to his hut as if nothing out of the ordinary had happened. He was cool, calm, and collected Arnold Mackenzie, the great man of Komalu, granite-hard and reliable. It was difficult to leave the tunnel, the birth scene of the discovery. He looked again at the diamond, turning this way and that, seeing its internal fire flashing through the clear, greasy planes, a fire that glowed mistily through the frosted surfaces. It was both incredible and ridiculous. It was worth many millions of dollars, yet he could transform it into worthless graphite or carbon-dioxide gas simply by exposing it to heat until it glowed red-hot.

It was time to leave. Mackenzie felt tension leaving his body, and the trembling in his stomach and legs had ceased. And then he heard Appleby's quiet voice behind him.

"What have you found, Mac?"

Instinctively Mackenzie's hand closed around the diamond, and he held it close to his chest as if to protect it.

BOOK TWO

CHAPTER 24.

"Two-thousand-point-twenty-five carats," Blohm said. "The second largest diamond yet to be discovered."

The crystal rested on the finely balanced scales, its greasy, glittering surface reflecting light from the anglepoise lamp on Blohm's table.

"I would grade it A-Two, pure and unspotted on superficial analysis," he went on. "It is irregular in shape, with clear cleavage indications. What shall we call it?"

"I can think of a damn good name," Mackenzie said. Sitting at the end of Blohm's worktable watching Appleby and Blohm's careful study of the diamond, he had wondered what he would have done if Appleby, cat-quiet and suspicious, had not come to the tunnel. Blohm's question touched something deep inside Mackenzie. The crystal had only one name and that was the Mackenzie; it was his by right of discovery. By accident, or divine providence, he had found the sum total of all that he had worked for in a continent he hated. In two short, dark hours he had found in one crystal the worth of twenty-one years of hard work. And now it was out of his hands, eventually to be squandered by a country incapable of standing on its own feet.

"How much do you suppose it's worth, Mac?" Appleby asked.

"The Lesotho was the last big one found," Mackenzie said. "Just over six hundred carats and worth millions. Two thousand carats? This lump has a starting price of twenty-four million quid."

"Enough to build Sotho's hospital," said Appleby.

Mackenzie grinned. "Maybe the little feller should hold an auction with bids starting at twenty-four million. Let De Beers, the CDM, Arabs loaded with extortionist oil money, consortiums, and syndicates fight their way up to what? Forty-eight, fifty million? That's what I call real money." Mackenzie glanced at Blohm. "Beautiful money, Arthur, beautiful! In Sotho's place, I'd go it alone and get the stone cut into a collec-

189

tion the world hasn't seen since the Cullinan was cleaved. He'd get a damn sight more that way."

"That's good sense, Mac," Appleby said. "What do you think, Ernst?"

Blohm shrugged indifference. "De Beers, the CDM, Arabs, diamond dealers—I could not care less. Just to see and handle such a crystal is enough for me. I am only concerned that it is taken to the president as soon as possible—and *safely* given to him."

"He's in Paris," said Mackenzie. "Raising the wind. Economic aid. Help me, O Western Powers, to spend money as if there are no tomorrows, or I'll ask the Russians."

"Don't start that again, Mac!" Appleby said sharply.

"I didn't start it. The whole damn continent's been at it for years." Mackenzie sighed noisily. "So what's the next move, Arthur?"

"I'll speak to Sotho by telephone—from the palace. Otanga will ensure secrecy."

"Be cryptic in your report," Blohm said. "Telephones, like walls, have ears." He fitted extension rings to his Pentax camera. "We must have a complete photographic record. Why not send prints to the president after you have telephoned him?"

"There's no scheduled flight leaving Angwana for three days," Mackenzie said. "Wouldn't advise using an Angwanan DC-9 just to get a package to Sotho. Magasi's sticky fingers might twitch. We could use the Aztec—with Magasi's permission, of course. One of us could fly to Freetown or Monrovia. There's daily flights to Paris from both cities."

"I don't want to leave Angwana," said Appleby. "I detest both Freetown and Monrovia. Ernst?"

Blohm shook his head.

"Will you go, Mac?"

"If Blohm agrees."

Blohm shrugged, then focused the Pentax on the diamond. "The sooner, the better," he said. "I'll have the prints ready this afternoon. If Mr. Mackenzie can get them on a flight to Paris today, the president will have them tomorrow. What will you tell Magasi?"

"I don't have to tell him anything," Mackenzie said. "In any case, he'll want to get rid of his latest diamond filch in Freetown."

Blohm snapped an exposure and said, "The stone must be put in a safe place. Somewhere known only to one of us. Arthur, you should be that one." He glanced at Mackenzie. "That is, if Mr. Mackenzie agrees."

"Can't you manage 'Mac,' *Doctor* Ernst Blohm?" Mackenzie said irritably. "Put it somewhere safe, Arthur, but don't tell me where it is, it'll put Blohm's mind at rest." He watched Blohm move the anglepoise lamp so that the diamond's heart sent back the light. "My God!" he said. "Now I know what diamond romantics mean by *fire*."

The Aztec was eating up the miles to Freetown. Magasi, at the controls, said, "Why are you going to Freetown, Mackenzie?"

"I'm sending a package to Sotho in Paris."

"What is in the package?"

"Just a routine report on the mine's progress."

"It could have waited on the president's return."

"Appleby thought otherwise," Mackenzie said. "Production's on the increase, despite stealing and primitive equipment. We thought an optimistic report might cheer Sotho up a bit."

"I could have sent a radio message from the mine or from the capital."

"Could have, but I thought it high time we had a trip to Vulture City. It doesn't do to stockpile, Magasi. You've quite a packet, by my estimation."

"Of little value, Mackenzie."

"I bet."

"I would like to examine the contents of the package."

"They're confidential from Appleby to Sotho. That's one bit of protocol I wouldn't advise breaking, unless you're prepared to risk your future."

"How can it affect my future, Mackenzie?"

"Just wait and see. I take it you'll spend the night with your lady friend—after visiting Zuncasi?"

"It is on the playing cards."

"Just 'cards,' Magasi. Leave out the 'playing.'"

"The package could have been sent by diplomatic bag," Magasi said. "I can insist on that, Mackenzie."

"I wouldn't if I were you."

"Why not?"

"As I said, it might affect your future."

Magasi frowned suspicion. "If you and Appleby are hiding something from me, Mackenzie—"

"Then it's for your own good—and mine. You believe that, Magasi."

Magasi drummed his fingertips on the yoked control column and stared through the Aztec's window to the horizon. Eventually he said, "I have come to trust you, Mackenzie. Send the package."

"Wise," Mackenzie said. "Very wise."

* * *

The flight from Freetown to Paris was scheduled for takeoff at 1600 hours. The Aztec landed at 1550, too late for the package's consignment. Magasi's rank-pulling was treated with contempt by the airport officials, his request for a flight delay rejected.

On their way into Freetown Mackenzie said, "You see, Magasi? Outside Angwana you're a nobody. What you could have done was to hold out a handful of dash. You *might* have got the flight held up."

"Why should I pay for what is my right, Mackenzie?"

"In Freetown?" Mackenzie grinned. "It's even worse in Liberia. Stop boiling; I'll get the package on tomorrow's flight—there's one at midday. The delay means you can spend a little more time wallowing in Freetown's fleshpots."

In his room at Queen's Hotel, Mackenzie opened the envelope, read Appleby's enthusiastic letter, then studied the photographs. Blohm had taken six exposures and made enlarged prints to bring the various shots of the diamond to actual size; on these he had drawn measurements of the stone's facets.

For ten minutes Mackenzie relaxed in a chair giving form to an idea that at first seemed ridiculous; but the more he thought about it, the less outlandish it became. There was nothing to lose, and instinct had served him well over the years.

He put envelope and letter in the drawer of the writing desk and locked it, then left his room and went to the receptions desk where he asked for a large envelope. Slipping the photos in the envelope, he joined Magasi in the hotel bar.

As he sat down at the table Magasi lowered the *Freetown Gazette* he had been reading. "Look at this, Mackenzie," he said. "Look, a big diamond has been found!"

For a moment Mackenzie was shocked, and then his eyes took in the headline: "*Big Diamond Discovery in South Africa.*"

"Over three hundred and fifty carats," Magasi said.

Mackenzie scanned the report. The Premier Mine near Pretoria had disgorged an irregular crystal weighing three hundred and fifty-three carats, with a possible value of over six million pounds sterling.

"Small stuff," Mackenzie said.

"Have you seen bigger?" Magasi asked.

"I saw the Lesotho. Nearly twice the size of this pigmy."

"If such a stone came into my hands—"

"Much whisky, expensive whores, and an early death. You'd blow the lot on trash, Magasi." Mackenzie looked seriously at him. "Would your ambitions stand up to handling all that wealth?"

"Yes."

"Which of the two: running Angwana or hotfooting it into Europe or South America for the good life?"

"I would like to be a citizen of the world, Mackenzie. Have you not said that everything has a price? Both people and possessions?"

"Don't forget status."

"That, too."

"You'd also buy enemies."

"Protection is easy to buy, Mackenzie."

"You should know," Mackenzie said. "Did you get a good price for your little packet?"

"When I look at this"—Magasi tapped the photo of the Premier diamond—"I feel that what I received was laborer's wages—a pittance."

Magasi's face expressed envy and bitterness, and Mackenzie said, "Cheer up. You never know your luck. You might take a walk one day and poke your beating stick into a bit of loose rock and another Cullinan might tumble out."

Magasi made a sound of disgust.

"It's true, you know," Mackenzie said. "Nothing's unique. Somewhere in the world—near the surface or deep underground—there's diamonds bigger than the Cullinan, bigger than anything seen before. Even Appleby's mine might contain such a stone." Mackenzie leaned forward and tapped Magasi's chest: "Remember that, Magasi. Next time you sell your stolen garnets and little fancy diamonds, comfort yourself with the thought that chance might lead you to something really big—and then your troubles would really start."

Mackenzie looked again at the press report. "Bloody fools," he said. "They didn't see the diamond until it reached the grease belt. That means De Beers won't have to pay a reward to the finder."

"Why is that?" asked Magasi.

"General rule. Rewards are paid only if a worker stumbles across an outsize diamond in the diggings."

Magasi was silent for a while, then he said, "Mackenzie? . . . If you should find such a stone in Angwana, what would you do?"

Mackenzie chuckled. "I'd have a quiet word with my friend Magasi —having assured myself that his complicity would be one hundred percent. That's on the premise that everyone and everything has a price— and you agree with that principle."

"Some facts are inescapable," Magasi said. "That you are not an entirely honest man is an inescapable fact."

"That's true," Mackenzie said. "That's very true." He looked at Magasi in silence to a count of five. "So that makes us birds of a feather. You as a black-faced cuckoo shrike and me as a white-faced owl."

Magasi finished his drink and got to his feet. "I have an appointment with my lady friend, Mackenzie—should my business concern you."

"It does," Mackenzie said. "As you well know. Have lots of bastards, Magasi."

Magasi dipped his head in acknowledgment.

Mackenzie watched the tall predatory figure leave the bar, then he got to his feet and went to the window overlooking the street. He saw Magasi emerge, hail a taxi, and climb in. Mackenzie raised his glass and drained it in contemptuous farewell.

He left the hotel and made his way through the humid, dusk-darkened streets, turning into narrow alleys and backtracking until he reached Abdullah Shakah's shop and workrooms.

Abdullah Shakah's speciality was strass, commonly known as paste, a term used to describe glass imitations of precious stones. Shakah's men could put fifty-eight facets on a one-carat piece of lead glass, back the resulting brilliant with material that reflected light, then put it in a setting that exactly matched its true and valuable counterpart whose future lay in a safety-deposit vault.

Shakah, his fat body clad in a soiled light-blue suit, greeted Mackenzie effusively, then led him through a beaded curtain to a room at the end of the shop.

"Do you wish our meeting to be strictly private, Mr. Mackenzie?"

Mackenzie nodded, and Shakah pushed a sliding door across the bead curtain.

"Now we can talk."

Mackenzie took the photographs out of the envelope and handed them to Shakah. "Look at these. I want a copy made."

Shakah looked at the photos in silence, then raised his head and looked at Mackenzie through heavy-lidded eyes. "I have never seen such a diamond."

"There isn't such a stone, and I don't want a cheap job. Crystal quartz is what I want."

Shakah hunched his shoulders. "It will be very expensive."

"Damn the expense. Have you got the quartz?"

"It will be difficult."

"Don't play with me, man! I want it now."

"It will take much time." Shakah studied the photos. "If such a diamond existed—"

"It doesn't," Mackenzie said, "and your interest ends there."

"I have the finest high-density lead glass."

"Quartz—and I'm in a hurry."

Shakah considered the photos and fingered the side of his beaky nose. "In quartz there will be a difference of three in the hardness scale, Mr. Mackenzie—compared with diamond—to say nothing about its specific gravity."

Mackenzie quoted from the reference book in his mind: "Diamond is ten on the Moh scale, and its specific gravity is three-point-five. Quartz, or rock crystal, is seven on the scale, and its specific gravity is two-point-sixty-five."

"Such knowledge!" Shakah stubbed a finger on the photos. "A memento perhaps?"

"Of all I hold dear. At the Komalu we found a ninety-carat irregular; these photos are enlargements of the stone. I'm leaving Africa for good—and yes, it is a memento."

"Three or four days," Shakah said.

"I want it tomorrow morning."

Shakah shook his head. "If you offered ten times the amount I would charge you, it is not possible. Tomorrow? Impossible! Mr. Mackenzie, I am not haggling. It is cold, hard fact. Glass would be a different matter, and the difference between the troy weight of diamond and my finest lead glass would be fractional—and likely to deceive. Even so, using glass, my workers would get no sleep tonight."

"How good would the job be?"

"Better than crystal quartz. Much better. Internal structure, graining, that slight frosting—so much easier to achieve with glass, Mr. Mackenzie."

"All right," Mackenzie said. "Use glass. Make it look like the finest white diamond rough. As if a dishonest Lebanese named Shakah is conning a rich innocent."

"Very unethical." Shakah smiled. "But how easy!"

"You should know," Mackenzie said. "Ten o'clock tomorrow morning."

"No sleep. Much eyestrain."

"That's why you're rich, fat, and greasy, Shakah. How much do you want to keep your mouth shut?"

"It is always shut if danger threatens my clients, but my workers —that is a different matter."

"Just name your price."

Shakah named it. It was high, but Mackenzie had no choice. "Do a good job, guarantee closed mouths, and I'll add a bonus. Do an indifferent job and you won't get a penny. One other thing—" Mackenzie paused "—I want a packet of your best paste—various cuts in amethyst, ruby, sapphire, and one or two diamonds. Keep 'em small and under a carat. If ever you're asked why I called on you, give them a list. Understood?"

"No, I do not understand." Shakah pressed a hand to his heart. "But I swear on my heart and the name of Allah that I will tell only of the little stones. You will bring cash, Mr. Mackenzie?"

"Yes."

"Then will that be all?"

Mackenzie looked at the photos, translating the images into the shape and feel of the diamond that should be called the Mackenzie. It certainly was not all, for the remainder was unknown to him; his action had stemmed from an instinct that was as unformed as a foetus accidentally conceived whose growth had however to be encouraged despite an unresolved future.

"That'll be all for the moment," he said.

Mackenzie left Shakah and walked through the dark, familiar streets seeing nothing he wanted and hating what he saw. He had, at least, a hunger for food and made his way to the hotel and ordered a meal. Halfway through dinner Bernard Manston appeared and sat down at Mackenzie's table.

"Mind if I join you, Mac?" Manston asked.

"It's usual to remain standing until permission is given."

"Old friends don't stand on ceremony."

Mackenzie indicated the half-empty bottle of wine. "Help yourself. It's vintage, so don't drink it like beer."

"Thanks." Manston filled a glass, tasted it, and nodded appreciatively. "Very nice. . . . See you've brought Magasi into town."

"He brought me. Dispatches to Sotho in Paris."

"Plus his usual?"

Mackenzie smiled. "He's under diplomatic privilege. Anyway, you know damn well he isn't peddling Sierra Leone stuff."

"True, true. Trouble is, Mac, a bit of his burnt cork rubs off on anyone seen with him. Know what I mean?"

"It washes off," said Mackenzie. "Know what I mean? For the record, Manston, I'm President Sotho's adviser on mining techniques in Angwana and honored guest of his government. Magasi is a necessary evil at the moment."

Manston sipped wine. "Very impressive. How's production in Angwana?"

"Up to scratch. Improved since I arrived on the scene. The CSO trading office here in Freetown will give you details, since it takes the whole of Angwana's production."

"What about a CSO presence in Angwana?"

"I thought you were an IDSO man, not a space-buyer for the CSO."

"I believe in keeping things in the family."

Mackenzie filled his own glass, then topped up Manston's.

"I wanted to have a word with you about a man from the Komalu," Manston said. "A chap named Partridge. He died in Aracaju. Worked at the mine when you were there. Can you tell me anything about him?"

"Not much. He was a sorter, as far as I remember. Pushed off—on leave, I suppose."

"Where—South America?"

"If he died in Aracaju, that's a pretty safe bet."

"Worrying, though."

"I don't see why. Nobody's immortal."

"An acquaintance of yours took a trip to Aracaju round about the same time. An American—name of Turner."

Mackenzie nodded. "I've met him. He's with Gem International."

"Not anymore," Manston said. "He upped and left. Now based in Geneva."

"Nice place, Geneva. Where's all this leading, Manston?"

"Well—" Manston rested his arms on the table. "It's like this, Mac —a set of odd circumstances with diamonds in the middle worries me. One of your miners, Juan Mandragez, Brazilian, gets killed and his body's shipped off to Aracaju. A day later a Komalu sorter, Partridge, is found dead in the same place. On top of that, your Mr. Turner, citizen of the United States, visits the same place at the same time." Manston tapped his head. "It hits me here—where I think."

"Then don't tap too hard. Partridge went walkabout as far as I'm concerned. Mandragez was killed in a tunnel collapse. And Turner? It's his job to go where precious gems are found and sold—illicit or otherwise. You know damn well fifty million dollars' worth escape from Sierra Leone every year."

"Painfully true," Manston said. "Well, Mac, thanks for the wine. When are you off to Scotland, the Land of the Brave?"

"Soon."

"That could mean tomorrow or weeks hence."

"Make it weeks."

Manston got up from the table. "Keep in touch, Mac. We've just had a friendly chat, right?"

"If you say so. About keeping in touch, Manston—I'll leave that to you."

"Fair enough. Travel hopefully, Mac, even if you don't arrive at your destination."

Mackenzie was still at table long after Manston had left. The warning he had been given was loud and clear; Manston was on to something, and he wanted Mackenzie to know that he intended hunting it down. But all the tracks were covered. Mandragez and Partridge were silenced forever, and Jamie was as safe as houses—he had too much to lose. The last danger of all was personal and involved no one but himself; the final danger would be focused on Magasi if the nebulous plan he had in mind evolved into positive shape.

There was no way Manston could expose the Komalu caper, no way at all, and Mackenzie ordered a second brandy, the irritation caused by Manston's appearance gone. There was no weak link in the chain of events from the Komalu disaster to the deposit of the diamond haul in the Geneva bank.

Mackenzie finished his brandy and left the dining room. He was tired and needed the sleep he knew would come easily to him.

Fifteen minutes after entering his room he was asleep, and no nightmares or images troubled his oblivion; not even the face of Dr. Franz Rikel in Lausanne, two hours forward in time from Freetown, facing up to self-diagnosis and the revelation that he was suffering from a guilty Roman Catholic conscience.

Ilbrahim Otanga's office was small and dark, and Appleby sat waiting for the telephone to ring. The only window to the room was set so high that it touched the ceiling. More like a cell, Appleby thought, and, like Otanga himself, shorn of luxury and decoration, demanding nothing but the bare essentials. If there were more Africans like Otanga, Appleby thought, there would be no substance to Mackenzie's assessment of Africa's future. It was hard indeed to sustain a liberal attitude to the abuses of power that certainly existed among the emergent nations; "time will tell" was a useful umbrella under which to shield one's hopes for a black continent to achieve dignity and respect.

Appleby looked at his watch; twenty-five minutes had passed since he had booked his call to Paris and the president. How guarded should he be when he spoke to Sotho? How would he reply to the president's questions?

There was virtue in being open and aboveboard. Mackenzie and others would call it naive, but Appleby was a geologist and gemmologist, not a politician. Surely political maneuvering could be left to those whose job it was?

Appleby made up his mind. He would tell Sotho the unvarnished and uncryptic truth, and to blazes with political, economic, and security cover-ups and cautionary measures.

The telephone buzzed its low tone, and Appleby snatched up the receiver. Otanga's voice came over the line: "Dr. Appleby—here is the president."

"Thank you, Ilbrahim."

Sotho's voice came over the line: "How good to hear from you, Doctor."

"Do things go well, Mr. President?"

"Moderately, moderately. . . . Doctor, this call—I am to take it that it has some importance?"

"It's difficult to assess," Appleby said. "I thought you should know that we've found—Mackenzie found something remarkable."

"Oh?"

"I should be guarded in what I have to tell you. I find it difficult."

"Then drop your guard. I take it you have asked Ilbrahim for a clear line—as far as it is possible?"

"Yes, of course."

"So tell me your news."

"The second largest diamond ever discovered." Appleby's reserve broke down. "It sounds small—four inches in length—but it's massive! Over two thousand carats and pure! There's so much to be done—"

"Wait!" Sotho's voice was sharp and imperative. "Wait, Doctor, let me think. . . ."

Appleby waited for thirty seconds, then Sotho's voice came over the line: "Doctor? . . . Do nothing. The diamond is in a safe place?"

"Known only to me."

"Who else knows about the discovery?"

"Mackenzie and Blohm. No one else."

"I see. . . . Two thousand carats? That is a lot, Doctor, and worth a great deal. Have you assessed its value?"

"It has a basic value of twenty-four million pounds. Its eventual value—many more times that amount."

"That is good news."

"When will you return?"

"In three or four days, Doctor. I cannot leave this conference. The Castro faction is strong here in Paris, and some of us are struggling to keep the scales balanced. How shall we call the diamond?"

"The Star of Angwana."

"A good name."

"Mr. President, Arnold Mackenzie is in Freetown and has photographs of the diamond. He's sending them to you in Paris on the first flight to France out of Sierra Leone. They should be in your hands within twenty-four hours. If I stay here at the palace, will you phone me when you have seen them?"

"Of course. Do you advise me to show them to anyone?"

"I would say not at this moment, Mr. President. There's much to be discussed, and the diamond is safe while few of us know."

"Does Colonel Magasi know?"

"No."

"Good. I will look at the photographs and hide them away from other eyes. How was it discovered, Doctor?"

"Mackenzie went to the tunnel, obeying an instinct he said, and found it where the drillers had finished their day's work."

"Mackenzie is a good friend, Doctor. Angwana must honor him. When he returns from Sierra Leone, please give him my thanks and best wishes. Tell him I look forward to shaking him by the hand. . . . Your news will give great power to my voice, Doctor; I shall speak with greater confidence. . . ."

The cable from the telephone ran along the baseboard of the floor and disappeared down to an underground network of similar cables; here the line being used by Appleby had been tapped by a connection that snaked away to join a cable leading to a locked, windowless room in which a tape recorder slowly turned its reels. On receiving disconnection sound, the recorder switched itself off and waited for the next call, when it would again open its ears and memory to every sound heard on Otanga's telephone.

In Shakah's back room the paste diamond glittered under a bright spotlight. The slight frosting on two of the facets was exactly right and contrasted with the icy, grained brilliance of the clear facets.

Mackenzie compared the replica with the photographs and said again, "Bloody marvellous!"

"You will notice, Mr. Mackenzie, how clean the photographs are. That is because I made copies of the originals. Here—" Shakah opened a drawer in his desk and took out the copies. "I thought it wise, since you omitted to mention it, to keep them clean and unsullied by my workers' hands."

Mackenzie took the copies. "I'd like the negs, too."

"They are with the copies." Head slightly cocked, Shakah added, "One more observant than myself would suspect that the diamond in the photographs is real, Mr. Mackenzie, and of the same size as the photographs."

"It isn't possible," Mackenzie said. "What about the assorted paste?"

Shakah unfolded a white paper packet and spilled out twenty variously cut stones. Mackenzie gave them a brief glance: "They'll do," he said.

Shakah was offended. "I would appreciate it if you examined them more closely, Mr. Mackenzie. My finest work *is* to be looked at."

"I'm looking at it now," Mackenzie said, and turned the diamond replica in his hand, so that a reflection of the spot sent back a dazzling star of light. "It's almost better than the real thing—bigger and better." He took out his wallet and drew out a wad of banknotes. "I've added a ten-percent bonus, Shakah; your workers have earned it. Just don't slip their cut into your pocket."

"If I did, their silence could not be bought." Shakah reached out and took the notes. "You will need a receipt for the assorted imitation gems, Mr. Mackenzie?"

"Yes, but make it out to one Joseph Magasi." Mackenzie opened his wallet and took out five high-denomination banknotes. "Worth a further silence bonus, Shakah?"

Shakah took the money. "What is in a name, Mr. Mackenzie? Mr. Magasi—he is colored?"

"Black as night, tall with a beaky nose set in a thin face."

"I remember him coming to me yesterday."

CHAPTER 25.

MACKENZIE sat in his hut looking at Shakah's glass replica. It was time to start the ball rolling; the question was, Where? He had the means but virtually no method. If he succeeded in switching the fake and the real, time had to be bought, but at whose expense? The false scent had to be strong, a scent so obvious that all noses followed it.

He looked at his watch; Magasi should be flying in soon. After landing at the capital's airport, he had left Magasi to go about Magasi business, and returned to the mine with Appleby in the Land-Rover. He had had four cups of tea to wash away the heat and dust of the miles between the airport and the mine and now wondered how events would shape up in the days to come.

The distant drone of the Aztec's engines came over the still air, and Mackenzie got to his feet and looked out the window, seeing the plane sideslip to lose height, then level out and touch down on the landing strip.

Within minutes of Magasi's climbing out of the Aztec and walking hurriedly to his section, a runner came to Mackenzie with a request for Mackenzie's immediate attendance on Magasi.

"Tell the colonel he may expect me in ten minutes," Mackenzie said.

"Yes, sah."

He timed ten minutes exactly, then strolled to Magasi's hut. Framed in the doorway, he said, "You asked me to call on you, Magasi?"

"I thought it would be better if we spoke in my headquarters."

"About what?"

"Please sit down, Mackenzie. Will you drink?"

"If it's Scotch."

Magasi opened a drawer in the desk and took out a bottle and two glasses.

"You'd get flogged in Saudi Arabia for possessing Scotch," Mackenzie said.

"We are not in Saudi Arabia." Magasi poured whisky into the two glasses and handed one to Mackenzie. "We will drink to our future cooperation, Mackenzie."

"Has it a future?"

"When I tell you what I know, a very great future. If I tell you that I know what you know, does that suggest anything?"

Mackenzie drank from his glass, savoring the bite of the spirit. "Something criminal? Political? Dishonest?" he asked.

"We went to Freetown, Mackenzie, and you sent a package to the president. What was in that package?"

"I told you: progress report on the Appleby."

Magasi smiled. "It was certainly that, Mackenzie. And Appleby spoke to the president from the palace. His call was monitored, and I have listened to the conversation between the two."

"And now you want to know where the diamond is?"

"Is it true?"

"It's true, Magasi. Interested?"

"My interest matches yours, Mackenzie."

"Mine isn't Angwana's."

"That is what I thought."

Mackenzie's glass was half empty, and Magasi made as if to top it up, but Mackenzie stopped the action. "I'll stay with this. So what do you have in mind?"

"Is it true that the stone is worth twenty-four million pounds?"

"Certainly not less."

"All that a man could wish for."

"I know." Mackenzie drank again and put down his glass. "Come out with it, Magasi."

"Very well. Tell me, Mackenzie, if you owned the stone and did not wish to guide it through conventional channels, what would you do?"

"Sit on it for a time. Eventually get it cut, and sell the diamonds piecemeal over a number of years."

"Would not the cutter talk?"

"Silence can be bought. You should know that, Magasi. You can buy it with money or a bullet."

"Yes." Magasi was silent for a space. Eventually he said, "You know where the diamond is?"

Mackenzie shook his head. "We agreed that only Appleby should know."

"Has it left the mining site?"

"I doubt it. Come on, Magasi—you're like a man wanting to pee but resisting a bursting bladder. You want that diamond—or part of it. You think I want it too. Let's agree that's the case, and you're not big enough or knowledgeable enough to handle it, but I am. I can't move without you, and you can't move without me. Am I right?"

Magasi nodded. "That is how I see it."

"And split down the middle?"

"That would be a good arrangement, but since we do not trust each other, there would have to be certain precautions—safety precautions."

"I can't think of any, Magasi."

"If I—" Magasi paused. "It is difficult, Mackenzie—difficult to put into words. . . . If one of us is in possession of the diamond, he is the most untrustworthy?"

"The man with the loot always is."

"But if I cannot move without your help, would it not be reasonable for me to hold the diamond until the time when we could dispose of it?"

Mackenzie exhaled noisily. "You beat the band, Magasi. You're climbing to undreamed-of heights. You're more intelligent than I thought. I imagined you to be the kind of fool who'd pinch a two-thousand-carat diamond and try to flog it in Freetown."

"I am not a fool!" Anger showed in Magasi's face. "I would not have asked you to come and discuss the matter if I was a fool."

"You realize you'd be carrying a big and heavy can?"

"What does that mean?"

"Let's suppose you get out of Angwana with the diamond, you'd be the one in danger, not me. I want no part in that side of the arrangement. Colonel Magasi would be the villain. That's the can, Magasi. That's the can you'd carry for a long time. Three or four years hence, when the stone's cut and unloading is under way and you exist under another name in another country, you might live in comparative peace."

"It would be worth it, Mackenzie. Worth it to you as well. You would have twelve million pounds, and I would have the same amount."

"You know I'd cover my tracks," Mackenzie said. "No matter what you ever said or did, you could never put the finger on me. I'd see to that. I've a long arm, Magasi—longer than the law."

"I understand that. Now tell me if you think it can be done."

Mackenzie chuckled. "Trouble is, we don't know where Appleby's hidden the stone, and you haven't got long. Sotho will return from Paris, and Appleby will carry the stone to the palace in triumph."

"You have a friendship with Dr. Appleby. Prevail on that friendship. Ask him where he has hidden the diamond."

"And link me with its theft? Bad thinking, Magasi, very bad thinking."

Impatiently Magasi got to his feet and went to the window, his hands clasped behind his back. Mackenzie watched the hands clenching and unclenching.

"You could always conduct a search," Mackenzie said. "Frame one or two workers. You're used to faking up a charge and exacting punishment. Appleby has a soft heart. Put on the old security act. Clear the site—me, Appleby, Blohm, and all the workers except those you've put under a firing-squad sentence. I might even give you one or two tips where to look."

Magasi's head jerked round, and he stared at Mackenzie: "You have an idea where it is?"

Mackenzie shrugged. "Guesswork based on a knowledge of Appleby. A gift you'll never have, Colonel. It's called intuition plus observation. I could be wrong, of course. Still, you'd make your search. But you'd better act soon—before Sotho returns. You're the strong man; use muscle and see what happens."

"That is good advice?"

"The best I can offer. If you find it, get out as quickly as you can. If you don't, bad luck, old boy. Whatever happens, you don't shoot the workers. You can't afford to offend Appleby." Mackenzie reached into his tunic pocket and drew out an envelope. "Care to see what the stone looks like?"

Magasi came away from the window. "You knew?" he said. "You came prepared?"

Mackenzie grinned. "You seem to forget that I like diamonds, too. Copy prints of those sent to Sotho. Actual-size pictures. Should be enough for identification."

"Blohm and Appleby, do they know you have these copies?"

"No."

Magasi looked at the prints. "It is as large as this?"

"Same size. If you get away with it, Magasi, it's my bet the world won't believe photographic evidence that the diamond was found. My guess is that Sotho will be accused of faking up the potential wealth of Angwana just to get foreign aid. The diamond's too big to be true. Second largest ever to be discovered. That's your protection. Mine, too, if we ever get that far."

"What of Appleby—will not he be believed?"

"He's a white Angwanan. That's ridiculous to begin with. No, he won't be believed. The only thing you need worry about is getting clear and staying that way. You'll need my help."

"Which you will give?"

"I want half that stone, Magasi. I'll want to know where you are every minute of every day, and you'll want me to know."

"In that, I trust you, Mackenzie."

"Good."

Mackenzie got to his feet. "I'll leave you to organize the search. I suggest dawn. You'll hear from me before then. Think of it as a game of chance, Magasi. You win or lose, that's all. If you lose, well, you can go back to filching. If you win—"

"I will buy the life I want, Mackenzie."

Appleby was alone when Mackenzie entered the work hut. The paraphernalia of geologist and gemmologist littered the tables: Oertling diamond balance, specific gravitator, and a spectroscope mounted on a microscope. As Mackenzie watched, Appleby placed a flask of copper-sulfate solution between the 'scope and the light source. "I've rough-polished a diamond, Mac, just one facet. Want a look at the spectrum? You get a better blue if the light is passed through a copper-sulfate solution."

"No thanks," Mackenzie said. "I'd be dazzled by Appleby science. You'll never get the Mackenzie under that microscope."

"The Star of Angwana, don't you mean, Mac?"

"Mine's a better title. When do we take it to Sotho?"

"As soon as he gets back from Paris. I'll be glad when it's out of my hands."

Mackenzie wandered round the hut, looking idly at the tools of Appleby's profession. A rack of shelves at the back contained rock specimens and bags of smaller rocks. Mackenzie picked up one and shook it, and Appleby said sharply, "Mac, please don't touch them—they're in order!"

"They're just rocks, Arthur, but I see your point. I always put things back where I find them. You know the tricksters with walnut shells—three of 'em, and you have to find which shell the pea's under? Watch this!" He took up two bags, one in each hand, then rapidly passed them to and fro over a third bag.

"Put them down, Mac!"

"All right, all right!" Mackenzie replaced the bags. "Care to see if I've put them back where they belong?"

"No."

"There's no need to get het up," Mackenzie said.

"I'm sorry. I haven't slept very well since you found the diamond. Anxiety, Mac, a great robber of sleep."

"You could always get Magasi to mount guard over it."

"Then I *would* worry."

Mackenzie completed his idle wandering round the hut. He came over to Appleby and straddled a chair: "Why is Blohm so cold and un-moved by the diamond, Arthur? It's as if it's a lump of common, worth-less rock."

"You'll never understand him, Mac. A mineral is a mineral as far as Ernst is concerned. In part I share his attitude."

"I don't. The Mackenzie is worth millions."

"The Star of Angwana," Appleby corrected.

Mackenzie shook his head. "It will always be the Mackenzie. When I'm back in Scotland and read about its future, I'll see a man called Mackenzie chiselling out the stone at the end of a tunnel and hear the voice of Appleby saying, 'What have you found, Mac?' "

"Suppose I hadn't come to the tunnel, Mac?"

"I don't understand."

"Ernst raised the question. I don't agree with him. I mean—I hadn't any doubts."

"About my honesty? I'll satisfy both you and Blohm. I'd have skipped it, Arthur. I'd have put that stone in my pocket, hung around for a few weeks, then out of Africa with the Mackenzie diamond." Mackenzie was smiling as he spoke. "A case of greed overcoming the strict principles of a dishonest Scot, Presbyterian in upbringing."

Appleby smiled in return. "I never know when you're joking, Mac."

"Perhaps you'll never know. Just as I'll never know whether you're an innocent or a canny, brainy geologist."

"I'm both, Mac."

"That's what I thought. By the way, Magasi's on the warpath. Brow black as thunder. I gather he's got an interrogation under way. Some-body must be following his example and pinching stones. He's gathered his bullyboys together for a roundup. Thought I'd warn you. I can smell floggings in the near future."

"One day he'll go too far."

"In Angwana?" Mackenzie made a sound of disgust and got to his feet. " 'They never will be missed, they never will be missed,' if you know the Gilbert and Sullivan song."

"I shall see Magasi," Appleby said.

"I wish you luck. You can't reason with that black bastard when he's in an even blacker mood."

"I can't sit back like you, Mac. Even when I know it's futile, I must object."

"Sure," Mackenzie said. "I know how it is. We keep our different flags flying, that's all. Kick Magasi's arse for me, will you? I'm tired of doing it for myself." Mackenzie looked through the open door. Three hundred yards away Magasi, with four of his men, was marching toward the miners' huts.

"There he goes," Mackenzie said. "I wonder how many of the sheep he'll select for the slaughter."

"None of them. It's time I objected!" Appleby pushed past Mackenzie and strode rapidly toward the huts.

"Thank you, Arthur," Mackenzie murmured. Watching Appleby's receding figure, Mackenzie put his hand into his side tunic pocket and felt the piece of glass Shakah had fashioned into the shape of the Star of Angwana.

Mackenzie turned and looked round the hut. So where had Arthur hidden the diamond? It *had* to be in the hut, yet he could see no logic in the assumption. It could be in Appleby's pocket or in with his personal effects, disguised with the cunning of a top-notch smuggler.

Mackenzie shook his head; that wouldn't be the way of Appleby, the man had no real guile in him. He looked at the workbench and the litter of instruments, at the heaps of minerals broken up for analysis. Where would a man who was highly intelligent, naive, and as straight as a Roman road hide an insignificant but incredibly valuable stone weighing a bare sixteen ounces? Somewhere so obvious that, like a paradox by Chesterton, it could be seen yet remain unnoticed?

You are Appleby, Mackenzie thought; you are basically a simple man, yet you must consider the possibility that predatory habits lurk in the characters of two men, Blohm and Mackenzie—men you like and trust so there's no need to go to great lengths in concealing the stone. Somewhere simple; perhaps obvious; to do otherwise might suggest that you mistrust your two friends.

Hands in pockets, Mackenzie wandered round the hut. Despite differing values, a stone is a stone is a stone, as Blohm might put it. Was there a clue in Appleby's behavior pattern? Equable, trusting Appleby, slow to anger, temper never rising above lukewarm; a calm worrier. *"I haven't slept very well since you found the diamond. . . ."* Neither have I, thought Mackenzie; and when I asked about demonstrating the pea-under-walnut-shells con trick, I heard the anxiety in your voice: *"Put them down, Mac!"* Put what down: bags of rock? Worthless minerals?

Mackenzie moved to the rack of shelves and looked at the bags of rock specimens, trying to remember which three he had handled. Time was running out, and he had to decide quickly; Blohm might enter at any minute or Appleby would return. Loosening the drawstring of one of the bags, he opened the neck and inserted a hand. Nothing there; just gravel-size pieces. He closed the neck of the bag and reached for another, opening its neck and fumbling in its contents. The specimens were bigger, related in size to the diamond, and he turned away from the rack to bring more light to bear on the stones. *Damn!* he'd drawn another blank. He was suddenly aware that his nerves were prickling and that sweat had broken out on his forehead. Another bag, quickly, quickly! Stop acting like a thieving schoolboy pinching sweets from a locker and calm down.

Mackenzie's hand was in the fifth bag when his fingers closed round a stone whose texture and temperature brought a flood of relief to his tense body. He withdrew the stone, glanced at it, nodded, and slipped it into his pocket. Tension left his body like a fast-receding tide, and he closed the neck of the bag and returned it to the shelf. Now, easy, easy. Calmly, casually, walk to the hut entrance and see who's around: Appleby returning, maybe, or Blohm stumping his way to the hut.

Through the open doorway he could see Appleby, some three hundred yards distant, talking to Magasi. There was no sign of Blohm. There had been no need for prickling nerves and sweat after all; he'd been as safe as houses.

Then apprehension and fear swept back like a tidal wave, and it seemed that every pore in his body opened and released a flood of perspiration. To be such a fool! He came away from the doorway, his left hand reaching into his tunic pocket for the Shakah fake. At the rack of shelves he grasped at the last bag he had searched, then halted the action. Which bag was it: this or that? His mind screamed, *Marshal your thoughts into some semblance of rational order!* He had to put the fake into the right bag. Confusion—bloody confusion! Start at the beginning. You looked into this one first, then this—this—and this. It had to be the bag his hand had instinctively gone to on returning to the shelves. He was trembling, and he cursed the mind that had sent panic flooding through his body. It was only when he had placed the glass imitation in the bag, tightened the drawstring, and returned the bag to the shelf that he closed his eyes and exhaled the breath he had held.

He pulled himself upright and tensed his shoulder muscles, then repeated his performance of strolling to the hut entrance where he leaned against the doorjamb and casually looked across the sprawl of the mining site.

Appleby was striding toward the hut, barely twenty yards away. Mackenzie forced a smile to his face and, when Appleby was in hearing distance, said, "Well, Arthur, did you give the bastard the length of your tongue?"

CHAPTER **26.**

W H E N Mackenzie entered his hut and closed the door, sweat was drying on his body and his spine felt cold. He had known fear for the first time in his life—apprehension, he was familiar with, but not fear. Panic had replaced cold deliberation, and he remembered the moment when he realized that his pocket still contained the Shakah fake. He'd lost his head, that logical, unsentimental head that had never left him before.

He poured a large measure of Scotch and drank it slowly, waiting for the alcohol to depress the last vestiges of fear. A long trail lay ahead, a trail that necessitated the buying of time, immediate time, plus the possibility of many more years before the diamond's potential could be realized.

A shadow of doubt crossed his mind. If he had acted on that doubt, he would have returned the diamond to Appleby's work hut and taken away the worthless imitation, but the shadow was thin, wraith-like, and vanished under the hammer blow of an obsessive sense of possession. The diamond was his. *He* had found it, had obeyed a devilish or divine order and pried the stone from its bed. It was the Mackenzie diamond, and to hell with everyone; it was his reward for sweating out so many years of his life on a continent he held in contempt.

Mackenzie drank another large measure of whisky, feeding an anger that seemed to spread to his limbs. His mind raged against the incompetence and innocence of the Appleby Mine, the naive brutality of Magasi, the academic simplicity of Blohm, and the muddled, inept state of Angwana. All of them—Appleby, the mine, Sotho, Angwana—deserved to be hit hard, every damned one!

He reached again for the bottle but checked himself. He pushed the empty glass away from him. Control and ordered thinking—he had nearly lost both. Anger and hate were good companions only when they could be used as controlled accessories.

He went to the door of the hut and opened it. A few yards away lights burned in the work hut. The niggling doubt returned. Suppose Appleby decided on further analysis of the crystal? With Blohm's departure imminent, it was in the cards that the meticulous German would seek further confirmation of the diamond's quality. So what? Mackenzie thought. Boo! Dr. Blohm—how's that for a joke? You see how careful you've got to be with criminals like Scotsmen and Magasis substituting fakes for diamonds.

"I want to tell you where the stone is," Appleby said to Blohm.

"Why?"

"Sharing might lessen the burden of secrecy."

"It would mean nothing to me."

Appleby said, "I dislike secrecy."

"Then weigh that dislike against your feelings toward Magasi," Blohm said. "I seldom agree with Mackenzie, but in this I am at one with him. If Magasi knew about the diamond"—Blohm spread his hands wide—"anything could happen. Magasi would murder every one of us to lay his dirty hands on the stone."

Appleby rose from his chair and went to the rack of shelves. "Please come here, Ernst."

"If you insist."

Appleby loosened the drawstring of a bag on the middle shelf and opened the neck of the bag. "There it is, Ernst, resting with its humble associates, volcanic excreta."

Blohm looked into the bag, and the crystal gleamed back at him. "Interesting," he said. "As interesting as a piece of glass or rock crystal. So now I share your burden, Arthur. One day it will be cleaved, cut, and polished into many times more stones than the Lesotho, and people will say how beautiful they are. Me, I will always remember a bright lump of carbon. Now draw the string and hide it again; Magasi walks as quietly as a cat."

Instinctively Appleby jerked his head and looked behind him.

"You left the door open," Blohm said. " You cannot be too careful."

Appleby closed the bag and said, "Showing you has helped."

"For our eyes only," Blohm replied, then added, "It has struck me suddenly how funny this is. An embryonic mining site with a seemingly very rich future controlled by two academics, a mining engineer—if we are to include Mackenzie—a sadistic Angwanan, simpleminded workers, and . . . the world's second largest diamond. It is incongruous, almost ridiculous. Security measures cannot be trusted, for the head of security is a dishonest, brutal man, and it is left to the two unworldly academics to guard a great treasure. I thank God I see the stone simply as a lump of carbon." Blohm shook his head in amused bewilderment. "Think what the great diamond men of De Beers would say if they knew such a stone was concealed with common minerals in a cloth bag on a shelf in a wooden hut. I find it amusing, Arthur. Strange and amusing."

"You think I should find a better way?"

"No," said Blohm. "Simplicity in this case is the best policy. No one could possibly pierce such naivety, such primitive security. Just one thought—would it not help if you were seen now and then anxiously keeping an eye, a surreptitious eye, on a spot some distance from this hut?"

"That's a thought worthy of Arnold Mackenzie," Appleby said. "I'll do that."

At one hour before dawn Magasi entered Mackenzie's hut. "Mackenzie?" he said quietly. "Mackenzie, wake up!"

Mackenzie stirred and came out of sleep. "What d'you want?"

"Where, Mackenzie? Where should I look?"

"Has the roundup begun?"

"In one hour. You know where the diamond is?"

"It's just a hunch, Magasi, that's all."

"Then tell me."

"Appleby keeps rock specimens in bags on racks in his work hut. Big rocks aren't bagged. My guess is that it's in one of the bags. I may be wrong. That's all I can tell you. Look and ye may find, Magasi."

"If it is there, I will find it, Mackenzie."

"Then what?"

"I have the Aztec ready for flight. After the trial I am reporting back to the capital, you understand. I have told Appleby that I am concerned about the security of this mine. He reasoned with me, but when I showed him the diamonds stolen by three of the workers, he weakened. You were right, Mackenzie, Appleby has a soft heart. I said I would not have them shot if I found no further evidence of theft among those working at the mine—but they would be beaten."

"You're learning fast," Mackenzie said. "You're the biggest crook of the lot and everyone knows it, and they let you get away with it because they've no choice." Mackenzie suddenly reached up and gripped Magasi's arm hard. "But I have that choice—you remember that. Be afraid of me, Magasi."

"We are partners, Mackenzie."

"As long as you walk a straight path of my choosing. Otherwise you haven't a hope."

"I recognize that you are essential. Mackenzie? . . . You were to tell me where to go?"

Mackenzie looked at Magasi's eager face. Across the Atlantic a fine and private place nestled on the coast of Brazil, a place where death was easily contrived and easily concealed. There wasn't a better hiding place for Magasi.

"South America," Mackenzie said. "Brazil. Get to Freetown and fly to Aracaju. That's upcoast from Rio. The Estancia Hotel. Hide up there until you hear from me."

"You'll come to this place?"

Mackenzie nodded. "And then we'll move on, Magasi. We've a long journey together." Accustomed now to the predawn gloom, Mackenzie saw that Magasi was in full battle dress. "You're dressed for the part, Magasi. I hope it's worth it. If you can't find the diamond, what next?"

"Appleby will be taking it to the president. I shall accompany him."

"That might be a better plan than the one you have."

"Which, Mackenzie? Which do you think?"

"This one, Magasi. First come, first served. What have you got to lose?"

"Listen, Mackenzie. At dawn we will come for you. And Appleby and Blohm. You will be held with the others while the search is made. Behave as if you resent my actions."

"Don't worry. I'll make it clear what I think of you."

A workers' hut had been cleared of trestle beds and all other bare comforts. There remained only a long communal table and four chairs ranged along one side. On three of these chairs Mackenzie, Appleby, and Blohm waited for Magasi to appear.

Appleby said, "Magasi is being unusually formal but just as sinister."

By the open door stood two of Magasi's guards, automatic rifles slung from their shoulders.

"He's playing a variation of his usual game," Mackenzie said. "Instead of exacting summary justice—to give it a name—he thinks this makes it all nice and legal and dignified."

They could hear the shuffling and shouted orders outside the hut as guards marshalled the workers into a single-line queue.

Blohm suddenly thumped the table in anger. "It is inconvenient!"

"Magasi *is* an inconvenience," Mackenzie said. "I reckon about one

hour of playacting and we can get breakfast. This is the same as letting
him pinch his packets of stones. Some might call it a small price to pay
for our independence."

"He had no right to haul us from our beds at dawn."

"Unfortunately," Appleby said, "he has every right under Angwanan
law."

"Which is of the jungle," Mackenzie said.

"Where is Magasi?" Blohm asked irritably.

"Dressing up, I imagine." Mackenzie stretched his long legs under
the table, leaned back in his chair, and cradled his hands behind his
head. "Sit back and enjoy the show, Doctor."

"We have sat here for—" Blohm looked at his watch "—for twenty
minutes, and for what?"

"The Magasi fun show," said Mackenzie. "Put on to remind you
what a big man with teeth he is. At least we can enjoy seeing the
bastard in full fancy dress. If I'm any judge of comic operas, he'll wear
every medal he's collected or invented. Should be amusing."

"Obviously you enjoy Roman holidays, Mackenzie."

"A pity this had to happen on the day you start your *German* holiday."

"I shall not go if the men's lives are in danger."

Magasi appeared five minutes later, and Mackenzie had been right.
Magasi wore full-dress uniform and ceremonial sword. He nodded to
the three men and took his seat between Appleby and Mackenzie.

"Thank you, gentlemen," he said. "I have been criticized by all of
you, accused of brutality and unlawful conduct. This is now a formal
court of enquiry, and I am investigating the theft of diamonds by three
of the workers. Punishment will be decided by the unanimous verdict
of those sitting at this table."

"Find 'em guilty first," Mackenzie said.

"They are guilty. Basa and Mhanka will testify that the stones were
found."

"Where?" Appleby asked. "And who are Basa and Mhanka?"

"Basa and Mhanka are two of my men. And where do ignorant
workers hide diamonds, Doctor?"

"The usual place, I suppose."

"Of course."

"I bet your men enjoyed getting them out," Mackenzie said. "What
did they use, Magasi—pneumatic drills?"

"You are offensive, Mackenzie."

Mackenzie smiled.

"You have the stolen stones, Colonel?" Appleby asked.

"Yes." Magasi opened the black wallet he took from his tunic pocket, and brought out a small, drawstring purse. The minute stones spilled out on the table. Mackenzie said, "Big deal, Magasi. How many?"

"Ten."

"They'd rope in a few pennies in Freetown. Why don't you just kick the three men up the arse and peddle the stones yourself? Save time all round."

"If the workers are allowed to steal, where will it end?" Magasi asked. "You will admit that I am right in this."

"Grudgingly," Blohm said. "It appears that only men at the top are allowed to steal."

"Magasi's point is that top men operate on a larger scale, using a different code," Mackenzie said. "It means that the colonel has the right of kings to murder and pillage. You must get your sense of values sorted out, Doctor." He looked toward the door and at the queue of workers. "Do we see the whole damn crew out there, Magasi?"

Magasi shook his head. "Depending on the verdict, they will see the punishment given to the thieves."

"You are prejudging the verdict, Colonel," Appleby said.

"They stole the diamonds. We will decide on the nature of their punishment."

"Like watching you shot at dawn?" Mackenzie said. "That won't be punishment but sheer pleasure."

"You're making it worse, Mac. Can't you hold your tongue?" Appleby's voice was sharp.

"That is good advice, Mackenzie." Magasi looked into Mackenzie's eyes, and Mackenzie saw that Magasi's face showed not resentment but a calm confidence. He's found it, thought Mackenzie. You thieving, stupid pig, you found it. Mackenzie cocked his head and raised his eyebrows in an unspoken question, and Magasi replied with a slight nod of the head.

"All right," Mackenzie said. "I'll hold my tongue but out of deference to you, Arthur, and your finer feelings. Get on with it, Magasi. Bring in the men. We're wasting time and I'm hungry."

Magasi had used a bullhorn to address the workers gathered in a circle round the men to be flogged. Now three of Magasi's guards, armed with eight-thonged lashes, were ready to inflict twenty-five strokes on the men tethered to posts.

Appleby said, "I can't watch this, Magasi."

"You are free to return to your hut. Dr. Blohm and Mackenzie also," Magasi said. "But it would look not good. It would show weakness, Doctor. Not good. They must see that the masters are strong men."

"With a keen sense of justice," Mackenzie said. "Due to your plead-ing, Arthur, the tenderhearted colonel reduced the sentence from fifty lashes to twenty-five. Best you should stay and count every stroke— Magasi's enthusiasm might push it beyond the twenty-five."

Magasi raised a hand, then let it fall, and the flogging began.

Appleby had no stomach for breakfast; black coffee was all he could manage. He watched Mackenzie eat his way through his usual large meal, marvelling at, but at the same time deploring, the man's indifference to the sight of men's backs opened raw and bleeding.

As if reading Appleby's thoughts, Mackenzie said, "I've seen it too often, Arthur. Years ago, my stomach turned. Not anymore. I've seen atrocities in Africa a damn sight worse than men getting twenty-five lashes. I wouldn't stand for it in Britain. Here, in Africa, it's the way of life. I'm case-hardened, Arthur. Where's Blohm?"

"In his hut, getting ready to leave."

"Seems odd going on leave. You'd think after this morning he'd stick around tending to the wounded."

"I can do that, Mac."

"When do you go on leave?"

"Leave?" Appleby shook his head. "I don't. Angwana's my home. Ernst will come back from Germany refreshed. It'll be good to see him again. I'm sorry you don't hit it off together."

"He doesn't like my survival plan." Mackenzie chuckled. "When I go and Blohm's back, you'll live in peace again. After all, you're so damned important to Angwana even your enemies are friends."

"That's a paradox, Mac."

"And a true one."

Work had recommenced at the mine. The jumble of sounds came over the hot breeze—the clankings and thuds and the far-off drill from the tunnel.

"Were those men really innocent?" Appleby asked.

"Search me," Mackenzie said. "And that's an appropriate reply. They protested enough. I wouldn't put it past Magasi to frame them. He's still got the diamonds, remember? You won't see them again. He says he's flying to the capital today to make his report. That's balls. He'll make an appearance and frighten his staff to death, then hop across to Freetown with the diamonds. How's that for a rough guess?"

"Sadly true."

Blohm came into the hut, ignoring Mackenzie's presence. "I have seen to the three men," he said. "I dressed their wounds. Surprisingly, they were less severe than expected. They send their thanks to the white doctor for his intercession on their behalf. How these people suffer!"

Mackenzie said, "Have you packed your bucket and spade, Doctor?"

"Yes." Then, as if he had not replied to Mackenzie's question, Blohm said, "Arthur, I shall not be away more than the three weeks. If I am needed in that time, do not hesitate to call me."

"Enjoy your leave," Appleby said. "Mac is staying until you return."

"That is very considerate of him."

"You'll miss the great diamond presentation, Doctor," Mackenzie said.

"It is only a diamond. Arthur will ensure that President Sotho suitably rewards the finder." Blohm looked at his watch. "The plane will leave in one hour."

Mackenzie got to his feet. "You won't care for your pilot," he said. "Magasi's your driver today. If I were you, I'd insist on a copilot."

"I have borne with Magasi's presence long enough to stand an hour in his company."

"And then it's Germany, Home, and Beauty." Mackenzie held out his hand, and Blohm reluctantly took it. "If I don't see you again, Doctor, I wish you the best. I'm sorry we don't get along."

Blohm tipped his head in acknowledgment. "I am sorry too, Mackenzie."

Watching Mackenzie leave the hut and stride toward his own, Appleby said, "It's just his manner, Ernst. It hides much that we don't see. Even a strong man like Mackenzie has his fears."

Blohm sat down and helped himself to coffee. "Many times I told myself that. It made no difference to my attitude. You could not find a better mining engineer than Mackenzie, but I think a better man could be found."

Mackenzie walked past the guards stationed outside Magasi's door, knocked, and entered.

Magasi smiled at him. "Well, Mackenzie?"

"I wondered how you were suffering the countdown."

"Countdown to what?"

"I take it you found the diamond?"

"It was where you said it would be. Look"—Magasi opened a drawer in his desk and took out the cloth-wrapped stone. "It is everything you said it would be. Shall I unwrap it?"

"No. I've seen it. From now on it's for your eyes only."

"What did you mean by a countdown?"

"Blohm is leaving when you leave. Suppose he asks Appleby for a last look at the fabulous diamond—what then?"

"He will assume that it has been stolen, and I will take charge of the enquiry. My flight to the capital would have to be cancelled. Naturally, no one will be allowed to leave the mine. And then a fruitless search. Mackenzie obviously will not have it, neither will Appleby or Blohm, and I am above suspicion."

"I said you were learning fast, Magasi," Mackenzie said. "You might yet prove to be a useful partner. I want a breakdown of your movements from the moment you take off today."

"I shall report the events of this morning to my department, then fly to Freetown. As soon as it is possible, I shall get to Aracaju and the Estancia. You wish me to report every stage of my journey?"

"Every movement." Mackenzie handed Magasi a slip of paper. "In Freetown you phone this number and speak to a man called Shakah. Tell him to tell Mackenzie that BD has arrived. That's all."

"BD?"

"Initials for Black Diamond. That's you, Magasi. And when you leave Freetown, you give Shakah another message: 'BD flies at ————' —and state the time of departure."

"And when I arrive in South America?"

"You call Shakah to say that BD has arrived."

"Black Diamond," Magasi said, and laughed. "It's a good name, Mackenzie. I like it very much."

"There's something else you might like," Mackenzie said. "It might appeal to the sense of humor you haven't got. Blohm is leaving with you. If Appleby finds that the diamond's missing and so is Blohm—do you get it, Magasi?"

Magasi frowned, then his forehead cleared. "He will be a suspect?"

"Long enough to get Appleby worried—and no one to track down the diamond with you over the hills and far away. Might be worth staying in the capital long enough for Appleby or me to contact you with the news. Make sure you see Blohm on his way to Germany without delay."

"Foolproof," Magasi said. "You have brains, Mackenzie."

"I don't know about foolproof with you carrying the stone."

"I am beginning to enjoy your insults, Mackenzie." Magasi put the diamond back in the drawer. "So. It is all over bar the yelling."

"Shouting," Mackenzie corrected. "Seems to be. I don't want to see you again until I arrive in Aracaju. Understood? You wait for me and keep under cover. No wine, women, or song. If you start wanting either, think of millions of dollars and live like a sexless, teetotal, tone-deaf hermit until I arrive."

"Mackenzie"—Magasi got to his feet, hand extended. "It is customary to shake hands when two men come to an arrangement."

Mackenzie took the hand and gripped it hard. Magasi winced, and Mackenzie said, "Double-cross me, Magasi, and you'll wish you'd never been born. Good luck, old chap."

The Aztec roared down the strip and lifted off to climb steeply before heading for the capital. Appleby and Mackenzie watched it out of sight, then walked back to the huts.

"I'm sorry he's gone," Appleby said, "but after this morning's horror perhaps it's just as well. Three weeks in Germany will soften the memory."

"I get the impression I'm part of the horror too," Mackenzie said. "Did he kiss the Mackenzie Star of Angwana before leaving?"

"No." Appleby smiled. "You just don't know Ernst Blohm."

"When I leave," Mackenzie said, "I'll go to the palace and handle it for the last time. It's mine, really. Pity you came up behind me in the tunnel, Arthur, I'd be far away now." He gripped Appleby's arm. "I'm serious. I would have kept it."

"I know, Mac. I knew all the time. In a way I can understand it— knowing you. Possession's an odd thing. Even I feel a sense of possession and won't like it leaving my hands. If it wasn't for Sotho—" Appleby paused, then shook his head. "No. I'm too frightened to be dishonest. What would I do with it anyway? Worship it in secret—hiding it from eyes other than mine?"

"Many would," Mackenzie said. "Christ! I need a drink, Arthur. Begone dull cares and all that. Your bottle or mine?"

"Yours, Mac. Ernst and I finished my weekly supply before he left."

There had not been a moment since he had made the switch that Mackenzie hadn't expected a panic-stricken Appleby to erupt from the work hut, incoherent with sense of loss. With Magasi and Blohm's departure the day had passed routinely. In the evening he had played cards with Appleby and, a little before midnight, had gone to bed.

When his door was urgently, violently rapped, he came awake instantly and heard Appleby's voice: *Mac! Wake up, Mac! Let me in!*

Mackenzie came out of bed quickly and unlocked the door. "What the blazes, Arthur? It's two-fifteen in the morning"

"The diamond's gone—gone, Mac!"

"Don't talk bloody rot!"

"I tell you it's gone!"

"Gone from where?"

"My hut. I put it in one of the bags of specimens!"

"The ones I mucked about with?"

"Yes—yes!"

"Do you think I've got it?"

"Of course I don't! It's gone, Mac. You've got to help me!"

"You've mislaid it," Mackenzie said. "You got flustered like the amateur you are, and looked in the wrong bags. Damn silly place to put it, anyway."

"What am I to do?"

Mackenzie gripped his arm and steered him into the hut. "You cool down first of all. Wait till I get dressed, then we'll go to the hut and search calmly. Don't be so agitated—it's bound to be there."

Appleby waited. Mackenzie's calm, unflustered manner had softened the edge of his panic, yet he knew that Mackenzie's assurance that the diamond was safe was a temporary placebo, given to calm him down.

"I know it's gone, Mac," he said.

"Shut up, Arthur!"

Then minutes after they had entered Appleby's work hut, Mackenzie said, "We'll have to assume it's gone and that somebody's taken it. Think, man, think! You're sure you didn't move it to another place?"

"I did not move it! Neither did Ernst. Mac, I saw it a few minutes before I left the hut to attend Magasi's mock trial. I don't know why I looked, but I did!"

"What d'you mean, Blohm didn't move it? He didn't know where the damn thing was."

"I showed it to him the night before Magasi roused us from our beds."

"Did he take it out?"

"No, he looked into the bag and said it was as interesting as a lump of glass or rock crystal."

"And when you looked, did you take it out?"

"No. It was there with the samples. There was no mistaking it. I used my torch. It was there."

"You've been a damn fool," Mackenzie said. "Why'd you show it to Blohm?"

"Because I trust him." Appleby covered his face with his hands. "My God! All I wanted was to share the responsibility!"

Mackenzie was silent for a few seconds, then he said, "We'd better put the finger on someone. Since only three of us knew of its existence and only two knew where it was—what's the ipso facto, Arthur?"

"Either Ernst or I have taken it."

"So if you've taken it, it's still at the mine. And Blohm's gone on leave. . . . Coincidence, Arthur? Blohm's indifference is a bit queer."

"Not Ernst."

"Sotho knew, of course," Mackenzie said, "and he could have told Otanga. . . . When you got back from the floggings, was Blohm left alone in here?"

"I don't think so. You and I came back for breakfast while Ernst cared for the men. You remember, he came to the hut and you asked him if he'd packed his bucket and spade."

"Then what?"

"You left. Ernst drank coffee."

"But did you leave the hut?"

"I may have. . . . Yes—I did leave him for a while—I needed the lavatory."

"And you came straight back? Ten minutes or so?"

"I came straight back."

"Magasi could have taken it when we were waiting on him, but he didn't know about the diamond. Did you take it, Arthur? That's a rhetorical question. You could ask me the same. Neither of us must leave, of course. We'd better get Magasi and Blohm back here. Do you want me to phone the palace?"

"Magasi will tear the place apart."

"We'll have to risk it," Mackenzie said. "There's no alternative. Why the hell didn't you get the stone to Otanga in the first place? All this could have been avoided. Damn it, Arthur, I could have taken it to the palace! Were you scared I might run off with it?"

"You did say it was rightfully yours."

"So it damn well is!"

"Ernst will have left for Germany."

"He may be waiting for a flight out of Freetown. Magasi can get him paged if Blohm's still there." Mackenzie looked at Appleby, his lips pursed. "You haven't asked me if I've taken it, Arthur."

"That's because I know you haven't been alone in this hut."

"I'd like you to be sure."

"I am sure. I've been alone here most of the day. The only times I've left it was to eat, to talk to you, and when I went to the lavatory. I know how you feel about the diamond, Mac; if I were not positive you hadn't been here alone, I would suspect you."

"Fair enough. I'll phone Magasi and get the bastard out here."

Magasi had not gone to bed. Waiting on Mackenzie's call, he allowed the telephone to ring three times before picking up the receiver.

"Mackenzie?"

"It's me. Are we on a security line, Magasi?"

"Of course."

"Appleby's discovered the loss of the diamond. Get moving, Magasi. What about Blohm?"

"I made sure he caught the twenty-two-hundred-hours flight to Frankfurt."

"Good. Appleby has agreed that I call you and Blohm back to the mine. I'll tell him you and Blohm will leave at first light. Now get the hell out of Angwana. I want you in South America quicker than the bullet that's going to get you one day can travel the distance between barrel and your black, thieving heart."

Magasi chuckled. "It's good to hear your insults again, Mackenzie."

"We'll wait for you, Magasi—and Blohm. We'll wait and we'll wait until we can wait no longer, and drive that bloody Land-Rover over the worst roads in Africa to the palace. You just disappear—and don't look like Colonel Magasi, understand? A real mufti job."

"Even my mother would not recognize me, Mackenzie."

"Now take your finger out and get!"

"Goodbye, Mackenzie."

When he returned to the hut, Mackenzie said, "Magasi's putting on his battle dress. He and Blohm are taking off at first light. That's what he said, anyway. I told him to treat Blohm with velvet gloves."

"How did Magasi take it?"

"Blew his top. I told him he wasn't informed about the diamond because he's a black, thieving pig of an Angwanan."

"He'll retaliate, Mac. You go too far."

Mackenzie shook his head. "Not me. Magasi'll go too far. If I were a palmist, Arthur, the first thing I'd notice is the short lifeline on the palm of Magasi's hand."

"And now he'll raise cain when he gets here. As from this moment I place little value on our safety."

"Then let's hope he crashes the Aztec on the way here."

"You forget Ernst will be on board."

"I forgot."

One hour later the Aztec took off for Freetown, its wing and tail lights blinking. An airport guard observed the takeoff and later confirmed that Colonel Magasi had been the sole occupant and pilot and had taken a heading due west to Freetown.

CHAPTER 27.

ERNST Blohm arrived at Frankfurt tired and dispirited. He
had imagined that his first sight of the pines near the airport and the
green fields on either side of the autobahn, so different from the arid,
troubled land he had left, would erase the memory of the day of his
leaving Angwana. Instead, the contrast sharpened recall and the cynical face of Mackenzie. The man was entirely materialistic, thought
Blohm, callous and unfeeling. Thank God he'd leave Angwana soon and
allow the Blohm-Appleby partnership to take up its old ways; even the
presence of Magasi would be bearable with the removal of Mackenzie's
enormous shadow.

There was no relief in his homecoming when he found his parents'
house empty of father and mother. Told by a neighbor that both had left
the day before to visit their daughter in Austria, Blohm bathed and
changed, then took a train to Mangfell, a town on the German-Austrian
border. It was nightfall when he arrived at Mangfell; he booked in at
a small hotel, telephoned his sister, and spoke to his father and mother.

The following morning, dressed in casual, tough clothes, he left
Mangfell early to walk the fifty-kilometer distance through mountainous
country to his sister's house, his spirits raised and his sight and lungs
responding to the crisp, clean air and all that he saw stretching out
before him.

The sky was intensely blue and cloudless. He left the main road
and took a track that climbed steadily upward to the hills and mountains.

Angwana was far away, Mackenzie and Magasi an unpleasant
dream; but this—the high mountains, the clear sky, the fine valleys, and
towering peaks—this was reality. As he walked, slowly because muscles
weakened by the hot African sun would take time to strengthen, he
realized that a moment of disenchantment had come when Mackenzie
had discovered the monstrous diamond. The discovery had nothing to

do with science and the abstract that needed definition by the application of scientific methods to establish causation of earthly phenomena; it simply pandered to the world's love of material gain—the purchase of luxury and better means to kill enemies, actual or real.

Blohm paused for a moment and looked out across the terrain of valleys, mountains, dark-green forests, and the great bowl of cerulean-blue sky. This is the true value, he thought. There is nothing here taken from the earth that is not put back. No gold, no uranium, no diamonds, no coal or oil. This is forever, not the diamonds round a rich woman's neck. And then, because his lost sense of humor had suddenly returned, he added, or in a belly dancer's navel.

Sotho, elbows on his desk and thumbs propping up his chin, pressed his hands together as if in prayer.

"We have neither Magasi, Blohm, nor the faintest idea where either of them can be. As Mr. Mackenzie has said, we must consider one, or both of them, as suspects."

"Ernst Blohm would never steal," Appleby said.

"I agree that it is unlikely," Sotho said. "But we must take the facts as they present themselves. We know that Dr. Blohm is in Germany, and we will find him. Of Magasi, there is no trace. So what course of action is open to us? Ilbrahim, where do we go from here?"

"The return of Magasi and Dr. Blohm must have top priority," Otanga said. "Finding the doctor should not be difficult, for we know that he flew from Freetown to Frankfurt. But Magasi—" Otanga paused. "After landing at Freetown, he disappeared. The aircraft he flew awaits collection at the airport. That is what he told the airport's traffic control. That was four days ago, and there is no Magasi."

Sotho looked up at Mackenzie. "Mr. Mackenzie, you are a very practical man. I would value your advice. What should we do?"

"As I see it," Mackenzie said, "it's not yet a case for international police involvement and might never be, since there's no proof the diamond existed. Just photographs and the word of three men." He shook his head. "So it's no police action, but it is a job for the diamond men— the International Diamond Security Organization. I know a man in Freetown, a man with tentacles and one of IDSO's top investigators. He *might* believe I found the stone. If he does, you can expect the CDM and associated bodies knocking on the palace doors."

"That cannot be avoided now," Sotho said.

"If you want me to bring him in, just say the word."

"Otanga?" Sotho said.

Otanga nodded. "It is very sensible. Mr. Mackenzie—this man—"

"Bernard Manston."

"Mr. Manston—you think he could find both Dr. Blohm and Colonel Magasi?"

Mackenzie nodded. "He'll find 'em—dead or alive."

Appleby said bitterly, "I'm entirely to blame! I assumed responsibility for the diamond's safety. It might as well have been put in the keeping of a child!"

"That won't do, Doctor." Sotho made a dismissive gesture. "I do not hold you in any way responsible. What alternative did you have— Colonel Magasi? If he had guarded the diamond, ostensibly to bring it to me, how safe would it have been? . . . Mr. Mackenzie?"

"As safe as a straw house soaked in gasoline and set alight. You wouldn't have seen him for dust. Point is, he didn't know about the diamond until I told him it was missing."

Otanga said, "That is not so, Mr. Mackenzie. His quarters were searched. The conversation Dr. Appleby had with the president was recorded and heard by Colonel Magasi."

"That puts a different face on it, Mac," Appleby said. "For me, it takes suspicion away from Ernst."

Mackenzie looked doubtful. "It's fifty-fifty now—Magasi *and* Blohm. They could have been in it together, which I doubt, of course. Even in crime, those two couldn't be partners. Every man has his price and a two-thousand-carat diamond is pretty damn likely to cover it, with change left over."

"Will you go to Freetown, Mr. Mackenzie?" Sotho asked.

"If you're sure I haven't got the Star of Angwana."

Sotho smiled. "Colonel Otanga personally conducted a search of both your person *and* belongings, Mr. Mackenzie. I think you are innocent."

"*Colonel* Otanga?"

"He now occupies the post once held by Magasi," Sotho replied.

"Good Lord!" Mackenzie looked down at Otanga. "Are you up to it, Otanga?"

"I have asked the president if the post can be temporary."

"Temporary or otherwise, you must be pretty sure Magasi's left the country and is not coming back."

"There is evidence, Mr. Mackenzie," Sotho said. "He has taken everything of value from his quarters. Money and all his personal possessions. Enough was left behind to suggest that he had abandoned more than his high position in the government. The Magasi faction in Angwana no longer exists, Mr. Mackenzie."

"Out of evil good can come forth," Otanga said. "Colonel Magasi had ambition; this he has abandoned—in my view for apparent reasons.

To him the diamond is worth more than the presidential throne."

"Was he really after that?" Mackenzie asked.

"Common knowledge, Mr. Mackenzie. Is it not also common knowledge in the West that prime ministers and presidents have opponents with whom they keep an entente—and not always cordial?"

"Some get assassinated," said Mackenzie. "Can't see you instituting a bloodbath for Magasi's supporters, Otanga."

"Ilbrahim has no such intention," said Sotho. "Neither have I. Action will be taken that no blood need be spilt." Sotho smiled, his dark, gnomelike face creasing. "Only their money will run from their veins. Dispossession can be harder than death." He clapped his hands together. "Enough, gentlemen. There is no time to lose. My aircraft is ready to fly you to Freetown, Mr. Mackenzie. When will you leave?"

"Within the hour."

"Magasi may have disposed of the stone," Appleby said.

"That's stupid," Mackenzie said. "No diamond thief carrying a two-thousand-carat stone is likely to flog it. Magasi or Blohm wouldn't risk selling it. They'd hide it and let it rest for a few years. It's one stone that won't be seen on the market for a long, long time." Mackenzie looked at Otanga. "One thing bothers me—"

"Yes?" Sotho asked.

"Suppose we find Magasi—wherever he is. . . . Look, Otanga, according to Dr. Appleby and what I've seen of you, you're a gentle person —a man of peace who never shows his teeth. Can you handle Magasi the way he should be handled?"

"Where Magasi is concerned, I have big teeth, Mr. Mackenzie."

"He's an ace bullyboy and you're not. My guess is, blood will fly in all directions. Make sure it isn't yours, or that of your men."

Otanga considered Mackenzie's advice, then said, "In extreme cases I believe in the death penalty. Whether he has the diamond or not, he deserves that punishment."

"But are you the man to carry it out?"

"I have lent him *my* teeth, Mr. Mackenzie," Sotho said.

Karl Raeder, detailed by Bernard Manston to find Ernst Blohm, said, "Another ten minutes or so and we land at Dakar."

Blohm, sitting next to him, said, "Good. Flying under a cloud of suspicion is not to my liking. You know, it is odd—I have led a comparatively blameless life, yet to be under suspicion strikes guilty chords within me, chords I never knew existed. Perhaps I have been complacent about my purity of thought."

"We've all got guilty secrets somewhere, Doctor," Karl Raeder said. "Look the average man or woman straight in the eye and say, 'I know what you did,' ten-to-one they'll color up and look guilty. I saw no such reaction in you when I found you at Keinerch."

"Things have changed since then," said Blohm. "I've protested my innocence too much, I think."

Karl Raeder had found Blohm in the mountain village of Keinerch after tracking him from Frankfurt. He had taken the mountain road out of Mangfell and systematically called on each village on the route. Two days after leaving Mangfell, he had arrived at Keinerch to find Blohm eating breakfast under a trellised canopy of grape-heavy vines. Raeder had politely explained his presence, shown Blohm his IDSO credentials, then asked if Dr. Blohm would answer a number of questions.

"And the purpose of the questions?" asked Blohm.

"A simple matter of theft, Doctor. This is not a police matter, you understand. There is no charge."

"Charge against whom?"

"You, Doctor." Raeder looked intently into Blohm's face. "You have recently left Africa. Arriving in Frankfurt, you called on your parents' home. They were away. You spoke to a neighbor and left Frankfurt, taking the train—"

"One moment," Blohm said. "My movements are not secret. If they appeared to be so, it was unintentional. You go too fast, Mr. Raeder. Let us take it from the beginning. I am under suspicion, is that correct?"

"Yes, Doctor."

"Then tell me the nature of the crime and why I am suspected."

"After your departure from Angwana it was discovered that there had been a diamond theft. I have no details of the theft, only that there are two suspects—according to circumstances—and you are one, Doctor. I was asked to find you and ask for your cooperation."

"Ridiculous!" Blohm snapped. "Steal diamonds? Herr Raeder, I am not a thief. And this other suspect, what is his name—Mackenzie?"

"I have not been told his name, only that he left at the same time as yourself."

"Magasi," Blohm said. "But it was always understood that he could steal." He thought for a while, then said, "You are at liberty to search my person, my personal effects, my parents' house, anything. You will find nothing, of course. Between Angwana and this peaceful village I could have disposed of many diamonds."

"Which you did not?"

"Which I did not. Now you will ask about accomplices and what I did here and what I did there—and you will find nothing because there is nothing to find. I have a better idea. Once you are reasonably certain that I am not a thief, I will return to Angwana. I take it you will come with me?"

"I have no authority either to insist on your return or to accompany you."

"I insist that you return with me." Blohm looked questioningly at Raeder. "Would you request permission to return with me to Angwana? If it is a question of expense, I will happily pay your fare."

"I will ask for permission, Doctor."

"And now, I insist on an immediate search, Herr Raeder, of everything I have with me, my parents' house—wherever you wish. But first, take me to my sister's house—it is not far. I would like to see my father and mother before we leave for Angwana."

A request in English, German, and French came over the speakers for passengers to prepare for landing. As the Lufthansa 727 began its descent Blohm said, "Herr Raeder, if we are met by Colonel Magasi, you will be shocked by our reception. Is it true we are to be met at Dakar by an Angwanan aircraft?"

"So I understand."

"Then we must expect Colonel Magasi and guns."

The aircraft awaiting Blohm and Raeder at Dakar was an old DC-6 carrying a minimum crew. There was neither cabin staff nor Magasi. "Where's your colonel with guns, Doctor?" asked Raeder. "I thought we were in for a hot reception."

"It may await us in Angwana," Blohm replied. "No doubt he will gun us down as we step off the plane."

Two hours later the DC-6 landed at Angwana where it was met by Appleby and Otanga. Blohm looked round the airport and said, "Well, Arthur, I'm here, you see? What happens now? The suspect has returned under friendly guard but without diamonds. Herr Raeder will tell you all he knows."

"I'm sorry, Ernst," Appleby said.

"Since the theft of diamonds is a commonplace, at both the mines, why was it necessary to look for me?"

"It wasn't a common theft, Ernst. The Star of Angwana's gone."

"I see."

Otanga came forward. "It was necessary to find you, Dr. Blohm. Colonel Magasi is no longer in Angwana. Your return may help us to find him."

"Full explanations when we get to the palace, Ernst," Appleby said.

"I expected to find not only Magasi waiting but Mackenzie also," Blohm said.

"Mac's in Freetown. He's been a tower of strength. Later you'll thank him, Ernst."

"And am I still under suspicion?"

"When you hear what the president has to say, you'll understand why we had to track you down."

Blohm smiled. "A pity Mackenzie is not here. He would see that I have not returned with my bucket and spade."

". . . so it was natural that suspicion should fall upon Colonel Magasi and yourself, Doctor," Sotho said. "Both of you left hurriedly. You were soon found, thanks to Mr. Mackenzie's advice, and your return convinces me that you did not take the diamond. Magasi, on the other hand, has disappeared. Certain conclusions have to be drawn. Ilbrahim will now tell you how things stand. Ilbrahim?"

"Dr. Blohm," began Otanga, "when Dr. Appleby and Mr. Mackenzie told us of the loss, you can imagine the shock all of us felt. Two men had left Angwana, Colonel Magasi and yourself. Both Dr. Appleby and Mr. Mackenzie recommended an immediate contact with you, and this was done. Naturally we expected Colonel Magasi to return. In many ways the colonel is a law unto himself. We received the news that you had been found and were returning to Angwana to assist us in recovering the diamond."

"But I am under suspicion."

"Technically speaking, Doctor," Otanga said. "Let me continue . . . Colonel Magasi has disappeared—of this we are now certain. Mr. Mackenzie has gone to Freetown to pick up Magasi's trail, for we know he was bound for Sierra Leone. We are waiting to hear from Mr. Mackenzie. It may be that the colonel is not involved, but of one thing we are certain, the diamond has been stolen."

"When, Arthur?" Blohm turned to Appleby.

"After you'd left with Magasi. I went to the hut. It was just after two in the morning. The stone had gone. I went to Mac and woke him up, and we searched the hut. Later Mac phoned the palace and spoke to Magasi, who said he'd return immediately to the mine and that you'd be with him. That's the last we've heard of Magasi. The call went out to find both you and Magasi."

"So Magasi is number-one suspect?" Blohm said.

"And you and I are next on the list."

"I understood Magasi knew nothing about the diamond."

Otanga answered: "The colonel's quarters were searched, Dr. Blohm. The conversation Dr. Appleby had with the president was recorded by Colonel Magasi; therefore, he knew of the existence of the diamond."

"But how did he know where to look?" asked Blohm. "Only two of us knew where it was—Dr. Appleby and myself."

"That's why we're suspects," Appleby said. "And we'll remain so until Magasi is found."

Sotho placed a hand on Blohm's shoulder. "Think of this, Doctor— such a stone can never be lost. Where could Magasi take it? Or any one of you for that matter? Mr. Mackenzie said that the thief would be a fool to take it to a cutter, and it is virtually unsaleable by dishonest means. Your photographs will be duplicated and sent to organizations throughout the diamond world. To quote Mr. Mackenzie, 'Such a stone would make a dishonest dealer sweat with fear.'"

Mackenzie's voice over the line from Freetown to Angwana was triumphant. "Magasi's as transparent as cellophane, Arthur. He covered his tracks like an amateur."

President Sotho, Otanga, and Appleby listened on connected telephones. "Three of us are listening, Mac," Appleby said. "The president, Mr. Otanga, and myself."

"Greetings," Mackenzie said. "Magasi left Freetown for Aracaju via Rio de Janeiro. He used a chartered aircraft, so the bastard has money to spend. I'm waiting now for news from Aracaju. How's that, O mighty President?"

"Very good, Mr. Mackenzie," Sotho replied. "You have friends in high places."

Mackenzie's chuckle came over the line. "Correction, Mr. President —friends in low places. Incidentally, Magasi's kept quiet about the diamond if he has it—which he has, of course."

"Ernst has come back," Appleby said.

"Give him my best wishes, then. He won't accept 'em, but pass them on. I take it he didn't have the diamond?"

"Of course not."

Sotho cut in. "Mr. Mackenzie, when do you expect further news of Magasi?"

"You mean his hideout?"

"Yes."

"Any hour, any moment. He should have reached Aracaju by now. I've an informant there—dishonest but reliable."

"That does not sound like a person to be trusted."

"Sometimes they're the best—they can be bought."

"Mr. Mackenzie," Otanga said, "the president has entrusted the recovery of the diamond to me. It is important that I find Magasi. Are you confident of success?"

"Pretty damn sure, Otanga. Just wait by the phone."

"We are very grateful," Sotho said. "I wish you well indeed. When can we expect you back in Angwana?"

"Soon as Otanga's caught up with Magasi and the diamond."

"Good."

"Champagne and fireworks, eh, Mr. President?"

"A celebration, certainly."

Forty-five minutes after the call they again heard Mackenzie's voice over the line from Freetown. It was no lighthearted chat. Mackenzie rapped out information, urgency strong in his voice. When he had finished, he added, "Nail the bastard, Otanga! Carry a gun and go with men with guns. Do you understand?"

"Perfectly, Mr. Mackenzie. I shall be leaving within the hour."

"Then good luck—and keep your powder dry. Call me in Freetown after you've settled Magasi's hash—you've got my hotel number."

"I will do that, Mr. Mackenzie."

CHAPTER **28.**

T H E Y had watched for five hours. At dawn Otanga and his ten
security men had taken up position to cover all vantage points in the
huddle of narrow streets and houses surrounding the Estancia. As
Aracaju woke up to begin its day before the midday heat closed working eyes in siesta, the security men, dressed in casual and, in some cases,
peasant clothes, became part of the town. They could have been casual
workers from the dock, or crew members come ashore the previous night
or in early morning.

Once Otanga was sure Magasi was there, it would be simple to enter
the Estancia and then—knowing Magasi, Otanga reckoned that it
would not be a simple task of saying "Please, Colonel, may we have the
diamond?" or "Have you seen anything of the Star of Angwana?" It
would undoubtedly be a brief and brutal encounter, and Otanga felt
pleasure that the "teeth" he had acquired from the president were very
sharp indeed. Time later to be the customary man of peace and of con-
ciliatory manners. As he waited in the strengthening sunlight he reflected that he had enjoyed showing his teeth in the purge he had conducted with the transfer of power from Magasi to his own gentle hands.
The Magasi faction had been castrated, and he remembered Sotho's
words: "It is almost worth the loss of the diamond, Ilbrahim. When all
is peace again, you will blunt those sharp teeth of yours."

But not yet, thought Otanga, and whether or not you have the diamond, Magasi, you are indeed a very dead man.

The hard object in its shoulder holster pressed against his body and
it felt alien. It had never been part of his body and he resented its presence. Each of his men carried similar weapons; he doubted that they
felt the strangeness of holstered, silenced guns; service under Magasi
had taught them to see lethal weapons as extensions of self and to use
them to express something essential to well-being. Change of allegiance

232

meant nothing to the men; Otanga or Magasi, it mattered little who issued orders to kill.

The glass door of the Estancia opened, and an old woman emerged to pour a bucket of water on the broken pavement outside the hotel. She paused and looked up at the sky, scratched a shrunken flank, and went back into the hotel.

Now a small, nattily dressed man came out carrying a brown briefcase. Certainly not Magasi, unless he had changed his complexion to an olive-brown and reduced his height by six inches.

Otanga looked at his watch: 9:02. He raised his eyes and looked at the crumbling facade of the Estancia. As he did so, the curtains of a room on the first floor parted and the windows were flung open.

"Sah?" whispered the man standing close to Otanga.

Otanga nodded. "That is Colonel Magasi. Tell the others to do nothing. Wait on my instructions."

"Yes, sah."

Otanga stared at the face scanning the street. As he watched Magasi yawned, and Otanga caught the flash of white teeth in the dark face. Then Magasi turned away from the window, and Otanga waited.

Magasi came away from the window, scratching at bug bites. They had come out again in the night, and more out of revenge than prevention, Magasi had lit a candle and spent an hour burning them off the wall. He poured tepid water out of the ewer and into a basin and washed, using the expensive French scented soap he had bought in Freetown. The fragrance of the soap lifted his spirits slightly, and he washed the whole of his body. He dried himself and dressed in the nondescript clothes that made him part of Aracaju's population. It was time Mackenzie came, he told himself. Time for Mackenzie to come and lead him to the life that contained no bugs that crawled and sucked his blood at night; time to begin the next leg of his journey to the good life. When Mackenzie came, it would be breakfast in the best hotels to which he would drive in the best of cars and in the best of clothes in the name of Joseph Preto, late of Sierra Leone, and a citizen of that country. Mackenzie didn't know all the tricks; it had taken real intelligence and wit to use the Portuguese for *black* and to prepare documents to prove that he was Joseph Preto, nationality, Sierra Leonean. *Preto Diamante.* Black Diamond. Clever.

Any hour now, Mackenzie would arrive. Shakah in Freetown had been informed that BD had arrived in Aracaju, and Shakah had informed BD that he was to stay in the Estancia, apart from leaving it for quick meals.

The scent of the French soap lingered in his nostrils as he came down the stairs. As he entered the lobby the desk telephone rang. The clerk answered it, and Magasi listened to the flow of voluble Portuguese. With an expression of anger, the clerk slammed down the receiver. "*A Policia!*"

"The police?" Magasi asked in English.

"They make jokes, senhor. Do we have any dead bodies to report. Pigs!"

"My telephone call," Magasi said, "should it come, tell the caller that I will return in exactly one hour. Do not forget that—in one hour."

"Yes, senhor."

"And my name is—?"

"Preto, senhor. I have not forgotten. Your key, please."

"I will keep the key."

"It is against the rules, senhor."

"But it is *my* rule."

The clerk shrugged his shoulders. The rule meant nothing to him, but Senhor Noni had instructed him to collect keys from those staying in the hotel. As Magasi strode out of the hotel the clerk reached under the counter and picked out a duplicate key, which he hooked onto the keyboard.

Five minutes later he looked up from his desk as a small colored man accompanied by two men came into the lobby.

"Yes?" the clerk asked.

"I would like information."

"Information?"

"For which I am prepared to pay. A man left here five minutes ago. He has a name?"

"All men have names."

"But this one?"

"He has a name, senhor." The clerk smiled. "What is a name worth?"

"Fifty cruzeiros."

The clerk held out his hand, and Otanga took five ten-cruzeiro notes from his wallet. "The name is Preto, senhor. Is it worth fifty cruzeiros?"

"Perhaps," Otanga said. "If the name also has a room number."

"Oh, yes. Senhor Preto has a room number." The clerk looked up at the keyboard. "It is one of those." There were twenty numbers on the board.

Otanga took out a further fifty cruzeiros. "For the number and a key. Later you will have twice the amount if you do not concern yourself with Mr. Preto and his visitors."

The clerk took the banknotes. "What visitors, senhor? And who is Senhor Preto?"

"Good. When he returns you will not tell him?"

"There is nothing to tell. . . . Senhor, he will be back in less than an hour." The clerk looked at the clock on the wall behind him. "In fifty minutes he will return." He unhooked the duplicate key from the board and handed it to Otanga. "He also has a key. His room is on the first floor."

Otanga and the two men made to leave the desk, and the clerk said, "Senhor, you will have one hundred cruzeiros ready when you have finished your business with Senhor Preto?"

Otanga climbed the stairs to the first floor followed by the two men. He reached inside his jacket and withdrew the automatic from its holster; behind him, the men followed suit. At the top of the stairs, the landing was furnished with a brass urn containing a dusty, tired plant bearing a single flower, once scarlet but now a faded rusty-red. There were three doors numbered one to three. Otanga glanced at the disc on the key in his left hand; "Number three," he said and went to the door, inserted the key, and turned the lock. He swung the door wide and stood for a moment looking into the dimly lit room, then entered slowly, his nose wrinkling in disgust. He motioned to the men to enter. "Search," he said. "You have time—search thoroughly."

The desk clerk had kept his silence. When Magasi entered the room, he saw the small black face of Otanga staring at him. Instinctively Magasi had glanced right and left, seeing the two men with drawn and aimed guns. He saw, too, the gun cradled in Otanga's lap.

Magasi heard the door slam shut behind him, and the sound broke the silence. "What do you want, Otanga?" he asked. "Why are you here?"

Otanga remained silent, his eyes fixed on Magasi.

"These men—the guns. They have no right to be here. I order you to give up your weapons," Magasi said.

"You have no authority," Otanga said. "You gave it up when you left Angwana. There are questions you must answer."

"I repeat—you have no authority."

"Only that which you had," said Otanga. "That authority has been given to me by the president. We found the diamond, Magasi. What have you to say?"

Magasi took two paces toward Otanga. "I have nothing to say to you."

"Why did you take the diamond?" Otanga asked. "Simple theft or for reasons of security?"

It seemed a loophole, and Magasi said, "It was safer in my keeping."

"Evidence I found in your quarters suggests that diamonds are not safe in your keeping. You are a thief, Magasi, a common thief, and on the run."

"The president will listen to me."

"He does not want to hear your voice again. I came to recover the diamond. I have recovered it. What does that suggest to you? With two guns behind you and this"—Otanga held up his gun.

Magasi exhaled noisily, as if he had been holding his breath. "Everything can be explained, Otanga," he said.

"With lies?"

"Tell me what you know."

"You and Dr. Blohm left Angwana. The diamond was missing. Dr. Blohm came back to Angwana from Germany as a suspect, and he returned of his own free will. You did not return. Suggestions made resulted in a search of your quarters and enquiries which led to my presence in Aracaju."

"Whose suggestion?" asked Magasi.

"Mr. Mackenzie's. It was he who had you tracked from Freetown to this place."

"Mackenzie!" Magasi showed his teeth and clenched his fists; then bewilderment replaced anger: "Why should he do that? It was the arrangement that—" Magasi paused.

Otanga said, "An arrangement, Magasi?"

"I will say no more."

"Tell me about this arrangement with Mr. Mackenzie," Otanga said. "You might as well, Magasi. Since your life is worth nothing, what have you to lose?"

"There is nothing to tell."

"I can wait." Otanga pointed to the table beside his chair. "Look at the diamond and the little diamonds, and weigh your life against their value. Mackenzie said that you would kill for a fraction of a carat. The floggings you carried out so that you could steal the Star of Angwana— Mackenzie was right."

Magasi looked at the table: at the great diamond and the packet of polished stones Mackenzie had given him for safe keeping.

Bewildered, he said, "But Mackenzie told me that— Otanga, listen to me. If I tell you everything, will you leave me here? You have the diamond. Go back to the president. Take the diamond to him."

"You will be left in South America," Otanga said, "and the diamond will go back to Angwana."

"I have your word?" Magasi looked round at the armed men.

Otanga nodded. "What have you to tell me?"

"Mackenzie told me where the diamond could be found. I knew about it because—"

"You taped Dr. Appleby's conversation with the president. We know that, Magasi. You say Mr. Mackenzie told you where the diamond was hidden?"

"He said he had guessed. It was where he said it would be. He suggested that I accuse the men of stealing and hold the trial. Why, Otanga, why? He was to come to Aracaju—together we would leave South America."

"Is that the truth?"

"Why should he do it?" Magasi stared at the diamond on the table. "Why should he tell lies? He has helped me before—many times. He wanted the diamond. He said it was his by right!"

"Perhaps he wanted to help Dr. Appleby and Angwana by ridding both of a very bad man, Magasi."

"It was Mackenzie. What I have told you is the truth."

"Then why did he tell us where to find you and the diamond? What is his gain, apart from becoming a most honored man in Angwana? The president has called him a good friend."

"Ask Mackenzie," Magasi said. "Hold him and question him. Use my methods, Otanga, you'll get the truth out of him. Then tell him I will kill him!"

Otanga got up from the chair. "What need is there to pull out his fingernails? We have the diamond, and Mackenzie was right." He picked up the stone and carefully inserted it into a leather case. Fingering the Shakah collection of stones, he said, "These too belong to Angwana."

"Mackenzie gave them to me for safekeeping."

"Then they are safer in my hands." Otanga gathered them into the paper fold and placed them in the case. "I made you a promise, Magasi. You can stay in South America and you will never return to Angwana." He locked the case, then reached into the inside pocket of his jacket. "This is your order of release—signed by President Sotho. You will recognize it. My discretionary powers allow me to serve it on you. Goodbye, Magasi."

"Wait!" Magasi said. "Take me back to Angwana. Let me plead my case."

"No."

"Please, Otanga, give me a fair trial. Let me prove that Mackenzie's guilt is as great as mine."

"It can't be. You stole the diamond, not Mr. Mackenzie. I found the proof in this room."

Forcing calm into his voice, Magasi said, "Leave me with my life, Otanga."

"For a few minutes," Otanga said. He moved toward the door, and one of the men opened it.

A spiral of indignation, of anger, rose up in Magasi. As the door began to close behind Otanga, he called out, *"Mackenzie, Otanga! Mackenzie!"*

Otanga left the hotel entrance and crossed the street. He waited two minutes, then, as his two men came out of the hotel and joined him, he looked at them questioningly. Receiving their nods, he said, "Tell the others to remove him. There must be no trace of Magasi left in the hotel."

"Yes, sah."

"When it is done, you know where to find me."

Otanga telephoned Angwana from his room in the Sergipe Hotel. As he waited for Sotho's voice to come on the line he unlocked the small leather case and took out the diamond. He felt no sense of wonder as he touched it; it was inanimate yet deadly, like so many diamonds lost and found in the past. From Appleby he had heard the seemingly apocryphal story of the Hope diamond, the stone of bad luck and tragedy; murder and suicide were the bedfellows of that famous blue messenger of death —forty-four carats of ill luck. Otanga put the stone back into the case. The Star of Angwana had started life well, and he shuddered as he thought of the scene in the shabby Estancia bedroom after he had left.

And now, many miles outside Aracaju, his men would be disposing of Magasi in the São Francisco River where life was more voracious than Magasi had ever been.

"Ilbrahim?" Sotho's voice came faintly over the line. "Are you there, Ilbrahim?"

"Yes, Mr. President. I have to report that all has gone well. I have the diamond."

"Good—good! And Magasi?"

"He had the diamond. And, sir, your orders were carried out to the letter. My men are now dealing with what is left."

"Return quickly, Ilbrahim."

"Tomorrow morning, sir. It would be wise if I am a normal hotel guest for the rest of today and night. It will also be good to act as a normal human being once again."

"No bitterness, Ilbrahim. And you must have no regrets. If you had brought Magasi back to Angwana, his end would have been much the same."

"I will try to find comfort in your words, sir."

"And sleep well, my friend, sleep well."

It was half an hour before Otanga could get through to Mackenzie in Freetown. The line was bad, and Mackenzie's voice came faintly through the sounds of interference.

"Mr. Mackenzie, I found it. I found the diamond!"

"Speak up, Otanga. I can't hear you!"

"I have found the diamond, Mr. Mackenzie!"

"I thought you would. What about Magasi?"

"He is dead."

"What?"

"Magasi is dead, Mr. Mackenzie."

"That's no great loss, Otanga. Who did it—you?"

"I was responsible."

"I didn't know you had it in you."

A burst of static smothered Otanga's reply. When the line cleared, Mackenzie said, "I can't stand this bloody line any longer. Otanga. Glad to hear your news."

"I have to thank you, Mr. Mackenzie."

"Save it till later, Otanga. When are you leaving for Angwana?"

"Tomorrow."

"Have a safe journey—and lang may ye reek!"

"Mr. Mackenzie. Please, when shall I see you?"

"Can't hear you, Otanga. Goodbye!"

Otanga replaced the receiver; there was much he would have liked to ask Mr. Mackenzie. But there was time for explanations and time for thank-you speeches made to a man who had served Angwana well.

He went down to the hotel restaurant to take lunch, the small leather case containing the stone under his arm, and near the shoulder holster he would wear night and day until he handed the diamond to President Sotho.

The palace Mercedes and the two army jeeps drew alongside the aircraft as it taxied to a halt. The man sitting next to the driver of the car stepped out and came to attention as he opened a rear door.

The plane's engines died, and its ramp folded out and down as Sotho, followed by Appleby and Blohm, came out of the car.

"Here is our excellent Ilbrahim Otanga," said Sotho.

Otanga stood framed in the cabin entrance; he dipped his head in a salute to the group waiting on the tarmac and walked down the stairs.

"Welcome home, Ilbrahim." Sotho reached out both his arms and embraced Otanga.

"Thank you, sir," Otanga said, and looked at Blohm and Appleby. "Mr. Mackenzie is not here?"

"He's gone home," Appleby said. "It's like the man not to wait for our thanks. I telephoned him after your news arrived. He sends you his congratulations." Appleby looked down at the small leather case under Otanga's arm. "Is it in there, Otanga?"

"Safe and sound, Doctor."

Sotho ushered Otanga toward the Mercedes. "I have yet to see the miraculous diamond," he said. "A simple ceremony at the palace, Ilbrahim. Senior members of the cabinet are gathered and a representative from the CSO. A great occasion, Colonel Otanga."

"I wish for civilian status, sir," Otanga said.

"When the emergency is fully over, Ilbrahim." Sotho smiled. "Sharp teeth are not to your liking?"

"No, sir."

Flanked by the jeeps, the Mercedes left the airport and took the road to the palace. Appleby, sitting next to Otanga, said, "Was it difficult?"

"Unpleasant, Doctor, rather than difficult. It was also puzzling, for Magasi involved Mr. Mackenzie in ways I cannot understand. Ways that even Magasi did not understand."

"What did you assume?" asked Sotho.

"That Magasi was lying to save his life. I think it is possible that he believed Mr. Mackenzie had assisted the government in discrediting him. Or he wanted me to believe that it was so."

"But all's well that ends well," the president said. "We have our diamond and lost Colonel Magasi. Mackenzie has indeed helped Angwana."

"Surprisingly," Blohm said. "If he were here, I would humbly beg his pardon for my faulty judgment of him. I have never been so wrong about a man in all my life."

"Arnold Mackenzie isn't the kind of man to bear a grudge, Ernst," Appleby said.

"You say he has gone?" asked Otanga.

"He left Freetown for Europe after you told him you had found the diamond," Appleby said.

"I would have liked to talk to him," said Otanga. "Magasi said strange things about Mr. Mackenzie. Accusations that bear little relation to the recovery of the diamond. But, as the president has said, all is well that ends well."

But as Otanga spoke the phrase he saw that it covered a multitude of sins: the journey to Aracaju under diplomatic privilege that was simply a cover for a killing, and the recovery of a diamond Otanga wished had never been discovered, for it involved the taking of life.

As if reading his thoughts, Sotho said, "The country is happier without Magasi, Ilbrahim. I would like to see you smile."

"I find smiles hard to come by, Mr. President. Perhaps when my men report that the evidence in the hotel room has been removed and thin air has claimed Colonel Magasi, I will, at least, know the relief that comes with the fact that I cannot be found out. Isn't that how the guilty hope to escape from conscience?"

CHAPTER **29.**

THE implication of Appleby's statement had stunned those assembled in the council chamber of the palace. The stone Otanga had brought back from Aracaju lay on the square of black velvet Sotho had ordered to be placed on the council table.

After Otanga had taken the stone out of the case, saying to Sotho, "Mr. President, it is my pleasure and honor to return to you the Star of Angwana," Sotho had taken the stone and held it in cupped hands. He had stared at it in silence for thirty seconds, then raised his head and looked first at Appleby and Blohm and then at the members of his cabinet. "Gentlemen. The Star of Angwana. The second largest diamond to be discovered."

Richard Walker said quietly, "My God! If you asked me to put a price on that, I couldn't do it!"

"I will say nothing about its disappearance or its recovery," Sotho continued. "The fact that it is my belief that Angwana will now be a happier state and—" Sotho smiled—"somewhat richer is sufficient to make us rejoice."

Appleby took a step forward, his eyes on the stone in Sotho's hands. "May I see it, Mr. President? I would like to hold it."

"If any man has the right to hold it, Dr. Appleby, you are that man."

And Appleby had taken it from Sotho's hands and looked into it, then raised his face, suddenly drained of pleasure. He looked at Sotho, then at Otanga. It seemed that he had difficulty in speaking, and then, when words did come, they were disjointed.

"This—this stone. . . . This is not—not the diamond!" He shook his head. "It is not diamond!" He turned his gaze on Otanga. "Otanga! This is not the diamond!"

"It is the stone I recovered from Magasi," Otanga said.

"But it's glass!" Appleby's voice was loud. "Do you understand? Glass!"

242

Blohm moved to Appleby's side. "Let me see it, Arthur." His judgment was immediate. "A rough replica of the original. Strass—good lead glass, and nothing more."

For a while there was silence in the council chamber. Sotho eased himself down into the great chair that dominated the council table, folded his hands, and looked down at the black-velvet square. Eventually he raised his eyes and said, "I do not hold Ilbrahim Otanga responsible. He has done his duty and done it well. We must now think quietly and in an ordered manner. The diamond has gone—someone has taken it. We must now find out who that is."

"Mackenzie," Blohm said. "He's the only one left."

They sat around the desk in Sotho's private room: Appleby, Blohm, Otanga, Richard Walker, and Sotho.

"Ways and means," the president said. "I thank God we did not invite the world's press to view the return of the diamond. Angwana would have been made the laughingstock of Africa." Bitterly he added, "So we must pay regard to Magasi's famous last words. It is all we have to go on."

"And so little," Appleby said. "The lying words of a dying man."

"We could be wrong," said Sotho. "We must find him—it is as simple as that. In this, perhaps Mr. Walker can help us?"

"If he's traceable, I can find him," Walker said. "I'd like to know time factors. Every detail of every hour between the discovery of the diamond and Magasi's flight. The same applies to Mackenzie's departure. Can I have a breakdown of events?"

Blohm nodded. "Every minute, every hour. The movements of the suspects, including my friend Arthur Appleby."

"You don't suspect me, Ernst?" Appleby said.

"Since I expressed the wish to apologize to Mackenzie, I doubt my judgment of any man."

"Does that include me?" asked Sotho.

"Yes, Mr. President. The fact that it gave you the chance to eradicate Magasi's opposition seems to be an excellent motive for staging the robbery."

"That is true," Sotho said. "It would have been a good plot. I plead not guilty, of course."

"Including Mr. Otanga, six men knew about the diamond," Walker said. "You, Mr. President, Doctors Appleby and Blohm, Arnold Mackenzie, and Magasi. One of the six is dead, so all but one sits at this table. Is it your wish, Mr. President, that I use my organization in finding Mackenzie?"

"I do so wish. Since I have decided to join the diamond empire of which you are part, it seems logical."

Walker reached across the desk and picked up the glass replica. "This could have been made in Freetown," he said. "Assuming it was, to whom did Mackenzie or Magasi go?"

"Magasi wouldn't have that intelligence," said Appleby. "He knew nothing about diamonds except what we told him. The president knows that Magasi regularly gleaned from the mine. A perquisite he was allowed for the sake of peace. In any case, I'm sure he didn't know about the diamond or the photographs until he and Mackenzie returned from Freetown and Magasi listened to my taped conversation with the president."

"It was Mackenzie," Blohm said with conviction. "Magasi was a petty thief, a brute, but nothing more. I can see Mackenzie's hand in every detail of the operation."

"I agree with Dr. Blohm," Walker said. "From what I've heard, Magasi's brainpower wouldn't be up tc it. Dr. Appleby, can you remember anything that might support Dr. Blohm's suspicions?"

Reluctantly Appleby said, "There was an occasion: Mac—Mackenzie was in the hut. He went to the rack of shelves where I keep bags of mineral specimens. I reacted and asked him to leave them alone. One of the bags he juggled with contained the diamond. He could have guessed by my reaction that that was where I'd hidden the stone. I don't know."

Sotho raised a hand to halt the flow of conjecture. "We must begin at the beginning. Mr. Walker has asked for a minute-by-minute account of the discovery of the diamond and its loss. Mr. Walker, I can offer you a trusted man to take notes, and a tape recorder to record every word."

"That would help," Walker said.

"In the meantime"—Sotho smiled—"with the exception of Mr. Walker, all present, including myself, are under house arrest. And that is not only funny but strictly legal."

In his office in Freetown Manston held the telephone receiver to his ear and listened to the voice of Richard Walker: "This is confidential, Bernard, strictly and highly confidential. . . . Just listen—you'll find this hard to believe. It's possible there's been a theft on a grand scale. A large diamond—two thousand carats in weight and a pure-white. Now get off the floor and don't tell me pigs might fly. I haven't seen it, but I've Dr. Appleby's assurance that it's a fact. . . . A few details—it's a cleavage, and think of the Cullinan, then knock off one thousand three hundred carats. That's a good description. I've seen photographs that

Dr. Blohm took and, what's more important, the glass replica that replaced the real thing. . . . First things first, Bernard. Where would you go to get a dummy made? . . . Fine. Get there and poke around. If you can use any pressure, then use it. . . . Yes, I can give you some names: Colonel Magasi and Arnold Mackenzie—I have to throw in the names of Dr. Blohm and Dr. Appleby." Walker looked apologetically at Appleby. "I'll take it further, Bernard—include any Angwanan with business in Freetown. . . . Of course I have my doubts, but I'm acting on a belief in the integrity of Dr. Appleby—enough, that is, to take it seriously. If you've no luck in Freetown, spread it. . . . No, there's the time factor—it couldn't have been made in Jo'burg or anywhere round the coast. Freetown's the obvious place. Pull out every stop, Bernard, and full pedal. . . ."

It was a job to Manston's liking; Walker's request touched off contact points in Manston's mind. There was only one man in Freetown capable of handling glass well enough to cut and polish using formulae most likely to deceive. He'd seen Shakah's copy of the Orloff, the Regent, and the Hope, made using color photographic reference only, and had been amazed. He also knew that Shakah was not above illicit deals. Honesty, Manston thought, as he walked the streets to Shakah's workshop, is a bendable thing in Africa, and somewhere along the line you got what you deserved or paid for.

When he entered Shakah's front shop, Shakah bowed his deference to a man he knew to be dangerous.

"You are welcome, Mr. Manston."

"I hoped you'd say that, Shakah. A quiet chat in your back and very private room?"

"If that is what you wish. There is an accusation?"

"Of what, Shakah?"

Shakah spread his hands. "One is constantly under suspicion in Freetown, Mr. Manston."

"There's more rogues to the square inch in Freetown than in the rest of the world. Lead the way, Shakah."

Seated in Shakah's musty overfurnished private office, and drinking the heavy black sweet coffee, Manston said, "Imitations, Shakah, fakes. What have you been up to lately?"

"I make no secret of my business, Mr. Manston. Rich ladies wish their diamonds to be reproduced in glass. I have even had De Beers request my services—also museums all over the world."

"How about a man called Mackenzie?"

"Mr. Mackenzie? The Komalu's chief mining engineer?"

"Was," said Manston. "Seen him lately?"

"Clients come and go. You will have more coffee?"

"As a delaying tactic, your coffee's much too sweet, Shakah."

"So." Shakah folded his hands in an attitude of repose and looked questioningly at Manston.

"So," said Manston. "I'll cast your mind back three or four days. A collection of twenty paste fakes: ruby, amethyst, sapphire, and diamond in various cuts."

"Oh, yes." Shakah reached for his receipt book and thumbed through the pages. "A colored gentleman—a Mr. Magasi. Here, Mr. Manston"—Shakah pushed the receipt book across the desk. "Every item is listed, as you will see."

Manston scanned the list. "All hunky-dory, Shakah. What about a replica of a two-thousand-carat rough diamond?"

"There is no such thing as a two-thousand-carat rough diamond."

"Rumor has it there is."

"Rumors!" Shakah spread his hands, dismissing the possibility. "Is there nothing else, Mr. Manston? My books are open to your eyes."

"It's the unwritten book I'm interested in."

"There is no such book."

"Then you've no objection to my looking round your workshop?"

Shakah hunched his shoulders.

"So let's go," Manston said.

From Freetown to Angwana the line was clear. Manston said, "I found nothing in Shakah's workshop. All the makings, of course. Chunks of glass, all the colors of the rainbow. A line on Magasi, though. If I'm to believe Shakah, Magasi bought the collection of paste Otanga brought back from Aracaju. Oily Shakah showed me a receipt made out to Joseph Magasi. But what's in a receipt, Dick?"

"What about Mackenzie?"

"Nothing. Shakah was obviously cagey. Look, Dick, it may be that Mackenzie's in the clear. Shakah described Magasi—a superficial description, it's true."

"Can't you bring pressure to bear on Shakah?"

"We've got nothing on him, Dick."

"There's a theory Magasi peddled the stone."

"Don't believe it. It'd be too hot. He could have hidden it, and Otanga was too quick on the trigger. Want my opinion for what it's worth?"

"Try me."

"Assume that there was a fantastic diamond in the first place, right?"

"Right."

"In Mackenzie's shoes, I'd set up Magasi. They were both in Freetown when, and if, the fake was made. From what I can gather, Magasi had areas of stupidity fed by greed—the best kind of fall guy. This is instinct only, Dick, but think about the fact that Otanga caught up with Magasi in Aracaju. Turner, Partridge—Aracaju sounds like Mac's favorite town."

"So where is Mackenzie now?"

"I can try to find out. Dick, do you believe in this diamond?"

"I trust the word of Doctors Appleby and Blohm, and there it ends. I've seen photographs and that's all. It's little to go on, and the further it gets away from the doctors—" Walker hesitated and looked at Appleby: "What I mean is, Bernard, the diamond becomes less believable. Just find out all that you can. Find Mackenzie and let me know."

Two and a half hours later Manston telephoned Walker.

"Not much to report, Dick. Mackenzie left on a flight to Switzerland. Geneva."

"When?"

"Round about the time Otanga was on his way back from Aracaju. Dick, Turner's in Geneva."

"I know."

"What d'you want me to do now?"

"Apart from keeping your ears and eyes open, I don't know. Just stay put. I'll contact you if anything comes up."

"Okay. Tell you one thing, if Mac has nicked the diamond, you've got to take your hat off to him. The man's got nerve."

Walker hung up and turned to Sotho. "Not much of use, Mr. President. Mackenzie is in Switzerland—or was." Mixed loyalties raged in him. "I would like the president to tell me how much trust he is prepared to place in me."

"You have my trust, Mr. Walker," said Sotho. "Why do you ask?"

"People I like may be involved," Walker said. "They may not be— I hope they're not. It means I will have to go to Geneva." He glanced at Appleby. "When friends are involved—I'm sure Dr. Appleby understands, his loyalty to Mackenzie parallels mine to my friends. It's the most I can do at this stage. If Mackenzie is there, I'll do all in my power to find the truth."

Sotho picked up the paste imitation of the Star of Angwana and looked into its depths. "What has Angwana got to lose?" he said. "If we have to cut our losses, we can thank God that we have a rich mine. I do not understand your reference to your friends who may be involved. That is your business and yours alone." He looked up at Appleby: "Doctor, will you accompany Mr. Walker to Geneva?"

"If you think it necessary."

"You are Mr. Mackenzie's friend and as personally involved as Mr. Walker suggests. Also, you will have no peace of mind until you have spoken with your friend."

Appleby looked at the prospect ahead. Would liking interfere with his approach, an approach diverted by Mackenzie's peculiar brand of humorous dishonesty? It would be all too easy for Mac to tell him to concentrate on Magasi, the *dead* Magasi, and wait for the diamond to surface. The only authority I have, thought Appleby, is the uncertain weight of a long friendship. And then he thought that Mac might prove his innocence conclusively, definitely, and Appleby's mood lightened.

"Of course, I'll go with Mr. Walker," he said.

CHAPTER 30.

TURNER was puzzled. When the knock came on the door of his hotel suite, he did not expect to see Mackenzie standing there, neither did he expect him to skate humorously over his discovery of a two-thousand-carat diamond, its theft, and the death of a high-ranking Angwanan suspected, and found guilty, of the theft.

And now Mackenzie had gone silent and withdrawn, and Turner found the silence puzzling. He moved over to one of the tall windows and looked out over Lake Geneva.

Mackenzie broke the silence. "We've done well, haven't we, Jamie? Together we've built up a pretty big holding, and what have we lost?"

"I haven't yet added up the score, Mac. I still feel like an exile. A bit like the dead atheist—all dressed up and nowhere to go."

"You'll adjust. You'll go it alone and do damn well."

Mackenzie went into silence again. Eventually Turner said, "If there's something on your mind, Mac, get it off."

"What do you feel about one last operation, Jamie?"

"I've had enough, Mac. The trip to Aracaju put an end to the chapter and story. I collected a ghost from that room at the Estancia, and it clanks its damned chains every night."

"You've never suffered from conscience before."

"Call it fear, not conscience."

"I know one way over fear and conscience." Mackenzie's mind recalled Mandragez and the bodies brought out from the Komalu Mine and his sickened reaction immediately smothered by the thought of the diamonds in Mandragez's dead stomach. He thought of the moment when he made the switch in Appleby's hut, and the spasms of fear that came and went in the days of waiting before he could take off for Freetown, and always the spasms were smothered by the two-thousand-carat diamond. "Profit, gain—if they're big enough, Jamie, misgivings vanish. It's a fact of life."

"Maybe I haven't had your practice."

"Could be. . . . Jamie? I've got to vanish—perhaps for a long time. I'd appreciate your help. I could demand it, but that's not my way."

Turner came away from the window and looked down at Mackenzie who sat slumped in the armchair. "You're not making sense, Mac. You've reached the point when you can grab your ambition. You don't need my help. We cut our holding straight down the middle, and that's that."

"Suppose this last operation dwarfs the Aracaju caper?"

Turner shook his head. "Not another. Look, Mac, you've come out of Africa with some kind of honor. You put the finger on Magasi and this president—Sotho?—he'll get back the world's second largest diamond ever and all's right with the world. He'll probably rename it the Mackenzie."

"They won't get the diamond, Jamie," Mackenzie said quietly.

"Why not? You said Sotho's man had gone to Aracaju, hit this colonel, and got back the stone."

Mackenzie shook his head slowly. "They won't get it," he repeated.

"You make less sense every minute," Turner said. Exasperated, he went to the drinks table and picked up a bottle of whisky. "Have a drink, Mac, and don't be a pain in the ass."

"I don't want a drink."

"I do."

Mackenzie chuckled quietly. "They can't get—they won't get it."

"Turn the record over, Mac," Turner said. "You're stuck in a groove. . . . All right, I'll play it your way. Why won't they get the diamond?"

"Because I've got it."

Turner went silent, then exploded. "You goddam fool! Have you lost your marbles, Mac? What the hell do you mean, you've got the diamond?"

"I took it because it's mine. If Appleby hadn't taken it into his head to come to the tunnel, there'd have been no trouble. I've got it, Jamie— and I want your help."

"You're crazy!" Turner stared at Mackenzie, disbelief showing in his face. "It's a great joke, Mac—great! And now you'll put your hand in your pocket and pull out two thousand carats."

"I can do that, Jamie."

Turner looked pityingly at Mackenzie. "In the first place, I don't believe you'd be fool enough to steal it. In the second place, a diamond of that calibre is more explosive than an H-bomb. My touch falters at the fifty-carat mark. Beyond that, I'm in trouble unless it's legitimate. Cut it out, Mac!"

"I did," Mackenzie said, and took the diamond out of his pocket.

"Hold it, Jamie. Feel it. Gaze into its heart, you bloody Yankee, and wonder!"

"You damned fool, Mac," Turner said. "You great damned fool!" He took the diamond to one of the tall windows and gazed into its heart. "Christ of the Andes!"

"What would you have done, Jamie?"

"Run in the opposite direction. You can't handle it, Mac—you can't! No one can."

"It's mine, Jamie. You've got to understand that. It's mine—don't you see?"

"I don't see!" Turner held the stone in both hands, seeing the life within the stone breaking through the rough surface. He held in his hands the dream of most diamond men, the dream of prospectors throughout the ages, the dream of the gold miner striking a rich seam: the dream of finding Eldorado. So a peasant laborer in the Chinese Republic finds a hundred-or-so-carat diamond and gets as a reward a job in a factory; and a three-hundred-carat diamond's found on the grease belt in De Beers. Chicken feed. But this was like discovering the secret of life.

"I don't get it," Turner said. "You told me Sotho's man had found the stone and was on his way back to Angwana. But why the hell you sent Magasi to Aracaju beats me. Do you have a fixation on the place?"

"It's as bad a place as any." Mackenzie grinned. "Otanga's carrying a glass replica, Jamie. I had it made in Freetown. Shakah—you remember him? Shakah made it. You want details?"

"No, I don't!"

"It wasn't difficult. I made a switch."

"I don't want to know." Turner placed the diamond on the low table by Mackenzie's chair and began to walk slowly up and down the room.

His eyes on the diamond, Mackenzie said, "We thought the Komalu was the big one, Jamie, but this—" Mackenzie's eyes were bright. "I've never had a sense of wonder. I've listened to you and others raving about diamond as if God's in it, or every beautiful woman that ever existed. Stupid, bloody romantics I called them. Couldn't they see that a diamond's only value was the cash it brought in? That's how I used to think until I prized this out of its bedrock. It's all right, Jamie, I haven't gone off my rocker. I can still see it in terms of the cash it'll bring to both of us. But this sense of wonder—I've got it, you know? For the first time in my life. The second largest discovered—maybe that's part of the wonder. I don't know. Or the fact that I found it. I can see it cleaved and cut into—how many stones? The Star of Sierra Leone made seventeen different stones, and that weighed only nine hundred and sixty-eight carats in the rough. The Lesotho topped six hundred and one and made eighteen cuts, and no syndicate was rich enough to buy the collection."

"It isn't on, Mac," Turner said. "No way at all."

As if he had not heard him, Mackenzie said, "We'll salt it away, Jamie, with the others. We've both years in hand, and we can afford to wait. We've time and money to find a cutter. Can you think of one honest enough to turn down two or three million quid for the job? That's the price we can afford to pay. Give it five years or so—we've time, Jamie." He picked up the diamond and held it between thumbs and forefingers of both hands. "All they've got are photographs and the word of two men it ever existed."

Turner had ceased pacing the floor, and Mackenzie looked up at him: "Who's going to really believe Appleby and Blohm, apart from Sotho? Magasi's dead, so he won't talk. And what do I stand to lose? The trust and friendship of Arthur Appleby. I'm sorry to lose that, but I can bear with it. I like the man, but I've never formed a close relationship with any man or woman, so what I've never had, I'll never miss. Partnerships, yes. Mine with you, Jamie—it's been a good one, but if I never saw you again, I wouldn't weep in my pillow."

"You're talking yourself into acceptance of an impossible situation," Turner said. "Don't you realize you're jeopardizing our partnership? The dogs will track you down—me, too. Do you want everything uncovered?"

Mackenzie shook his head. "I'll be away from Geneva by the time Appleby and Blohm recover from shock." He picked up the diamond and held it out to Turner. "Take it, Jamie. Salt it away and I'll be off."

"If I take it, I'll get it back to Angwana." Turner looked hard at Mackenzie. "I never took you for a damn fool, Mac, but you've turned into the biggest clown the world ever saw. I know IDSO better than you. I must know it better than you, otherwise you wouldn't be holding that stone. Walker and his memory man, Manston, are already sniffing around us two. Walker sounded warning noises at me a few weeks ago. We're already connected, Mac. They've got no evidence, but they *know* we're connected. How long d'you think it'll take them to get to me?"

"I still say we can handle it, Jamie. We're rich enough to cock a snook at 'em. They can only act on proof—and they haven't got it."

"They've the power to gang up on me. They can close those great bronze doors in Charterhouse Street. I don't want that, Mac. Those doors have got to remain open for J. D. Turner."

"You don't need the CSO anymore."

"Oh, yes, I do, Mac. I need the CSO very, very much. Send the stone back to Angwana. Send it back—get rid of it!"

"No!" Mackenzie's voice was loud, emphatic. "What I have, I hold! You don't understand what it's like, Jamie—what it's like to find a diamond like this. You know the saying possession is nine-tenths of the law? And what's the one-tenth that's left? Who owns it? I'll tell you: a small African state that's as primitive as a shithouse hole at the end of the garden. What the blazes have they done to earn this diamond? Sweet damn all! With my help they've got a good mine established. It's my diamond, Jamie, and half of it could be yours."

"No, Mac," Turner said. "I want no part of it."

Mackenzie was silent for thirty seconds, then he smiled and Turner saw a return of the old Mackenzie. "All right, Jamie," Mackenzie said. "All right. There's a long trail ahead. I'm sorry you won't be with me."

"You don't know what you've started, Mac. You say it's only a matter of days—even hours—before the storm breaks and the world gangs up on you. What about me? Do you think I won't be included? Every damned investigator will nose out connections from Sierra Leone to South America, the USA, and your partner, James Drake Turner. There won't be any goodwill, Mac. No more whispers, because Arnold Mackenzie is a super-duper mining engineer and Turner's one of the best American diamond buyers, and you've got to give and take a little. Shouting, Mac—a yelping pack of international diamond bloodhounds out for a kill, and I mean a kill. Everything we've built up—finished!"

Quietly Mackenzie said, "Unload, Jamie. Tel Aviv's sympathetic to a deal on the side. The Israelis didn't like the CSO's countermove against their forty-percent increase on polished stones. Unload, Jamie—every stone in our holding. You can do it. Spread the cash. A bit here and a bit there. Japan, Jamie. The yen's almighty powerful against the dollar. Split the holding between Israel and Japan."

"You're forgetting one thing—I'm left with no status. I'll be discredited. So there'll be no charge, no prison bars, but a damned great stigma for friends and enemies to see. It'll be like the mark of Cain!"

Mackenzie's voice was still quiet and controlled: "You've borne the mark without pain for some time, Jamie."

Turner, standing by the window, was silent. He heard Mackenzie sigh and then his quiet voice again. "Just do one thing for me. Sell my part of the holding if you don't want to flog the lot. I trust you in this, Jamie. Later I'll contact you. It'll be some time, but I'll contact you."

"Do you want money now, Mac?" Turner turned away from the window. "I can let you have as much as you want."

Mackenzie shook his head. "I've enough to hold out for a time. When I need cash, you'll hear from me, but stay in Geneva—make it your base so that I know where you are."

"Don't you trust me, Mac?"

"Here's my authority and all legal to handle my share." Mackenzie took an envelope from his pocket and handed it to Turner. "That's the extent of my trust, Jamie. Good enough?"

Turner took the envelope. "I'm sorry, Mac. I'm sorry I said that."

"For a man who has everything, why should I worry about a few million dollars? Spending money, Jamie, that's all. When the hullabaloo's over, what I'll have'll make our Swiss fortune look like the widow's mite."

"Send the diamond back to Angwana," Turner said again.

Mackenzie raised his eyebrows in mock surprise. "With love from Mac? No, Jamie, once I set a path I follow it. I don't see crossroads and side roads. I set a goal and make for it by the most direct route. You know me. I'm a big fish in a big sea—"

"Blinded by your own metaphor," Turner said. "And you want this minnow to swim alongside you!"

"You might enjoy the trip." Mackenzie picked up the diamond. "Sometime in the future I'll make landfall and come ashore. A few years, maybe." He looked into the heart of the stone. "And this will spawn the finest collection ever seen."

"And who'll see it, Mac?"

Mackenzie looked up from the diamond. "I'll see it, and that's all that matters. Jamie? . . . I'll have that drink now. You can wish me Godspeed or go to hell—it doesn't matter."

"I can help, Mac. I can help you get the stone back to Angwana. God, I'll even take it back for you! Go into hiding. Disappear. They won't want you if they've got it back."

"They're not going to get it back. It's mine." Mackenzie smiled again. "And what would you tell them back in Angwana, that I'd turned looney? I'd lost my mind, flipped my lid? Not that, Jamie. Not Arnold Mackenzie. I've some pride. I've one helluva lot of pride. I've carved my way through that bloody rock called Africa. I dug an escape tunnel to what I want out of life. This diamond's my crowning glory. Come hell and high water, they won't get it." He took the glass of Scotch Turner had poured and raised it. "Here's to us, Jamie. It's been a good and profitable association."

"We're rich men," said Turner, "and that's all we can say."

Mackenzie drained his glass in two swallows. "It's better to be miserably rich than miserably poor. I'm away, Jamie." He picked up the diamond and slipped it into his jacket pocket.

"Where will you go now, Mac?"

"Here, there, and everywhere for a bit—it's better you didn't know. Walker or Manston would get it out of you, to say nothing of the little black men of Angwana." Mackenzie got to his feet and held out his hand. "I'm away, then. Round about now, the storm brewing up in Sotho's seedy palace is the joke of the century."

Turner took Mackenzie's hand. "Is it the heather and lochs of Scotland, Mac?"

"Aye, it'll be the Western Isles eventually. Somewhere off Oban and one of a few hundred islands. You'll hear from me." Mackenzie gripped Turner's hand hard. "Goodbye, Jamie."

He released Turner's hand and began to walk to the door. "Mac?" Turner said. "One last effort. Let me return the diamond to Angwana."

"Over my dead body," Mackenzie said, and took his first steps into the wilderness.

CHAPTER **31.**

T H E decision to die with as free a conscience as possible came to Dr. Franz Rikel after a night of pain, and a self-diagnosis that finally confirmed the presence of a malignant growth whose development would be both rapid and terminal.

Since his return from Sierra Leone he had felt a growing weakness and the introduction of pain, despite the clean air and gentle sunshine of Lausanne. And coupled with weakness and pain was a lessening resistance to the religious conditioning he had received in his childhood. An ever-loving God awaited him in the very near future; the Devil faced him in the past and the present in the shape of Mackenzie.

He had gone to confession and told the gray priest-face, dimly seen behind the grill of the confessional, the story of his complicity in the death of the Komalu miners. His penance had been stiff but conventional; added to the penance was the direction that he should confess his guilt to the authorities involved and accept punishment for his crime. Only then could he face God at least partially cleansed of sin.

The means to facilitate a speedy confrontation with God were at hand. In this, Rikel was in opposition to his early religious upbringing; the term *suicide* was a cover name for self-murder. Balanced against present pain and the more extreme pain to come, the risks involved in slipping painlessly away from life were preferable to those of stoically suffering the agonies he knew would come.

Rikel called in his lawyer and made a confession. It was witnessed, and copies were sent to the government-controlled Diamond Mining Company in Sierra Leone, the Central Selling Organization in London, and IDSO in London and in Freetown.

Within a day of their arrival Bernard Manston read the confession with interest and satisfaction. He'd been right all along the line; Turner

256

and the emeralds he didn't buy in Aracaju, the whispers about Mackenzie, the Aracaju deaths—a beautiful operation now blown, blown,
blown! A stomachful of diamonds; two thousand carats and the same
amount as the so-called Star of Angwana. Coincidence, or some grisly
joke made by the God, or Goddess, of Diamond?

A confession meant that Rikel could be called to give evidence.
Manston telephoned Lausanne and spoke to Rikel's lawyer. When he
had finished his conversation with M. Tergot, Manston hung up and
said, "Bugger it!"

He picked up the telephone and booked a call to Angwana and
Richard Walker, enthusiasm undimmed by the news that Rikel had
taken the easy way out.

It was late at night, and on the eve of his departure from Angwana,
that Walker took the call from Manston.

"I've got a bombshell for you, Dick!" Manston's voice was ebullient.
"A thousand-pounder. A blockbuster! Will you listen while I read you
something—something bona fide, witnessed, and hunky-dory?"

"I'm listening."

Manston read Rikel's confession. When he had finished, he said,
"That's it, Dick. Do we blindfold Turner and Mackenzie before we
shoot 'em?"

"Don't be so damned cheerful!"

"It's good news, isn't it?"

"Not when friends are involved. I don't care what happens to
Mackenzie. Jamie Turner is, or was, a friend. That's not your concern—
forget it. Can we get hold of Rikel?"

"Not a hope. He's with the angels, Dick."

"What do you mean?"

"Dead—and never called me 'Mother.' Do you want a copy of Rikel's
statement?"

"Yes, but send it to Geneva, the Hôtel des Bergues. One to the CSO
as well."

"They've got one already—and the DMC here in Freetown."

"I'll have a word with the CSO in London before Appleby and I
leave for Geneva tomorrow morning."

"Then you'll see Turner?"

"Yes. Appleby's saddled with the responsibility of recovering the
diamond. Turner might be able to help. Rikel's confession is a stroke of
luck, both bad and good. If he knows anything about Mackenzie and
the diamond, Turner might break under this latest development."

"Where does the bad luck come in?"

"I can anticipate the CSO's sentence. I'll be the one to deliver it.
Like Appleby, I find old friendships die hard."

"You're as bad as Appleby, Dick. Apart from giving Turner the kybosh, do you really think you're going to track down a diamond that probably doesn't exist? I mean, two thousand carats in one lump! It's laughable, Dick!"

"There's a quotation that fits it. 'If, as is commonly believed, history repeats itself, then I cannot imagine any event that can be called unique.'"

"In other words, somewhere there's a diamond as big as, if not bigger than, the Cullinan. I've another for you: 'Seeing's believing.' Look, Dick, I'd like to join you in Geneva, if that's okay. I'm on leave, so I can be spared."

"Why do you want to come?"

"Personal pleasure—professional pride, if you like. A jigsaw puzzle that's given me headaches is nearly completed. Turner's face when he realizes he's had it and I've fitted in the last piece."

"I can't stop you coming, unless I pull rank."

"And will you?"

"No. Meet up with us in the hotel. Bring my copy of Rikel's statement."

"What time at the hotel?"

"See if you can make seven o'clock—evening, Swiss time."

As Walker put down the receiver Otanga, sitting at the desk opposite him, said, "News relevant to our search, Mr. Walker?"

"Perhaps. We were certainly right in doubting Mackenzie's honesty."

Walker left Otanga's office. As he made his way to Appleby's room he wondered whose best friend diamonds were. "Damn!" he said aloud. "Damn!" The information he was now carrying to Appleby was a sharp sword; a sword that would sever Appleby's tenacious hold on a long-standing relationship. And tomorrow, in Geneva, that same sword would put an end to his friendship with Jamie Turner. He thought, too, of Joan waiting for news in the apartment on Riverside Drive; what would be her reaction on receiving news of Jamie's disgrace? Some women loved lame dogs, bad boys, and the rejected. Hitherto untapped maternal affection might pour out of her and cover Turner in a protective blanket. The sword he carried was an unreliable weapon, but he had to use it; he had no choice in the matter, and there was no comfort in the thought.

"With luck," Walker said, "he's still in Geneva."

The presidential DC-9 was two hundred miles south of Geneva, and the flight from Angwana had seemed interminable.

Appleby sat with Richard Walker, tired but sleepless—a condition he had suffered since the loss of the Star of Angwana.

"The Hôtel des Bergues," Walker said. "The last time I was there, I warned a friend against keeping bad company."

"The American?" Appleby asked.

"Yes. Jamie Turner. I still think of him as a friend. I doubt if he'll see me in that light—there's something between us that's more personal than Angwana's lost diamond and the Komalu operation. If a sick man in Lausanne hadn't decided to die with a clear conscience, this confrontation with Jamie wouldn't have happened."

"I'm in the same boat," Appleby said. "I've known Arnold Mackenzie for years and enjoyed his company and friendship. I've disagreed with him but respected him. I try to see him as a thief and a murderer, but I can't. I see a big man with a ready smile—a man of strength, a man to be trusted."

"Manston is flying in from Freetown," said Walker. "Perhaps it's just as well; he'll correct any weakness we show to Turner."

"What will happen to Turner?"

"I don't know if the law can touch him. That's up to Sierra Leone. My guess is that they won't. But he's finished in the diamond world. The Angwanan stone is another matter—if it ever existed."

"It does exist," Appleby said.

"There's very little proof, Doctor. I believe you, but it's only a belief based on character assessment of yourself and Blohm, and that's not worth tuppence in a court of law."

Through the port window Appleby saw the distant Alps, rose-tinted by the early evening sun. "I was a very young man when I first saw those," he said. "At the age of seventeen I spent two weeks with my hammer and chisel chipping at rocks. It's where I first got interested in geology."

Turner sat by the window. He was very still, looking across the lake, a copy of Rikel's confession in his hand.

"What do you say, Jamie?" Walker asked.

"What do you expect me to say? It's a good story. Is there a court of law involved? Do you have proof? If there's a charge, who's making it?"

"No charges have been preferred," Walker said. "The company in Sierra Leone have a copy of the Rikel statement. It's up to them to bring charges."

"Do you believe Rikel?"

"Yes."

"Based on circumstantial evidence. You must *want* to believe it, Dick." Turner looked away from the window and faced Appleby. "What about you, Doctor? You're on another tack. Which road are you on: the missing two-thousand-carat ghost or Mac's so-called murder operation in Sierra?"

"One backs the other," Appleby said. "I've tried not to believe Mac stole the diamond, but this confession confirms my belief Mac is guilty. I want to find him and the stone."

"And is there a diamond?"

"I was with him when he found it. Please be open and honest with me, Mr. Turner. What happened in Sierra Leone is terrible—I find it hard to believe that Mac could do such a thing. My sole object in coming here is to find him and help him."

"You sound like a friend."

"Of long standing. I beg you to be open and honest."

"I thought I was too crooked to be open and honest." Turner again looked out the window, his back to the three men. Dusk was deepening into night, and reflected quay lamps glittered and danced on the lake. A pleasure boat, strung with colored lights, slid along the water, and he could hear the sound of music.

"Have you seen Mackenzie?" Walker asked. "Is he here in Geneva?"

"Open and honest, huh?" Turner said. "Obviously I can't manage the second—goes against the grain. But the first? Okay. Mac came, and Mac went a few days ago. He told me what he'd been up to in Angwana. How the mine was getting under way and had developed under his guiding hand—Mac isn't a modest man."

"The diamond," Appleby insisted. "Did he show you the diamond?"

"Plural, not singular, Doctor. He had a few with him. Most diamond men do. Good currency if you're hard up."

"You know damn well he means the big diamond," Manston said.

"I know damn well you can keep your mouth shut!"

"He has the diamond, Mr. Turner," Appleby said.

"Good for Mac. He's earned it."

Appleby took a deep breath and exhaled slowly. "If I told you the whole of the story, Mr. Turner, perhaps you'd change your mind."

"There's nothing to change."

"Nevertheless, I'd like you to know."

Appleby related the events following Mackenzie's discovery. When he had finished, he said, "So I'll ask you again—did Mac have the diamond and where is he?"

"Where is he? Here, there, and everywhere. In other words, I don't know, and that's the truth. I'll tell you this for what it's worth—and I'm talking to you, not Walker and Manston—there's been a change in Mac. Maybe it's because he's left Africa for good. It's as if the Mackenzie we knew, or part of him, was the costume he wore to live in a country he disliked. He's different—quieter. As strong as ever, but quiet—*and* resolute."

Manston said, "If Mackenzie *had* shown you the stone—assuming he had it, of course, Mr. Turner—what would you have done?"

"Told him to mail it back to Angwana with a gosh-I'm-sorry message."

"Why?"

"Too hot to handle."

"Is that what you told him?"

"It's what I *would* have told him, Manston. I'd have also told him that Angwana wants only the stone and not his body. I'd even have suggested my taking it back to Angwana personally. Knowing Mac, I know what his reaction would have been—a big Scots grin and directions how to get to hell the quickest way. How's that for supposition?"

"Tell me more and I'll let you know."

It was one way of truth-telling, Turner thought. "Okay," he said. "I'd have told him that contacting me in Geneva might put a rope round my neck. I'd have pleaded with him to return the stone. 'For God's sake, Mac,' I'd have said, 'You're a rich man. You don't need a two-thousand-carat pure. Buy your chunk of Scotland and live in peace.' And I know just how Mac would have responded. He'd have laughed and shrugged it off. Guilty or not guilty, Mac would have laughed it off. Good old Mac!"

"I have to find him," Appleby said. "If you have any clue, I'd be grateful."

"I don't know where he is, Doctor. Believe me. If I did, I think I'd tell you."

"Was he travelling under his own name?" Manston asked.

"Why should he?"

"Had he changed his appearance? He's a conspicuous man."

"I can help you here," Turner said. "He'd dyed his sandy-red hair black—eyebrows, too—and he'd started a moustache. Walked with a pronounced limp as if he had a false leg. Oh, one other thing, he's now five feet six in height and weighs a hundred and forty pounds."

"In other words, he's the Mackenzie we've always known."

"I told him his disguise wouldn't fool a donkey." Turner looked at Walker: "We believe in loyalty, don't we, Dick?"

"Not when it's blind."

"Or when you stand to gain by denying it."

"I'm not enjoying this, Jamie."

"You will, Dick, you will. You'll tell Joanie what a shit I am and press your suit sharper than a Seventh Avenue pants presser."

"I thought you didn't care what she thought." Walker looked at Appleby and Manston: "This has nothing to do with either of you—it's personal. We'll keep Joan's name out of it, Jamie."

Abruptly Manston said, "I've a gift for you, Mr. Turner: Rikel is dead. I've thrown that in for obvious reasons. See what I mean? The case against you and Mackenzie is weakened. My guess is, you won't be taken to task, neither will Mackenzie. I mean, all we've got is a dying man's deathbed confession. What court of law would respect it? Defense could say he was round the bend. Eventually, the Komalu killing and pinch will just be something that might have happened. So why not tell us about Mackenzie and the diamond?"

"I've told you. Now shift your ass out of here."

"I can't wait," Manston said. He turned to Walker: "What now, Dick?"

"Jamie?" Walker said.

"Yup?"

"I've spoken to the CSO—they've seen the Rikel confession. I've now got to be their spokesman. . . . You are no longer persona grata in the CSO or in any other associated body. An account of your activities with Mackenzie is to be circulated wherever gemstones are mined, bought, and sold. Your brokers will be informed, and all credit, naturally, will be denied to you. If you consider the CSO's action libellous, you can sue. I'm sorry, Jamie; it needn't have happened. You were respected and liked."

"I'll consider action for libel," Turner said. "Poor old Mac's name will be mud, too—not that he'll mind. You'll hear me out in this, won't you, Dr. Appleby? Mac's resourceful, full of spunk—an unbeatable guy, right, Doctor?"

"All of those things," Appleby said. "He's also dishonest."

"If he has the great diamond. Why don't you take a leaf out of Rikel's story and do an autopsy on Magasi's body? Maybe he swallowed it."

Walker turned toward the door. "Goodbye, Jamie. I'm sorry."

"Don't be. You read my sentence real fine. Give those old bronze doors in Charterhouse Street a fond farewell embrace for me. Now, get out—all of you! I didn't ask for your company!"

Walker and Manston moved toward the door. Appleby hesitated, and Turner said, "I'm sorry, Doctor, you're with them, so I've included you in the eviction order."

"I understand," Appleby said, and walked toward the door.

"If you do find Mac," Turner said, "give him my respects."

Then, as Walker closed the door behind him, he heard Turner's raised voice: *"And I mean respects!"*

Long after they had left, Turner sat in the chair by the window, looking out over the lake and remembering the night when he had looked at diamonds and Joanie had come quietly into the room and begun the final act to the end of their relationship. He could see no Riverside Drive streetlights nor Jersey Palisades in the distance, only the reflections on the lake and the street lighting along the Quai des Bergues. The Riverside Drive memory merged with the equally clear memory of standing with Carol and watching the dancing, golden oysters on the lake, and he seemed to be standing with Joanie and Carol looking out on a scene that was neither night nor day, a strange composite of places and persons.

The mental imagery made him frown. He had rejected his marriage in favor of life with Carol, so why should Joanie intrude on his thoughts? Was it the fear of losing Carol that had turned his thoughts to other comforts, other loyalties? Carol would soon learn about Mackenzie, Rikel, and himself—the whole sordid story. Richard Walker would see to that—in the line of duty. Of course Joanie, too, would know—Walker would make damn sure she knew and at first hand.

Oh, yes, he told himself, the mother in Joanie would want to comfort her bad boy seeing the trouble as the cause of his flight from her side; but would Carol stand by him and comfort him with words of love and promise of a future carved out of the mess?

Perhaps he wanted them both. Perhaps he wanted Joanie to say: "Don't worry, Jamie, you've been through a bad time, but I'm here and I'll stay with you, no matter what happens. Now, you take Carol to bed and make love—you'll feel so much better afterwards. You'll have the best of both worlds, Jamie: Carol's sense of fun and lovely body, and me, standing by to ward off all the nasties."

The defiance he had shown to Manston, Walker, and Appleby drained out of him, and his shoulders drooped. He was nothing but a sham—an indulgent, spoilt child reaching for the moon.

The lights of Cologny across the lake beckoned him. Life was there: amusements and beautiful women; a place for a rich man to buy whatever his fancy demanded. Bodies and liquor in which a troubled man could drown himself. Then, as he got up from the chair, he thought of Mackenzie, his deceptively honest face with its red fuzz of beard, a man on the run with no beautiful bodies and liquor telling him to forget and enjoy life.

In a sudden, angry motion Turner drew the curtains across the window, cutting out the lake and the lights of Cologny.

Later, the bottle of whisky he had opened now half empty, he began to cry drunken tears of self-pity and called on both his wife and Carol to help him.

It was midnight when a knuckle rap on his door pierced his fuddled senses. He got out of the chair and weaved his way to the door and opened it.

Appleby said, "I'm sorry. I had to come back. I want to talk to you."

"You can come in. You won't get any sense out of me but come in."

Appleby followed Turner into the room, closing the door behind him.

"There's a drink if you want it," Turner said.

Appleby shook his head. "I just want to talk about Mac."

"I thought we'd finished talking about him."

"Walker and Manston are leaving Geneva," Appleby said. "All they intend doing about the Angwanan diamond is to keep watch in case it surfaces. That's all. It's in my hands now, and mine only. I have nothing to do with the Komalu incident."

"There's nothing I can do for you." Turner reached for the bottle, then checked his hand. "What the hell! I can't get plastered the way I'd like."

"I'd like you to trust me," Appleby said.

"Sure—I trust you."

"When you talked about Mac and what might have happened, I read between the lines."

"What did you read?"

"Roughly what you told him when he showed you the diamond."

"Yes." Turner slumped deeper into the chair. "Roughly what I told him. Trust's a mighty funny thing. I trust Mac—always have. Always will. Maybe I'm as crooked, I don't know. Dick Walker gave me a kind of sentence of death, do you know that?"

"Yes. If I had been disgraced in my world, I would call it a death sentence."

"Like Mac, I'm rich enough to shrug it off, but I can't. Mac will laugh it off. . . . I wish to God I could. What do you want, Doctor?"

"The truth."

"About what?"

"The diamond. Did he have it?"

"You know damn well he has it. He showed it to me. I wanted him to return it. We'd collected enough trouble already. The Komalu? You guess whether that's true or not. I called Mac crazy to hold on to it. Now I've told you, but what has he got to lose? If you're the friend you say you are, okay. One day you might catch up with him and try friendly persuasion. I wanted no part of it. I told him I wanted no part of it. He wasn't angry; took it quietly enough. He said he was sorry to lose your trust and friendship. He really said that."

"He still has my friendship," Appleby said. "If I could see him, I'd prove it."

"And that's where I can't help you. He had a drink and left. He didn't tell me where he was going. I'd tell you if I knew. Maybe."

"If you offered to send the stone back to Angwana, couldn't you have persuaded him to leave it with you—for disposal?"

"That's why he called on me. No, I've got to be careful, even with you, Doctor. You can suppose that it's why he came to Geneva—I could salt away the diamond for use later on. Since I care for the safety of my neck, I refused, or would have refused."

"A pity," Appleby said. "You could have agreed and then sent the diamond back, or given it to me."

"Foresight of a different kind." Turner shook his head. "Hindsight's with me now. Sure, telling Mac I'd take care of the diamond, then double-crossing him for his own good sounds like the right course of action. I didn't take it. If I'd known about Rikel's statement, I could've convinced Mac."

"Did he really organize the Komalu accident? Was Rikel telling the truth?"

"No comment," Turner said. "You've heard the lack of evidence. Form your own opinion, Doctor. What now? . . . I've told you a damn sight more than I'd tell Walker and Manston. Do you feel it your bounden duty to report back to them?"

"No. From this moment, what lies ahead is a personal matter between myself and Mac. What about you, Mr. Turner?"

"If he needs my help, it's there, and to hell with Manston and his dogs. Mac's the kind of survivor I want to survive."

"Despite the fact that association with him has brought you so much trouble?"

"I was an active and willing accessory, not a lamb being led to the slaughter."

"Other lambs went to the slaughter," Appleby said. "Mackenzie's law as applied to colored Africans—the expendability of life in the jungle." Appleby moved toward the door. "Thank you for talking to me, Mr. Turner. You have my word that what you've told me won't go beyond this room."

"Would it make any difference?" Turner asked. "What will you do now?"

"Look for him. I shall go to London—make it my base. All I know is that he'll make for Scotland."

"You may have to wait a long time."

"Then I'll wait. I shan't return to Angwana until I have found both Mac and the diamond." At the door Appleby paused. "Would your trust extend to contacting me if you hear anything about him? Where he might be?"

"Perhaps. If I think it's in his interests."

"Thank you. I'll let you know where I shall be staying in London."

Turner heaved himself out of the chair and made his way unsteadily to the door. "A word of warning, Doctor—stay clear of Manston. He's a bastard. He'd hound Mac to his grave for the sheer pleasure of it."

"Not the most pleasant of men," Appleby said.

CHAPTER **32.**

T H E discrediting of Mackenzie and Turner was done with the certain knowledge that it would eventually leak out to the press. The Angwanan diamond was not mentioned; as far as De Beers and the mining combines producing and controlling eighty-two percent of the world's gem diamond production were concerned, the diamond did not exist.

The Central Selling Organization circulated Rikel's statement in full and appended their sentence of ostracism.

Jewellers, the term used to cover cutters and those who sold gems, mounted and unmounted, were also informed that Arnold Mackenzie and James Drake Turner were to be considered undesirable and that any trade with either man would render the trader unacceptable to the CSO.

Like wildfire, the news spread through the diamond clubs and bourses throughout the world. In New York Sol Grunwald, flushed with success, heard the news and felt a moment's sadness as he recalled his last meeting with Turner.

Tony Klein and Swede Petersen saw only the scale of the operation. The blacklisting, the deaths involved, meant nothing; each saw only millions of dollars safely salted away and not one cent of it theirs.

And Joan Turner received copies of Rikel's confession and the CSO's sentence, accompanied by a letter from Richard Walker:

My dear Joan,

I've been reluctant to write this letter since I am deeply involved on two counts—my relationship with you and Jamie, and my particular function in the diamond industry. I am also in the position of reluctantly hoping that what I have to tell you might finally put an end to the affection you may still have for Jamie, but make you think more of me.

I had no other choice but to act as I did. I became involved on such a high level that there was nothing I could do to protect Jamie—assuming that I wanted to protect him. Others, too, were involved and less sensitive regarding Jamie's future, so, even if I had been moved to connive in a cover-up, I'd have had no chance of success. I personally delivered the CSO's sentence of diamond death to Jamie in Geneva at the Hôtel des Bergues and hated doing it. He reacted with a mixture of defiance and defeat. The defiance I could understand, knowing Jamie—he could always put up a good front, and I don't mean that unkindly.

After you've read Rikel's statement, you will see just how deeply Jamie was involved. It's easy to gloss over illicit diamond buying, even the odd bit of smuggling, but murder is another story. I blame Arnold Mackenzie, of course, an evil genius if ever there was one—and he must be held responsible for the Komalu miners' deaths. But Jamie knew the miners would die and that makes him an accessory.

No charges can be brought as far as I can see at this moment. The only suggestion of proof is contained in Rikel's statement, and Jamie refuses to confirm that Rikel has told the truth. So, as far as the law goes, Jamie can stay in Geneva a free man.

According to Rikel and what I've deduced, Jamie is a very rich man; this would explain his generosity to you when he left the States. Over the years, he and Mackenzie must have stacked up an enormous amount—as you will see from Rikel's statement many millions of dollars are involved.

The devil of the piece is missing—gone to ground—and is being looked for in connection with another theft in which Jamie is involved because of his past association with Mackenzie. Jamie has been questioned but can tell us nothing about his "friend"—or won't. You see? I alternate writing kindly of Jamie and throwing in bits of disapproval. That's because I happen to be in love with you and the old Adam tells me, "Hit Jamie Turner hard—make her see what a louse he is —how untrustworthy and ready to take part in a killing for profit—reduce him in size so that you add cubits to your own stature."

I could tell you more "to press my suit sharper than a Seventh Avenue pants presser," as Jamie put it, but I told him I would not. And in telling you this, in part, I've broken my promise.

If a storm breaks, I don't know how severe it will be. I do sincerely hope it doesn't get into the hands of snooping journalists. If it does, it won't be due to any action on my part. I'll come to you at the drop of a hat, Joan. Call me if you need me and I'll catch the first possible flight to New York.

With all my love, as ever,

Richard

Richard Walker was not looking forward to the interview. He sat in Robin Dickson's office with its framed prints of horses, and photographs of family, and waited for Carol Grantham.

When she entered, he smiled his welcome and said, "Please sit down, Carol. Would you like coffee?"

"If it would help what appears to be a social occasion."

"It's more than that, I'm afraid."

"Then I'll have coffee."

She sat down and watched as Walker poured two cups from the percolator and took a seat opposite her. "I want to talk to you both as a friend and in my capacity as security chief—and I don't know how to begin."

She took the cup of coffee from him. "There's always the beginning."

"Which means I have to let you know that, unwittingly, I learned something about your private life, Carol. It wouldn't be my business if it didn't concern someone close to you—or who might be close to you."

"Who?"

"Jamie Turner."

"I see." She stirred the coffee in which she had put no sugar. "He comes under the heading of my *very* private life."

"There's a danger of it becoming public."

"I don't see why." Suddenly disliking him, she added, "Unless it's to do with your liking for his wife."

"That was uncalled for," Walker said. "Jamie told you, I suppose."

"He mentioned it."

"I want you to read something, Carol." He picked up the Rikel statement and handed it to her. "I suggest we stop talking until you've read this."

He saw her expression change as she read—defensive hostility to him gave way to hurt bewilderment. She looked up from the statement, silent and questioning.

"And this, please, Carol." Walker handed her the CSO's statement of ostracism.

For perhaps a minute after she had read it, she was silent, her head lowered. "Is this true?" she asked. "Was he an accessory?"

"Yes. I'm sorry, Carol. I know you were with him in Geneva. I accidentally saw you with him. I assumed that what I saw was a fact. That you and he—you know what I mean, Carol."

"Your assumption was right."

"I have to ask you—did you know anything about Turner's association with Mackenzie?"

"Why don't you ask me if I said, 'Goody goody, lots of lovely money and diamonds and to hell with dead bodies?' " There was bitterness in her voice. "Did it cross your mind that I'd helped them with my expert knowledge of diamond and how to tell the good from the bad?"

"It didn't cross my mind," Walker said. "Listen to me, Carol. Dirt rubs off. To put it bluntly, anyone closely connected with Jamie Turner isn't welcome in the CSO."

"I see." Carol looked beyond Walker. Two pigeons had settled on the sill outside the window, and she watched them preening their feathers. Eventually she brought her gaze back to Walker. She said, "My job with the Corporation isn't all that important. This"—she tapped the Rikel statement—"hits something more important and personal."

"I had to tell you, Carol."

"Yes, I see that. I'm sorry I said that about his wife and you—I was on the defensive. It's just that—how is one supposed to feel when someone you like, or might have loved, suddenly changes, like a Jekyll and Hyde character, into a thief, murderer, and liar? Can you believe anything he's said? Worse still, you remember things you've said and thought—the sort of things people think and say when they're in love, or think they're in love."

"Did it go as far as that?"

"It went as far as that and was meant to go further."

"If Rikel hadn't exposed him," Walker began.

"I'd have cheerfully played corespondent."

"Past tense—Carol?"

"Yes—I didn't mean to. Perhaps I did. I'm confused, Richard. Hurt. Where does it go from here? Do you think dirt has rubbed off?"

"I had to check," Walker said. "All I want is your assurance that you knew nothing of his association with Mackenzie."

"I knew nothing—*nothing!* It was stupidly romantic, and we looked across the lake dancing in the sun and talked about a future with an apathetic wife got rid of. I'd have a man full of fun and a lover free and easy without a care in the world. We played it tender, and he was considerate with the right degree of sweet sadness you expect from a lover."

She smiled without humor. "It doesn't take long for love to turn into something very unhygienic, does it, Richard?"

"I don't know, Carol. I'm still in love with his wife."

She went back to her sorting table and tried to concentrate. After twenty minutes of useless work she left without excuse and taxied to her flat. She telephoned cancellation of her weekend flight to Geneva, then sent a telegram to Turner: *"Saw Richard Walker stop not only Lake Geneva is polluted stop flight cancelled stop goodbye stop Carol."*

And then she wept, not because she had lost someone she loved, but because she felt she had been the victim of gross deception, her body invaded by something alien and despicable.

The late flight from Kennedy Airport to Europe rolled out to its takeoff run, waited for clearance, then surged forward down the path whose lights seemed to zoom into infinity. After the Boeing had lifted off and steadily climbed to course upcoast to Newfoundland, it veered to take a bearing to Geneva.

Joan Turner looked through the cabin window and saw the lights of the American coast disappear, and faced the hours ahead when she would think of no one but Jamie, disgraced and alone in Geneva. She had read Richard Walker's letter and then the indictment he had enclosed. She had felt no shock. Her reaction had been simple, as simple as a doctor diagnosing a treatable illness needing care and attention to guarantee recovery of the patient. She had made no moral judgment, neither had she felt the need to seek confirmation by calling Walker. She had booked a flight to Geneva, packed a suitcase, taken a cab to the airport, and boarded the Boeing 747. A short wait in transit at Heathrow and then Swissair to Geneva and Jamie. Only one niggling thought intruded on her instinctive desire to be with Jamie: What did Richard mean by "I could tell you more 'to press my suit sharper than a Seventh Avenue pants presser' . . . but I told him I would not"? Was Jamie disgraced but *not* alone?

Many seats away from Joan Turner, Sol Grunwald lighted a cigar with a match torn from a matchbook. At ten o'clock the following morning he would enter the double bronze doors of Number Two Charterhouse Street and attend a sight; there he would sit with Mr. Dalmon and spend three hundred grand on, he hoped, top-quality rough diamonds.

It was a pleasure to limp through those bronze doors and to be treated with respect; synonymous with the thought was memory of the last time he had seen James Drake Turner in the diamond corridors of the CSO. There was no welcome there for Turner; those solid doors were slammed shut against him forever, and Grunwald felt sorry for the man.

Before leaving for the airport, he had sat with Sadie and weighed his success story against Turner's. "Two ways a guy can go it alone, Sadie: honestly or dishonestly, and the honest way ain't easy. From experience I speak, Sadie. Today we are rich and our grandson has fifteen thousand bucks in trust and my brother's wife has her brooch for services rendered. And why are we rich, Sadie? I will tell you. For riches an honest guy must suffer the attentions of hoods who mean him harm. I speak from experience." And as he spoke Grunwald remembered the men's toilet in Dakar and the toilet at Kennedy Airport. "You will never know, Sadie, what I have suffered so my sister-in-law gets her diamond brooch and my grandson fifteen thousand dollars."

"You set zircon in the brooch, Sol, not diamonds," Sadie said.

"So, does Dave's wife know the difference? She enjoys them like diamonds. You think she needs that clasp as an investment? It is the gift that counts."

It was a minor dishonesty, Grunwald thought as he drew on his cigar; but the Turner-Mackenzie act was on a Mafia scale.

"What does the Talmud say?" Sadie had asked.

"About what?"

"About Turner."

Grunwald searched his memory. " 'When the righteous man dies,' " he quoted, " 'it is the earth that weeps. The lost jewel will always be a lost jewel, but the possessor who has lost it—well may he weep.' "

And in Turner's case, I would weep, Grunwald said to himself; and then, his thoughts now directed to fat, comfortable, law-abiding Sadie, another quote from the Talmud entered his mind: "He who weds a good woman, it is as if he had fulfilled all the precepts of the Law."

Joan Turner had arrived at the Hôtel des Bergues and, half afraid to confront Jamie, had ordered coffee, which she now drank in the lounge. She drank it black and strong and felt its bitterness bite into her tiredness.

At 10:15 she asked for and was given Jamie's suite number, and she took the lift to the first floor. After her third pressing of the door buzzer she was admitted by a gray-faced, still-pajamaed Turner, and as he stared at her she saw the look of a demolished man.

"Jamie?" she said. "I had to come, Jamie."

"Had to?" He walked away from her and slumped into a chair. "No one has to—except to clear up the mess."

An empty bottle lay on its side on the carpet, and clothes littered the room.

"Walker told you, I suppose?"

"He wrote to me."

"So you came to see the wreck. You've got every right to gloat, Joanie. Have yourself a great time. I drink until I can tell the world 'Shit!' Liquor's great . . . there's a point where everything's a damn big joke—Walker, the CSO, diamonds, even death's laughable because it's common—dead common."

"So's life," Joan said.

"That too. Last night I laughed myself sick at a thought—you always hate the one you love—ain't that something, Joanie?"

"Who do you hate, Jamie?"

"Every goddam thing when I'm drunk, every goddam thing!"

"I said who, not what."

"Two women—you and someone else."

"I don't want to know about the someone else."

"Why should you? She's sperm under the sexual bridge by now! How's that for metaphor? I've got the biggest hangover in Christendom and I can dream up a lulu like that."

"That leaves me, Jamie."

"That sure leaves you, baby." A smile twisted Turner's face. "The one you wanted walks out, and the one you didn't walks in like a faithful dog either anxious to comfort her master or bite him hard."

"I didn't come to bite you."

"Then lick my hand, sweet bitch, and tell me all's forgiven."

Joan walked to the window and looked out across the lake; she heard him mutter, "Golden oysters dancing on a polluted lake."

"What did you say?" she asked.

"The view from here is pretty, isn't it?"

The venom in Turner was oozing out like pus from a lanced boil. Soon, she told herself, the core itself would be ejected. To further the escape, she said, "It's a lovely day and the lake's an incredible blue—it is nice to be here."

"Jesus!" Turner got up from the chair and staggered as the sudden action hit the thumping in his head. "Why the hell don't you do social work in skid row? Swab up the piss those winos spill out on the sidewalk, and wash their stinking bodies, then go to bed with them for rehabilitation's sake?"

"Is that how you see yourself?"

"Sure—why not? Isn't that what you came to see? Take a long loving look, Joanie—ain't I the best lookin' drunk you ever did see?"

She said quietly, "Stop whining, Jamie."

Nausea suddenly rose up in him. He said in a small voice, "I want to be sick, Joanie."

Her arm was round his shoulders as he heaved and retched in the bathroom, the smell and contents of his vomit revealing little trace of food but slime tinged green with bile. When the spasms were over, she supported him to a stool, then filled the bath.

"Thank you, Joanie. Thank you," he said, as she sponged his body.

When he was clean, she helped him out of the bath and into a bathrobe.

"Bed, Jamie," she said. "No talking—that can come later."

Like a child, he allowed her to put him to bed, grateful as she settled him down. A little before he went into sleep, he said, "I couldn't get a hard-on, Joanie, even if my life depended on it."

"You don't need one just now," she said. "Go to sleep, Jamie. I'll be here when you wake up."

"Promise?"

"I promise."

The sun was setting over the Jura, its last red-gold shafts striking the peak of Mount Blanc, when Turner, mistrusting his ability to keep down the meal ordered by Joan, ate scrambled eggs on thin brown toast. The coffee helped, and he watched her refill his cup. Color had returned to his face, and sometime during his sleep—he had no recollection— she had used his electric shaver to remove his two-day stubble of beard. But he felt weak, drained of strength.

"Hardly the end to a perfect day, Joanie," he said. "I'm ashamed and sorry. I'm grateful, too."

"How long had you been drinking, Jamie?"

"Seems like a lifetime. I don't know. I'd make up my mind to go out on the town, then do nothing about it and phone down for whisky. I'd decide to go to bed, then sit by that bloody window and watch the dawn come up. . . . We've got a lot to talk about, Joanie, haven't we?"

"I've read that doctor's statement and the CSO's little piece. It's spilt sour milk as far as I'm concerned. It's the future, Jamie, that worries me—and I don't necessarily mean ours."

"A pariah doesn't have a future—except with other outcasts."

"What can I do to join the low-caste group?"

"Do you want to?"

"If it means I can be with you."

"Like a nun joining a leper colony for the sheer pleasure of catching the disease just to please God? I'm an accessory to murder—you've got to understand that and I've grown rich in the process. Very rich."

"I know."

"So why don't you counsel me to empty my pockets or go to Sierra

Leone and admit my guilt and take what punishment they care to dish out?"

"I dismissed that notion on the way over, Jamie. I'm not a saint, neither am I particularly honest. As for the money you've made, you'll need that to reestablish yourself."

"In what?" Turner said. "There's not an honest dealer who'd touch me now and forever."

"There'll be other things—other interests. It's early days yet."

"Yes," Turner said. "It's early lousy days—and I'm not going to Sierra Leone because I'm scared shitless and always will be."

"I have to ask you this," Joan said. "I can take it, Jamie. I really can. I can't lose what I've already lost, can I? Richard hinted that he could tell me more that didn't seem to have anything to do with diamonds and Mackenzie, so I've got to ask you. . . . Is there someone else—another woman?"

"There might have been, but there isn't."

"I see."

"You don't see." Turner got to his feet. "I've been riding on diamonds and good old sex in the belief that it was the good life—the real success story!"

"Sex?" Joan asked. "We didn't see much of that, Jamie."

"It went into hiding when the Mackenzie caper started and the diamond flow began to build up. Collection trips and hot-seat flights to Geneva. When we'd topped the two-million mark, I thought of nothing but doubling that figure and doubling yet again. The last trip to South America was to be the biggest and best of the lot. It was the last, Joanie, the last great caper! Mac and I had made it, and old Simon Legree Sex came out of hiding. Oh, boy! How that old bastard came out of hiding! I was glad—don't get me wrong. It helped wipe out something so obscene it twisted my gut!"

Joan said quietly, "Tell me about it."

"It was in South America. You read Rikel's confession, but it didn't end with his story. I went to a fleabag hotel in Aracaju and saw a bedbug on the forehead of a dead man. Malaria. He'd been used by Mac to get the diamonds from the miner's body shipped from Sierra Leone. I'd seen Partridge—that was the man's name—the day before and taken the stones from him. I closed his eyes before I left the room."

"Then you came back to New York and we talked," Joan said. "Next day you left for Geneva—and what, Jamie?"

"Sex—and that's all it turned out to be!" Anger had strengthened him, and he walked about the room, arms tightly folded. "It's the great traitor of all time. When you rely on it as if you've found God, it lets you down. It blinds you, then opens your eyes to see everything in bright, sordid light!"

"I never saw it like that, Jamie," Joan said. "Even when we didn't quite make it together, it was a comfort. This girl, Jamie—did she mean so much to you?"

"I thought so. I saw her as wiping part of the slate clean. Change of identity. I was always good at pushing dirt under the carpet and forgetting all about it. Dirt and people. Mac can do it with ease, but he's selective—he chooses the dispensable. Mastery over conscience—he's got that to the nth degree. I guess I wanted to be like him. When he came here with this fantastic diamond—two thousand carats, Joanie!—it scared the pants off me. . . . When I told him I wanted no part in it, he just smiled and told me it was okay and that he'd go it alone. He needed me badly, but he played it *so* cool. I could have taken the diamond off him and, at the same time, called off the dogs, but I didn't. Now, he's gone off into the wilds, and what do I do? I beat my goddamned breast and sick up my guts because I've been found out."

He ceased pacing the floor and stood in the center of the room, near exhausted of words. She watched anger leave him, saw it leave his face and the very stance of his body, so that he seemed smaller, defenseless. Then he walked slowly to the chair by the window and sat down, burying his face in his hands. Eventually he took his hands from his face and said without vehemence, "When Mac outlined our last operation, I told myself my hands would be clean. All I had to do was collect from Partridge and hotfoot it to Geneva. After all, I'd bought illicit for Gem International, and that was all I was doing with Mac. I've just tried to do the same thing with love and sex. I wanted to prove I could do without you and Carol."

"Is that her name?" Joan asked.

"Yes. I met her in London months ago. It's all over now. Dick Walker saw to that."

"I wonder why I'm here, Jamie."

"You came at the right time—for what it's worth. When Dick Walker, Appleby, and Manston left, I wanted both you and Carol. I needed what both of you could give."

"And now there's only me."

"You came at the right time," he said again. "I want you to stay."

"For how long? Is it a case of any old port in a storm?"

"I don't know for how long. I'm not lying or pretending anymore. I need you—and that sounds like a line from an old movie. How do you put it in good English? I feel I cannot cope with the future deprived of your help and guidance? Question is, for how long can you take it? Maybe Dick Walker's a better bet."

"Don't be so damn contrite and humble!" She spoke sharply. "Do you want me to believe you're nothing but a worthless, guilty slob?"

"Convince me I'm not."

"It might take years to do that, Jamie, if you keep mea-culpaing all over the place and doing nothing about anything."

"You're a nice woman, Joanie."

"Yes," she said, "I think I am. I'm also hard, and ready to share past dishonesties with you, but no more cover-ups, Jamie. No more dirt under the carpet. You say we're rich?"

"Very. We've got millions, Joanie—millions!"

"Then, we'll spend the years using it to neutralize the dirt and the stink. Don't ask me how, because I don't know. It's to be thought about, Jamie. One thing's important, though—no further contact with Arnold Mackenzie."

"I can promise no more deals," Turner said, "but if Mac needs help, I'll help him—all the way, Joanie." He looked at the bottle of Bell's whisky in the liquor cabinet. "Poor old Mac, who's going to help him?"

CHAPTER **33.**

MACKENZIE was on his way home. He had reached that bi-furcation of roads in England known as Scotch Corner, where the A1 ends to become a motorway, and an A-road branches west to Brough and Penrith and merges with the M6 up to Carlisle, Glasgow, and the winding roads to Oban and the Western Isles.

In the weeks of backtracking through France after he left Geneva, Mackenzie's beard had grown; now reaching maturity, it was fiery-red and trimmed so that anyone observing him with interest would have dubbed him a mariner.

His longest stay in one place had been the three weeks spent in the Auvergne. The hotel at the Viaduc des Fades, poised high above a great dam spanned by a railway bridge, had given him a kind of peace, and he would have stayed longer had not the yellowing leaves of the trees reminded him that autumn and winter came early to Scotland. He made his way to Normandy, ever watchful and on the alert. On a little used stretch of coast near Fécamp he used money to bribe a passage across the Channel.

A few miles off the coast of Kent a boat had been lowered over the side of the fishing smack, and Mackenzie had rowed through the night to a beach where he left the boat to be carried away by the tide.

He had little money left, and he was more than five hundred miles from Scotland. When he reached the Kentish village of Breznett, he put up at the King's Head, a small pub-hotel. There he telephoned Jamie Turner.

He recognized Joan's voice as soon as it came on the line; in re-sponse to his cheerful, bantering voice, she said, "I'll bring him to the phone. When you've finished speaking with him—get out of his life."

His conversation with Turner was brief. He was told that Rikel had blown the Komalu operation and that Appleby was in Europe.

"Where is he now?" Mackenzie asked.

"Last I heard he was in London. That was weeks ago."

"You've had a bad time, Jamie?"

"Yes. I've been blacklisted, Mac. I'm a bad smell wherever diamonds are mined and sold. You've still got the diamond?"

"Of course. Look, Jamie, send me some cash. Not much—fifty quid will do; I'm on my way to Scotland. Once I'm at Oban, I can use the bank. Cable that fifty quid to me here at the King's Head, Breznett, Kent —have you got that?"

"I've got it."

"Who's on my track, Jamie—apart from Appleby?"

"I don't know. Manston and Co could be. I haven't heard a whisper since they called on me the day after you showed me that damned diamond."

"All right, Jamie. You won't hear from me for a time. . . . Maybe when the spring comes I might turn up in Geneva. Don't forget, if you move on, notify me via the Bank of Scotland in Oban. Get off the line now, and send that money."

And now he stood by the roadside at Scotch Corner and waited for a friendly lorry driver to respond to his hitchhiker's thumb sign.

It was well after midday when a lorry bearing the name *Patterson of Glasgow* pulled up and, obeying a gesture to come aboard, Mackenzie climbed up to the cabin and sat next to the driver.

"If Glasgow's good enough for you, that's where I'm going," the driver said.

"Glasgow'll be fine. Just fine."

"You'll be travelling far?"

"Northwest."

"To the Isles, maybe?"

"Aye."

The driver snatched a glance at Mackenzie's brown, bearded face. "You're a Scot, I can tell that. You've been away for a long time?"

"Too long."

"Would that be in foreign parts?"

Mackenzie grinned. "You've only to cross the border from Scotland into England to be in foreign parts."

"That's true enough."

Six hours later, a few miles outside Glasgow, Mackenzie asked the driver to drop him and offered an English pound note. The driver shook his head. "I'd take it from a Sassenach but not from a fellow Scot. I reckon you can ill afford it, mister, unless"—he tapped the side of his nose and winked—"you robbed the Bank of England."

"Nothing like so small," Mackenzie said "I steal diamonds worth millions."

He watched the lorry grind away, its right-hand blinker glowing orange in the darkness. Loneliness closed round him, and he heard a train's bugle call from far away. He looked at his watch: 8:30 and night had closed down on Scotland. He shouldered his pack and made his way into the town. He'd find somewhere to eat and sleep, and tomorrow would see him in Oban and the Western Isles.

Mackenzie strode into the town bearing on his back the articles that kept a man decent and clean. And packed away in a heart of socks, underwear, sleeping bag, and other bare essentials, the Star of Angwana lay hidden. His silhouette as he passed lighted shop windows resembled that of a tall hunchback.

Appleby shivered against the cold wind blowing down the street. He had thought it would be warmer in London in October, for England's Indian summers were still talked about by exiles in Africa; the biting northeast wind slapped the face of nostalgia and false memory.

He entered the hotel that had been his base since his arrival in England with Richard Walker and felt the welcoming heat as he emerged from the revolving doors and entered the lobby.

He asked for his key at the reception desk, and as he made his way to the lift the receptionist called him back. "A message, Dr. Appleby, from a Mr. Turner, calling from Geneva."

"What is the message?"

"He said he would call again at six o'clock."

In his room, Appleby peeled off his heavy topcoat, then rang room service and ordered tea. When it came, he sat by the window looking out on the gray street. Rain had begun to fall, and he thought of the clear skies and sun in Angwana.

The search had to end soon. The weeks had passed in fruitless journeys; he had asked questions and taken boats to islands with strange names set in dangerous waters, looking for a man who could be anywhere on the face of the earth. Switzerland bordered France, Italy, and Germany. Mackenzie could be in any of those countries. All he, Appleby, had to justify his base in Britain was the conviction that Mackenzie's homing instinct would lead him back to Scotland. But Europe contained a thousand places where a man could go to ground.

London was depressing. It stunned him with the speed and noise of its traffic, and the City itself, a towering mass of glass and concrete, seemed to threaten and tell him that he had no place in Britain. That was certainly true, he told himself; I have no one here—no relatives, no nearest and dearest; and the only man I can call my friend is also a kind of enemy.

Remembering a fruitless journey to Scotland, the result of a faint memory of Mac's once calling Oban a "jumping-off" place, Appleby was in a quandary. If Turner had no positive information to warrant a further search for Mac, a return to Angwana had to be considered; it would be an empty-handed return, which Sotho would readily forgive. But it was not only the Star of Angwana Appleby wanted, it was also the act of trust and friendship accompanying the diamond's return. So what to do? Return to Angwana or wait and hope in London or Oban or wherever lack of inspiration sent him? Perhaps Turner *did* have good news, perhaps Mac had had a change of heart and given the Star to Turner.

Appleby's spirits lifted. Turner wouldn't go to the trouble of telephoning from Switzerland unless he had something worthwhile to say. Mac could even be with him in Geneva—that would be incredible. And why not?

Appleby looked down at the darkening, rain-wet street and remembered other times—his long association with Mackenzie and the enjoyable meetings when Mac's sardonic humor made for lively argument that was never ill-tempered.

Murderer, thief, and confidence man—that was Arnold Mackenzie. Trusted friend, reliable, bluff Mac—that also was Arnold Mackenzie. As he waited for the telephone to ring Appleby wondered which of the two he would eventually face.

He drank his third cup of tea and watched the hands of his wristwatch tick away the seconds to six o'clock. Promptly on the hour his room telephone uttered its discreet *cheep-cheep*, and he picked up the receiver after the second signal.

"A call for you, Dr. Appleby. From Geneva. You are through, Geneva. . . ."

Turner's voice came over the line: "Dr. Appleby?"

"Yes, Mr. Turner. I'm here. Have you news?"

"He's in England. Or he was five days ago. I called you several times, but you were away."

"It's good of you to call, Mr. Turner. Where is Mac?"

"He was in Kent. A village called Breznett. I sent him some money. Listen, Doctor. He's on his way to Scotland. I can't give you details because he didn't give me any. All I know is, he may be making for a place called Oban."

"I was there a little while ago."

"One other thing. He has an account with the Bank of Scotland in Oban. That's all I can tell you. I'm breaking trust in telling you, but I'm taking you at your word that everything you do will be in his interests."

"You have my word, Mr. Turner. Neither Richard Walker nor Manston is with me, or will be with me. Did you speak to Mac?"

"Yes. Over the phone."

"How did he seem?"

"Same voice, same manner. I told him about Rikel and that you were in England."

"So he knows I'm looking for him?"

"Oh, yes, he knows. Look, Doctor, why not wait? He told me he might turn up in Geneva next spring. Go back to Angwana. If and when Mac turns up, I'll let you know."

"No." Appleby's voice was firm. "It's now or never. You've given me hope, Mr. Turner—real hope. I think I shall find him now."

"Be careful. You know I think well of Mac, but if he's cornered—"

"Mac would never lift a hand to harm me."

"You'll never get him to part with the diamond."

"We'll see, Mr. Turner. Thank you for calling. Would you like me to let you know what happens?"

"I'd appreciate it."

As Turner hung up, Joan said, "Why did you say you thought well of Mackenzie?"

"Because I do. He's a difficult man to dislike, Joanie."

"I find it easy."

"He and I are financially and officially apart. That's the best I can do."

Turner's decision to use Mackenzie's authorization to act with power of attorney and divide the Turner-Mackenzie deposit of diamonds and cash in the Banque d'Helvétie had been a token gesture toward disassociation from Mackenzie—a gesture approved by Joan. It was, at least, the beginning to the end she most desired: a total break with Mackenzie. The holding had been split down the middle, and the bank now handled two accounts, one in the name of Arnold Mackenzie and another in the joint names of J. D. and J. Turner. The gradual unloading of the diamond was an operation set some time in the future, the how and where deliberately avoided until events either forced Turner's hand or the climate suggested more favorable conditions.

"What will you do if Mackenzie asks for your help, Jamie?" Joan asked.

"I'll give it. There's no one that Mac can turn to. I can't give him much, but what I can give—he has only to ask. That's something you can't change, Joanie."

* * *

The island of Luing had changed little in his years of absence; shapes and land contours were the same, but miniaturized. Mackenzie had walked the miles from Cuan Sound, past the primary school he had attended and the war memorial, and along the track that led to Black Mill Bay, remembering it as a busy place with an iron jetty built to serve the quarry boats bringing slate from Belnahua.

He stood on the grass clearing and looked around him. The jetty had gone but pieces of its rusting skeleton littered the rocks below the clearing. A dead swan lay a few yards away, part of the detritus either washed up by the sea or left by boats using the bay.

And it was quiet but for the lapping of the tide and the cries of gulls; in Mackenzie's memory the bay rang with the shouts of men and the clanking of machinery, lively with teams of horses and traction engines tugging at loads of slate glittering with silver-gold pyrites.

The difference between memory and present-day reality pleased him. In his walk from Cuan Sound only one vehicle had passed him—a post bus serving Cullipool, Toberonochy, and the scattered crofts on the island.

He looked out across the bay to Lunga and the smaller islands of Fiola Meadhonach and Rubha Fiola; the curve of the bay obscured Belnahua, and he remembered his father rowing from the quarry island, skirting Cullipool until Black Mill Bay came in sight.

A green-and-white boat lay at its moorings beyond the dead swan and where sloping rock led to the sea. As Mackenzie looked, a man left the boat and made his way toward him. A vestigial memory stirred in Mackenzie. Thirty-five years ago, when he and his parents had left Belnahua and the islands, there had been a lobster man noted for his ability to poach the salmon, or take his boat to Scarba and come back with a freshly killed deer. The sea-booted man approaching him must be in his seventies, Mackenzie guessed; but the tall, thin figure matched his memory of the younger man.

Above the bay, where a cliff rose ten or so feet, a line of crofts, five in number, huddled together in various stages of neglect or repair. As he watched, Mackenzie saw the man pause and look in his direction before entering the last but one of the crofts.

Mackenzie hoisted the pack onto his shoulders and made his way around the grass clearing and along the top of the cliff. The man from the boat stood in his doorway, and Mackenzie, pausing at the gate, exchanged glances with him before slipping the loop of nylon rope securing the gate and walking up the short path to the door. He had taken three paces when a black Labrador came to meet him, barking and showing her teeth.

"Easy!" Mackenzie said. "Easy now." He held out his hand. The bitch hesitated, nosed his hand, and, in response to a face and voice that showed no fear, licked the hand held out in friendship. "Come," Mackenzie said, "come, you old black devil."

The man at the doorway nodded a greeting, and Mackenzie saw him as he was thirty-five years ago. "I've come looking for a boat," Mackenzie said.

"For what purpose, mister?"

"I want to go to the islands. Will you take me?"

"Mebbe."

"You were down there with a boat—would it be yours?"

"Aye."

"I'd like a few words with you, Mr.—"

"Livingstone. John Livingstone." He looked down at the dog fawning around Mackenzie's feet. "Shuna's taken a fancy to you, mister. You'll come along in?"

The living room of the croft was tiny and cluttered. A black puppy sleeping on a chair was swiped off by Livingstone; it landed on its feet and, bewildered for a moment, looked up at Livingstone and then at Mackenzie.

"You'll take a chair?" Livingstone said.

Mackenzie slid off his pack and lowered it to the floor. As he sat down he said, "What about the boat?"

"There's a few people needing a trip round the Isles this time of the year," Livingstone said.

"I'm one of the few," said Mackenzie, "and it's not a pleasure trip I've in mind."

"You'll be having a name, mister?"

"Mackenzie. Arnold Mackenzie."

"A name to respect," Livingstone said. "I married into the clan."

Mackenzie reached into his pack and withdrew a half bottle of whisky. "We could drink to that respect—if you've a mind to."

"I've the mind and the thirst."

Two drinks later Livingstone said, "There's little to see now on Belnahua—a graveyard of a place. The crofts are in ruins, some worse than others. There's better islands to visit."

"Like Scarba for killing the deer and the waters for poaching the salmon?"

Livingstone's eyes narrowed. "You've been here before?"

"I lived on Belnahua with my parents. My father was a quarryman. I was born on that island, Livingstone. We left for Oban when there was no more work."

"Did you, now? I remember well the exodus. A plague might have hit the poor place." A smile added more creases to Livingstone's lined face. "And there was a man who killed the deer and poached the salmon."

"You're still the man, Livingstone. Do you know what it means when a man's world-weary?"

"I've not had the time to think about it."

"It means you want to get away from the world and its people. I've travelled much and I'm tired, Livingstone. I want away from it all. I want an island where I can live without being seen through to the spring. Maybe then I'll move on."

"You'll have to wait on the tide," Livingstone said. "That'll be this afternoon."

"I can wait."

Livingstone stroked his unshaven chin. "There's been many a stranger spending weeks on the islands studying the botany, I think they call it. They'd have no mind to be spending a winter out there."

"I have the mind," Mackenzie said. "With the help of a poacher like yourself, winter's no problem. I'm a rich man, Livingstone."

A smile twitched Livingstone's mouth. "The way you look does not suggest it."

"I'll need provisions. Can you get me some?"

"Hubert Duncan will be stopping by in his old car. What is it you want?"

"Bread, meat. Cans of food. Enough to see me through until you bring me a boatload."

"It can be got from Cullipool."

"I'll need whisky too."

Livingstone nodded. "My kinswoman Meg Mackenzie keeps a few bottles for souls in need."

Mackenzie reached into a pocket of his duffle coat, took out a roll of banknotes, and laid them on the table. "Get me what I want. There's many more where they came from. I'll pay you well, Livingstone—for a still tongue in that wise old head of yours."

Livingstone picked up the notes. "You'd better write me a list," he said. "I've no memory one day to the next. You'll bide here while I'm away?"

"If there's no one calling on you."

"There'll be nobody."

The tide was rising when Livingstone returned. Mackenzie watched by the window as Hubert Duncan helped Livingstone carry two cardboard boxes up to the gate, where Livingstone waited until the sound of Duncan's car died away in the distance.

Livingstone came into the croft. "I've got what you wanted, mister. If you're ready, there's enough water to get us out of the bay."

The last of the Labrador's puppies tugged at Mackenzie's trouser cuff, and Mackenzie reached down and picked it up. It was the last of Shuna's litter of seven, and Livingstone had had difficulty in disposing of the other six. "You'll be a wee bit lonely on Belnahua," he said.

"There'll be little wine, women, and song."

"You could take the puppy. A dog's grand company for a man living alone."

"Why not," Mackenzie said.

"Shuna's getting too old to have the mite tugging at her teats. You'd be doing me a favor, mister."

"Maybe it'll work both ways," Mackenzie looked into the puppy's bright brown eyes and grinned. "I've seen eyes like that in a little black man named Sotho."

"Would that be true?"

"A good name for a dog, d'you think, Livingstone?"

"It's as good as any. You'll take him, then?"

Mackenzie nodded. "If I run out of food, he'll make a couple of meals."

Livingstone frowned. "You'd do that?"

"I've eaten worse in my time." Mackenzie shook his head. "I'll not eat it. He'll live to serve all the bitches on the islands."

CHAPTER 34.

LIVINGSTONE'S boat stuttered and gasped its way out of
the bay and headed for Belnahua. Dusk had settled over the islands, re-
minding Mackenzie of the long winter nights of his childhood. The
puppy, tucked inside Mackenzie's duffle coat, whimpered, and Mackenzie
smoothed its head. "Easy, Sotho. Easy."

Shouting above the noise of the engine, Livingstone said, "You've
enough provisions, mister?"

"I've enough, but I want you back in three days, remember?"

"I'll be here."

They were nearing the island, and Mackenzie could see the ruined
crofts.

"A fine place for a man to rest his head," Livingstone said.

"It'll suit me fine," Mackenzie said. "Just remember I want nobody
to know I'm here."

"I'll not be telling a soul."

"You'll maybe be asked. If you have to, say I came to Luing, then
went back to Oban and up to Thurso. I'll have your guts for a bagpipes
if you let me down."

"You've paid me well—you need say no more. Will you stand by
with the rope?"

The boat bumped against flat smooth rocks, and Mackenzie threw
the rope, then stepped out, taking the puppy from his coat and placing
it on the grass a few feet above his head. He picked up the rope and
hitched it round an angled rock, and Livingstone said, "That'll do,
mister."

Livingstone climbed out of the boat carrying Mackenzie's rucksack.
He handed it to Mackenzie, then reached over the side of the boat and
hauled out the fully packed seaman's duffle bag. Mackenzie took it from
him and lugged it to higher ground.

"Shall I help you find a place?" Livingstone asked.

"No. You'd best get back."

It was near nightfall, and Livingstone looked across the firth. "With October getting along," he said, "I doubt you'll get visitors. Hector Galbraith might drop anchor or Laughlin McLaughlin might call in for a bit of iron, but you're safe till early spring."

The wind was freshening and whipping up the sea. "I'll be going, then," Livingstone said, "if I'm to be warm in my house with a toddy."

"Three days," Mackenzie said. "I want you back in three days and no more."

"I'll not let you down. I've got your list, mister."

"Look after me, Livingstone, and I'll look after you."

Livingstone smiled. "You've started doing that well, mister. Will you cast me off?"

Mackenzie watched Livingstone crank his engine into life, then move away from the island riding the heavy swell inshore until it reached rougher water where it pitched and tossed in the sea that was getting more agitated as the sky darkened.

Carrying the rucksack and duffle bag, Mackenzie trudged up the rocky beach to the center of the crofts, the puppy close at heel. It began to rain, and Mackenzie put down his burden and pulled the hood of the duffle coat over his head. He had to find somewhere habitable, something at least with the semblance of a roof. In one of the larger crofts he found a part that was still slate-roofed; a room twelve feet square and floored with chipped slate. There was a rusting fireplace with a chimney-piece that was sound; three wall shelves that had somehow resisted decay; and two windows, one of them intact and facing out across the sea, the other facing Cullipool and bare of frame and glass. It would do for the night, Mackenzie decided; tomorrow he'd scour the island for something better.

The puppy was pulling at his trouser cuff, and Mackenzie picked it up. "You little black bastard. Getting hungry, are we?"

A flight of gulls suddenly swirled over Belnahua, shrieking in a burst of bad temper, and Mackenzie thought of the vultures in Sierra Leone. A strong draft was blowing through the window space, and Mackenzie put the puppy down and went outside. A few yards away a partly rotted wooden door lay on the turf. He picked it up and carried it back to the croft. He placed the door against the window, securing it with rocks.

Mackenzie looked through the intact window, out across the wild sea; in the rapidly falling dusk he could see the revolving beam on Fladda lighthouse shimmering through the rain that was falling steadily.

He came away from the window and methodically sorted out the contents of duffle and rucksack; sleeping bag, cans of food, bread, cartons of Long Life milk, two bottles of whisky, tea bags, instant coffee, a small saucepan, two enamelled metal plates, a mug, a Primus stove and a liter bottle of methylated spirits, a white plastic container that held a gallon of water, a dozen boxes of matches, and a packet of candles, one of which he now lighted.

Methodically he stacked provisions and utensils on the shelves, the cans of food neatly arranged as if on display in a shop. When he had finished, he went back to the rucksack and extracted the diamond from its bed of socks and underwear. In the light from the flickering candle the crystal gleamed yellow. He looked around the dimly lit ruined room, then, remembering Appleby's hiding place in the work hut, he went back to the shelves and put the diamond behind a can of baked beans.

The puppy was worrying at his feet, and Mackenzie took a can of dog food from the shelf and opened it, spilling its contents onto one of the enamelled plates.

He watched the puppy eating and scattering the food in its excitement and hunger, then reached for a bottle of whisky, unscrewed its cap, and drank straight from the bottle. That was better; the spirits sent a core of warmth down to his stomach. He scanned the shelves and planned his evening meal: stewed steak and peas and potatoes, followed by coffee laced with whisky. In the end, he carved a thick slice of bread, opened a can of stewed steak, and ate it cold.

When he had finished, he unrolled the sleeping bag, took off his boots, and climbed into the bag. For a while he lay on his back thinking of the weeks and months ahead. The long wait had begun, and he felt no apprehension, no fear of discovery and retribution. Even his choice of sanctuary—a ruined island and hostile climate instead of some refuge in warm southern Europe—he looked upon without regret. It was lousy, he told himself, but it was home.

A warm, wet tongue licked at his ear, and he reached up and pulled the puppy to him so that it nestled in the sleeping bag. "Sleep, little black bastard," Mackenzie said. "Sleep. Tomorrow we'll walk the island and find a place fit for one man and his dog to live in."

Appleby looked across Cuan Sound to the island of Luing. He knew from the map he had studied that beyond Luing lay the islands of Mull and Scarba, Belnahua and Shuna, the mountains of the Jura and a thousand scattered islands to the north and the south.

He had asked questions in Oban—questions answered with a shrug or a monologue spoken in the soft brogue of western Scotland. Had they seen such a man? No such man had been seen on the regular ferry services to Mull or Lochaline, and such a stranger would have been noticed now that the season was over and the holidaymakers had gone away. There were the ferries at Seil and Corran, where boats could be found fishing for the mackerel and laying and lifting the lobster pots and willing to take the tripper around the islands. Would he not be trying Easdale on Seil, and Toberonochy and Cullipool on the isle of Luing?

And the two Banks of Scotland in Oban had been unhelpful; many Mackenzies had accounts with them, but the gentleman must understand that customer accounts were sacred and absolutely no information could be given.

He decided to move southwest of Oban and down to the islands lying in the Firth of Lorn, and now, after a ride in the post bus from Oban, he waited for the Luing ferry regretting the fact that he could not drive a car and had to rely on local buses and the limited passenger service offered by the GPO postal vans. It had never crossed his mind that he would need a driver's license to hire a car in Britain, or, for that matter, even to drive one. He had been naive and Angwanan. In Africa he hadn't needed a license to rattle the Land-Rover or the prospecting truck over the wastes of Angwana.

Appleby looked across Cuan Sound to the Luing jetty. The ferry's mooring ropes had been cast off, and the square boat was crabbing its way across the fast-running tide. As it maneuvered into the Cuan jetty he walked down the seaweeded slope, waited for the mooring ropes to be made fast, then went aboard. Maclean, the ferry master, called down from the cabin: "We'll be crossing in thirty minutes or thereabouts."

"Do you have a moment?" Appleby asked.

"Aye."

"I'm looking for someone. A friend. You might have seen him."

Maclean climbed down from the cabin. "And would I be knowing your friend?"

"He could be on one of the islands."

Maclean looked amused. "I can take you to only one out of hundreds, and that's Luing over yonder. There's tours from Oban, or there was. Better wait for the spring. This time of the year's no good for visiting the islands." He looked up at the sky and the fast, scudding clouds that had begun to pile up to the north. "There's a bad spell on its way."

The tide was flowing fast through the Cuan Sound. "Twelve knots," Maclean said. "When the tide comes in, the current runs at twelve knots. This friend—what manner of man would he be?"

"Big—well over six feet. And travelling light, I think. He may have grown a beard—it would have been red. He's a Scot and his name's Mackenzie."

"Would he be related to Mistress Mackenzie of Cullipool? That would be Meg Mackenzie."

"I don't know."

"Mark you, Mackenzie's not an uncommon name in Argyll."

"But have you ferried a man fitting that description?"

"I've no recollection. Mebbe he crossed in my time off. When would your friend be likely to have crossed?"

"Within the last week."

"And I came on yesterday. There was no man with a beard or a big man travelling light, but old Johnnie Livingstone travelled heavy."

"Livingstone?"

"He has a wee house at Black Mill Bay and a creaky old boat he takes through the Corrie Vechan—that's the Grey Dog in English—and risks the lives of those he takes with him. But he's a good old fellow, even though he clips the English when they want a trip round the islands. Mackenzie is a clan—like my own name, Maclean; and we're flung all over the world. Canada, now, you'll find thousands of Mackenzies and Macleans, to say nothing of Campbells and Duncans, Maclarens and the like. I mind the time during the war—I was attached to a Canadian battalion. It was like a gathering of the clans if you cut out the Frenchies."

"Yes," said Appleby, "I'm sure the Scots are spread over the globe, but, Mr. Maclean, this Mrs. Mackenzie—Cullipool, did you say?"

"Aye. Some call it the capital of Luing. Look there, now," Maclean pointed to the Luing jetty across the sound. "That's the Luing post bus waiting there. I'll be crossing to get the post. It'll take you to Cullipool. Ask anyone where Meg Mackenzie lives. Mebbe she knows your friend. Mackenzies know all about the Mackenzies—those on the islands, that is."

Appleby looked back at the waiting Oban post bus; the old people he had travelled with from Oban had gone.

"The last ferry from Luing is at six tonight," Maclean said. "If you miss it, sound the siren at the top of the jetty. It'll cost you a pound."

"I'll remember that," Appleby said. "You said you'd just come on duty. . . . Can I see the other man?"

"He'll be away in Oban till Monday. If you want to find Donney Kilmartin, you'll need to start in the first pub in Oban and, mebbe, you might find him before you reach the last." Maclean eyed Appleby. "And you don't look like a man to drink his way from one pub to another."

There's nothing to lose, thought Appleby. At least he had found a Mackenzie, and Mac had come from the western islands of Scotland. Perhaps memories were still fresh in the minds of the people of Luing.

"You seem to be the only passenger," Maclean said. "I'll cast off, if you're coming."

"Yes," said Appleby, "I'm coming."

* * *

The post bus took the winding, narrow road toward Cullipool, rattling over iron grills set in the road and splashing through patches of loose cattle dung. "It's late in the season for visitors," the driver said. "It'll be near dark by four o'clock. If you're not staying on the island, start back early!"

"I want to call on Mrs. Mackenzie."

"Meg Mackenzie? I'll be stopping a few yards from her house in Cullipool."

Appleby said, "I'm looking for a friend who might have passed this way. His name's Mackenzie. A big man. Bearded, probably, and travelling light."

"Would he be related to Mistress Mackenzie?"

"It's possible. I don't know."

"Well, now—I seem to recall passing such a man. Would he be carrying a pack on his back?"

"It's likely."

"It's not an unlikely sight to see men with packs on their backs." The driver chuckled. "And it's not an uncommon sight to see them walking back to catch the last ferry across the Sound. Like the tourist cars coming over. They drive to Cullipool, take a look at the black sand and piles of old slate, and drive straight back to the Sound wondering why they came in the first place."

Rain spattered the windscreen, and the driver switched on the wipers. The sky had now massed into a fast-moving blanket of gray cloud, and the wind had increased; Appleby could feel its force slapping against the minibus.

"This man you saw—the man with a pack—where did you see him?"

"A mile or so back."

"When?"

"In the last day or so. Monday, would it be? Or Tuesday. Donney Kilmartin would've been piloting the ferry. You could ask him."

"I've been told I'd have to roam the pubs of Oban to find him."

The driver laughed. "Aye. That's Donney. A hard-drinking man. He'll be back on Monday as sober as a procurator fiscal and talking to no one until the whisky fumes clear from his head."

The road skirted a rocky black beach, past two fishing boats bearing Mull and Oban registrations, then curved toward a huddle of crofts dominated by a sharp, rising hill topped by a church.

"This is Cullipool," the driver said.

He whipped the steering wheel right, then left, and scudded to a stop in a slate-chipped clearing. "Straight ahead," he said. "That row of houses—the fifth along. That's Mistress Mackenzie's house, and you owe me twenty pence for the ride."

Meg Mackenzie liked the thin, polite man sitting in her warm parlor and felt sympathy for the bony face so full of anxiety and tiredness, and the hesitant manner in which he had introduced himself.

"Would you be a medical doctor?" she asked.

"Not that kind," Appleby said. "I'm a geologist and gemmologist. I diagnose stones, not people. Mrs. Mackenzie, I'm looking for someone who bears the same name as yourself: Mackenzie, Arnold Mackenzie."

"Of the islands?"

"I believe so. He would have left as a boy—or as a very young man. I've known him for twenty years or more—in Africa, which is now my homeland. I want to find him, Mrs. Mackenzie."

"Arnold Mackenzie." She folded her hands in her lap. "There was an Alastair and a Duncan Mackenzie. Good boys and went to college like my own nephew, Laughlin, but that was years ago. Laughlin was given his degree last year. You'll be interested in his photograph, Doctor?" Meg Mackenzie pointed to a framed photo of her nephew in cap and gown. "He's in law, Doctor. One day he'll be procurator fiscal of Oban, mark my words. He's a fine lad. When he comes back to the island, he likes nothing better than to sail with his uncle Johnnie Livingstone from Black Mull Bay in that old boat of his with the engine that coughs and splutters, but always brings them back safe and sound."

"Livingstone?" Appleby questioned.

"My brother-in-law. He lost his wife, my sister, poor man. Johnnie's old, but a braver man would be hard to find."

"Mr. Maclean, the ferry master, told me about him," said Appleby.

"Everyone knows everything about everyone on Luing," Mrs. Mackenzie said. "Johnnie lays his lobster pots and takes visitors on trips through the Grey Dog or lands them at Scarba to look for the whirlpool. I'd not trust my life to Johnnie's old boat—it's as old as the man himself."

"My man is Arnold Mackenzie," Appleby said. "He'd be touching the mid-forties mark. Say he was born in 1932—does that ring a bell, Mrs. Mackenzie?"

"Luing had many people in those days, Doctor, and many of them Mackenzies," she said. "Belnahua, across the water there, quarried slate, and Luing was filled with the young and the old. When the slate wasn't good enough for the houses, populations died, leaving us as we are now —an island of pensioners. There were Mackenzies, Macleans, and

Campbells and McLaughlins. It was like the gathering of the clans." She shook her head. "I've no recollection of an Arnold Mackenzie—none at all. Ask Johnnie Livingstone, Doctor. . . . Will you take a cup of tea with me, or something stronger?"

Looking at the rain beating against the window, Appleby said, "I'd like both, Mrs. Mackenzie."

Reluctantly Johnnie Livingstone allowed Appleby to enter the tiny living room of his croft. The room was made smaller by the pile of clothing and blankets and cardboard packing cases heaped in the center of the room. Appleby saw that one case was labelled "Bell's Whisky."

Seeing Appleby's interest, Livingstone said, "I like to stock up for the winter—before the weather breaks. I've no mind to leave the bay for a while. You say Meg Mackenzie sent you, mister?"

"She thought you might be able to help me find someone."

"Well, now—" Livingstone shifted his dog off a chair. "You'll sit for a while?"

"Thank you."

"Will you take a dram?"

"That would be welcome. I feel the cold, Mr. Livingstone. Years in Africa thins the blood."

Appleby watched Livingstone take a bottle from a sideboard littered with ornaments and framed photographs. "This friend," Livingstone said as he poured large measures into glasses, "he'd have a name?"

"Mackenzie."

Livingstone's hand jerked slightly, causing whisky to run over the side of a glass. When he came away from the sideboard and handed Appleby his glass, his eyes were averted. "Africa, you say? A far cry from Luing and the islands. You'll be going back to Africa?"

"As soon as I can—I've been away too long. As soon as I've found Mackenzie."

"That's not an uncommon name, mister." Livingstone drank from his glass.

"A Scottish needle in a Scottish haystack," Appleby said. "It's possible he'd be on one of the islands."

Livingstone smiled, showing toothless gums. "Tomorrow, or the next day, I could take you out in the boat. Scarba's a good place to visit, and there's the island where Columba buried his mother."

"Mackenzie is a big man, possibly with a beard. He may have been seen on Luing a few days ago. Have you seen such a man?"

"There's few come to Black Mill Bay this time of the year." Livingstone had drained his glass; he got up from his chair and refilled his glass. "Men with beards are not an uncommon sight in Scotland, mister. I've taken many round the islands."

"The man I'm looking for may have taken a boat from Luing," Appleby said.

"McLaughlin in Cullipool has a boat, and there's Galbraith in Toberonochy."

"You didn't take him, Mr. Livingstone?"

"I've not been out in the boat for the last fortnight."

"Mrs. Mackenzie thought she'd seen you out a few days ago."

"The woman can't see that far!" The tone of Livingstone's voice had changed, become edged. "Meg's a fine body, mister, don't misunderstand me. She takes fancies into her head. She saw nothing of my boat. See Galbraith or McLaughlin—maybe they took your friend."

Appleby looked at his watch: 2:30. "How do I get round the island?" he asked. "Is there somewhere I can stay the night?"

Livingstone shook his head. "You'll find somewhere to stay on the other side of the Cuan. The Trish and Truish—that's a pub. They'll give you a bed."

"It was a long walk to your house, Mr. Livingstone. Can I get a car —a taxi?"

"There's Hubert Duncan who has a car, but he'd be away in Oban for a few days. There's no taxi on Luing."

Appleby had had enough. He put down his glass and got to his feet. "A needle in a haystack," he said. "It's time to give up."

"Mister?"

"I'm very tired, Mr. Livingstone. Dispirited. I've come a long way to find Mackenzie—a very long way."

"You must badly want to see the man. Do you have good or bad news for him?"

"I want to see him—nothing more." Appleby looked at the heaped goods, the new waterproof clothing and blankets, the case of whisky. "Eat and drink well, Mr. Livingstone. Thank you for your trouble."

"It was no trouble." Livingstone's face had relaxed, and his voice was soft. "You'll be making for Cuan Sound and the ferry?"

Appleby nodded.

"It's close on four mile," said Livingstone. "You'll be in time for the last crossing. You didn't tell me your name, mister."

"Appleby. Dr. Arthur Appleby."

"If I see your friend, Doctor, I'll tell him you were looking for him."

Appleby looked into Livingstone's lined face; there was knowledge of a kind in the pale-blue eyes. "Tell him," Appleby said, "that Appleby is staying at the Gleneagles guest house in Oban before returning to Angwana empty-handed."

"That's a lot to remember, Doctor."

"Since you haven't seen him nor are likely to, does it matter if you forget?"

For a moment Livingstone was silent, then he said, "I'll not forget."

The pile of clothes, blankets, and packing cases again caught Appleby's eye. "I'd like you to tell him that no one else is looking for him. Just Arthur Appleby who wishes him well."

"You talk as if I knew where Arnold Mackenzie is hiding from the world," Livingstone said, "when I've never set eyes on the man."

Appleby smiled, suddenly liking the weather-roughened old man. "Talking to you has helped, Mr. Livingstone," he said. "I'll be back. I doubt if you'll run out of whisky, but, just in case, I'll bring a bottle with me."

As Appleby took the rough track from Black Mill Bay to Luing's one main road, he faced the gusting, cold wind in better heart than he had been in for many weeks. Mac *was* out there somewhere. Livingstone had told him so. How else would the old man have known Mackenzie's Christian name when he, Appleby, had not mentioned it? Mac would get the message along with the cartons of food and whisky and the clothes and blankets, and whatever Johnnie Livingstone had bought on the mainland.

The last mile to the Cuan Sound was hard-going. The wind had strengthened, and it was dark with early nightfall. He stood on the jetty, cold, wet, and hungry, but sustained by hope. From across the sound the ferry lights gleamed green and red. As he watched, the ferry moved away from its moorings to strike a diagonal course against the tide. Appleby looked at his watch: 5:30. He'd made the last crossing, with half an hour in hand.

Maclean greeted him as he came aboard. "Did you find your man?"

"Not yet. I talked with Mrs. Mackenzie and Livingstone."

"And how did you find Johnnie?"

"Interesting. He's a deep man, Mr. Maclean."

"You'll not be getting to Oban tonight," Maclean said, "unless you call out the taxi."

"Livingstone mentioned a pub called the Trish and—some other name."

"The Trish and Truish. You could stay there, or the Stag Hotel on the other side of the Atlantic Bridge."

"I'll settle for the pub. I feel in the need of company."

"You'll find it at the Trish. Will you be wanting a lift? I'll be leaving at six or soon after. I take the ferry to its moorings, and then it's for home. I'll drive you to the Trish. Maybe your friend called there."

Mackenzie had called in at the pub. Appleby stood at the bar with

Maclean and listened to the landlord: "Aye. I recall such a man. He took a dram and bought a bottle of whisky. He used Scottish money."

"And then?" Appleby asked.

"He went. He bade me good morning, shouldered his pack, and was away."

Appleby felt his body and mind relax. The pub was warm, and a cassette player was blaring out Scottish music. He ordered another round of drinks. Raising his glass, he said, "To absent friends."

"I'll drink to that," Maclean said.

Mac's only a few miles away, Appleby thought. Tomorrow or the next day Livingstone would steer his old boat to Mac's island, unload the goods he had bought, and deliver the message he said he would not forget.

Tomorrow or the next day, and on into the winter if necessary, Black Mill Bay would see him muffled up against the wind and the rain, watching and waiting for Mac or Livingstone to break silence, then he would persuade Mac to give up the diamond, and tell him to go in peace.

Maclean had bought another round of drinks. "And what shall we drink to now?" he asked.

It was Appleby's third large whisky, and he felt slightly drunk. "To Angwana and the Star of Angwana."

"That's a queer toast," Maclean said. "I've heard of neither."

CHAPTER 35.

THE intermittent flash from Fladda lighthouse briefly illuminated the island of Belnahua, then allowed it to rest in darkness until the next flash one minute later.

Mackenzie stirred the mixture of baked beans, stewed steak, and potatoes in the saucepan on the Primus and watched the heat bubbles in the light from a single candle.

During the day, with the puppy chasing scents and unseen prey, he had walked over the island trying to identify the place where he had been born, but memory had failed him. It could have been the very place he had selected the evening before when Livingstone had put him ashore. Belnahua was a dead island, a place of dereliction and rusting iron machinery and crumbling crofts.

The Fladda light glowed again and was gone. Mackenzie tipped half the contents of the saucepan onto a plate. As he ate he saw in his mind's eye all that lay beyond Belnahua: the length and breadth of Britain and the Channel separating France from England and Europe itself and down through France to Spain and Africa.

It was all so far away: Jamie Turner in Geneva, Appleby and Blohm, Partridge dying in Aracaju, and poor Mandragez who died happy. So far away. The sun would be hot in Sierra Leone and Angwana, and men would be dreaming of cool winds and unattainable homes where larks flew instead of vultures. Mackenzie looked at the sleeping puppy and smiled. Here, on Belnahua, gulls screeched and cold gales whistled through the ruins of crofts and piles of rusty machinery —a fine realization to the dream of castles and lochs and the salmon leaping. He was sleeping rough and eating a mess of stew, a blanket draped over his shoulders to keep the whistling drafts from chilling an already chilled body.

There was sense in it somewhere, he thought. If Jamie had gone along with him and taken care of the stone, he could have faced them and laughed in their teeth. But why hide both himself and the diamond? Why not just the diamond? The Viaduc des Fades and the Hôtel de la Gare in the Auvergne where he'd rested and known such peace; he could have buried the stone and marked it well. Better, far better, than nursing it like a two-thousand-carat succubus in a cold slum of a heap of old iron in the Firth of Lorn.

He had cooked too much, and the puppy had a full belly. Pulling the blanket up from his shoulders and over his head, Mackenzie went outside and scraped the remains of his meal onto the ground, spits of rain hitting his face like tiny needles. A few dim lights were showing on Luing, and out in the firth he could see the port and starboard lights of a boat making slow progress north.

There was nothing to do but eat, sleep, and wait through the short days and long nights that lay ahead, unless he came out of the cold, hands empty of diamond, and faced his accusers. He shook his head, negating the thought, and went back into the derelict croft.

Long after he had climbed into the sleeping bag, the puppy asleep in the crook of his arm, he lay awake listening to the island's sounds and seeing the star-flash from Fladda lighthouse shafting through the one intact window. He'd have to do something about that, he thought; a screen to cover it at night so that he could use light not observed by passing boats or eyes in Cullipool.

It would be fine to have a bright Tilley lamp to lighten his darkness, and blankets and a folding bed. What else would Livingstone bring him? Waterproof clothing, a butane heater and gas cylinder, gallons of fresh water—the list of goods he'd paid Livingstone to buy in Oban ran through his head and relieved the depression that had hovered over him, threatening to descend and engulf him in darkness blacker than the night outside.

Shortly after dawn Johnnie Livingstone finished loading up Mackenzie's supplies and equipment, boat-hooked his way out of the shallows, then took the craft into deeper water and headed for Belnahua. He could see little through the misty rain, but the course to the island was as clear in his mind as if he could actually see it. Keeping well away from the coast of Luing, he hugged the waters off Lunga, confident that he could not be seen by Meg Mackenzie or any other early riser in Cullipool.

Mackenzie was waiting on the rocky beach when Livingstone moored his boat. Together they carried provisions and equipment up to the croft. When it was done, Livingstone said, "There was a man came to the bay asking questions."

"What kind of man?"

"A good man, I think. He said his name was Appleby. A doctor of some kind."

"I see. . . . You sent him away?"

"Aye—but I think he'll be back."

Of all people, it had to be Appleby, Mackenzie thought; it had to be poor old Arthur. "Did he have anyone with him?"

"He was a lonely, cold man, mister. Not used to this part of the world, I'd say. He was a friendly man—a good man. There was a message should I see a man named Arnold Mackenzie." Livingstone searched his memory for Appleby's exact words. "I forget all the words he spoke."

"Remember what you can, Livingstone."

"It was something like he's staying at a house in Oban called Gleneagles . . . and will be going back to Africa. I've lost the name of the place."

"Angwana?"

"That was the name, sure enough. He said he wishes you well and he did not want to return to Africa empty-handed."

"Anything else?" Mackenzie's tone was brusque.

"Only that nobody else was looking for you."

"He said that, did he?"

"It's what he said, mister." Livingstone looked at the case of whisky, then at the half-empty bottle standing on an upturned cardboard carton. "I need a dram," he said. "Cold mornings eat into old bones."

"Help yourself, then."

Mackenzie went to the window and looked out across the firth. Luing was an island of old people, Livingstone had said, and subsisting on social security; an island that closed its doors with the advent of winter when high winds came and rain shrouded the islands. In Mackenzie's mind were memories of long summer nights with fleets of small boats plying between Belnahua and Luing, and homemade music coming from the lamp-lit crofts; there was no recall of long, dark nights, loneliness, and angry seas. He turned away from the window. "If Appleby comes again, you'll tell him nothing, Livingstone!" He spoke almost angrily. "I want you out here again in a week and every week until spring."

"Aye. I'll keep to our bargain."

"There's money in it for you. As much as you'll need for the rest of your life and beyond."

"You're paying me well enough as it is, Mr. Mackenzie. You need not take on so."

Contrite, Mackenzie said, "I'm sorry. I thought of things as they were. . . . I want you to be friendly toward Dr. Appleby. He is, as you say, a good man—a good and trusting man."

"He said he was your friend."

"Well-meaning friends can be dangerous friends," Mackenzie said. "Livingstone, if I should want to leave Belnahua for another island, how far north can you take me?"

"A fair distance in summer. In my old boat, not far when the bad weather comes. Mine's an island boat, mister, and there's bad water up north."

"Then it seems I'm holed up here," Mackenzie said. "You'd better take another dram and be off before the old ones stir in Cullipool. I'm depending on you, Johnnie Livingstone. Don't let me down."

Livingstone wiped the neck of the bottle and put it back on the cardboard carton. "I won't let you down, Mr. Mackenzie—and the old ones won't be astir yet. I'm away, then." He paused at the makeshift door Mackenzie had erected. "Will you tell me something?"

"What?"

"Is it something bad you've done?"

"I'll answer you with a question, Livingstone. Do you own the land you live on?"

"No."

"Suppose you found gold in your vegetable patch. What would you do with it?"

Livingstone smiled, showing his gums. "I reckon I'd keep it."

"Then that's your answer. Make of it what you will."

Appleby drove through the dark, misty morning in an ancient Morris 1100. "Borrow the old car, Doctor," the Trish and Truish publican had said. "There's no police traps on Seil, and what's a driving license between friends?" At 8:15 he ran the car up the ferryboat ramp and crossed to the Luing jetty; by 8:25 he was driving up the steep hill away from the Luing jetty and on the road to Black Mill Bay.

The mist was like fine rain, and visibility ended at two hundred yards; he drove slowly, braking as shadowy forms of cattle or sheep crossed the road.

It was close on 9:00 when he parked the Morris on the clearing near the row of crofts. He could see little beyond the beach of rocks where Livingstone moored his boat, and there was no boat to be seen.

Appleby sat in the car and waited, drinking coffee poured from the thermos flask given him by the publican's wife in lieu of breakfast. As he watched and waited the misty rain thinned, and the shadowy shapes of the islands of Lunga and Scarba faintly emerged. Another shape, small and moving, appeared around the furthermost tip of the bay, and Appleby wound down the car's side window; a chugging, coughing sound came over the mist. As the sound grew louder it took recognizable shape.

Appleby watched the boat turn and glide into the shallow waters of the bay, then make for the sloping ridge of rock that served as a mooring. The sound of the boat's engine died, and he waited for Livingstone to secure the craft before getting out of the Morris and walking down to meet the old man.

"I'm here again, Mr. Livingstone," Appleby said.

"Aye. So I see."

"You've been out early."

"I've lobster pots need seeing to. There's bad weather on the way." Remembering Mackenzie's injunction to be friendly, he said, "I've not had my breakfast yet. I've enough for two."

"Thank you. I left early and I haven't eaten."

"Then come away in, Doctor." Livingstone began to walk toward his croft. "I've no news for you, but you're welcome to share my table."

It was when they had eaten and Livingstone was pouring his fourth cup of strong tea that Appleby placed a roll of banknotes on the table.

"That's a fair bit of money," Livingstone said. "Why would you be putting it on the table, Doctor?"

"I was hoping you might consider it fair payment for any help you might give me."

"How much would that be?"

"A hundred pounds."

Livingstone lit a cigarette and inhaled deeply. When he had expelled the smoke from his lungs, he said, "Do you know the Scots, Doctor? Did you ever hear of clan loyalty?" Without waiting for Appleby's reply, he went on. "I'm not of the Mackenzie clan, but I married into it, you might say."

"Mrs. Mackenzie's sister."

"Aye." Livingstone pointed to the roll of banknotes. "And that might be the price of loyalty should I know and tell you where your friend is?" He inhaled too deeply and coughed. "Damn things! If I were a young man, I'd give them up. . . . So I am part of the Mackenzie clan, Doctor, and where your friend is, I'd not be telling you if I knew."

"I'm sorry," Appleby said. "If I've offended you, I'm sorry. I have to find Arnold Mackenzie. Offering you money—such action I'm not used to. You see, I know Mac is out there—somewhere, and I'm sure you know where." Appleby looked round the room. "Yesterday there was a pile of food, clothing, and equipment. Now it's gone."

303

"There's not much of a shop on Luing," Livingstone said. "When one of us goes to Oban, we buy for the island."

"I believe that. Do you remember the message I asked you to give him?"

"If I see him—yes, Doctor. I'll not forget. I've no objection to giving such a message to a Mackenzie."

"But you'd object to telling me where he is?"

"I'll not tell on a Mackenzie unless the police and the procurator fiscal himself gave me good reason. Would the police and the procurator fiscal be telling me?"

Appleby shook his head. "It concerns neither. It's between Mackenzie and myself."

"I'll bear it in good mind."

A sudden gust of wind buffeted the croft, and Livingstone looked through the window. The misty drizzle of the morning had given way to driving rain and fast-moving masses of gray cloud. "I'll not be moving far from this table today," Livingstone said. "When white horses reach the bay, there's skirling weather on the way."

Leaping white-capped waves were tossing Livingstone's boat on its moorings, and across the firth the sea was breaking against Scarba and Lunga in great explosions of white foam.

"If your friend is out there," Livingstone said, "have pity for him. Leave the man in peace."

"That's why I'm here," Appleby said. "And I'll come back every day until he allows me to leave him in peace." He got to his feet and held out his hand. "You've been kind and hospitable, Mr. Livingstone— I think we understand each other. I'd like to repeat one thing—please bear it in mind: I *am* Arnold Mackenzie's friend."

Livingstone took the proffered hand and shook it. "I know that," he said, "and if I were in a position to tell the Mackenzie that, I'd tell him he's a poor man hiding from a good friend who wishes him well."

The roll of banknotes was still on the table, and Livingstone averted his eyes. He saw Appleby to the Morris, fighting back the impulse to tell him that he'd forgotten the money, but an old, well-ingrained mendacity won. When he returned to his croft, he picked up the roll, telling himself that when Appleby came back, he'd return the money.

It looked fine with the windows of the croft blacked against the night and Cullipool eyes, and the light from the Tilley lamp, and the heat from the butane heater, and there, in the frying pan, four rashers of bacon, and the eggs ready to be broken and the yolks and whites dropped into the hot fat. It was fine, too, to see the coffeepot bubbling on the meths burner and sending out its appetizing aroma.

The light, the warmth, and the transistor radio playing Scottish music, the smell of frying bacon and coffee, had lightened Mackenzie's spirits, so that he thought, if the nights can be like this, a man could live indefinitely in quiet, warm solitude. Perhaps, come better weather, he'd move up north and find a bigger island; one that he could buy. There were such islands, and money talked loud.

The black puppy was curled up in an old basket Livingstone had brought; the young dog's day had tired it, and now, with a full belly, it was fast asleep, twitching now and then with dog dreams.

Mackenzie ate the eggs and bacon and drank two cups of coffee laced with whisky and sat in the folding chair Livingstone had bought in Oban. It wasn't exactly *the* life, but it was *a* life and certainly worth living. On the thought, he got to his feet and went to the shelves where he took the diamond from behind the stacked cans of food. Returning to the chair, he held the crystal against the glare of the Tilley lamp. Even in its rough state he could see the fire and color trapped in the stone. God! It was worth keeping! The moment he'd held it in his hands and then heard Appleby's voice, he knew it was his. He *had* to have it, and the desire was beyond reason, like the diamond itself.

Appleby was still the problem, but how big a problem? He was out there somewhere, either on Luing or on the mainland, and could do nothing but watch and wait. And even if one morning he stepped ashore on Belnahua and asked for the diamond, all he had to say was, "What diamond, Arthur? Can't a man escape from the world without being persecuted? Ask Magasi."

Rikel. Poor Franz Rikel spilling beans that couldn't be counted to a number great enough to move the Company in Sierra Leone to take action, and even if they did, where would they get supporting evidence? Partridge was dead, and Jamie Turner valued his own skin too much to open his heart and confess. . . . Magasi—another character dead and gone, and the world hadn't lost by his death. All was circumstantial evidence and nothing more; the proof of the final pudding was the diamond, and they would not get that. One day the diamond men would stop tearing their hair and biting their nails at the one that got away. They'd soon wonder, if they weren't wondering already, whether the diamond had ever existed. Poor, rich Jamie discredited. . . . With the millions he had, what did it matter if diamond doors had been slammed in his face? He could cock a real snook at the diamond kings.

Shakah. Abdullah Shakah. It was possible he'd blow the gaff, and it didn't matter. All he did was to copy photographs supplied by his friend and client Arnold Mackenzie and produce in finest lead glass an impossible diamond—a glass diamond, a confused term to describe the Star of Angwana.

Only four men knew for sure the stone existed; one had it, and three did not, and of the three only two mattered, Blohm and Arthur Appleby. Blohm was unimportant, and that left Arthur. All he could do was prowl round the islands and, if he struck lucky, say, "Please, can I have Angwana's diamond back?"

Poor Arthur, he'd find the Scottish winter hard to bear. Not enough flesh on the man to stand up to the gales and the cold, hard days to come.

Mackenzie drank a four-finger measure of whisky, then poured another. He looked at the sleeping puppy and felt a wave of affection for its quiet acceptance of himself and the environment it shared. He called to it: "Sotho! Here, boy!" The puppy stirred and raised its head, and Mackenzie beckoned it with a snapping movement of thumb and forefinger. The dog's tail wagged, and the small, fat body came out of the basket and toward him. Mackenzie picked it up and sat it down on his lap beside the diamond. "Know what that is, you little black bastard? That's the world's second largest diamond, and you don't give a damn!"

Mackenzie was a little drunk, knew it, and he didn't care. He reached out and switched off the transistor radio, and the island was suddenly loud with the noise of wind moaning through the ruined crofts and the thunder of the sea pounding the rocks. "You hear that?" Mackenzie said. "That's the world shouting 'We want Mackenzie. We want Mackenzie!'" The puppy stood up on its hind legs and tried to lick Mackenzie's face. "Lick, lick, lick—that's all you can do, you black bastard! You sit your fat little arse on the world's second largest diamond and that's all it's worth to you!"

The whisky, the food he had eaten, and the warmth of the croft closed round Mackenzie, and he was suddenly tired, desperately tired. Without removing his boots or any of his clothes, he carried dog and diamond to the sleeping bag and climbed into its enveloping comfort. He turned out the Tilley lamp and darkness blanketed down.

The butane heater glowed in the dark, and Mackenzie listened to the wind skirling round Belnahua and the sea pounding at the island, and the sound comforted him. Storms would come and go as the months wore on and autumn slipped into winter and winter into spring; but it was the storms he wanted, storms and inhospitable seas to keep unwanted visitors away, and periodic calms when Livingstone would cough his old boat to the island with supplies.

In the Atlantic beyond the Outer Hebrides the weather had freaked into a cauldron of elemental forces, building up into a complex system that waited until it had achieved maximum ferocity before moving southeast. It roared over Lewis and Skye, narrowing its width to raise its wind to hurricane force, driving the sea before it in towering waves that tore at the Island of Rhum. Concentrating its forces, it stormed the Sound of Mull, then the Firth of Lorn, and struck at Luing and the surrounding islands.

At the height of its fury the noise of the wind and sea woke Mackenzie. He listened to the thunder of waves and the screaming of the wind, told both sounds to go to hell, and pulled the sound-muffling flap of the sleeping bag over his head. The puppy stirred and whimpered, and Mackenzie stroked it to sleep; then he, too, slept, oblivious of the storm battering the island.

Two miles away from Belnahua the Cullipool islanders left their sea-attacked crofts and trudged up the steep hill to Saint Peter's Church. The church stood high, a sanctuary against the sea sweeping over the black beach and onto low-lying land.

At 2:00 A.M. the teeth of the storm bit hard, hitting into the islands and tearing at rock as it forced the sea between high- and low-rise islands.

It came at Belnahua with a thunderous sound of destruction, blasting at rock and fissured slate, at the sprawl of derelict crofts, and ripping away topsoil and undulations—a giant scythe that razored the surface of the island.

In Saint Peter's Church, old Larich Campbell was pedalling the ancient harmonium and singing in a high, quavering voice:

> "O Lord, whom winds and seas obey,
> Guide us through the watery way;
> In the hollow of Thy hand
> Hide, and bring us safe to land."

At first light the storm had moved south, dying as it went and touching Glasgow with its final gusts. In Cullipool the villagers looked down from Saint Peter's at their crofts barely showing above the level of water. Half a mile downcoast Laughlin McLaughlin came away from the wreck of his fishing boat and looked at the flooded land around his house, deploring what he saw. The garden that his wife, Fiona, had nurtured over the years after ridding it of slate and rocks lay under three feet of water, and he thanked God that the house itself had been built on rock high enough to miss the floodwater level. As far as he could see down the coast, jetsam had piled up two hundred feet away from the high-tide level. Hubert Duncan's house had suffered; the gaping hole in the slate roof resembled an ugly black stain.

McLaughlin swore in Gaelic, cursing the devil that sent troubles to a harmless island inhabited by the aged. He looked north and up at Saint Peter's on the hill; the church would be crammed with people from Cullipool; later he'd do what he could and take food and drink to them. He thought of his lobster pots and those of other lobster men on the island; not a hope that any string of pots had survived or, for that matter, the men themselves, Hector Galbraith and Johnnie Livingstone, whose crofts stood hard on the sea's edge.

He lifted the binoculars from around his neck and focused them out to sea and the scattered islands. The lighthouse on Fladda stood white and firm against the gray sky; he'd have to get out there somehow; at the height of the storm its light had gone—the underwater power cable from Luing must have been snapped. A chunk of Scarba had gone, he noticed; the jetty built by the Cadzow brothers was no longer there.

McLaughlin swept the binoculars round to the peaks of Mull and then, because he had missed something he had seen since childhood, slowly ranged the binoculars back again, picking out landmarks and islands. But the low island with its serrated surface formed by ruined quarriers' crofts was gone. Instead, a low, featureless mound like a sandbar left by a receding tide met his gaze. For a moment he looked at what remained of the island, then, coming up from the wrecked fishing boat, he called out to his wife: *"Fiona! Come here—Belnahua's gone!"*

Appleby watched dawn break as he sat in the public bar of the Trish and Truish with the publican and his wife. Two oil lamps cast a yellow light in the bar; sometime in the night, power had been cut, and Appleby, unable to sleep and hearing the sounds of activity in the pub, had left his room and joined the publican and his wife.

"A wild night," the publican said. "One to remember for a long while. There's no telephone and no electricity."

"Will the ferry be running?" Appleby asked.

"I have my doubts, though it's a strong old boat. You'll be getting to Luing again, Doctor?"

"If I can."

The sun rose, tinting the broken cloud rose-pink. "A pretty sunrise after an ugly night," the publican's wife said. "If the Lord taketh, then giveth back, I don't see His point."

"It has point if man takes and gives back," Appleby said.

"You're thinking of your friend, maybe," the publican said.

"The storm might have helped change his mind, but, knowing him, I doubt it. It's time I left for the ferry."

"Not before you've breakfast inside of you," the publican's wife said. "It's been a long time since I cooked on an oil stove."

The storm had left a trail of havoc. As he drove to Cuan Sound he frequently stopped to move fallen tree branches off the road. On the steep fall of the road leading to the ferry he was held up for half an hour while men moved stones and rubble from a wrecked house.

The ferry was at its moorings but riding high on a sea that reached the top of the jetty slope. Maclean was not on duty; instead, a black-browed, sturdy man in a tattered thick-knit sweater waved Appleby and the Morris onto the boat. Appleby guessed it was Donney Kilmartin.

It was slow going from the Luing jetty to Black Mill Bay. Low parts of the road were still under water, and there had been earth slides where the road cut deep between banks.

When he reached the bay, he got out of the car and looked at the row of crofts, seeing exposed roof timbers jutting out and upward, a black, skeletal design against the bright morning sky. The dead swan had gone, so had the rusting remains of the jetty; and piled up against the low cliff, marine detritus formed an untidy wall of ship timber, bright orange and blue nylon ropes and floats, and a litter of plastic waste flung overboard by passing ships.

He found Johnnie Livingstone huddled in a blanket and sitting in the ruins of his living room, the old dog Shuna at his feet.

"Mr. Livingstone?" Appleby said.

Livingstone turned his head slowly, looked at Appleby for a brief moment, then looked through the broken panes of the window. "The boat's gone," he said. "My old boat's gone."

"The storm?"

"It cannot be replaced."

"I wanted to know—"

"There's little enough to know," Livingstone interrupted. "My boat's gone. There's nothing left worth putting together. Maybe your man's gone too."

"Where is he?"

"He could be anywhere after last night. I've no boat to go to him."

"Then we must get one."

"I doubt if there's one left on the island."

"You know where he is, don't you, Mr. Livingstone?"

"Aye. I know where he is."

"Will you tell me?"

"I've no boat to go to him," Livingstone repeated.

"I can get a boat—from Oban, if necessary." Appleby reached down and laid a hand on Livingstone's shoulder. "Will you take me to him if I can get a boat?"

"I'd be breaking a promise. He paid me well to keep a promise that I cannot keep for I've no boat." Livingstone brought his gaze back to Appleby. "Would you tell him I couldn't keep to the promise?"

"I'll explain the circumstances."

"He's got a wee dog with him—one of Shuna's. God help the man and the dog."

"Is he far away?"

"Belnahua's but three miles away."

"Belnahua? Is that where he is?"

"Aye. He's in a croft a small way from the landing beach." Livingstone shook his head. "I told him it was a dead place, but he said it was what he wanted. I fancy he knew the place a long time ago."

"McLaughlin," Appleby said. "Was that the name of the man you said had a boat?"

Livingstone shook his head. "Hubert Duncan came by at dawn. Laughlin's lost his boat."

"Then it's Oban," Appleby said. "I'll get a boat from Oban."

Livingstone turned his head and nodded toward the mantelshelf. "The money you left, Doctor—it's in the mug."

"I don't want it," Appleby said. "Please keep it."

Appleby stood on Belnahua with Andrew Stewart. Apart from gulls flying in and screaming their arrival, there was no life on the island.

"There was something to see before the storm," Stewart said. "Shells of quarriers' crofts and the machinery. Now it's rubble. Not a wall standing nor much of a surface."

"There was a man here," said Appleby. "He'd taken shelter in a croft near where we're standing now."

"Now there's nothing."

A day had passed since Appleby had left Livingstone and driven to Oban, where he had spent the rest of the short day searching for a boat to take him to the island. Night had fallen when he found Andrew Stewart and his small cabin cruiser.

They had left Oban soon after dawn—the sun rising in a clear sky—anchored off Belnahua, and rowed to the beach. They had walked the entire island and found nothing, no sign of life. Once Appleby had shouted, "Mac!" then realized the senselessness of calling out on a bare island whose entire length and breadth he could see.

"If he was here," Stewart said, "he's here no longer." He moved away from Appleby and stirred thinly scattered slate rubble with his foot. A glint of metal caught his eye, and he bent down and scooped his hand under the rubble. He straightened up and said to Appleby, "A fifty-pence piece, Doctor—minted last year."

"It could have been dropped by a visitor," Appleby said.

"Maybe. We'll see if we can find anything else."

An hour later Appleby looked at the small pile they had found: a spoon, a fragment of blanket, an unopened tin of corned beef, a few shards from a smashed whisky bottle, and an enamelled metal plate.

Stewart said, "They're all recent. None of this was left by a tripper."

On one of the glass shards part of a label still adhered: "Bell's Whis——" Appleby read. "It wasn't left by a tripper," he said. "Mac isn't here any longer."

He looked out across the Firth of Lorn and to the islands; somewhere out there, at the bottom of the sea or borne by strange currents, Mackenzie was either resting or being carried along by the tides until washed ashore like the dead swan in Black Mill Bay. And the diamond? It could be anywhere: under Belnahua's rubble or with Mac's body. The way and time ahead stretched into an infinity of conjecture. If Mac never surfaced and the island were searched from end to end with nothing found, what then? Better to cut losses and return to Angwana and confess failure. He had to be rational. He said to Stewart, "Can you tell me what the chances are of his body coming ashore?"

Stewart shook his head. "These are strange waters. There's been many a man lost forever in the seas round the islands."

"There must be a chance."

"Last night's seas could have carried him anywhere. Out into the Atlantic, maybe. And there's rocks, Doctor—a body would stand small chance of staying in one piece, if you see what I mean."

"I do see what you mean."

Stewart looked out to his cruiser lying at anchor. "We should be moving, for the tide's well out. Will you come to the island again?"

"No. All that I came for has gone."

Appleby stood in the stern of the boat as Stewart took it away from the island. Somewhere below the waters that could resemble a mountain range or a whale's back rested a stone whose worth was far beyond the reach of any man's pocket.

An irregular piece of pure carbon weighing two thousand carats; a pure-white and the second largest diamond to be discovered. For millions of years it had waited for Mackenzie to discover it, only to be hidden again, perhaps forever. Much clearing up had to be done; a report to the police and the consequent search of the islands for Mac's body. The diamond was another problem. It was senseless to make its loss an official or public matter. Hordes of amateur treasure seekers, and not a few diamond men, would invade Belnahua with their trowels and shovels.

Mac *would* have taken the stone with him—it was in the nature of the man. Of that, Appleby was sure, and it marked the end to the Star of Angwana. Appleby watched the low hump of Belnahua diminish in size, aware that on two occasions he had been only three miles from the living Mackenzie.

The wind was strong and cold, driving down from the northeast, and Appleby huddled deeper into his overcoat, wishing for Angwana's sun and the companionship of Blohm and the remote mine. The island now barely showed above the dancing, sunlit water; then, as Stewart wheeled the cruiser around Easdale and into the Sound of Insh, all that was left of Belnahua disappeared from sight.

JAMES BROOM LYNNE

James Broom Lynne was born in London and trained at English colleges of art to become a graphic designer. Since 1947 he has specialized in book design, and therefore had a long association with the publishing world before becoming a writer.

Mr. Lynne made his literary debut in 1963, when his play, The Trigon, *was produced in London, and subsequently in New York, Australia, Africa, Germany, and Scandinavia. The author of seven novels published in the United States (three under the pseudonym James Quartermain), James Broom Lynne lives in Suffolk, England, with his wife and family.*